# Flow of Thoughts

# Flow of Thoughts

Hukmdev Narayan Yadav

PRABHAT
PRAKASHAN

*Published by*
**PRABHAT PRAKASHAN PVT. LTD.**
4/19 Asaf Ali Road,
New Delhi-110 002 (INDIA)
e-mail: prabhatbooks@gmail.com

ISBN 978-93-5322-001-3
**FLOW OF THOUGHTS**
*by* Shri Hukmdev Narayan Yadav



*Edition*
2025

*Price*
₹ 600.00 (Rupees Six Hundred only)

*Printed at*
R-Tech Offset Printers, Delhi

*Dedicated to*

*My father late Shri Rajgir Yadav, a freedom fighter and my mother, Mrs. Champa Devi and my political guide Dr. Rammanohar Lohia*

# Author's Note

My public life began early in the 1960's, when I got elected as the *mukhia* (head) of our village *panchayat*. It was third year of my graduation. My father was a freedom fighter. He was a humble village farmer. In those days I could never imagine that the journey which started from the village *panchayat* would take me to the highest house of the nation. I salute the great people of this county who have bestowed this much respect on a simple person born in the house of a modest farmer. I got elected thrice to Bihar legislative assembly. As a member of that house, witnessed various changes and participated in them. In 1967 non-congress governments were formed in many states including Bihar. While all this was going on, Congress faced split in various states. The face of politics changed. Many legislators, who got elected, came from modest families. Backward classes saw rising awareness. New leaders started emerging amongst backward classes and scheduled castes and scheduled tribes, resulting in socio-political awakening. The stream of social, political and economic change started gaining momentum. Powerful leaders stared emerging at state level. Membership of Bihar legislative assembly provided an opportunity to meet many great leaders. There were many leaders, who still have an influence on my life. Due to their simplicity, morality and good behavior, they are revered in the society even today.

During debates in the legislature, my voice would be humble and thoughts firm. While in house there were stern denial and corroboration through arguments, but outside the house, members would respect each other. Democracy drew strength from these leaders. All of them had been influenced by the freedom movement. Many of them were freedom fighters.

A government with agreement was formed in 1967. In the Bihar assembly, socialists, Jan Sangh is, communists and feudalists were all part of the government. A practical form of non-congressism was seen. The moral impact of Dr. Rammanohar Lohia and Pt. Deendayal Upadhyaya was evident. Division of United Socialist Party resulted in the fall of government of agreement. Shoshit party came into being, which formed government with the support of Congress that would last for forty days. This government could not survive due to a split in the Congress. Two mid-term polls were held. The year 1974 witnessed widespread student agitations. The movement spread far and wide under the leadership of Loknayak Jai Prakash Narayan. Legislators resigned from the legislative assembly. SSP leader with mass appeal, Karpoori Thakur led initial resignations of seven members. I was one of them. Emergency was declared. People were sent to jail as prisoners. While in jail, l got to learn and understand so many things in the company of these enlightened people who were fighting the oppressive forces.

General elections were held in 1977.I had to file nominations from the jail itself from Madhubani. Despite fear and threat prevailing all over, people's mandate brought a change in government for the first time and the Janata Party was formed. Unfortunately, internal dissensions and personality clashes caused the fall of the government even before it could complete its full term. Chaudhary Charan Singh led the government which was formed with Congress support. A party called Lok Dal was formed. I was proactive during the split and a founding member of the Lok Dal. Just as the Shoshit Party government in fell in Bihar after a very short term due to Congress,the Lok Dal led government met the same fate as Congress withdrew its support. Lok Dal sent me to Rajya Sabha in 1980. At the end of 1989, elections for Lok Sabha were held. Janata Dal was formed. I too fought the election from Sitamarhi. After a lot of ups and downs,a government led by VP Singh was formed. Chaudhary Devi Lal was sacked from the cabinet. Chandra Shekhar led the split in Janata Dal and formed government with Congress support. Soon Congress pulled the plug and government fell. I was a cabinet minister in that government. While 1991 elections were going on Mr. Rajiv Gandhi was assassinated. A minority government was formed. Thereafter, an era of coalition governments began.

I joined the BJP in 1993. Socialist thought got divided and inherently led to a leadership crisis. In the national interest as well as to move ahead in my political career with principles and ideals I decided it was better to be a part of BJP. It gave me an opportunity to hold various positions in the organization at state and central level. I started working with full dedication under energizing leadership of Shri Atal Bihari Vajpayee, Shri Lal Krishna Advani and Dr. Murli Manohar Joshi. I have been a *swayamsevak* since 1950; therefore, adjustment in BJP was smooth. In 1999 got elected from Madhubani and Shri Vajpayee gave me an opportunity to serve in various departments as minister of state. I was fortunate to have worked under the leadership of Dr. Ram Manohar Lohia, Chaudhary Charan Singh, Shri Chandrashekhar and Shri Atal Bihari Vajpayee. Along the way found leaders like Shri Karpoori Thakur, who remained a good friend. He gave a lot of respect. Later on, joined anti-congress stream and the journey is still on. Madhubani sent me to Lok Sabha four times, and I deeply acknowledge support of people there. I represented the most enlightened constituency of Bihar. Almost all the leaders showered their affection. My political journey was starting to bring about social, economic and political change. I happened to witness a lot of change. I got to see many leaders. I even saw leaders talking about principles and ideals sinking deep into swamp of regionalism and family rule. People who preached socialism entrenched society into family rule, individualism and casteism. Regional politics provided many leaders from backward and scheduled caste communities an opportunity to move ahead. Their leadership emerged in full flow at regional and national level. Exploited society saw a ray of hope. However, they were misguided into the darkness of casteism. Those who emerged out of anti-congress wave, went on to become supporters of enjoyment, fear, confusion and corruption symbolized by Congress. Amid this darkness, a ray of hope emerged. A new awakening took place under the leadership of Shri Narendra Modi. People rose above all narrow considerations to support him. Dream of Dr. Ram Manohar Lohia and Pt. Deendayal Upadhyaya was fulfilled.

In the 15th Lok Sabha I got an opportunity to speak on various issues. Leader of the party, Mrs. Sushma Swaraj encouraged me a lot, and I owe my heartfelt gratitude to her. I had an opportunity to read a book on the speeches by Shri Vajpayee delivered in the parliament on coalition politics. I was inspired by the book to get a book of my own speeches published. Associates from Prabhat Prakashan assured that they would execute this task and I am thankful to all of them. Socialist leader Madhu Limaye used to say – you must write. Many of my articles were published in newspapers. My wife Sudesh Yadav, who has been a dedicated BJP worker, always encouraged me to get my speeches published. I extend my thanks affectionately to her as well. I extend heartfelt regards to all the leaders, who have sent across their good wishes. I would be ever thankful to the villages, poor-laborers-farmers who have always extended their support to me. I deeply indebted to all those great leaders, whose company provided me a vision and positive path. I will remain thankful to readers, who would overlook language errors and focus on feelings. I am a villager – therefore, please forgive my writing mistakes. With lots of affection.

**—Hukmdev Narayan Yadav**
15 August, 2018

# Contents

# 1
# An Open Letter to the Colleagues of Janata Dal

There is no gainsaying the fact that society holds primacy over an individual and so holds true in case of national interest vis-à-vis societal pursuits when it actually comes to lending a serious thought to humanity at large. I am of strong conviction that humanitarian spirit can hold a strong base in the periodic table of political arena only when it is invariably espoused with elements of unconditional love, compassion, generosity and of course, the jewel of selfless sacrifice.

Since I don't happen to be a part of administrative hierarchy, I find it a bit inconvenient to voice my opinion through the means of formal communication. It doesn't specifically concern me alone; rather, the same is true in case of every individual residing within the territorial jurisdiction of our beloved nation.

All of us, who have joined the socialist movement, had been associated with different ideologies. At a certain point of time, we all were in the same party, while at some other points in time, in different parties. As per my own experience, whenever the ego of a few leaders got hurt or whenever there was a setback to their personal interests, at that time they could remember neither the ideology, nor the slogans of socialism, nor their colleagues; but, when they were in power or held any position, at that time they remembered all these things. The downfall occurred in all political parties, especially of socialists because of permanently adopting a non-Congress strategy as an ideology and it would remain an unprecedented incident. Neither a positive ideology would emerge nor a creative vision would be developed from negative ideas, negative strategies and negative ideology. We have made negative strategies as the basis for all social and political issues. As a result, feelings of hatred, deceit, revenge, enmity and retaliation have become stronger. Whatever is happening today is the bane of that destructive politics in which we had a key role to play. In such a situation, don't we have any duty? Can't we introspect ourselves? Is socialism a philosophy of life or just a means to nurture the interests of a handful of people?

Since I have been your companion in this journey of rise and fall, I felt like politely requesting you. There will be many reactions to this. **The person in power and the party in power would always try to suppress the opposition, but nobody succeeded in doing so. From Prahlad to Lohia and Jai Prakash Naraian all are witness to this. Whether it is an individual or an organisation, whenever anyone came to power or acquired it** by force, the ego prevailed upon them. They might not have raised selfish slogans of caste, community or party, but they have been rooted in individual selfishness and desire. What's the difference between the rule of the Congress and that of the Janata Dal? The result of the despicable games played by the Chief Ministers of Congress to keep their power secured are witnessed today. In the Congress regime, whichever caste the Chief Ministers came from, they decimated the efficient, talented, knowledgeable and idealistic officers of the same caste who opposed them, based on a policy and sheltered those belonging to the other castes who flattered them. Same thing is happening even today. **When the grindstone of caste moves, it grinds the people without any mercy and doesn't even differentiate between kith and others**. It tortures the kith more vis-a-vis others. If we assess on this criteria, what is the difference since then and now? At one point in time, because of opposing late Lalit Naraian Mishra, eligible freedom fighters and social workers like Dr. Vaidyanath Jha, Digambar Thakur, Dr. Shivchandra Jha, Choudhury Ramakishore Rai and Bhagirath Jha were seriously attacked at the polling stations by hundreds of people of their own caste during the elections. Their murder has still been a serious blot on the system, and the present-day society is still made to come to terms with its consequences. In the same fashion, as I happened to raise my voice against Lalu Prasad Yadav, in the last Lok Sabha elections, in Darbhanga, attempts were made to burn me alive. A murder conspiracy was hatched on the day of the election. My supporters were beaten and even today, are framed under false charges. Their lives, assets and reputation are more unsafe today than during the Congress regime. The opponents of Mishra brothers were opponents of Brahmins, now the opponents of Lalu are opponents of Yadavs. In my opinion, it was neither Brahmin opposition at that time nor Yadav opposition now. Instead **the person in power becomes the symbol of that caste and, by spreading caste-based hatred, tries to intoxicate the whole society**. At that time where were our national and regional leaders of socialism? They were also equally at fault as others, as they were also getting votes because of Lalu's blind and intoxicating logic of the Yadavs and backwardness. They not only kept mum when people like me were getting burnt alive, but were also eliciting a sense of pleasure out of it. How come Lalu was then worthy of reverence and is being condemned today? When the Chief Minister goes to Darbhanga, he snacks with the mastermind who had a principal role to play in hatching a conspiracy. In front of him, those people are coercing the administrative officers. When veteran leaders like Ram Lakhan Singh Yadav and Ramsharan Yadav are grumbling in Parliament, who am I to say anything? Reason being internal conflict within the party. There was a time when respected Ramsharan Yadav was trying to pull the carpet from under my feet as I was opposing Laluji. Ramsharan Yadav used to breathe fire at me, but today all those people are burning in the same fire of revenge, retaliation and counter violence while writhing with pain. Why are Ram Sundar Das and the Central leaders who once protected him worried now?

The people who talked of social justice were contesting against Bommai for the national President's post. At that time when they were supporting him then, where was their philosophy of social justice? Existing MPs and MLAs of Janata Dal from Bihar have sacrificed the old relationships and they are scared of supporting me. They didn't hear my appeal. If you still have that manifesto which I have published and distributed at that time, I request you to kindly go through it. All the Chief Ministers and national leaders of Janata Dal have requested me in the larger interest of the party to be out of electoral politics. Then I told you that I am contesting as Shri Chandrasekhar told me so and I will only withdraw if he says so. Just a day before the voting, at 4 o'clock in the evening, Chandrasekhar told me to withdraw and I withdrew. You all have experienced the consequence of that evil deed and you are going to experience the remnant thereof. Where did issues like backwardness, social justice and Yadavs disappeared at that time? You can't give national level positions to the underprivileged, you murder the people of character, you felicitate anti-social and people of heinous character, then how justified your demand is to elect an individual from a deprived class to the post of the President of the country. Just remember that the elders in *Mahabharata* had lost their respect because one Abhimanyu was killed in deceit. But today the same thing is happening at every step.

When there was a fight between late Charan Singh and Karpoori Thakur, that time many of you took the side of Karpoori Thakur associating yourself with me and as a result, suffered the wave of casteism and got insulted. Didn't the current Chief Minister and his colleagues by taking the side of the late Charan Singh hurl highly disgusting abuses at Karpoori Thakur? Didn't you generally address Karpoori Thakur with many derogatory, disrespectful and insulting words? Where did the soul of those who used to regard Karpoori Thakur as their role model and took his name with respect disappear? Today those people who became the target of anger of Yadavs and those people who bore the insults for the sake of Karpoori Thakur are slowly getting eliminated. Those people who insulted and hurled abuses at Thakur are today enjoying the power and using his name. Similarly, at last I paved a separate path for myself. As I went along with Chandrasekhar, I was called as middle man Raibahadur and what not? Today to save your position why are you getting ready to kiss the feet of Chandrasekhar? My family fought against the British, I became a rebel during the

Congress regime, but so far I have never experienced the kind of hatred which I am experiencing in the Janata Dal regime. When life is endangered and when opponents get beheaded, then what's the difference between esteemed Brahminism and nationalism? I want to awaken your soul and wisdom. Has our blood turned into water with the flux and flow of time? Do we want to destroy everything by becoming voluptuous after reaching the third and fourth stage of our life?

Revenge can't be taken against a particular community, caste or class because of some historic incidents. **Due to some prevalent social, economic and political systems, our ancestors would be treated as untouchables, down- trodden and suppressed and were victimised. Today we want to take revenge against their progeny for the crimes committed by their ancestors; is this humanity? Replacing fanatic Brahminism with any extremism based on Yadav caste, backwardness or any other issue will only become a cause for destruction of the society.** The society is suffering from the ill-effects of revenge, repression and retaliation. All through Jagannath Mishra and Lalu Prasad have been playing the same politics against each other. They are not foes; in fact they are comrades of each other. We have also seen that **the person who seemingly works for the oppressed is no better than the oppressor in any sense**. In other words, he outdoes anybody as far as the elements of indulgence and corruption are concerned. Only a few politicians, administrators and rulers are managing the show, and they are spewing all sorts of venom to fulfil their ulterior motives. The way Chief Ministers of Congress ruled by delegating power in the hands of administration, adopting the same path Lalu Prasad is also ruling the state. **Path is the same but passengers are different. We have to see the path, not the passenger**. Come, let us learn from the past, but let it not get repeated. By liberating ourselves from the fear of future, let us get ready to do our duty by standing on the foundations of today. In order to achieve the objective of creating an egalitarian society, a new age of knowledge and wisdom has to be built on the edifice of generosity and humility.

Before I conclude, I would like to request all of you with all humility at any demand because of opposition, if there is any danger to myself or my family, you will take care of me. Wake up, get up, take a vow – we will fight together, we will die together and build the new age together in a spirit of close cooperation.

**Mr. George, why did You Choose to Observe a Conspicuous Silence at that Time?**

Respected George sir,

There were attacks on you and your colleagues and many of you and they received mild injuries. Vehicles were damaged and the programme was stalled midway. The news about this incident was published in various newspapers. Mr. Abdul Gaffur, Mr. Nitish, Mr. Vrishin Patel, Mr. Shahabuddin and Mr. Sanjay Lal were travelling along with you. Although all of them are well-known leaders from Bihar and also MPs, yet the police couldn't provide them adequate security. This incident was shameful, painful and very scary. The constituency which apparently seemed peaceful had become brazen. Even during 1978-79 when there were attacks on you while you were touring Muzaffarpur, reservations were introduced by late Mr. Karpoori Thakur. You both of supported him due to which the people opposing reservations attacked you. Today again, you and your colleagues were attacked, but this time the attackers were those supporting reservation and those who shouted the slogans of social justice. Why did it happen? One should lend a serious thought, as to how this unfortunate incident happened in the protection of the same government and by those people for whose ideology and the party, you bore insults, faced hardships and toiled to form the government. Earlier, whenever such attacks were carried out by our political opponents, we always attributed them to be opponents of democracy and agents of feudalism. Today, the same thing is happening and our own colleagues are involved in it.

During the last Assembly elections when Nitish Kumar was distributing the tickets of Janata Dal, you all were quietly supporting him. So that day itself you had invited; lawlessness, terrorism, aggression and lunacy in the state. Criminals and arrogant people were made candidates by denying tickets to genuine candidates. My close aides were hanged; I was the only one to oppose it. At that time, the Lalu and Nitish team got the support of Choudhury Devilal, V.P. Singh, Mulayam Singh and Raghunath Jha, the close confidant of Mr. Chandrasekhar. They were getting tickets for their relatives, followers and disciples; all those people having good character, and those who struggled a lot, committed, talented, sincere people who always came second in elections were denied tickets. I strongly opposed this, and when I was bewailing this at the residence of Mr. Chandrasekhar, then Ajit Singh, Raghunath Jha, Yashwant Sinha were also present. Ajit Singh was smiling at my helplessness. Secret tie-ups had been made with Pandit Jagannath Mishra. At that time when I was exposing all these things, you all kept quiet and were supporting Lalu. While the government was formed, I vehemently opposed it but you all were supporting Lalu. Till the end I was agitating and watching the people of Bihar that by handing power in the hands of Lalu, we were inviting total destruction of Bihar. I wrote an open letter addressing the colleagues of Janata Dal, and sent a copy to you also. You all must have had a copy of that letter which I brought out when I was contesting for the post of national president of Janata Dal. You also requested me over phone to quit from the race. Where did ideas like social justice, socialism and special opportunities vanish, when Chief Ministers like Lalu, Mulayam, Choutala, Biju, Ajit Singh and also Mr. Devi Lal for whose sake I always kept my entire life at stake, were supporting Bommai. You and your colleagues were holding ministerial posts in the government at that time. Lalu was considered a hero, a mass leader and the saviour of social revolution. You all were eulogising him and I was getting grinded in the grindstone.

During the 1991 General Elections in Sitamarhi on the day of filing of nomination, in front of Mr. Harikishan Singh, his supporters attacked me in the Assembly, abused and insulted me, and at that time you all kept quiet. You all still kept mum even when lunatic the Yadavs kept on insulting me at Parihar, Rasoolpur, Sahugachi of Sitamarhi by provoking small children in various schools to hurl abuses at me. You were silent even when in Darbhanga, during the elections, rogue Yadavs pelted stones, shoes and sandals at me and attempted to burn me alive by throwing diesel at me. Only god knows what all were the abuses that were hurled and thrown at me at a rally in Madhubani. All these things happened when I was a minister in the Union Cabinet. The administration proved inept and inefficient; protection was not provided; there was absence of proper security; I was going around with only two security guards provided by the Central Government. My jeep was stolen from the premises of the Assembly Club of Patna. Culprits were driving the jeep by putting a fake number plates and the flag of Janata Dal. You did nothing when, in Pirocha village of your constituency, my in-laws and two other relatives of mine were killed in police firing. No action was taken against the accused reported to the police personnel. Sitamarhi is on the south and Darbhanga on the east of Muzaffarpur, which is your constituency, but at that time you were unable to register anything; instead, you were supporting injustice, riot and atrocity.

**You were in the government along with all those people who participated in the movement of 1974, who supported the state of Emergency, who bootlicked Sanjay Gandhi and who called Jai Prakash a fascist, are now in your government even today, such people are still in your group.**

You all supported the undemocratic arrest of Lal Krishna Advani. No civilised person would like to hear the kind of derogatory and insulting remarks made by Lalu about Mr. Advani. Didn't you remember your good manners when you went on rampage on Holi at the residence of the Chief Minister? Caste-based public rallies were taking place and the whole society was reeling under corruption in Bihar; political kidnappings and killings were increasing; criminals were getting rewarded; MLAs were given a freehand to exploit or misuse the post of president; whimsical decisions were taken about MLAs; memberships were revived after cancelling them; people were appointed in unconstitutional ways; communalism was promoted under the guise of language; corrupt, greedy and immoral officers were getting promoted in the administration;

ministers were dancing along with officers under the influence of alcohol in public places; development activities were stalled; economy was facing rough weather. In the Bihar Service Commission, postings were given by receiving graft; warnings of the High Court were getting overlooked; opponents were terrorised; workers like me struggled between life and death then, why did you all choose to maintain a stunning silence? By supporting that government, you all were grabbing your share of political advantages. What prompted you to be up in arms just before the election is best known to you only.

The Bharatiya Janata Party was steadily growing in Bihar; the people, who were opposing Lalu, were showing inclination towards it, then you people tried to create an illusion to stop the backward communities which were opposing Lalu from joining the BJP. That was a political move of yours. Many of your supporters would either join Congress or help the Congress when the opportunity came. In future also they will leave and go there only. Samajwadi had lost its direction and destination, both. In Gorakhpur, the convoy of Mr. Advani was attacked. Can that be termed as the behavior of Samajwadi? Didn't the hatred and negativity towards Congress make us commit all sorts of bad deeds? In future, all of you shall stoop to any low because of the hatred and negativity towards BJP? The founders couldn't even imagine that Samajwadis would stoop so low for the sake of power and position. Nehru, Indira, Rajiv and Narasimha Rao were all links in the stream of an ideology and stream of a political culture. Whoever was ever connected to that stream, they all will go back to them. Only those people keep opposing Congress who take the path of nationalism, socialism, morality, righteousness, cultural social harmony, generosity and sacrifice. I feel deeply pained and touched for whatever has happened to you. I sympathise with you. So I request you to let there be two political streams. You all swallow the poison and go back to the Congress or else come to the BJP to strengthen the ideology of nation building, indigenous, self-reliance, self-rule and self-respect. Here organisation and principles are above everything. Ego, idolisation, glorification, adoration and veneration of human being is in itself a sort of ailment and obviously symptomatic of being ill. In India, there will be a decisive battle between two streams of ideologies. It will be termed as an ocean. **Self-respect of a nation can only be achieved when we adopt the culture of ownership over the culture of slavery**. We want complete freedom; talking about economic freedom is a will-o'-the-wisp. Similarly, slogans of political and social freedom are also incomplete and one sided. All other freedoms would remain incomplete without cultural freedom. **Cultural slavery is slavery of the soul**. India wants absolute freedom and citizens want complete liberation. You kindly survey the northern villages of your own constituency where Muslims are in a majority and take pains to find out whether the Hindus living in those villages have cultural and political freedom. Is socialism meant to provide freedom to Hindus from the exploitation of upper castes? Is waging a struggle to grant freedom to Hindus from the exploitation of Muslims and vice versa wrong and inhuman? Socialists and altruists have to steer clear of this illusion. People of all communities should have the freedom to observe their religious duties. It's not that Hindus should disenfranchise on dissociate themselves from their culture and religious worship and others be allowed to dominate them. Communal harmony is a part of social harmony. We have committed a lot of sins for the sake of votes. Now think of creating hurdles in the mainstream of the nation. If not today, sooner or later you all shall join the bandwagon some way or the other. My request is, the sooner the better. Come, welcome to all of you.

*Panchajanya, 7 August, 1994*

□

## 2

# Recognise the Values of Lok Nayak

It's a long story that when and how Jai Prakash became Lok Nayak. The journey of Jai Prakash as a Marxist, Gandhian, socialist, supporter of Bhoodan (donating land) and then as complete revolutionary is very long. It is very interesting to know how Jai Prakash, the great soldier of freedom struggle and the inspiration of great revolutionaries, joined the movement of land donation after turning into a socialist. He commented on this strategy in his book titled *From Socialism to Sarvodaya*.

People, who consider economic disparity is the only disparity, do not understand the caste system of India. People born in wealthy and upper-caste family cannot feel the pain of backward and lower-caste people. There are fundamental differences between the philosophy of socialism and a society based on equality. Privileges and special opportunities are fundamentally different from each other. In his long journey of life, Jai Prakash had experienced this. While Lohia gave the message of *sapt kranti* (seven revolutions), Jai Prakash gave the message of complete revolution during the time of Bihar movement. According to him, it is necessary to bring the complete revolution in order to establish economic, social, cultural, intellectual and political equality. Individuals and society can be rejuvenated through transfiguration. There would be many people agitating for political power change, but there will be very few people agitating to bring about a change in social, administrative and systemic powers.

There should be an analysis of the people who were responsible for the Emergency. People who shouted slogans of complete revolution ran away from it when they got to see the full form of complete revolution. At Gandhi Maidan in Patna, where Jai Prakash was conferred the title of 'Lok Nayak', at that very same Maidan, on his 75th birth anniversary, what happened? How did Jagjivan Ram, the erstwhile Defence Minister was made to flee from that Maidan? It was all due to the reservations given to the backward castes. At that time Karpoori Thakur was the Chief Minister of Bihar. He provided 26 percent reservation for backward castes, women and poor people belonging to upper castes. He announced that out of 26 percent reservation, 12 percent will be for extremely backward castes, 8 percent for backward castes, 3 percent for women of all categories and 3 percent for economically poor people belonging to upper castes. Later on, the definition given by the Supreme Court on reservation due to the controversies that came up because of the Mandal Commission was based on the formula given by Karpoori Thakur. At that time whatever was said about Karpoori Thakur is known to everybody; all that would remain a blot on the so-called civilised society. Even today, that has an impact on the minds of backward and lower castes. Karpoori Thakur was the colleague, disciple, friend and supporter of Lok Nayak due to which Lok Nayak was insulted. Karpoori had put economic sanctions on reservation, and excluded the income-tax payers from the benefits of reservations. Neglecting and insulting Jai Prakash was one of the main reasons for the failure of Bihar movement.

Complete revolution couldn't be realised as there was no economic, social and cultural revolution. People with vested interests had joined the struggle for change of political disposition; in the end they ditched the movement. Complete revolution cannot come without decentralisation of administrative power, cleansing of political power and empowering the villages. Although the movement of Jai Prakash failed temporarily, it had agitated the society in reality and in the long run. The fire which broke out from the agitation was growing bigger and bigger with each passing day. The fire kept burning; not just one leader, many leaders kept taking birth and marching ahead with that torch. Sometimes they also might stray off their path even after taking a vow in the name of Jai Prakash, still the name continues. It's not the person but his name that becomes immortal. In a true sense, Jai Prakash was an illuminating source to ensure victory and he was beyond failure.

**Lok Nayak's Love for the Public**

My concern is as to what kind of people I would like to live with in this society. Certainly, I wouldn't like to live in the society of liars and murderers, who don't have tolerance, companionship and kindness towards each other.

*(Excerpts from the speech given by Mr. Jai Prakash Narayan on the occasion of accepting the post of General Secretary of the Socialist Party in 1948.)*

**For the Sake of Votes, the Storm of Reservation Politics Making the Earth Red**

It's very difficult to understand whether it is politics of reservation or reservation of politics? Politics of reservation and reservation of politics—both are intervened with each other. Politics has become the means for fulfilling the short-term interests of power. Politicians have become the means to fulfil those interests. It's become difficult to recognise the accomplishment.

There is no difference left between the ruling party and the opposition and between people supporting and opposing. Even those who are supporting factually don't know who they are lending support to. **It's the bane of negative politics. It is the fault of directionless struggle to achieve some temporary gain. It's an illusion of change and losing direction and path. The term 'reservation' is also in the same state. There should be an extensive debate on philosophy, principles, abstract, subtle and gross aspects of issues related to reservation, such as reservation for whom, why, how and how long, for long term, short term, immediate basis. Whatever is done is based on the consensus of the nation; the results arising out of it**

**remain permanent in the life of the nation for a very long time.**

## Special Opportunities

Reservation is a distorted form of Dr. Ram Manohar Lohia's vision of special opportunities. An agitation was started on privileges versus special opportunities. Some communities in the Hindu society enjoy certain privileges based on birth. They have the privilege of education, holding high positions and reputation. These privileges were given only to those people born in specific castes, others howsoever qualified or eligible they might be, were deprived of these privileges. A barricade has been formed; it was not so in the olden times. The class or castes used to be very transient and were formed for different reasons. When the class and caste became static, then they took a firm shape. Today, the class is getting transformed into a new form, which in due course would take the form of caste. The children of MPs, ministers, IAS and IPS, doctors, engineers and businessmen are claiming their right over the profession of their parents. Capability, eligibility, potential and talent are getting neglected. Whichever caste they belong to, the values and character of the people of the privileged class remain the same. New castes are getting formed from the same system in parliamentary democracy, and this may become the reason for danger in future. When the children of farmers become farmers, children of businessmen become businessmen, children of industrialists become industrialists, children of officers become officers, then what will be the future of India? It becomes very clear when the antiquity of this philosophy is seen, where children of Brahmins were made Brahmins, children of Kshatriyas into Kshatriyas, children of Vaishyas into Vaishyas and children of Shudras into Shudras. For this very reason India became very static and today we see the ugly face of it. People having privileges are hiding their inefficiency, ineligibility behind this shield. This is the main reason for the slavery of India. When Mahatma Gandhi gave assurance to everybody that everybody would be given equal opportunities and special opportunities are given to people who are at the lower rung to climb up, then life came back into the nation and everybody stood united. The country got freedom. Whenever the entire nation stands in a spirit of solidarity it can be said to be the golden period of the nation. The principle of special opportunities was put forth to end privileges. The philosophy was to form an egalitarian society, free from all sorts of exploitation. Individual with total freedom and well-governed system. The way a patient is brought to health by giving medicine and special diet, similarly, those communities which were suppressed and faced all sorts of exploitation have to be helped to rise in society by giving special opportunities. Similarly, by giving special opportunities to the ailing children of the Mother Nation they have to be helped to reach the physical, intellectual, psychological and spiritual heights. But it should be borne in mind that once the patient gains health, those privileges should be withdrawn. If a patient even after gaining health still considers himself a patient, then all the family members get irritated and feel sad. The entire nation is also like a family, which to be looked at in a similar perspective.

### Lohia's Dharmayudh

With regard to special opportunities, Lohia said, "Attack on the caste should mean development of all, rather than development of a particular stratum. Development of a particular stratum brings some changes in relationships within the caste system; however there won't be any change in the caste-profile (caste system)". He further said how even the people belonging to lower castes change once they reach the higher echelons. They try to mix with the top strata people and in the process they imbibe all the bad qualities of the upper strata people. Lower-caste people who reach to the top because of reservation do not treat the poor and weak people of the same caste with affection. Their lifestyle becomes exactly like that of upper strata. Those people who continue to progress on reservation become weak in course of time. Once when they are given special opportunities through reservation, then it becomes their responsibility to progress ahead. However, today through reservation, they want to ensure privileges for them and their future generations till eternity. Lohia warned the people who do politics in the name of reservation to be alert on various issues. Even before the lower caste awakes, the Brahmins with their ability to mislead and cause a sense of doubt may directly or indirectly defame the people following this strategy. Secondly, people belonging to Ahir and Chamar castes, which are slightly superior castes among the lower castes, instead of extending the benefits of this reservation among all other lower castes try to enjoy benefits all for themselves. As a result, Brahmins and Chamars may change their places but the caste system remains the same. Thirdly, selfish people, belonging to the lower castes, in a bid to empower their own people may take undue advantage of this policy and may stoke infighting and employ ammunition to burn the caste. Fourthly, every occasion of election or selection may create situations of conflicts and abuses between the Brahmins and lower castes. Some bad elements among the oppressed castes may repeatedly use such instruments when overcome by an overpowering urge to take revenge on a particular Brahmin against whom they have some grudge, or may even try to eliminate the entire Brahmin community. If they fail, they may create doubt in the entire environment. Fifthly, they may make economic and political issues very ambiguous or else, may push them into the background. To fulfil their interests, some reactionary elements among the lower castes may misuse the policy against racism. Besides he didn't consider it right to provide reservation in the education system. Everybody should get equal opportunities for education or children of lower castes can be given special education, but precluding any child from entering into an educational system based on caste cannot be demanded as a right under any circumstances. He said that the commission didn't do any justice by recommending reservations in education.

## Need for New Leadership

All those people who utter the name of Lohia, or who talk about socialism and shout slogans for a society based on equality, having lost their path, consider that special opportunities are the only goal to be achieved. Hatred, jealousy, violence, selfish motives and acquisition of political power are the core principles of their special opportunities. If these principles could bring the abolition of caste system, equal education, economic equality, decentralisation of power, indigenousness, self-rule, village development, priority of agriculture, curbing corruption and overconsumption, etc., it could be considered a step forward towards realising the vision of an egalitarian society. When one tries to visualise the philosophy through one or two programmes, the whole society crumbles. Where did programmes such as inter-caste marriage to abolish caste system, ban on private educational institutions to provide equal educational opportunities, four-tier structural system to bring about decentralisation of political power, setting minimum and maximum income limits to remove economic disparities, setting limits on expenditure to end corruption and consumerism, foreign investment to promote indigenousness, total boycott of industrial and consumer-based items, constitutional freedom to local units to inculcate self-reliance, according priority to agriculture for rural development, allocation of 60 percent of budget for the development of villages disappear? Because of economic disparity between backward classes vis-á-vis upper classes and forward classes in backward classes have taken birth. Brahmins have joined the league of backward and lower castes; similarly there are backward classes among Brahmins too. People who do politics on reservation will be eliminated the day the blind opposition to reservation ends. **Reservation in government jobs alone will not transform the nation. They only want votes; they don't care for their sake even if the earth becomes red in the name of caste, language and community.** Principles developed on the philosophy of nationalism, equality, firmness, generosity, fair practice, harmony, affection and spirituality only can bring about welfare of the humanity. Today there is a need for such a leadership. Will all wise men think about it?

*Panchajanya, 25 September, 1944*

□

# 3

# Whether to Stay Away from the 'Battle' of Samajwadi or to Cooperate with the BJP

Mr. Hukmdev Narayan Yadav, a staunch Samajwadi (socialist) and former Minister of State for Textiles in the Cabinet of Mr. Chandrasekhar has recently joined the BJP. Mr. Yadav, who considers district Darbhanga in the Mithilanchal region of Bihar as his land of action, is known as a supporter of Gandhian and Lohia's ideology. Those who assess his seniority and potential are not ready to accept that his decision to join the BJP is a move by an opportunist.

Before joining the BJP, Mr. Yadav wrote a letter to Mr. Lal Krishna Advani, requesting him to maintain the sanctity of those in media who provide extensive and emotional base to a nation which is passing through the state of slumber to the state of awakening. In the letter he mentioned that BJP is slowly and steadily climbing the steps of success. It is the responsibility of the BJP to clarify their policies to make public their vision and direction in the current scenario and on their ideology of eternal nation, culture and civilisation. He sought BJP's clarification on the policies of BJP to remove the caste equations on which so far Congress is ruling. If the BJP has intentions of building India based on Gandhi's ideology, Lohia, and Pt. Deen Dayal Upadhyay, the BJP should start an ideological debate. There are some people in both Hindu and Muslim communities who plundered or supported the people who have looted the country. People who consider these people as their ancestors will never be able to protect the dignity and decorum of the nation.

The BJP should make their perspective clear on all these issues, so that the misconception of all the followers of Gandhi, Lohia and JP get cleared and collectively all of them join the stream of BJP.

## Questions to George Fernandes

Hukmdev Narayan Yadav wrote another letter to the Janata Dal, George Fernandes and posed some questions to the politicians who blindly oppose the BJP and consider them to be symbols of socialism, Lohia's ideology and revolution. The letter was as follows:

Respected George sir,

We all formed alliances even earlier to stay in power, but couldn't discharge our duties. Every time we cheated the nation and its people. We were worshipping the Congress, whom we, as non-Congress people, termed as decadent and wicked. You considered Viswanath Pratap Singh, who used to bootlick late Sanjay Gandhi, as your ideal. Didn't you remember the unity of Samajwadi at that time?

During the last elections in Bihar, when there were attempts to burn me alive and when there was a severe blow to rights of civilians, where did your vision go? Even Chandrasekhar, in whose cabinet I was a minister, too chose to observe silence, thinking that he would get the support of Lalu when required. When I was a contestant to the post of national president of Janata Dal, you all supported Mr. Bommai; where was your caste policy and socialist philosophy then?

The letter written to me by you when I was the Minister of Textiles bears witness to it. I set up an enquiry committee and was about to send a request to cancel the licence of Pepsi to the council of ministers, but by then the government had gone. The Finance Ministry had asked to return 20 percent of the excise duty to the traders. The allegations were found to be true during the investigation. Madhu Dandavate, who regarded himself to be the greatest socialist, was the Finance Minister at that time. If the same thing had been done by any other party, you would have called it a commission and dealing of an intermediary. Where was the philosophy of socialism at that time?

When Dr. Lohia, Deen Dayal Upadhyay and Acharya Kripalani were contesting the by-elections, Jan Sangh was supporting Dr. Lohia and the socialists were supporting Deen Dayal Upadhyay.

In 1977, Jan Sangh had become part of the Janata Party, in which you and I were ministers. Even V.P. Singh's Government was formed with the support of the BJP. I am reminding you all these episodes of the past because we have an age-old relationship with the BJP. Between the Congress and the BJP, Samajwadis always preferred BJP. On issues like nationalism, language and religion, BJP has always been better as compared to the Congress and the communists.

On issues relating to economy, we were closer to the communists, but on other issues, communists spread poison. Is it right, the way people are getting suppressed in Bengal, opponents are getting rooted out, civil rights are getting curtailed? The irresponsible behaviour of the Janata Dal Government in Bihar, is it democratic? If not, why are they getting the support?

Significant issues like equality in education, setting limits on income to remove economic disparity, inter-caste marriages, administrative reforms, code of conduct for ministers, shape of cabinet of ministers, development of rural India, programmes to bridge the gap between rural and urban areas have always been on the agenda of the Samajwadis.

But you haven't taken up willingly any of these issues, after coming into the government. So my suggestion is to relent on opposing the BJP blindly and let there be a considerate distinction between the Congress and the BJP. Either all Samajwadis keep away from this battle and not contest the elections or support BJP for the complete elimination of the Congress. Forming tie-ups for the sake of power are always detrimental and so will be the case in future also. In the name of communalism and blind opposition, we shouldn't let the values and principles of democracy, civil rights, constitutional and fundamental rights suffer.

You all are talking about polarisation under the influence of hatred from the past, fear of the present and lure of the future. I am taking inspiration from the present, I am once again appealing to you—either stay away from the battle or select one force between the two. Many among the Samajwadis used to go with the Congress and many would go even today. Let them go; I am not stopping them, but my humble request is that at least for once, all the Samajwadis should join the BJP, forgetting about all past grudges because nation building can only happen if transformation, speed and sharpness reign supreme all around.

With all sincerity, love and affection for all.

*Panchajanya, 18 April, 1993*

□

# 4
# Whirlpool of Corruption

The whole system is suffering because of corruption. From Parliament to streets, debates are going on to uproot this problem. Dr. Lohia used to say that vision, direction and determination—all the three factors are very important. Corruption is an abstract term. When it is extensively described and solid measures are taken to uproot this problem, then only its gross form becomes visible. Corruption has affected the conduct, thinking, behaviour and nature of people. The insect of corruption takes birth and gets nurtured and grows on the garbage of consumerism. It gets the protection of the caste system. All political parties, bureaucrats, and so-called intellectuals, to some extent, get united to protect people of their own caste. Secondly because of class character and selfish interests, all corrupt people keep protecting each other. They have the expertise in bringing principles to this end.

There is a nexus between professional corruption and political as well as administrative corruption. The relation between profession and power is very old. The whole system gets entangled in this and keeps wriggling. How can a society which is deeply sunk in the quagmire of consumerism, fear and illusion, put up a struggle? Many retired Lok Sabha and Rajya Sabha secretaries enjoy the privileges due to compassion and grace of government. Cabinet Secretaries, who are at the top of administrative hierarchy, get the benefit of government's ex-gratia after retirement. Can we expect them to remain unbiased, transparent, righteous, fearless and sincere?

After retirement many people get benefits by becoming advocates, advisors and consultants in various reputed government, business and industrial establishments. Can we expect any positive measures from them to eradicate widespread corruption in these establishments? A judge who has become an advocate of a company, how can he be expected to be fair against the irregularities of that company? When he himself gets into the company of a political party, then he tries to overlook all its corrupt practices. Can a law be passed so that no judge after retirement can take up any salaried or non-salaried position in any private or government company, or become an advocate, or join any commission, etc. or any political party? Same rule must be put in place in respect of the officers of Indian Administrative Services. In case any decision maker tries to pass on the benefits to any of his relatives up to two generations, they should be disqualified from all the positions for their entire life.

Is it possible? I can tell that this is not possible, the reason being the deep nexus between politics, administration and business. Caste system is the major reason for this. Till such time as there is a law to limit wealth accumulation and expenditure, the consumerist society keeps suffering from corruption. Top 20 percent of the people constitute 52.7 percent and the bottom 20 percent of the people contribute 5.2 percent of the national income. Gifting an aeroplane on the wife's birthday, feasting lakhs of people during marriages and spending hundreds of rupees aren't called corruption? Building a mansion worth thousands of crores and constructing a helipad on the rooftop, isn't it a crime? Isn't it a corruption to draw dearness and other privileges amounting many times more than the basic salary? In IPL, behind selling and purchasing of players for crores of rupees, many secret games are played. Can a law be made to curb extravagance and profligacy? This can't be done, as there is no strong determination or willpower or genuine love for the nation.

Minimum and maximum income should be defined. There should be 1 : 10 or 1 : 20 difference between the salary of the

President of the country and that of the watchman. A law should come in place with consensus in the Parliament. There is a string of voluntary organisations in the country. It was said in Parliament that from 2005-06 to 2008-09, in these four years, these voluntary organisations received foreign donations amounting to a total of rupees twenty-eight thousand seven hundred and seventy-eight crores. Some NGOs are working in the interest of some multi-national companies, especially in the field of agriculture. They are active in causing huge loses to the domestic companies, while benefitting the foreign companies. In this, many people are shielded by bureaucrats, politicians and businessmen and also the so-called intellectuals' members of their family involved in it which helps them in getting the aid.

**Nobody is above the Constitution and rule of law in a democracy. Decorating and nominating the ineligible, undeserving for membership of the Rajya Sabha also comes under the category of constitutional corruption. Aren't there allegations of corruption against the Chief Justice of India and other judges? What harm will it bring, if prosecution is carried out against the officers of Indian Administrative Services, judges, the Prime Minister and the President of India under general procedures?**

**The character of political organisations has changed. Lakhs of rupees are spent on political rallies. Offices have five-star facilities. Wherefrom does the money come? Here the officers, workers and businessmen arrange for the money.**

Wherefrom do the farmers, labourers and villagers get money? People get positions on the basis of the amount of money they manage to collect. It is obvious that whoever makes these facilities and money available to politicians and political parties, would like to get some favour in some form or the other. This is also a major area of corruption.

Retired bureaucrats and business houses greatly influence politics. Over the last 10 to 15 years, corruption has gone up in the same proportion in politics as well as in administration. The income of 90 percent of farmers, labourers, rural and urban poor hasn't increased in proportion to the increase in the income of these people. This is a sort of strategic corruption and no government has any policy or means to overcome this problem.

A comprehensive and integrated approach should be in place to curb and weed out corruption. It is very difficult to exercise control over this by just keeping a vigil on government offices alone. It requires extensive thinking. There is a need for making stringent laws against it. Reforms should be made in the electoral process and amendments be made in the Representation of People's Act (RPA) to ban criminals and corrupt people from contesting elections. The political parties which give tickets to criminals and corrupt should be derecognised. Anybody convicted by any court or arrested and released on bail against corruption charges has to be debarred from contesting elections and be declared ineligible for holding any position in the organisation of political parties. On many occasions, there has been emphasis on these aspects nonetheless though nothing concrete has so far come up due to lack of political will.

Whoever has the authority to nominate in politics will find eligible candidates in their caste only. New definitions are given, decision is not ethical but can't be said to be illegal. But when a decision is not ethical, how can it be called legal? If corruption has to be removed, the form of Parliament has to be changed based on the principles given by Gandhi, Dr. Lohia and Deen Dayal Upadhyay. Today our country is governed by an elected government and the affairs of the government are taken care of by the bureaucrats. In other words, people are servants to government and government is a servant to bureaucracy. Dr. Lohia said in the Lok Sabha that in order to uproot corruption, it is very essential to end the caste system, set an upper limit on expenditure, define minimum and maximum income, all office-bearers of political organisations should make their wealth and assets public, a permanent commission should be set up to regulate this. All the representatives of the people are supposed to declare their wealth and assets but there is no control over it. Nobody can understand how come their income increased by leaps and bounds. There should be a balance between the salaries, dearness allowance and other perks of employees and officers of the government and private companies. There should be a regulatory authority over private companies also as public and government financial institutions have a stake in them.

Stashing black money in foreign countries should be considered anti-national and such people should be awarded life imprisonment and their wealth confiscated. The amount deposited in the Nation Building Fund for 20 years should be removed from the category of black money. Through this, crores of rupees from lakhs of people can be used for development activities. There are many solutions but who is going to do it? Talks are going on to bring back the black money stashed in foreign banks, but so far it couldn't be found out who are the people who have deposits in foreign banks and what's the amount? To take practical steps on this issue, character, conduct, behaviour and the face of the Parliament has to be changed. There is no alternative except fighting a battle of righteousness for transformation. This can be done only with extensive support of the people.

*Jansatta, 11 December, 2015*

□

# 5
# Lohia in the Present Times

Everyday there are discussions on corruption, dynasty politics, terrorism, casteism and democratic dictatorship—newspapers, magazines, TV channels keep discussing these issues, but debates are conducted for the sake of discussion. Some people are engaged in it fulltime and some people are called upon for holding debates. Nothing is becoming clear, as if some intellectual entertainment were going on in the dark, no fruitful discussions arc happening. Discussion can be fruitful only when a result is expected. People don't have comprehensive understanding of the issues involved. It is a very basic principle that unless the root cause of the problem is known, how can any solution be found out? Awareness of the form, speed and direction of the problem should be there and this is known as direction and vision.

Dr. Ram Manohar Lohia was one of the modern thinkers of Indian socialism. He used to think holistically on all the aspects of the problem. He used to explain the problem both at macro and micro levels by analysing the issue both by narrowing it and expanding it. Politics is related to economics, social policies and administrative policies. As is the intention, so are the policies and as the policies reflect the intentions, it is a very common rule. Lohia used to decide a policy only after thinking about it extensively and then would propose new rules to solve the problems of society.

Corruption is an abstract term. People can understand only when it is presented in a concrete form. Moral corruption takes shape when there is economic, ethical, moral and ideological corruption. A consumeristic society needs wealth in abundance. There is no limit to consumerism and morality is lost in consumerism when only one rule stays — whatever has to be done to ensure one's own comfort, facility and prosperity, should be done. In other words, wealth should be accumulated at any cost. Through money people are lured and threatened. There is no morality and fearlessness left in society which is influenced by lure and fear. According to Lohia, there are means described in Indian philosophy to suppress and eliminate the consumerist behaviour. The Marxist philosophy has taught the means to fulfil one's wants and desires.

Both of them are incomplete philosophies. Desires do arise and assume humongous dimension. They cannot be doused successfully. Most of the people who tried to suppress became hypocrites and imposters. Those who tried to fulfil their desires in a systematic way turned violent and dictators. Lohia had suggested binding them in a limit — there should be freedom to earn but there should be a cap on expenditure. Tax should be levied on expenditure rather than on income. The difference between minimum and maximum should be 1 : 10; this has to be reviewed from time to time. When there is a rise in the national income, it should be raised from bottom to top. Pt. Deen Dayal and Mahatma Gandhi had talked about the last man. If the President of the country gets 10, a watchman in the village should get one. Today islands of wealth are built in the ocean of poverty. Every year a few people join in the league of the affluent either because of increase in their salaries, dearness allowances and other perks or due to the implementation of recommendations of the Pay Commission. New islands of wealth are being built by the flesh, blood and bones of the 90 percent of the population. There is a rule in socialism *"na sou se kum, na hazzar se zyada, Samajwadi kay yahi hain takaza"* (neither less than 100 nor more than 1000, this is the demand of socialism). Why don't people evolve a national consensus on this?

Lohia had initiated a debate in Parliament on setting a cap on expenditure—nobody should be allowed to spend more than rupees 1,500. Today instead of 1,500, may be the limit can be extended up to 15,000 rupees. People of the country should act not for themselves only, but also for nation building. Capital should be used for building the capital, to increase production rather than consumption. Consumer items are produced and luxury items are produced. For 20 years money should be collected in assured savings scheme and after 20 years that amount should be returned with interest and profit. With the savings earned through this, all foreign debt can be paid back in five years.

This cannot be done unless people's representatives, bureaucrats, businessmen and industrialists agree to it. Lohia said that only a strong-willed and determined political leader can make a law on this and implement it, even if he doesn't come into power for the second time. Nation building can't be expected by a leader who wishes that his body should be wrapped in tricolour and his pyre should be lit along with the salvo of 21 guns. Nobody should be a Prime Minister beyond two terms or 10 years.

People should reach the peak, rising from the ground. The Ganges originates from Gangotri. Gangotri is sacred, that's why Ganga is sacred. If there is garbage in Gangotri, then how can Ganges be pure? In politics, the people who run the government and organisations are like Gangotri, from where the Ganges of administration and organisation flows out. When Gangotri itself is dirty, then how can society and administration be clean and upright? Today bureaucrats, businessmen, industrialists, actors are made politicians, then who will talk about farmers and labourers? The programmes at the top should be rolled out according to the energy and vision emerging from the ground. The top will be strong and experienced when it grows from the ground.

Today, the ground is lifeless and a mute spectator. Government and organisations are run from the top. Those people who don't know the way for themselves are prescribing the path for others. Lohia wanted to make leaders of nation from among the people who are familiar with language, lifestyles, values and living conditions. **A sense of belonging to the nation won't be there in the ideas of people who believe**

**in foreign language, foreign lifestyle, foreign food habits, foreign buildings and foreign culture and traditions. There are some pretentious people who appear to be indigenous but behind the scene, they have relations with people espousing foreign culture.** Lohia had given many rules but people dared to discuss only one or two rules. If the nation debates on the principles of Lohia in Parliament and comes up with laws accordingly, the transformation of the nation will take place.

*Jansatta, 24 March, 2013*

□

# 6
# One More Letter of Yadav

Respected Rajendra Yadav: A letter written by Mulayam Singh Yadav was published in *Jansatta* (10 September). You are a famous author and a literary person, so you have published that letter. Many people write letters to Mulayam Singh Yadav, but they don't get published in any newspapers and most probably will never get published. As you said, just because you have 'Yadav' as your surname, you are often associated with Mulayam Singh and Lalu Prasad. Even I have 'Yadav' in my name, and for that reason I am commenting on this letter. This is not a reaction as I am not a reactionary. I believe in constructive criticism and positive thinking. This is the Indian school of thought. I am in the BJP and many Yadavs like me are in the BJP. Sharad Yadav is also in the same government. As long as the caste system continues and as long as an individual gets imprisoned based on birth, till then, from birth to death, he is going to get grounded between the grindstones of caste system. I am not aware of ideology. I have never met you nor have ever talked to you over phone. Whoever is in politics is there because of his or her influence. There is something attractive in their personality; even if we consider that as a bad quality, it's not going to affect them anyway.

The BJP is continuously widening its influence. It has its own path, its own ideology, principles and ideals. **BJP, by overcoming all sorts of opposition, obstacles and resistance has established its own identity.** Communists and socialists are all thinking on the lines of reactionaries in the name of so-called progressive-thinking revolutionaries. **Negative**

**thinking engenders hatred.** Political racism is more dangerous than the caste system based on birth. Communism, socialism, capitalism and nationalism are abstract terms; their actual form becomes visible only when they draw the action plans. In 1967, I became an MLA for the first time in Bihar. My ideal figure, Dr. Lohia was still alive. Communists with red cap and red revolution and socialists were in the government along with yellow-capped Jana Sangh. In eight states of India, similar coalition governments were formed. The principles and ideals of Jana Sangh at that time were not as generous as the BJP is today. Truth and facts can't be evaluated based on insistence, persistence and bias. Ram, Krishna and Shiva didn't belong to the BJP alone; they equally belonged to Lohia and Gandhi as well. Deity is in every individual and every particle of India and they are going to be there. Ayodhya, Mathura and Kashi are not only religious places of India but they are centres of cultural unity.

The rivers and religious places of India are the symbols of national integrity. Every Indian has reverence for Gokul, Vrindavan, Govardhan, Barsana, Mathura and Dwaraka, but Yadavs have a greater emotional connect with them. It is the duty of Yadavs to protect the proud history, geography, culture, tradition, name and fame. If BJP says this it is termed to be reactionary, Dr. Lohia also used to say the same thing and we call him a socialist. Lohia has founded the ideology of Indian socialism. There is no fundamental difference between cultural nationalism and cultural socialism.

In politics, strategies apart, there should be coordination of power and tactics. Immediate, short-term and long-term goals have to be set. Purity, fairness and transparency are our ideals. From time to time, the grindstone of caste has grinded the people of the same caste and history is the witness. The advice and suggestions given by you as a literary personality is welcome. Everybody respects scholars, but a request is that it would be better if you don't force your ideological commitment on others through your writings. Thinking has to be done holistically within a complete mind. Preaching should never be in the order of accusation.

**A Pest Called Corruption**

Corruption is discussed all over the world and it is quite natural also as corruption is rife and ubiquitous, whether it is capitalism, or socialism, feudalism or communism, nationalism or consumerism. Actually, corruption is not attacked at its root and so far the factors responsible for it are not known very clearly. Without knowing the reasons, how can a solution be arrived at? It is also possible that reasons, therefore, may be known but the requisite degree of willpower to treat the problem may be sadly lacking. Without a strong willpower, it is very difficult to fight against it. There is some weakness somewhere; it is very important to find out the weakness also.

Socialist thinker Dr. Ram Manohar Lohia said, **"The pest of corruption takes birth and gets nurtured and grows on the garbage of consumerism."** However bitter it may taste, it is true. Power goes into the hands of whomsoever; all qualities, such as eligibility, capability, talent, scholarship enter into that caste. In the eyes of selectors, only people of their caste appear to be eligible. Right from birth till death all people at all social platforms remain engulfed in the vicious cycle of caste. When one is holding a post, then many people of his clan will go to meet him and naturally he gets the votes of his clan. Due to caste system, it influences the selection of officers also. The influence and pressure from the clan poses hurdles in taking a fair decision. Even in the form of advisors, one is surrounded by people of one's own clan. If we look in the light of our conscience, we will be able to see the truth and facts. It is possible to fight against a foreigner and others, but it is very difficult to fight against people of our own caste. Lohia says, "When the caste mill runs, it doesn't differentiate between one's own and others; sometimes it tortures people of the same caste more than others." I experienced the same twice in my political life. As a matter of fact the intensity is much more than that meets our eyes.

In 1968, when I supported Karpoori Thakur against V.P. Mandal, then I heard all that. And for the second time when I supported Chandrasekhar against Lalu Prasad, I had to suffer great humiliation and I can't describe the pain I experienced.

There are certain evergreen people, among all castes. Usually, power comes and goes, leaders keep changing but for those people, positions and posts are always preserved and they are always protected. People keep embracing the worst and the most corrupt officers, contractors, extortionists and mafia people of their caste. A head of a caste may belong to any political party but his presence will be there in all courts. People may stay in different parties, but they inter-mix with each other. On political platforms, in Parliament and in the Assemblies, they keep opposing each other but on social occasions they are seen hugging each other. They felicitate the most corrupt persons in social functions. A person, as he gets corrupt, receives that much respect from his caste. Do Parliament and Assemblies have the courage and determination to stop this?

In Parliament, ministers are bound to give replies. Ministers give those replies which the department prepares for them. Ministers don't have much time to supervise each and every issue of their ministry. So many scandals take place in the ministry, but ministers get to know about them only when the issues are raised in Parliament or get published in newspapers. There is an understanding in the administrative system from top to bottom that when they quit the posts, they get adjusted somewhere or the other. Some smart and manipulative officers stay evergreen. Whichever officer is expert in managing corruption, he will be that much more popular. Lohia has said, "People who sit in the number one chair keep changing, but those who sit in number two position, they become permanent slaves; they; don't change. Whosoever be the king, they engage in the slavery of that person."

For being in service for a long time, they have relationships with many leaders, professionals, industrial houses and managers of multinational companies. Mutually, they keep extending favour to each other. There will be a little influence of caste even here; this is the reason why after retirement these people get appointed in some or the other government, cooperative, semi-government or public sector undertakings and non-governmental establishments. Keep favouring and when the time comes, accept the results of the favours. Lohia has said, "People retiring from administrative services and judiciary have to be prohibited from taking up salaried or honorary positions in any government or non-governmental institution." Will leftist, rightist, communist, socialist and nationalist political parties, authors, and thinkers support this? Till the time the answer to this question doesn't come in affirmation, we will keep sinking deep into the quagmire of corruption.

Since urban comforts, facilities and means increased in politics, corruption has started brewing. The time period of 1952 to 1972 has to be studied. Activities of big leaders, whether at national level or at regional level, used to be run from small houses. But today, why can't it be so? When they could run with such minimum comforts, why can't the leaders of today do so? When they could live with such simplicity and purity, why can't today's leaders live like that? After becoming an MLA in 1967 and continuously being active in Parliament and State Assembly, the author introspected himself, "Today, why is there this downfall?" One reason is, from the time people from princely states, business and industrial houses and retired personnel from administrative services have started coming into politics, since then comforts, facilities and luxuries in politics have increased.

**The system of levying tax encourages corruption. Tax has to be paid on income. Earn, loot and consume. Tax has to be paid on the savings, but there is no tax on expenditure.** Lohia has said and even initiated a debate in Parliament that **there should be a cap on expenditure; there should be a legal ban on the mentality of consumerism.** People should be subjected to pay taxes proportionate to their expenditure. Tax keeps increasing in proportion to the expenditure. **Every citizen should have complete freedom to earn but there should be a ban on expenditure.** Whatever capital is saved will be used for reconstruction of the nation. This way India, by becoming free from consumerism, will be able to reconstruct itself with its own capital based on nationalist ideology.

## The Pretentious Politics of Grants

Any individual or institution can't be powerful due to the support of compassion, grants, and favours. In independent India, politics is run by these three things; the games of politics of grants and grant of politics are going on. When the grants prove insufficient, money is given on the grounds of compassion and favour. These provisions are made in order to benefit some specific institutions, individuals and communities. Earlier, during the feudal system, people used to depend on donations. In a democracy, the same thing has got converted into grants and compassion. On the basis of discretionary grants, there has been vigorous attempt to favour people close to them. **If the intention is right, there would be allegiance**. With allegiance comes the direction. When funds are given from the state treasury on the basis of discretion, compassion as favours, then political, social and administrative downfall ushers in, due to which cracks have crept into the economy. Because of grant-based economic policies, corruption, scandals, bungling have grown in society and everywhere wrong means are being adopted. Various methods are taken to receive grants, compassion and favours from the state treasury. Voluntary organisations have been formed; many corrupt practices are followed. Not all voluntary organisations follow scrupulous means; some of them are doing very good work and their good work has been appreciated. But the writer in his 38 years of political life has seen that many NGOs have taken grants under false documents. There is an institution called CAPART under the Department of Rural Development. Thousands of crores of rupees have been given in grants through CAPART, and no audit has been conducted on this. "There are no accounts or records, whatever they say is hundred percent right." It has the protection from the leaders in power and from administrative officers of highest ranks. They were posing problems for organisations doing good work; if an audit is conducted on this, a big scandal would break out. Grants of small and large amounts are being given to thousands of organisations across the country. Funds are spent in the name of rural and agricultural development; money is spent like water for child welfare and development. Number games are going on in the Planning Commission and in secretariats of agriculture, finance and rural and agriculture development ministries. Statistics get manipulated; name of the economists living on grants are made popular through promotions and they are asked to prepare statistics. These prejudiced economists are misleading people and cheating the nation. Making plans and allocating funds as per those plans, prioritising the plans and collecting data on those plans are very easy. All that can be done on a computer while sitting in an air-conditioned room; however an assessment of the reality on the ground can't be done either through computers or through the theories of economists. Why is it that 90 percent of the grants is spent on management, establishment and administration?

This writer has a wealth of experience of working as the head at village, block and district level and has also worked as a minister in the Central Government. He has the experience of overseeing the work done by all the democratic institutions in villages. During 38 years of political life, it has been perceived that regular chanting is done in the name of farmers, villages, labourers and the poor; they are remembered as the saviour of problems, but they get cheated. **The way in a temple, various tasty delicacies are offered to the deity and then the priest feasts on them to his heart's content, similarly, in villages farmers and the poor are shown different plans and programmes meant for their development, but ultimately the person who is presenting the plans happen to take away all the money meant for the villagers. The status of those villagers and the poor remain the same with no substantial improvement.** However, through various figures it was proved that there is all-round development in the lives of these villagers. It's not that there is no development, but even if 50 percent of the total budget allocated had been spent on the programmes, the villages would have become heaven; Gandhi's down-trodden, Deen Dayal's last man and Lohia's poorer class would have been enjoying the benefits of that heaven and prosperity would have reigned in villages. Farmers would have been rich, the poor would have been free from the grips of poverty. Solutions should be worked out after identifying the cause, remedies should be given without any bias. All the people involved in this bungling have to be exposed. In order to rebuild rural India, a new economic policy based on agriculture has to be prepared and a new economic system has to be strengthened. To create public awareness, even the common people have to take part in developmental activities. Nation building has to be treated as a great sacrifice and should be performed very sincerely, making others perform.

The most burning and immediate serious issue is the scandal related to the grants given for chemical fertilisers, pesticides and seeds. Government spends thousands of crores of rupees on these grants; grants are given to the producers of chemical fertilisers in the name of farmers. Many factories have been set up, the production has more than doubled than the capacity based on which the grants has been given. Subsidies are given on chemicals to produce fertilisers, subsidy on raw material, chemicals and then again grants on the production. With all these grants after producing more than double the total capacity, still there is an acute shortage of fertilisers in the country. DAP, urea are not available on time. Always there is a severe crisis for DAP at the time of sowing and for urea at the time of spraying after irrigation. Data shows that there is no shortage of fertilisers; fertilisers are available at high prices, but the ground reality is diametrically different. Facts don't get verified. *'Kabira baanche aakhan dekhi, pandit baanche pothi likha'* (Kabir says what has been seen, learned says what's written in the book.) Villagers and farmers are witnessing the truth directly; however that truth keeps getting hidden in the data in secretariats. Whatever scam is carried out by factory owners in the name of fertilisers, is it an ordinary issue? In an agriculture-based country, plundering in the name of agriculture is a national crime. By giving wrong figures of production, shortage of fertilisers is blamed. By giving wrong figures of seeds, wrong sowing is shown. Production figures are wrong and on top of that fertilisers are adulterated. The natural fertility of land gets lost because of the inferior quality of fertilisers. Salt is getting used and heavy subsidy is given on inferior and adulterated fertilisers. Priority is given to agriculture due to which farmers are getting loans and avail various subsidies. Now planners and economists should tell who is benefitting from these subsidies and loans. The producers of fertilisers are eating fertilisers. The homes of planners and fertiliser producers are becoming prosperous.

Pests are not getting killed by pesticides, but farmers are committing suicides. No producer gets caught. No government is able to catch them. Farmers' suicides are continuing. The looters are devising new ways of looting under the name of new schemes.

Steel and plastic pipes are given for irrigation. Farmers get these pipes on subsidy at one-and-a-half times higher than market price. It is the same situation for all equipment used for canal irrigation. Same brand motors run by electricity and motor pumpsets are given at different rates by different banks in the same district. Who is going to save the farmers and who is going to break this vicious cycle? The interest on the bank loan gets doubled by the time the grant reaches the farmer. Tractors are sold by tractor companies on subsidy, but the accessories of tractors are sold at almost 30 to 50 percent higher vis-á-vis the market rates. Farmers makes purchases under duress. These are never reviewed. Will any economist, planner or a Nobel laureate tell the reasons thereof? What punishment should be given to those people who are letting the industrial houses make profits in the name of farmers? Who are the culprits? Because of the subsidies given to farmers, the price offered to farmers is valued very low; as a result, the minimum cost price given to farmers for their produce is far less than the investment. The real cost is be one-and-a-half times more than the support price decided by the government. The people who export and import enjoy all types of subsidies. FCI also gets subsidies, the goods eaten away by two-legged rats are shown to be eaten away by rats and shown as wastage. All this is happening in the name of agriculture. It reminds me of the proverb *'hari anant, hari katha anant'* (God is infinite and the story of God is infinite). There is no end to the troubles of farmers; the plight of villagers can't be watched. Saint Aurobindo had a dream – make heaven on earth and transform India. But because of rulers who have been running the government for the last 50 years, villages have become hell and farmers have been reduced to daily-wage workers. The government has to fight against it. India has to be transformed through public awakening and public participation. The seeds of nationalism are hidden in the culture of agriculture but the flag of cultural nationalism has yet to be hoisted.

*Jana Satta, 1 February, 1999*

□

# 7
# What Kind of Socialists?

It is said that Janata Dal belongs to the socialists. I don't know why my heart gets jolted whenever I hear the word 'socialist' and the images of Acharya Narendra Dev, Dr. Lohia, Jai Prakash Naraian and Karpoori Thakur get flashed in the mind. It is not very clear when and how Janata Dal became socialist. Have all the socialists of present-day joined Janata Dal or people who stayed back in Janata Dal after 1990 have mostly fallen down. People in the Janata Dal consider themselves as followers of Choudhry Charan Singh; this too is false. Where is the simplicity, sincerity and nationalism of Charan Singh in them? To call opportunists, consumerists, authoritarians, luxury-loving and fanatics as socialists is an insult to all those great people, who treading on the path of socialism sacrificed their entire life and never compromised.

In 1990, for the first time elections were held for the post of national president of Janata Dal; I was also one of contestants for that post. It was a straight contest between me and S.R. Bommai; all national leaders at that time including V.P. Singh, who claim to be a supporter of social justice and secularism, instead of supporting a leader belonging to the backward class, like me, supported Mr. Bommai. Where did the socialism of Lalu Prasad, Mulayam Singh, Sharad Yadav, Ram Vilas, Ajit Singh, George Fernandes and others go at that time? Upper-caste people had occupied all the five chief national positions. I demanded one post by taking a stand of opposition, then where did the social justice disappear? In 1991, when I was a minister to the Government of India, I was burnt with diesel, mobil-oil was thrown at me and sandals were hurled at me, just because I was opposing the politics of dictatorship and fanaticism of Lalu Prasad. There were attacks on me, my supporters and my relatives because, among the Yadavs, I was the only one openly opposing Lalu. All those who were expelled from the Janata Dal today were at that time watching like mute spectators and describing Lalu Prasad as the Messiah of social change. I was a minister in the Central Government, even then no security cover was provided to me and even the government, in which I was a minister, didn't do anything. All those people who supported silently that injustice are raising a hue and cry today.

Today they are proving truth and facts, but had the disciples of Lohia raised their voice at that time, Bihar and India wouldn't have been in such a bad state. The duality that is present in Janata Dal today is not because of principles, but it is the struggle over personal issues, selfish interests, violence, counter violence and due to the feeling of revenge. At present the path of Lohia's ideology is going towards the BJP. Lohia has said, "Reform, otherwise break up." Today they are not reforming; instead they are breaking up. They are blindly following individuals. I have very close links with thousands of Janata Dal workers; they are flourishing the way the saplings planted by me are flourishing. They should think in peace and join in the cultural and spiritual stream of nationalism. This is the call of the times and the age.

*Jansatta, 20 August, 1997*

□

# 8

# Transformation Calls for Determination

October 12 comes every year. This year too it had come and gone. On the day of 12th October, the death anniversary of late Dr. Ram Manohar Lohia had been observed. Many articles were written on him, he was remembered and forgotten. The people who remember him remember in many ways. They remember the passenger but forget the path pursued by him. It has been inherent in the nature of India that idols of the individuals are made and worshipped, but never the path followed shown by them. Due to idol worshipping, their mentality has become gross. By holding on to gross and not thinking about the subtle leads to loss of the path. Holding on to the body and leaving out the ideology has become customary in India. Lohia has said, "Follow the path, don't look at the passenger." There is a danger of becoming a blind follower in walking behind the passenger, while looking at him. Worshipping the individual becomes the goal of blind following. Individuals have both virtues and vices. It is very difficult to progress on the path of socialism but it is very easy to get distracted from it. An individual reaches the top after putting in a lot of hard work and practice, but within a flash he may slip and fall into an abyss. The path of suppressing and controlling desires cannot prove successful; both paths are one sided.

The desire to enjoy is as natural as waves rising in an ocean. Stopping the waves from rising is like stripping an ocean of its identity and there will be a reaction to it. Stopping action leads to reaction and with that rises the wave of reaction. Creative thinking doesn't make way for destruction. Due to obstacles, rebellion takes birth. If obstructions are stopped, then the rebellion will also stop. Attempting to remove the obstructions is one stream of thought and creating hurdles through rebellion is another stream of thought. There are means in the world to enjoy and human beings have the desire to enjoy. It depends on the person how he utilises the resources. Along with the sanctity of resources and goal, the sanctity of the medium is also very important. Today attention is not given to either the resources, or the means or the goal.

Reform of an individual doesn't reach the full scale without bringing in the elements of reform in society. Society will definitely change when individual changes, but the individual gets influenced by vices in society. When both individual and the society get reformed simultaneously the process of change becomes easy. When passenger and the passage are right, progress becomes fast. If the path is right, even the weakest will achieve the goal sooner or later. But if the path is wrong, the passenger gets lost and is not able to reach the destination. There is a need to correct both the path and the passenger. The disciples of Lohia have to think about this. Thought has to be spared on how to maintain the sanctity of the medium along with the sanctity of resources and the goal.

In parliamentary democracy, through Constitution and legislation, society can be reformed. Morality remains strong under the protection of legislation. If there is no protection for morality by legislation, it becomes impotent. Through legislation, such rules should be made by which an individual is stopped from blindly running after desires. Desires are endless; every second new waves keep rising and the old waves die down. One has to think holistically to control and regulate them. Exceptions to legislation pave the way for the downfall. A protected class takes birth because of exceptions. Taking advantage of exceptions, human beings try to fulfil their ambitions. By forming gangs, he starts groupism. There is a hunger for power in a democracy. Today struggle is going on for equality in the world. Many strategies are devised to suppress this struggle. Everybody wants equal opportunities. It is essential not to have exceptions for availing equal opportunities.

For what are the struggles going on today? Decisive battle is going on between protection and reservation, conservation and reservation, privileges, special opportunities, exploiters and the exploited, rulers and the ruled and administrators and the ill-treated. A legislation should be made in a democracy to stop this. In a feudal system, a king continues to be in power till the time he wishes so or till he relinquishes and goes into the forest. Sometimes he would be thrown out either by way of defeat in battle or through assassination.

In democracy, it is the rule of representatives. Everybody has equal right to be the representative, but this is only in words. How will others get an opportunity, if only one person continues to be the member of an elected institution? In an organisation, only few people continue to occupy the position by turn, then when and how will other eligible members will get the opportunity? Gaining experience and eligibility while working is the foundation of democracy. Opportunities to work are not given and this apart, people are told that opportunity will be given upon acquiring eligibility. This is a philosophy of deceit. If a legislation is made that nobody can be a member of any elected body for more than 15 years or three terms, then a way is made for others to come in. One institution that is either Panchayat, or the Assembly or the Parliament has to think keeping this in mind. All other institutions wherever members are elected through election, the same rule should be applied. Whatever may be the organisation whether it is a political party or a cooperative society the same rule should be made applicable. An individual should not hold any post whether in an organisation or in the government as a minister for more than two terms or ten years. One man one post and right to one employment. Reservation should be given even in political organisations and institutions. Because of democratic processes only, the dynasty politics, dictatorship, caste system, individualism has come into Parliament of India. Now, this has to end.

It is meant to end privileges through special opportunities, to end caste system. It is end to protectionism through reservation, it is to give full opportunity to develop talent, capability, eligibility, and personality. But when special opportunities become privileges and reservation becomes protection then the paths get altered. Direction turns opposite. Instead of uprooting caste system, it strengthens caste system. Lohia's vision is distorted by misinterpreting it. If family members of the people who got reservations keep getting reservation, then they become protected. Eligibility, talent and character is not respected among protected communities. Privilege is another form of special opportunities. Because of caste system, economic rights have been reserved in Indian society. It was a kind of category but with time as that class lost momentum it has taken the form of caste. According to Lohia's philosophy, classes are formed by progressive groups, and when classes lose momentum they become castes. An ailment of thousands of years old can't be treated in a day. Today the mentality of people who got reservation and special opportunities is also turning into the same, by which India went deep into the quagmire. Change is not going to come by exchanging the positions of Brahman with that of a night soil collector. New system is not going to be formed by turning out the existing system.

As long as the ladder stays erect, there will be people sitting on the lower and higher rungs, but when the ladder is pulled down, people on all the rungs will become equal. Some people want to bring equality by putting the ladder upside down. This is destruction. On the other side, people who talk about social harmony are not ready to sacrifice. Manure is required for the dwindling plants, the day upper caste people start preparing manure, that day the society becomes green. Relinquish the seat and let the exploited, backward and lower caste people sit on that seat. They preach sacrifice but they never sacrifice. Earlier it was difficult to find eligible candidates among women, lower castes and the backward castes, but from the time reservations have come, eligible people are becoming visible among them. In the name of eligibility, search is going on for people who can boot lick. The vested interests of caste are given the name of principles and ideals, due to which the principles have become distorted. Bonded labour are getting recruited in politics. Tigers and lions are maintained as in circus. Tension is escalating between backward and lower caste people. Everybody is running on the policy of appeasement. Because of appeasement, cultural distortions have started coming in. In our country, people shy away from treating brothers and sisters equal, though they find respect in bowing in front of foreigners. We feel ashamed of hugging each other by bending down, but we find respect in prostrating in front of someone else.

In the last phase of his life, Dr. Lohia tried to bring together socialists and nationalists. However, the philosophy of freedom of speech and controlled action couldn't succeed. Actions become aggressive due to freedom of speech. There is no discipline; due to continuous agitation against the government, discipline has eroded. On the other hand, due to discipline, freedom of speech and independent thinking are lost. Lohia tried to contact Deendayal and started building a relationship. He thought of combining freedom of speech, temperament to struggle and legislature through discipline, dedication and loyalty. To build an egalitarian society by combining nationalism and socialism, to bring the feeling of cultural harmony by liberating from cultural slavery, to describe concepts like foreign and indigenous correctly, to bring in modernism in ancient systems in the Indian context, he thought of starting this process on the plains of Ganga and Yamuna. But it was not acceptable to time. Both the people who wanted to combine the ideologies—mediators of both ideologies passed away prematurely. Will the people who are pursuing the path shown by Lohia and Deendayal give a new direction to the nation by thinking over it? Can they fulfil the incomplete dream of combining both the ideologies? Can they bring new light in this darkness? Overwhelmed by cultural and spiritual feelings are they ready to transform India on the foundation of nationalism and cultural harmony? India needs transformation; there is no alternative to it. Transformation is possible only through determination. Lohia is no more, but he has laid the path— that path, fully empowered and eternal, lies in front of us even today. People who run after power and enjoyment couldn't understand Lohia. Today there is a need to think over it.

*Jansatta, 3 November, 1997*

□

# 9
# All Parties have Looted Bihar

Bihar holds the distinction of having been endowed with many unique features. Bihar is amazing by itself. Bihar moves on its own, irrespective of who it is governed by. Whatever is happening, it is not because of one day, one person or one government. Whoever came, shouted the slogans of reform and slogans remained just slogans only. Lawlessness, corruption, racism and fanaticism have increased in the name of reforms. The trap of anarchy was laid in the name of system and people got trapped in it. The movement of land annexation was started in the name of land reforms. Activities to destroy crops have been started in the name of bringing about desired degree of amelioration in agriculture. Corruption has been promoted in the name of controlling corruption. Lack of discipline increased among state government employees. Slogans have become the order of the day. Whoever has come has put the burden of racism and communalism on the state treasury.

In the name of maintaining the caste balance, caste imbalance has been given rise to. Though the schemes run for the uplift of backward classes, the backward classes were exploited the most. Some state officials' houses were embellished with the money meant for the betterment of lower castes. State treasury was looted like the Mughal emperors to please some people belonging to the minority community. Still, there was no improvement in their lives. Poverty and helplessness of minorities worsened. Some of them were made white elephants who kept on shouting slogans in support of minority communities. By creating illusion in the minds of the upper caste people, attempts were made to unite them together, but even among them unemployment and poverty kept on rising. The politics of caste got transformed into racism. A coalition was made between racism and communalism. Due to this coalition, factionalism, disintegration, consumerism, authoritarianism have cropped up. Due to the destruction in politics, there was administrative breakdown in the whole state. The negative politics and non-Congress politics changed this destructive ideology into authoritarian politics. The trend of coalition has started. All the principles, ideals, policies and rules have washed away. Because of racism, individualism got strengthened. The whole organisation started revolving around individuals. Democracy has been personified; corruption and crime have entered into politics only because of this. Instead of holding elections in organisations, the system of nominations has started. To ensure their power in the organisation, a circle of very cheap and sycophants people of their own caste has been formed and in that circle talented and sharp political 'Abhimanyus' of the same caste have been slaughtered.

All this was happening quite naturally. Violence, lawlessness and fanaticism started rising automatically. The support of these elements was sought during elections. Slowly, these elements started overpowering the politics. Now too much water has flown under the bridge. Only one tradition has been going on right from the time of Sri Krishna Singh to Lalu Prasad. The train is running on the same track and attempts are being made to let the train run on the same track; the Congress which was opposing Sri Babu was no less racist. It becomes very clear from the castes of those administrators who were at the helm under these governments. Whichever caste the Chief Minister belonged to, overnight all talents would get accumulated in the same caste. The moment they went out of power, all talents of that caste would disappear. Whoever has held power in the organisation, they have made the organisation a racial organisation. They all would have got exposed had any journalist or organisation done any research on this. But barring a few, all of them appear to be the different sides of the same coin. Karpoori Thakur alone appears to be a singular and extremely talented person. A backward class person like Karpoori Thakur was insulted in the land of Bihar. During the rule of Lalu, repentance had to be done for that crime.

The question is, whether Lalu alone can be held responsible for this present sorry state of Bihar? For the betterment of Bihar, everybody should think over it sans any prejudice. Earlier, during the rule of Congress, keeping Gandhi Maidan and platform of Patna Station as hostage, money has been taken from the bank. Crores of rupees have been embezzled under the Koshi project. To have their majority, re-polling was ordered at many polling booths in the constituencies of opposition candidates even when they were still alive. At some of the polling booths, re-polling has been done thrice. The government system has been misused. The opposition candidates of the same caste were politically lured, having been offered positions and privileges. To suppress the opposition, all means were adopted. Who did all these things? Those who did all these things, did they belong to the backward caste or to lower castes? Lalu Prasad has extensively misused this government system which has become corrupt with racism. He was brazenly misusing the power and spread fear to protect his own interests. Maximum killings of people belonging to backward caste people occurred during the rule of Lalu. Almost a dozen of committed, agitating and veteran Yadavs were expelled from the party by Lalu. They were not given tickets and if given tickets, they were defeated by his own administration. Rebel candidates were made to contest; when they got defeated, they were given money. For example, Hemlata Yadav, who defeated Vinayak Prasad Yadav, the candidate of Kisanpur constituency, was made the chairperson of the Social Welfare Board. Reason should be found out as to how this happened? Congress leaders also used the same strategies. Because of racial fanaticism, many times people get insulted only on the basis of caste. Only criminals, sycophants and rowdies got the opportunity to progress. This was what was happening in Bihar and even today the same is going on.

On the issue of corruption, all corrupt people stay united. Caste doesn't come between them. They are very obedient, humble and generous. In the formative years of Lalu Prasad's rule, Chief Secretary Arun Pathak and Inspector General Arun Kumar Choudhry, both were Brahmins. Both of them got extension of service. Later on a Jain and Scheduled Caste member came to occupy those posts. Members of the main castes have joined the Cabinet. Tickets were given to them and they were elected using all sorts of ploys. The upper caste members who joined Lalu's Cabinet were blindly following Lalu more than the backward caste. At the time of elections, among the officers against whom allegations were levelled and against whom the Election Commission ordered an enquiry largely belonged to the upper caste. Whether it was an issue of corruption or malpractices during elections, Lalu didn't show any bias nor caste preference in these matters; instead he gave equal opportunities to all corrupt and boot-licking people. The whole of Bihar is deeply caught in the quagmire. Assembly was made the centre of corruption. When Radha Nandan Jha and Gulam Sarwar were holding the post of Speakers, all assembly etiquette was overlooked and broken.

Both the Congress and the Janata Dal Governments were protecting scams. If any independent commission, Parliamentary Committee or Assembly Committee conducted an enquiry into these issues to find out as to which MLA or MP sought or recommended the transfer, appointment or promotion of which officer, it will be known who were involved. Money, recommendation and caste — all three were needed. Officers belonging to extremely backward or sub-castes among the Scheduled Caste, who didn't have much of a political clout, are affected the most. The character of dominant castes among backward and Scheduled Castes is more or less the same. If a survey is conducted, it will be seen that the proportion of MLAs from dominant castes is about three to four times higher than their actual demograph. During the rule of Sri Babu, Bhoomihars were four times vis-á-vis their number and Rajputs were five times as against their number. During the Government of Jagannath Mishra, due to the power of numbers, Brahmins used to get five times more seats in the Assembly. Dominant caste among backward classes were getting the seats but not according to their numbers. Wasn't it racism? Whose share they were gobbling? Awareness dawned upon those belonging to the backward castes thanks to socialist movement and special opportunities and policies of Lohia. Yadavs, Kurmi, and Kushwaha started coming into the front line. Because of Karpoori Thakur, Akshyabat Roy and Bhupendra Narayan Mandal, new awareness prevailed upon the lower castes. Lalu Prasad was taking undue advantage of that new force. The families of most of the Janata Dal members were worshipping the idols of many Congress leaders at that time. In every government, whatever caste was in power, members of that particular caste got more seats, disproportionate to their number. Everybody was eating into the share of extremely backward castes. Lalu Prasad had snatched away more seats from upper caste people. Even today Muslims seats are not commensurate with their number. It's a different issue that this time their number has increased. Extremely backward and extremely lower castes are like orphans even today. Nobody wants to uplift them. Everybody wants to rise up on their backs. Upper caste people who didn't like Karpoori Thakur, are blindly supporting Lalu today. They were harbouring their dreams of coming back into power by climbing up on the backs of extremely backward castes and by creating a storm against Lalu. Do the politicians, political parties and social activists want to get the politics of Bihar out of this labyrinth?

*Jansatta, 2 March, 1996*

□

# 10

# Desire to Change the State of Inertia

The big battle of Parliament elections ended in the first year of the latter half of the last decade of this century. Right from the beginning, people started predicting the outcome of these elections and once the results were announced, they started analysing the results. But it was unfortunate that most of the analysts, intellectuals and writers were not liberated or they didn't want to be liberated for they were critics of rulers as well but supported the same issues indirectly. Moral values didn't change even when situations and circumstances changed; the basis of ideals and principles do not change. Because of selfishness, greed and fear, ethical and spiritual values can be established even if policies and ethics are changed. There should be a balance among state, religious and ethical powers. Due to lack of spiritualism and nationalism, the light of love can't be spread around. The results of this election set many directions. Along with Gandhism, many issues including communism, economic liberalisation, materialism, Hindutva and secularism were put to test, when some proved unsuccessful, some others ended in fiasco. Voters haven't totally rejected anything nor have they accepted anything completely. It became clear that voters haven't accepted the policies of any political party in toto. In case of regions, communities, castes and groups, people have shown different mentalities. All voters of all communities of a particular region didn't vote on the basis of a single issue. It appears that while voters were in favour of change and liberalisation at the same time they were held back by inertia. This was seen very clearly in Bihar. The mentality of voters was not the same in the region in the heart of India. The areas which were under the influence of communists have accepted them once again; still they expressed their anger and opposition against their policies and style of functioning. They couldn't find an alternative to communism. Maybe, nobody wants to give them that alternative. The feeling of fundamentalism came into racism; feeling of resentment and fighting has increased. Without moving from their position, everybody talks about change. **Equality of all regions means everybody should imbibe the virtues of all religions and sacrifice the vices of all religions altogether.**

The results were different in north India, central India and in south India. In north Bihar, if we draw a line from Hazipur to Sitamarhi and go up to Kishanganj in the east, the results would appear to be similar. This region is a stronghold of the Congress and Samajwadis used to give tough competition. In this region, the population of Yadavs, Muslims and Maithil Brahmins was impactful. Janata Dal has influence over Yadavs and Muslims and there was a slight division in that. Maithil Brahmins were loyal to the Congress but there too, there was a division. The population of others in forward castes was not so influential. Population of the other backward castes was very high but it was divided at many places. There the influence of Janata Dal was reduced; there was anger against the alliance of National Front and Left Front but there was no other party which would attract respect and political space for them. There were no irregularities in them. This time around, the extreme backward classes got the capacity to take independent decisions. Earlier they used to cast their vote having been influenced by the powerful castes. This time also, they were not completely free but they tried to some extent. There was influence of National Front and Left Front over 20 to 22 seats in 14 to 15 districts of this region. Brahmins, the Yadavs and Muslim-dominated areas were inclined towards the BJP. The voters of Congress couldn't free themselves from the strappings of Jagannath Mishra. At some places, the supporters of the Congress voted for the Congress to stop the BJP. In turn, the BJP supporters posed obstacles to the Congress. Yadavs constituting 20 to 25 percent couldn't give resistance aggressively and attackingly. Muslim voters were divided but at the time of voting, to defeat the BJP, they voted massively in favour of National Front and Left Front alliance. Congress didn't allow the forward classes to get united. In the battle among racism, nationalism, Hindutva and communism, racism compelled the voters and this benefited the alliance of National Front and Left Front. In Viashali, in the by-elections, wife of Mr. Satyendra Babu contesting on the Janata Dal ticket was defeated by Lovely Anand there Raghuvansh Singh was elected. This time Rajput voters were elected on caste basis; Vrishin Patel Kurmi was contesting there on the Samata Party ticket. Similarly, in the west of Sitamarhi-Hazipur line, the results were different. In this region, people of Rajput, Kurmi, Bhoomihar and Vaisya communities formed a combined front; there are no Brahmins and Maithili Brahmins, due to which the BJP and the Samata Party won many seats.

In 9-10 districts of central Bihar, the pattern was different. There the caste polarisation happened in a different way. Here Yadav, Kurmi, Rajput, Bhoomihar, Kushwaha and Muslims exercised major influence. Among the backward castes, Kurmis were very aggressive. However, there was no proper polarisation among those opposing Lalu. Suporters of Lalu just saw the caste of the candidate and cast their vote blindly for Lalu. Opponents of Lalu first checked the caste of the candidate and then, if the candidate was of their choice, they voted for alliance of National Front and Left Front due to which the alliance benefitted. Voters of backward caste cast their vote to Samata Party alliance from a political point of view.

The trend of voters of Monghyr and Bhagalpur was also similar to that of north Bihar. In the south, influence of caste was relatively low. Population of Yadavs and Muslims was not very influential. The BJP built its base over there. So the BJP got the benefit. The candidates of National Front and Left Front alliance won with a lesser margin in 1991. Caste equations had more impact this time due to the feeling of revenge and retaliation. Bigger issues became secondary. Yadav voters were also disappointed by the failure of Lalu's administration, corruption and the style of functioning, but they didn't have any alternative in their caste. Even extreme backward castes were highly disappointed but there was no political party ready to give them a respectable position. Muslim voters were ready to cast their vote for anybody because of their opposition to the BJP. The Congress loyalists couldn't free themselves from their affection for Congress. Certainly, there was strong opposition to Lalu; they were very aggressive and attacking in their speeches, but at the time of casting votes, they were a little pessimistic and indifferent. Janata Dal was very successful in the Congress strongholds. It appears that there must have been a secret understanding between the top leaders of the both the parties.

*Jansatta 21 May, 1996*

□

## 11
# Ethical Power Versus Legislative Power

A heated debate has started off inside and outside Parliament on the decision of Lok Sabha Speaker. Debate is the truth of democracy but when it happens with chagrin, impulse, angst and injustice, truth gets overshadowed. To know the truth, both heart and brain have to be combined. Many articles delving into the bottom of the truth were getting published in newspapers and magazines on switching of parties, Parliamentary ethics and political organisations. Of course, there is a difference of opinion but it is very sad to notice lack of vision. Lack of vision leads to darkness. Along with the power of education and intelligence, the use of the power of right has proven dangerous to democracy.

Severe agitation is going on for autonomy of legislature, executive and judiciary, which is very destructive and disintegrating. When all the three can't work in agreement with one another, how can a national coordination be made possible. The majority rules in Parliament; the cabinet rules over the majority and Prime Minister rules over the Ministerial Council. When the will of one person is implicitly followed in Parliament, doesn't it become tantamount to parliamentary dictatorship? When there is a synergy between legislative and the ethical power, then only discipline is followed naturally. How can it be possible to control others in the organisation in the name of discipline when they themselves tend to become arrogant?

Anti-defection law was brought in to protect from political party dictatorship and arrogance of power. Where has the philosophy of freedom of expression gone? When a solitary person takes a decision and works, based on his conscience, he becomes corrupt. But when a party does so according to the wishes of its leaders, it becomes an issue of principles. In the year 1969 and even now, what did the Left Front do during the election of the President? It is a sin to caste vote for the candidate supported by the BJP, but is it sacred to vote for the Deputy Speaker of the Rajya Sabha along with the BJP? Speaker, Lok Sabha functions in the interest of the nation, but what about the feelings of the MPs? Do they consider the anti-defection law right? How much injustice was done by this law? To put it the other way, it can be said that it is a severe blow to the very foundation of the parliamentary system. Difficult to say anything. Which political party was left, whose Speakers of Assembly didn't create ruckus, taking advantage of this law? The same people who criticised the decision of respected Rabi Ray, have behaved indecently on the decision of Mr. Patil. Shivraj Patil had given a new direction to this law with his decision. Granting relief to the members from party dictatorship and from whimsical behaviour of the council of leaders is also the responsibility of the Speaker. In case of dichotomy between legislative power vis-á-vis ethical power, the latter is to be supported.

*Jansatta, 1 September, 1992*

□

# 12

# Bread Politics in the Politics of Bread

Everybody wants bread, whether it is from the pan or from the factory. When it comes to bread, there will be a talk on the baker of the *roti* and seller of the *roti* and even of those people who do politics over bread. When the people doing politics over it are talked about, everybody, including Food Department, Department of Civil Supplies, and Food Corporation of India will come into the picture. It is also essential that all businessmen and traders join in. Bread has a strong link to votes and votes have a strong link with wealth, privileges and resources. Money and resources can only come from business. Money, and subsidy quota and permits—these are the things which will give privileges in business. The farmer, who produces grain for the bread, has neither money nor quota. There is a mad rush for permits. It is only because of this that nobody bothers about the farmer who produces the grain for the bread. Once, when the grain comes out of his house and reaches the market, then bread and its story begins. This is a small reflection of the trial farmers are usually riddled with.

Elections have been announced in many states of the country and in many states, elections have to be announced. Elections of Delhi Municipal Corporation are going to take place very soon. The prestige of Central Government sitting in Delhi will be tested. It will be an acid test for the goodwill and popularity of the Prime Minister. It is linked to the future of party, along with his future; it is a very tough situation. Votes have to be garnered. All efforts are being made to that end in mind. Hardly had the echo of scandal of Harshad Mehta subsided, when the echo of sugar and molasses scandal started being raised. When this subsides, the sound of bread scandal is going to be heard. Money is required for generating election funds. Some departments have expertise in collecting money. After Finance and Defence Departments, Food Department is the biggest centre for collecting money. Food Ministry keeps looking for new methods to collect money. Bread has also come into this new field. Immediately after the programme of Prime Minister on 15 October 1994, Modern Industries set up two factories on Lawrence Road in Delhi. Functions were organised, spending lakhs of rupees and during the function, it was announced by the Prime Minister that the bread which is going to be made in this factory will be sold at a price cheaper by 50 paise. For this the producers will be provided the grain at a cheaper rate. To make bread, *maida* (refined wheat flour) and sugar are required. When wheat is given at a cheaper rate, then sugar will also be provided at a cheaper rate. Both Food Department and Food Corporation play a major role in the distribution of these items. When government factories get wheat and sugar on subsidised price, only then they can produce cheaper bread. Other private manufacturers are also forced to sell their product at cheaper rates. If they don't get wheat and sugar at subsidised prices, they can't survive in the market. When their factories are on the verge of closure, then foreign companies will be invited to produce bread in the name of liberalisation. There is a huge scope for commission here. Why do bread-producing public companies go into losses? Why did their products, such as Rasika and cold drinks were stopped? What is the reason for incurring losses? What is the reason for closing down many of its units? Even after receiving subsidies, why are they running into losses whereas private companies, even without getting any subsidies, are earning profits and are serving the consumers? To beat the domestic companies in the competition, public undertakings are given subsidies. Is it liberalisation? Bread consumers are urban people. Two to three percent of the population living in cities, markets and big colonies eat bread produced in the factories. Since they are debaters, spokespersons, journalists, opinion builders, authors, rulers and administrators, those stricken with poverty need cheap bread. The author was at one time the Minister for Food Processing, so with firsthand knowledge and personal experience one can say that Modern Bread is the centre of the scandal. Because its headquarters is in Delhi and all top leaders sit in Delhi only, so they become the targets of their lobby. They have their lobby in the ministry. All sorts of things happen there. There are 13 units all over the country making Modern Bread. While they have 17 franchise units, these franchises give royalty to them over bread. Whatever royalty they earn, accounts for profit only. They don't get any benefit from these franchises; instead, by showing all nonsensical expenditure they bungle with money. If an investigation is done on 13 franchises by a Parliamentary Committee, the role of franchises in reducing their loss will be established. The subsidy and wheat at cheaper rates given to Modern Bread might not be given to its franchises. Instead on their name, Modern Bread avails cheap wheat, sugar and other privileges. When Modern Bread becomes cheaper by 50 paise, franchises too get compelled to sell at the same price. When their prices fall, without subsidies they would go into loss. So either they have to run the business in loss or close down the factory. On those factories, they manage to get financial assistance and bank loans. To recover their loans, financial institutions would auction those factories, and then foreign companies will buy those factories in the name of big companies or NRIs. Private factory owners, through their associations, establish links with Food Ministry, PMO and the Municipal Corporation. Deals are struck in crores of rupees. By eating cheap bread, the voter would hail the Prime Minister and money will reach the Congress Party election fund. Burden has to be borne by those who don't eat bread, neither produce nor sell it, but just produce the grain for making bread. Most of the franchises are in states like Haryana, UP, Rajasthan, MP; close to Delhi and in those places where elections are going on and also in those places where elections are going to be held soon. The author had already written two letters to the Chief Election Commission in this regard, but they also kept quiet. Is it right to make such announcements just before elections? By now the commission hasn't been settled with private producers. Here franchises of Modern Bread are thinking of cancelling their contract. CBI has done an investigation and exposed a scandal of several crores in Modern Bread Industries. Files have been suppressed and the case has been closed. The officers of Modern Bread in collusion with private manufacturers caused huge loss to the government. What did Parliament think on this issue? Will Election Commission think of cancelling this announcement? Will the opposition and other leaders raise this issue in Parliament and debate over it? Matter will progress, when rotting wheat in the Food Corporation godowns will be given to flourmills in the name of cheap wheat. Wheat will not be sold in the PDS centres because wheat prices will go up. The Food Corporation sells the grain at a much higher price than procurement price. Till now crores of rupees are given in subsidy. Has the plan to make the country go pauper by colluding in the name of liberalisation, nationalisation, politicisation, and xenocentrism already set in motion?

*Jansatta, 14 November, 1994*

□

# 13

# The Storm of Change Rises and gets Settled here Itself

Politics in Bihar and Bihar in politics, both are very surprising. In Bihar, the code of politics is of caste, corruption, indulgence, selfishness and strategies. The storm of change starts right from here and also ends here itself. The waves of agitation rise and break down. All isms, including socialism, communism, racism, consumerism, dynasty politics and feudalism—everything is getting an opportunity to flourish in Bihar. Sometimes such isms are witnessed to be in force all together. No political party could give a proper direction to Bihar. Everybody says that Bihar has mines, abundant water sources, fertile land, people here are hardworking, it has political consciousness, it has leaders who are excellent orators; after all, why is it that Bihar is eternally poor, weak and disappointed? Nobody is bothered about the holistic development of Bihar. The politics of Bihar is not working for Bihar; instead it is working in fulfilling the vested interests of a few individuals and a few groups of individuals only.

Way back in 1967, a coalition government was formed in Bihar which consisted of Sanghatita Socialist Party, Praja Socialist Party, Jana Sangh, Communist Party, and Janata Party of Kamakhya Narayan Singh as coalition partners. Mahamaya Babu was elected the head of this coalition. This can also be seen as a government of non-Congress parties under the leadership of the Congress Party. In that there was an alliance between communism and feudalism and alliance between socialism and capitalism and there was cooperation between nationalism and consumerism. But that government didn't last long and whatever government was formed in its wake, it could continue only for 45 days. Bindeswari Prasad Mondal was the leader of that government. Later, under the leadership of Bhola Paswan Shastri, a non-Congress government was formed by dissolving Bindeswari Prasad's government. In that there was an alliance between communism and feudalism and alliance between socialism and capitalism and there was cooperation between nationalism and consumerism. In 1967, the trend of unprincipled, power-hungry political alliances started and downfall of politics had started with politics was going downhill. Even today there are some ministers who have assumed the office of ministers in various governments since 1967. Along with ethical, character and democratic downfall of legislative bodies, there has been a severe degradation of the administrative machinery as well. Both of them are interlinked. In this same Bihar, political leaders like Karpoori Thakur, Bhola Paswan, Jaglal Choudhury and Ramanand Tiwari were born, whose life was without a blemish and who didn't leave behind anything for their offspring. But unfortunately, those leaders of Bihar couldn't be the ideal of Bihar; rather, such leaders have turned out to be our ideal who believe in racism and who are destructive. To acquire Chief Ministership, racism has been promoted and after becoming chief ministers, they gave shelter to communal forces and racism. When the frenzy of racist and communalist elements got the support of the power, that be, crime, kidnapping and terrorism started spreading all around.

Where some drops of nectar were found due to negative politics of non-Congress ideology, at the same time there was seen a cup of poison as well. Everybody was happy after sipping the nectar, but nobody touched the poison. Today that poison is working disaster across Bihar. Even now there seems to be nobody who can consume that poison. Everybody has enjoyed the nectar together called change of power and ending of the political hegemony which came from the churning of ocean of politics; but everybody has left out the poison called racism, corruption and communalism which came out of that churning. Socialists and communists characterised by waging a crusade against injustice, atrocities, political and administrative corruption have also started swimming in the comforts of power. Through agitation they could reach the seat of power but subsequently they forgot about the politics of agitation. They changed socialism to individualism and communism to authoritarianism. When two agitating political parties drown in the quagmire of indulgence, obviously the influence of criminals, extortionists, kidnappers would get into politics. On one hand, political parties who relentlessly engaged in bringing about change in power, administration and politics, turned away from all those principles and started building caste equations. On the other hand, nationalist parties have been engaged merely in intellectual propagation. They were of the opinion that intellectual propagation would bring about some ideological change and that social development comes only through ideological change, so they continued on that path. Everybody gave up running agitations to fight against those issues which keep affecting the day-to-day life of the common people and which have an impact on the worldly life of masses at large. Non-Congress parties also started moving in the ideological flow of Congress. The duel between two political ideologies has ended. No political party has any long-term ideology for public agitation. They want to live by reacting to each other. Instead of being action-oriented, they want to acquire power by being reactionary. Janata Dal has started this kind of politics and now it is burning in the heat of the same politics.

Along with Lalu Prasad, all of them who are colluding either directly or indirectly in looting the state, are equally responsible. By making MLAs comfort-loving and abusing resources, Lalu imprisoned their conscience. Pretentious agitations, pretentious opposition, sham Assembly can't show the way to Bihar. There is a need for such a nationalist party that has the guts to end the politics of indulgence, corruption, privileges and misuse of resources and is able to control the legislature and executive in the light of the economic condition of the people of Bihar. The Assembly will become such a mirror in which the reflection of sacrifice, generosity, self-respect, self-reliance and nationalism can be seen clearly. Bihar needs this kind of politics and in politics, Bihar wants to embrace the ideological path.

*Jansatta, 26 July, 1994*

□

# 14
# Battle of Righteousness has to be Fought Against Oneself

It is very difficult to embark on a definitive conclusion as to when and who started the caste system. It has come into existence with time for reasons ascribed to societal impact. From the time when eligibility was decided by birth, this imprisonment in the dock has been going on in society in many forms. Class has taken the form of caste. Profession has been linked to birth; children born to people in any profession were made heirs to the same profession. No significance was attached to knowledge, intelligence, potential, talent and eligibility of those children. Talent was eclipsed from the time when teachers, lecturers, doctors, warriors, rulers, administrators started entering the field on the basis of birth from those houses and slowly the whole of India was drowned in complete darkness. When the whole society was neck deep in this quagmire, then individuals too got drowned in the same quagmire. Since ancient times it has taken many forms—from feudalism, capitalism up to socialism. In the cycle of time, in its journey from the *Satyug* to *Tretayug, Dwaparyug* and ever up to *Kaliyug,* it has kept on changing its form. As from the point of view of political ruling system, it has become multi-dimensional.

If one observes organisations of political parties seriously, it becomes very clear that the reigns of the party are in the hands of one particular individual of whichever caste and in that party, all eligible people pop up from that specific caste only. In whosoever's hands the government goes, in his caste only all virtues take birth. This is the magic of this caste system.

Leave alone the political parties, take any social organisation and review its activities of the past ten or twenty long years—it becomes very clear that caste has laid its influence on that organisation, which means the caste system is everywhere and everybody is getting crushed under that system and crying. Yes, it is true that a few people forming their own groups keep running this system and reap benefits and profits in the name of caste. Why does it happen so?

In case some researcher undertakes a research on this aspect and studies the organisational structure of all political parties in Bihar and investigates people, from bottom to top, based on caste, then it becomes amply clear that all political parties are under the influence of one or the other caste. This means, that the caste system has assumed its political form. It is a different issue that there are attacks on the caste system. They keep accusing and counter-accusing each other; the reason for this is that an individual from birth to death keeps revolving in the system like a plodder at all times and keeps receiving blessings, cooperation and support of the people of his caste. He is surrounded by people of his caste. Slowly, caste spells its influence on his conscious, subconscious and unconscious mind to such an extent that slowly he acquires the values of his caste. When he imbibes those values, it gets reflected in his thinking, behaviour, nature, actions and in everything else. When it is engrained in every drop of his blood, then what's the use of superficial opposition? People who talk about the welfare of the nation, society and human being are also seen painted in the same colour. This disease has to be cured from the root. It implies that the poison mixed in each drop of blood has to be cleaned up.

While talking from the dais, people may be nationalists, socialists and humanitarians, but when they come down from the dais, they all become racists. By the speeches delivered from the dais, one can't judge the character, personality and leadership of an individual. Writers, journalists, editors, rulers and administrators, though aware of this secret, still try to be ignorant of it. It is such a strong poison that can only be destroyed through the battle of righteousness. Today's caste system is a system that had been developed long ago, based on one's profession. Similarly, today the caste system is getting built in the new process. The class is getting transformed in accordance with the political and economic system. This is also going to pose problems in India in the times to come. Children of traders become traders, children of industrialists become industrialists, politicians' children become politicians, MLAs' children become MLAs. Children of MPs and ministers become MPs and ministers. An individual born in a particular clan will exert pressure to get the same position. The coming times will get drowned in its darkness. Similarly, organisations and institutions also get drowned in the quagmire. When a few groups and gangs or factions dominate organisations, the same people turn by turn keep managing the institutions and organisations and in turn the political caste system gets formed. In a democratic system, the structure of political institutions and organisations should keep changing. Today because of the caste system, an individual is able to hide his ineligibility, lack of potential and lack of skill.

Political parties were assessed based on principles, policies, ideals and ideas. But all these are intangible. The organisations' shape, structure and form are built by the people who run these organisations. With this thought, Mahatma Gandhi formed the national organisation during the national movement. He was like a glowing sun at the centre and a circle was formed all around him by people like Nehru, Vallabhbhai Patel, Jagjivan Babu, Azad, Lajpat Rai, Malaviya, Subhas, etc. coming from different regions and different castes and different classes. After seeing those leaders, people were convinced that Congress represented the entire nation. This faith became the public perception. Public perception became public determination and from determination arose the elements of public strength and public strength mothered democracy. Slowly, the leaders in power have dented this consent and its structure, both. Because of that dent only, lower castes and backward castes are enraged today. Today, there is a need for such a party and individual who can drink that poison. Only that party can do this supreme sacrifice and establish ideas like equality, generosity, love, nationalism, humanity and sacrifice in the minds of the public. It should not be just preaching, but has to be shown in deeds. When there will be feelings of sacrifice and generosity among forward classes and castes, then the feelings of humbleness and obedience would develop among the lower castes; then only the nation can get transformed. This is a flow, which has to be strengthened. When the nationalists, eligible people of character and talented leaders from among minorities, lower caste and backward castes get the deserved respect, then aggressive, violent and destructive leadership has to give way. When there is coordination among nationalist, economic, political, agriculture, education, judiciary, legislative and social policies, then individualism and feudalism have to be replaced from every bit of the nation with nationalism. Democracy will become successful, prosperous and empowered when each and every individual gets equal opportunities in each and every field. Will the Indians be able to fight this battle of righteousness with the instrument they have got in the form of ballot paper through their right to vote?

*Jansatta, 07 November, 1994*

□

# 15
# Who Loves the Backward and the Lower Castes?

Certainly, MPs and MLAs exercise their franchise for the election of the President, but they are not the only ones to script the destiny of the nation. Indirectly, they are representatives of people's ideas and opinions. The feeling with which they were elected or the feeling with which they are doing politics, in accordance with that feeling they have to cast their vote, rising above political party affiliations. If party membership gets cancelled for not following the orders of the party, how can voting be unbiased and independent? If snatching the ballot paper of a voter by force constitutes the body of crime, can't it be called a crime to snatch the ballot paper of an MP or an MLA in the name of discipline?

If it is a crime to demand that a person belonging to lower caste or backward caste only should be made President by looking for a highly eligible candidate from amongst them, then the Father of the Nation was the biggest criminal. People who say that there are none among lower and backward castes in the entire country who is eligible for this post are insulting those people. Those people have to do introspection. Leaders like Sankaran, Buta Singh, P. Siva Sankar, Ramsundar Das, Ramnaresh Yadav, Jagannath Pahadia, Siddheswar Prasad, Dhanik Lal Mandal are in what way inferior to anybody? People who talk about lower and backward castes in the name of social justice don't think of their interest. They are sequestering those communities and groups. Lower castes and backward castes supported by the BJP or communists are declared on political party basis to be untouchables and people who demand the right to vote as guided by their conscience, have to fight against all political parties to liberate the voters. Why is it that a particular class of people only are raising this demand to satisfy their political interests? People of the country have to learn from this.

As all organisations, political parties and all parliamentary systems are under the control of people from upper castes, so there is no difference between the psychology, thinking, perspective and their direction. Even while staying away from each other, they all are travellers of the same path. While people of lower and backward castes, though being in the same boat, still stay in isolation. Why till today, nobody from backward or lower caste was given the post of president of any political party? If at all, anybody was given the post, he was made a puppet. Whoever had the vision of equality and who are talented and smart were killed in the political *chakravyuh*. Whenever any opposition party came into power, there were severe attacks on lower castes and backward castes.

Slogans were for their development but leadership was in the hands of their opponents. Why were important portfolios not given to lower caste and backward caste in the cabinets of both V.P. Singh and Chandrasekhar? They were offered portfolios of ministries claiming to have done them a favour. Without taking names, it can safely be said that in comparison to whoever they considered experienced, veteran, stalwart, capable and eligible, the lower castes and backward castes in their own ministry were, if not more, but definitely less on any count. People who were accused about certain types of crimes were still given significant posts, but why the backwards and lower castes accused of similar types of crimes were not allowed to stand even for the second term? Lower castes and backwards should never tread the path of upper castes and classes. Whoever imitated the upper castes, they only pushed the people of their community into the path of downfall. People who fought for social justice have nominated a candidate from lower and backward castes for the post of President of the country, but why didn't they nominate candidates for Rajya

Sabha and Legislative Council from those communities? When I contested against Bommai for the post of national president of Janata Dal, at that time I was standing alone. Where did this philosophy exist at that time? At that critical juncture, all those people chose to leave me alone, who at one point of time had encouraged me to contest for the post.

In the governments of Rajiv Gandhi, V.P. Singh, Chandrasekhar, P.V. Narasimha Rao, whosoever was nominated for positions of governors, ambassadors, judges, members of UPSC, and chairmen and members of various other commissions and chiefs, directors of different public undertakings, etc., among them why were there no candidates from backward and lower castes? At that time, it was argued that there were no eligible candidates in these communities. This is the ladder of democratic system on climbing which an individual reaches the top. If filtering is done only at the bottom, which plant would be seen in this forest? Everybody wants to reach the goal by using lower castes and backward castes as steps and by chanting their name. But sadly, nobody harbours love for them in his heart. Negativity in the heart and pretention of love in the mind, this is what is proving dangerous for the nation. Names of Gandhi, Lohia, Jai Prakash, Marx and Deendayal are getting misused. A few leaders, by behaving like Kaalnemi, are misleading the talented navigators of the nation and thus making the nation lose its direction and lifeless and regressive. Country should think consciously. Upper caste people should be liberal and lower caste and backward castes should be humble. Then a new nation can be built.

*Jansatta, 5 July, 1992*

□

# 16

# Difference between India and Bharat

Since 1977, I have been able to witness the metro city of Delhi very closely. In due course, when I was not an MP, even then I used to stay in North Avenue. Staying in the midst of distinguished people, an ordinary person can't realise the truth about his status or situation. He lives in his imaginary world. By the grace of God, for the last one year, I have also been living like any other commoner in the midst of ordinary people in a densely populated New Multan Nagar area of west Delhi. I am used to seeing both India and Bharat in the same country; but now I am seeing two cities in the same city. That part of Delhi where distinguished people reside can't be compared with that part of Delhi, where ordinary people live. Foreigners, by seeing Parliament House, India Gate, President's House, and the areas where quarters and residences of high-ranking officials live, go back with certain images of Delhi. These mesmerising images lure them.

Where ordinary people live, in those areas what is the condition of electricity, water and toilets? In addition to regular bus service, for transport white line, green line and STA services are there. All of them are equally crowded, though only fares are different. I gained experience of travelling by these modes of transport with different names. In distinguished areas those vehicles are challenged which vent out heavy exhaust fumes, but in ordinary areas, those vehicles are more in number. At what cost people are living in these areas! They are like insects and pests and a burden on earth. The area in which I live, there one has to undergo a lot of trouble to get drinking water. There is no schedule of water supply. Staff of all departments keep playing cards the whole day. Without taking money, they don't do any work and they don't let any outsider do any work. What should a helpless citizen do? If a telephone rings, consider it as a message from God. Not for days, for weeks, the telephone remains under repair. No response comes even after making a complaint. When a distinguished person lives in the midst of ordinary people like an ordinary person, then only he gets to realise the truth. Don't say anything about sanitation, cleanliness and don't listen also as both of them are crimes. Parks are like resting places of pigs. Distinguished people are very rare; that's why it is priceless. But the life of an ordinary man is very easy so there is no value to it. Whoever lives in Delhi enjoys the status of being a Delhi resident. It is also their helplessness. Sometimes they enjoy visiting the distinguished areas of Delhi and see some distinguished people. That pleasant feeling is like a resident of hell sometimes getting an opportunity to visit heaven. There is no despondent for being a resident of hell, but he enjoys and gets lost in the breeze of heaven. The villages in India and in Delhi present a true picture of the real Bharat. The struggle which takes place between the real and the fake is coming to the forefront and is becoming true. Who is going to listen to me, because I am also an undistinguished and very ordinary person.

*Jansatta, 22 October, 1992*

□

# 17
# Today there is no Opposition

When society and nation get embroiled in one circle, they keep going in rounds in the same circle; unless they come out of the circle by breaking free their inhibitions, no new light and new direction can be seen. Everybody talks about breaking the circumference, but can't get over the element of fascination. Today all over the world, political, economic, social, administrative, communal and ideological inertia is setting in. New direction and new light are not in view due to loss of momentum and inertia. The whole world is grunting and thrashing about, but running away from bearing the pain of liberation. When a snake sheds its old skin, it experiences more pain than experienced at the time of birth. After that it gets transformed. Society and nation can also get transformed only if it sheds its old skin, which is painful—getting scared of shedding the old skin but at the same time wanting to enjoy the pleasure of transformation. This is the height of ideological inertia and political inertia has become the toughest problem. New ideas are not coming; accepting old ideas completely as the premise is communalism. Political communalism is burning the world more than religious communalism. Everything has been politicised, but politicisation of community and communalisation of politics have become the major reasons for all the troubles humanity at large is faced with in the current scenario. This is called ideological inertia.

It is very common to face opposition in politics and it has been there for a long time. When the differences between the treasury bench and opposition disappears, when party gets mingled in opposition and opposition gets mingled in the party, then it becomes very difficult to analyse. One can only see the difference—who stands in the middle of the two. However, it is not at all easy to stand in between. This has become an issue of research to find out who is in opposition and who is in favour of the government.

If the Congress is in power at the Centre, in many states the BJP, the Left Front and the Janata Dal are in power. All are in power and also in opposition; simultaneously the same individual has to play both the roles on the same stage. All parties, in power and opposition, need to do introspection. Instead of looking into themselves, they are looking at others. Whatever is coming out of the womb of accusation, criticism and negative things will be destructive only. Everybody is behaving the same way to get into power and retain it. Policies, ideals, principles, rules, conduct, ideologies and ethics—everything is getting sacrificed to retain the power. The goal is to stay in power come what may. Against which BJP has called for a pan India close down, on the same issues if Congress is calling for a close down, then what is the truth? If the Central Government is a culprit, then who is responsible for making and safeguarding this government? That is also to be taken into account. To get the Mandal Commission implemented, Janata Dal started the Mandal *rath* (chariot of Mandal). Mandal Commission could not be implemented in Bihar and Orissa where Janata Dal is in power. People who try to hide their misdeeds by blaming others will be self-deceiving. **We see the world only with two eyes, but the world sees us with infinite eyes. Two eyes may not be able to see the complete picture, but infinite eyes can't be deceived. While the Congress carries out the role of an opposition in the states ruled by the BJP, Left** Front and the Janata Dal, even all the non-Congress parties perform the role of opposition in Congress-ruled states. All ruling parties are enshrouding their sins. How long would they keep acting to camouflage their inaction, inability, failure, lack of organisation and appetite and for power.

At certain points of time, socialists and communists have resorted to cordoning off, *Satyagraha,* strikes and closedown. By way of holding demonstrations and public meetings, they try to express public feelings. It would give happiness when opposition lacked resources to fight against the resourceful ruling party, but today it is a face off between the resources. There is a hidden ego in the clash of resources. Ego becomes immoderate because of resourceful and resource-short situations. But when all parties are playing the role of both ruling and opposition, then where is the scope for lack of resources? Secret resources are collected. These journeys are part of it. Political parties make their secret resources public through these journeys, that is, it is the way to convert political black money into white. Then against whom are these close downs done? If the policies of the Centre are against the interests of states, then just say whose policies are in the interest of states? Whatever money gets collected to do close downs, demonstrations, rallies and conferences, that burden has to be borne by the impoverished, weak and the meek public of states. People are giving funds because they know that the opposition parties are also ruling parties in some or the other state and they will return this money in one form or the other.

Can't stay together, so the process of getting separated continues. They can't uphold the ethics of democracy in their government and even in the organisation for that matter. In the name of bringing stability to the government, they keep playing all dirty games to hold the influence of individuals or groups of individuals. For their selfish interests, they keep giving protection to criminals. They keep cleaning the people who earn money by all illegal means with political soap. Whenever the opportunity comes, they don't hesitate to offer the posts to their family members and sycophants. In the name of Ram, Rahim and Mandal, they try to hide the internal demons. All are equal sinners and righteous. Now such a system is required by which everybody is annihilated simultaneously, then only a new era will be built. This world and especially India will be freed from this cunning and *Kalanemi* type people only when people of equal intelligence and when all have the same goal. Heard everybody, seen everybody, understood everybody and knew everybody, then what for is the delay?

The country is riddled hardships because of these fake strikes and wriggling. Today, the true opposition is only that, which is not in government in any state. A political party which is either supporting a government or part of the government in some state or the other can't afford to be in opposition in true sewage of the word. People who are unable to demonstrate their virtues at a smaller level, how can they prove themselves at the bigger level? What can they show in a short span of time? Nation and the world has to think in these hard times and complicated situations. Vidur in the Mahabharata had said that for the sake of family, individual, for society's sake family, for society and welfare of conscience, nation has to be sacrificed.

*Jansatta, 26 November, 1992*

□

# 18

# A Vow 'Awaken the Village— The Impoverished, the Farmer'

The meeting of the national executive of BJP Kisan Morcha, expresses its concern over the fact that little or less attention is paid to the agriculture sector in an agro-based country like India, based on the priorities of Mahatma Gandhi to keep agriculture in the top place, cottage and village industries in the second place and big industries in the third place. If budgets had been allocated on that basis to agriculture in the Five Year and annual plans, the status of villages and farmers would have been transformed. The farmers' wing of BJP reiterates that vow and in the BJP regime, agriculture is accorded top priority and sufficient amount is spent on its development. To build India as per the ideals of Gandhi, Lohia and Deendayal and to bring prosperity and comfort in the lives of rural people and to create opportunities for employment, the following strategies should be adopted:

- ☐ BJP should take immediate action on the issues discussed in *'kisan ka adhikar patra'* (A letter on the rights of farmers). On 1 August 1996, the delegates of Kisan Morcha submitted the letter of rights along with memorandum to the President.
- ☐ A network of cottage and village industries should be established to reduce the number of people dependent on agriculture. Those countries have become rich where population has come down. Countries where dependency of population on agriculture has increased, poverty has increased in those countries. In 1920, in America, 89 percent, in England 18 percent and in India 55 percent of

the population was dependent on agriculture; by 1985-86 it came down in America to 3 percent, in England 2.5 percent and in India 71.4 percent of the total population.

- The gap in the per capita income of people living in rural and urban areas has increased. In 1950-51, it used to be 1 : 2, but in 1995-96 it became 0.5 percent in urban areas as income per family grew at the rate of 52 percent, while in rural areas per household income could grow only 7.8 percent. Very strong measures have to be taken to reduce this gap. Urban development is linked with rural development.
- Village-oriented political, financial and administrative powers have to decentralise. It is very much needed for social equality, harmony and self-reliance.
- Farmers should be given remunerative price in accordance with the costs incurred by them. Measures should be taken to reduce the cost. Agriculture has to be given privileges at par with industry. Pesticides, fertilisers and seeds should be made available at cheaper rates. Systems should be devised to supply electricity required for irrigation at a minimum rate and up to a fixed period on priority basis. If loss is incurred on crops due to lack of power supply, the loss should be compensated.
- In the commission of agricultural costs and prices, two-third members should be from amongst agricultural graduates and scientists who are engaged in agriculture-related activities and from the consumer class. The price of crops should be announced before the sowing starts. Announced price should include the cost of farm equipment and all through the year those farm equipment and related parts should be made available at the same price.
- Non-commercial crops should be irrigated for free and no tax should be levied on such crops.
- According to fixed price policy, prices of agriculture output and industrial output should be decided. Unless the cost of industrial output is not known, till then the profit can't be estimated. Whatever is the price at the time of the new harvest, it should be increased not more than 10 paise per

kilo till the time next harvest comes. The price of the factory output should not be more than one-and-a-half times of its cost.

- ☐ The interests of farmers should be kept in mind while deciding the EXIM policy of agriculture output and farmers should also be able to participate in deciding what policy and measures should be taken to do so.
- ☐ Every panchayat should have a *galla godam*, where farmers can keep their harvest and recieve interim payment from the bank. There should be a provision for sufficient purchase centres.
- ☐ Insurance schemes should be implemented for crops, farm cattle and also damages caused by natural calamities.
- ☐ Sugar industry should be free from licence and ban over vacuum pan technology should be removed. By removing control over molasses, farmers should be given bonus from that income; there should not be any ban on farmer's oil mill.
- ☐ By rejuvenating dead rivers, canals, ponds and lakes, resources for irrigation should be increased as this will also help in flood control.
- ☐ Act related to draught relief fund and revenue should be amended; land acquisition act should be modified. Land meant for agriculture should not be acquired to develop residential areas and government offices and other projects. Compensation should be given at market rates. One person from the families of displaced farmers should be given employment in these projects and from the profit earned from these projects, they should be given bonus every year.
- ☐ Measures should be taken to provide basic amenities in rural areas. Emphasis should be given to issues like education, health, electricity, transport and self-employment, etc. on a priority basis. Top priority should be accorded to construct toilets for rural women.
- ☐ Emphasis should be laid on businesses linked to agriculture, such as poultry, pig and cattle rearing, pisciculture, silk production, food processing, forestry and fruit production should be expanded.

- Land reformation programmes should be linked to agriculture development programmes. Farmers should have representation in boards and commissions set up to handle revenue-related issues. Along with delimitation of land, limits to income has to set in all fields. To convert fallow and useless lands, national *bhoomisena* has to be set up. Rural unemployed youth should be engaged in this activity.
- Programmes should be made to develop the forests. Afforestation programmes should be run through *bhoomisena* and along with the conservation of forests, the interests of people living in forests also have to be protected. Rules should be made to use the forest products and resources by tribals and people living in forests and they should be given privileges. Farmers who grow forests in rural areas should be given all amenities and financial support. Forest departments keep troubling the farmers and don't allow them to cut trees—this torture has to be stopped.
- Livestock is the basis for agriculture; it is declining continuously. Emphasis should be laid on conservation and increase of livestock. To put a total ban on cow slaughter, an act should be passed in Parliament.
- A comprehensive debate on agriculture, farmers and rural development won't happen in Parliament. There should be a Parliament session once a year devoted to agriculture. To ensure sufficient representation of farmers from rural areas, they should have sufficient representation in Parliament and State Assemblies and constitutional arrangements should be made. Reservation should be given in government services to students who study up to higher secondary level in rural areas.
- The balance should be paid at the earliest along with interest to sugarcane farmers. Repayment of government loans should be stopped. Sick and shutdown sugar factories have to be revived. Wherever cane is burnt in the field or cane gets dried up due to delay in fixing the procurement price, compensation should be given. A system should be

set up to procure jute from jute producers. All shutdown or sick sugar mills have to be revived urgently.

- ☐ Permanent solutions should be worked out to stop floods and drought. To discuss the reports prepared by all related commissions and committees, a high-level rights commission should be set up. Flood-affected farmers should be given compensation of at least 1,000 rupees per acre towards crop damage.
- ☐ Farmers were severely affected by urea, animal husbandry and sugar scandals. They are not just, economic offences; instead, national crimes and treason. All the accused should be punished for national crime and treason.

To awaken the element of self-respect among the farmers and bring national awareness among them, they have to be brought together. National Committee takes a vow that following the principles of contacts, relations and unity, they will be ready to agitate. By worshipping the pride of village, nation's pride will be worshipped. We achieve cultural and spiritual nationalism by awakening respect for local language, local attire, local food, local habitat, local culture, local values. We bring consciousness among farmers to remove corrupt scamsters and people's enemies from power. To root out people who run on fear, indulgence, illusion and corruption from power we call villages impoverished farmers to wake up and get united.

- ☐ The suggestions given by BJP Kisan Morcha for the betterment of farmers.
- ☐ All the persons involved in scams should be punished, working upon them as treasonaries.

(The proposal passed in National Working Committee of BJP Kisan Morcha on 19-20 August at Daruhera.)

☐

# 19

# Is it Necessary for Politics to get out of Caste Polarisation?

There is an era of downfall which cannot be stopped. Downfall is a trend; the whole world is influenced by it. Nothing including ideology, principle, idealism and system can stay without getting influenced by it. Ravan was not any single individual. He was symbolic of Ravan's tendency. The battle between Rama and Ravan was not any battle between two individuals, rather it was a battle between two tendencies. It has been going on since time immemorial. The battle between good tendency and bad tendency, selfishness and charity and individual good and good of the whole society is still continuing. This battle is eternal and permanent. Nothing is going to happen by saying, '*satyameva jayate*' (truth always wins). Mighty falsehood suppresses the voice of meek truth. Truth wins only when the people fighting for it are strong. Strength of people on the side of truth comes from ethics, ideals and expansiveness. Strength wanes because of narrowness and individualism. Narrowness and individualism slowly attack and weaken the permanent values. Righteousness, generosity, goodwill and ideology continuously get weakened. People with such tendencies believe that they can completely destroy those values and destroy them from the root. However, till date they couldn't do so; still the battle is going on and it will continue to do so.

Systems keep changing with time. Values keep changing in accordance with the changing systems. With changing values, legislature keeps changing. When inertia sets in the changing legislature, it starts protecting the system and then illegal activities start taking place. Systems should get furbished, based on eternal and permanent values. Without losing its antiquity, they should continuously get modernised. Furbishing in politics, economics and social policies should be done to impart momentum to each other. Similarly, the policies of administration should change accordingly. The mentality of enslaved India was different to democracy that came in after Independence. To attain political equality for which nations of the world were struggling for centuries, India got it along with Independence. However, initiatives were not taken to bring social equality. Caste system was a major hurdle on the way to social equality and it is the root cause of economic disparities in the society. Caste system is nourishing these inequalities. The same trend has got into politics and is showing its impact. Communal and racial violence and counter-violence caused due to hatred and jealousy have shaken the very foundations of our society and is troubling the whole world. Moral and ethical values are getting destroyed. The political system of India is writhing in pain and calls for total transformation, but even now it is not accepting the truth. Bhishma, Karn, Drupad, Bhim and Draupadi, while committed to their vow, wanted to stop the battle of Mahabharata and requested Krishna to suggest ways to stop the battle; but could they give up the ego of their vow, could Krishna fulfil their wish?

Working in 1964, a new trend set in politics. Non-Congress strategy was started, the results of which came to be seen in 1967. Like in Bihar, in eight other states non-Congress parties came into power. The leadership in those governments was in the hands of politicians who had defected from Congress. Jana Sangh and communists were part of those governments. Socialists and feudalists were enjoying power as they were part of those governments. All those governments have collapsed in the same way. Leaders, who defected from the Congress, only formed the governments and aborted the non-Congress governments with the assistance of the Congress. With that started the process of downfall of authoritarian politics. Caste equations, polarisation of vested interests, criminalisation of politics and corruption in administration began. The writer became an MLA of Sanghathit Socialist Party in Bihar Assembly, way back in 1967. Bindeswari Prasad Mandal was an MP and he was made a minister. Later, making him a minister courted controversy. With assistance from the Congress the Sanghathit Socialist Party was divided and Bindeswari Prasad Mandal was made Chief Minister of Bihar. That government also ended with the division of Congress. Under the leadership of Vinodanand Jha and Bhola Paswan, the senior-most leaders of Congress, the Congress was divided. Many veteran socialists defected to the oppressed party of Bindeswari Prasad. Many veteran Congress leaders joined Binova Babu's Loktantrik Congress and dethroned the government of Bindeswari Prasad Mandal's oppressed party and made Bhola Paswan the Chief Minister. In due course, all disconcerted Congress leaders went back to their old party whenever they got an opportunity. They wanted to be in power but when the opportunity was not seen, they went back to the Congress to be part of the government. Even after that, the parties opposing the Congress joined the government of Congress. At that time nobody was untouchable to anybody. Will the leaders of today clarify this and will the voters ask for clarification? Most of the voters of today don't know anything about this.

The era of 1974 has ushered in the Bihar movement which had emerged from the student movement. Lok Nayak Jai Prakash Narayan led that movement. Writer has been elected to that Assembly for the third time. MLAs have resigned. Under the leadership of Karpoori Thakur in the beginning six people tendered their resignation; the writer was also one among them. Emergency was declared across the country because of this movement. When all the leaders of opposition and a few Congress leaders were put in jails, at that time Communist Party of India started a fascist movement in support of Indira Gandhi and describing Lok Nayak as fascist. In due course, 1977 elections were announced. All non-Congress and communists came together. Janata Party formed the government in alliance with all parties. Today they are part of the National Front. Along with Samata Party, Samajwadi Party, Janata Dal, few from the Bahujan Samaj Party also joined that government and became part of that Front. Even the BJP leaders were part of it. There was no question of untouchable or otherwise. Those communists who were with the National Front are also part of the United Front today and who were with the Congress at that time. Those who called Lok Nayak fascist and supported the dictatorship during the Emergency of Indira Gandhi today are forming a front with those leaders, who were put in jails during the Emergency. Who will question it and who will give the answer to it? Parliament was a witness when Congress was divided; Indira Gandhi came into minority and was running the government with the support of the communists. In its journey from Jana Sangh to Bharatiya Janata Party, the latter always supported the non-Congress parties and leaders with political sincerity. In 1990, Viswanath Pratap Singh became the Prime Minister with the support of BJP only. In Bihar, Lalu Prasad became the Chief Minister for the first time only with the support of BJP. Whenever Congress got into trouble and the danger was lurking in the corner, it took the support of Left Front. Left parties have defended the Congress in bringing down the Janata Party Government. Left Front played a secret role in bringing down the Janata Government. It was the conspiracy of the Left Front to get Mr. Advani arrested and oppose the promises made by V.P. Singh. Left Front always wanted to hoist the red flag in the heart of India, that is, the states lying in the plains between Ganges and Yamuna. Socialists used to stop their *aswamedha* horse in Bihar while travelling from Bengal. In Uttar Pradesh, their identity was almost nil. The wave of political, economic and social furbishing set by Dr. Lohia had maximum impact on Bihar and eastern Uttar Pradesh. The new generation among the backward castes is highly influenced by Dr. Lohia. A new consciousness was awakened among the backward castes. The writer was also regularly going to the Shakha till 1962. But influenced by the social revolution of Dr. Lohia he became a member of Sangathit Socialist Party. There were many such people. In 1977, due to the politics of Jan Sangh and Lokdal, most of the Chief Ministers were made from these two groups only. As Choudhury Devi Lal in Haryana and

Karpoori Thakur in Bihar, Ram Naresh Yadav in Uttar Pradesh and Nilmany Raut in Orissa became Chief Ministers, then in the states lying in the heart of India the flag of Lok Dal was flying high. They all were from the farming community and from the backward castes. They had the image of a poor farmer. At the same time, in Bihar, the issue of 26 percent reservation had come up. Janata Party MLAs started opposing it openly. Coincidently, the MLAs of Jana Sangh faction were also in the frontline of that agitation. Kailashpati Mishra, the then Finance Minister of Bihar Government and also highly respected leader of Jan Sangh emphatically supported reservation. Support of Atalji and Nanaji was also there. Even after these, because of a few local leaders the image of Jana Sangh has turned out to be of anti-reservation. Kailashpati Mishra has tried till the end to keep Karpoori Thakur as Chief Minister. In that government with the support of Kailashpati Mishra, the kind of work done by Karpoori Thakur was not done by any other government in Bihar. It was unfortunate that, that government has gone.

The opportunity which Left Front was looking for has come. The ill-effect of the degrading politics of backward and lower castes is that power has gone into the hands of Mulayam Singh and Lalu Prasad in Uttar Pradesh and Bihar. To protect their power, both of them gave birth to the fanatics of casteism in the name of social justice. Left Front colluded with them and gave rise to caste fanatics and tried to convert the base from socialist to communist. The companionship of Lalu and Mulayam Singh has attempted to increase their influence over Yadavs and other backward castes. Left Front and regional parties have their influence in coastal states of India, while in states in the heart of India the competition was among the BJP, Samajwadi and supporters of lower caste. Today the distorted form of Samajwadi is based on racism and Dalitvaad. In the coastal states, the competition is between the Left parties and the Congress. Even regional parties are against the Congress. Politics of racisim is stopping the flow of nationalism. The day BJP establishes its dominance in Bihar and Uttar Pradesh, from that day the influence of Left Front will reduce in West Bengal. That is the reason why the Left Front wants to stop BJP.

In the blind race to gain power, Lalu and Mulayam Singh are overlooking this truth. **If we study the history starting from the freedom struggle to current struggle of anti-Congress, it can be inferred that from the beginning Left Front always gave top priority to fulfil their own vested interests. They want change but for their own benefit.** BJP had supported every change and supported every non-Congress leader. But it is unfortunate that it became untouchable for everybody. Other parties couldn't expand but BJP expanded itself.

The result of political downfall in Bihar is polarisation of fanatics and criminals. At one time slogans used to be raised for Jagannath Mishra—*Jagannath ke char naath;* Rajo Raghunath, Pabhunath and Kamalnath—today all these are confidant commanders of Lalu Prasad. They were working for him during the Lok Sabha elections. Isn't it a mystery? People who used to carry ashes against reservation have joined the group of Lalu Prasad. All those Samajwadis who agitated along with Akshayvat Roy, Bhupendra Narayan Mandal and Karpoori Thakur were grunting in 'gas chambers of Hitler'. Jagannath gave birth to the fanatics of racism. It was there even earlier, but it was subdued and hidden. Criminals, corrupt and persecutors have become the people to be worshipped in their respective castes. Even after committing so many scams, Jagannath is revered by everybody; similarly Lalu Prasad has also become person worth revering. Left parties are supporting him. Their strategy is that lawlessness should continue in Bihar so that they get an opportunity to come into Bihar. After 1977 no party has carried out any purposeful agitation. When purposeful and decisive agitation against economic disparities and administrative corruption ends then racist forces come up. Politics is now done by entering the *chakravyuh* of racist polarisation. In the name of castes and races, new leaders are being made and politics is going deep into this quagmire. Country is plunging into deep depths. Politics has become quarrelsome, pretentious and indulgent. There is a need for a new form of it. May be politics is writhing in this labour pain. Transformation of the nation is bound to happen.

- In the system that changed with times the expectation of development of politics has become regressive.
- With growing dominance of BJP in Uttar Pradesh and Bihar, the influence of the Left will diminish in West Bengal

*BJP Samachar, 16-30 June, 1996*

# 20

# National Policies have to be Developed for the Development of Agriculture

The Bharatiya Janata Party Kisan Morcha held its national working committee meeting under the chairmanship of Hukmdev Narayan Yadav on 19-5-1996. During the meeting, discussions were held on the present status of agriculture and rural areas of the country and the following proposal was passed.

The national working committee of Bharatiya Janata Party Kisan Morcha is deeply worried about the fact that even so many years after Independence a national policy on agriculture couldn't be worked out, due to which farmers and rural people are getting neglected. Prioritywise, agriculture and cottage industries should have first and second positions respectively. If there would have been a network of industries based on agricultural produce, then because of cottage industries, the problem of unemployment wouldn't have increased to such an extent. There have been serious scams and corruption in projects initiated in the name of rural development and poor farmers. Many schemes have been initiated by the Central Government to better the situation of economic and social status of farmers, however, the benefits of those schemes couldn't reach the target groups. The only reason for this is in political and administrative framework, these programmes have not been given a respectful and deserving place, because of which, proper energy didn't spread among poor farmers and rural population. Collective consciousness and the feeling of social interest couldn't develop in them; as a result they couldn't come together to fight against exploitation, corruption and social disparities. As the feeling of nationalism and social harmony didn't become prominent, they didn't develop the feeling of unity among themselves. Programmes like adult literacy, informal education, *anganwadi* and nutritive food have been started for poor farmers and rural population, but the benefits did not reach them. If that amount was spent on irrigation, electricity and rural transport in the villages, they would have transformed the villages with their efforts. But instead of their efforts, villagers had to depend on the programmes of the government. Only scandals took place in those programmes and schemes. All the money spent was fake.

The growing influence of foreign culture along with foreign investment, consumer technology, foreign industries has made farmers and the rural population of India dependent on others and become parasites on others. Local culture of rural India is slowly getting extinct due to which the local values have become corrupt. To make India self-reliant and self-respected, the feeling of indigenous, self-rule and self-dependence have to be awakened among the rural population and farmers. This work can be done only with strong willpower, allegiance towards nation and devotion and until such a government comes at the Centre, this grand initiative cannot be completed successfully. Just for a few days, a government was formed at the Centre under Atal Bihari Vajpayee, and whatever direction was set by that government for the nation, they substantially inspired the rural people.

The cycle of time tells that a small famine comes once in every five years and a medium-level famine once in every ten years and a severe famine once in every thirty years. For the last three to four years, a major part of the country was experiencing conditions like famine. Because of floods, drought and natural calamities, farmers have been ruined completely. They are not getting the compensation when crops get destroyed. If crops are good, they don't get the right price for their harvest and they don't get electricity, fertilisers, seeds, pesticides, farm equipment and other agriculture-related items in time. Whatever grant comes in their name already gets distributed among the corrupt administrators and politicians. Seed Corporation and Fertiliser Corporation play a major role in devouring these grants. Small and marginal farmers are given grants for boring, wells and pumpsets. Most of the loot happens in these programmes. If the grants meant for 'Jawahar Yojana', 'Indira Awaas Yojana' and 'Samekit Gramin Vikas Yojana' had been utilised sincerely and properly, villages would have been transformed by now. By devising policies leading to racial differences, communal appeasement, slogan shouting, farmers were cheated on. They all can be united only through creating a feeling of national consciousness, cultural awareness and spiritual nationalism.

Animal husbandry and urea scandals are like robbing the interests of farmers and poor people. In the animal husbandry scandal, it was not only economic loss and rampant corruption, but had that amount been utilised as intended, prosperity would have come in the lives of lower caste, backward castes and tribals. They were deprived of development and on the other hand, it caused a major loss to the national exchequer, thereby causing severe unemployment as well. By not getting urea in time, crop yield fell, which caused loss to the nation. This is not only an economic offence but also unpardonable treason. Action should be taken against all the people involved in these scams and they should be awarded stringent punishments.

Farmers get cash income by growing crops like sugarcane, cotton, jute and soya bean, but day by day their production is reducing. Farmers of the country are not getting proper price for their harvest, whereas by paying more to foreign farmers, these products are being imported. The condition of sugarmills is very bad. The mills run by the cooperation of government are either totally dead or sick. Why the balance of payments to farmers is getting delayed? On one side their payments are getting delayed, on the other hand, they are pressurised to repay the government loans. National Committee demands that sugarcane and jute mills should be modernised and farmers should be paid the balance amount immediately with interest. Total freedom should be given to set up sugarmills and licencing system should be removed, molasses should be deregulated and from that farmers should be given bonus. This year, compensation should be given for whatever sugarcane was left in the field or was burnt. Parliament should call for a special session in which there should be elaborate discussion on agricultural policy and problems of farmers.

Commission for Agriculture Prices should have two-third of members from among the farmers. In all the boards and corporations, commissions and institutions should have representatives from villages and rural areas. A national commission for prices should be set up which will decide upon the cost of industrial output by which a balance would be struck between agriculture and industrial output prices. **A system should be devised to give grants directly to the farmers instead of paying through institutions.** A system should be set up to purchase soft grains and other crops on the support price. As there is no system in place to purchase, farmers are forced to sell their crop at lower prices.

The irrigation systems should be completed quickly and those which are halted due to issues related to environment and other controversies, have to be started immediately by solving the issues so that these facilities can be availed fast. Sluice gates, solid embankments, and small dams should be constructed at various places on small and medium rain-fed and perennial rivers so that rain-water can be collected in them by which farmers can avail cheaper irrigation facilities by their own labour. The groundwater levels are steadily dipping down. If we don't implement schemes to irrigate with minimum water possible, the water levels will dip so low that plants will not be able to absorb water on their own through their root system. Due to the disorganisation of irrigation dams and irrigation canals, water gets collected at some places, due to which farming can't be done on most of the land. So water outlets should be organised immediately. Dependency on electricity has increased due to modernisation of farming, but as there is no availability and certainty, it is causing a lot of loss to agriculture; so electricity should be made available to agriculture-related activities on priority basis.

Soil erosion due to indiscriminate deforestation is raising the level of river beds; as a result the problem of floods is increasing.

Measures have to be taken immediately to protect forests. Programmes like social forestry and afforestation programmes run by cooperative societies have to be run at full speed. In afforestation programmes, unemployed rural youth should be involved by setting up forest soldier units. Afforestation programmes on government fallow land should be done on a war footing. Cows and farm cattle are very important for agriculture-based countries. Without farm cattle, agriculture will be incomplete. It is very essential that cow slaughter should be banned completely and farm cattle should be protected and conserved as it is very important for economics of agriculture. Priority should be given to programmes of development of cows and other farm cattle. Politicians and other people involved in scams like animal husbandry and urea have to be arrested immediately. By confiscating the black money lying in foreign banks, it should be utilised for rural development and for developing irrigation facilities. Investigation should be done to find where all the money allocated for rural development was spent and action should be taken against all people accused of it. The Famine Act of India is very old, so it should be reformed. Proper provisions should be made to compensate farmers commensurate with the loss of crops. If necessary, payments should be made based on the market price existing at the time of payment. If land has to be acquired for industrial and business activities, then one member from the family of landowners should be given employment according to the eligibility.

Bharatiya Rashtriya Kisan Morcha works for the development of poor farmers and for the rural population of the country, so that along with getting their rights they should move forward to promote the feeling of self-governance, self-respect, self-dependence, nationalism, culture and values. When they awaken, then the country awakens. If they sleep, the country also sleeps off. The National Working Committee of BJP Kisan Morcha is deeply thinking of conducting extensive programmes to generate awareness of national consciousness and culture in rural areas.

**In another proposal passed by BJP Kisan Morcha they have demanded for a CBI enquiry into scandal related to animal husbandry.**

BJP Kisan Morcha has expressed serious concern in its national committee meeting on various issues. For small and marginal farmers, many programmes have been started to provide irrigation facilities; in Bihar, lot of scams and scandals happened in these programmes. Pumpsets and boring are given in Bihar, under this programme starting from 33 percent to 80 percent subsidy; less this facility is provided free of cost to Scheduled Castes and Tribes. In this programmes, whatever balance amount is made available to farmers is adjusted as loan from banks. Banks used to charge interest on full amount till the time the whole grant was received by farmers. The entire amount received as grants used to get adjusted against the interest. Grant was not given without taking commission; half of the total grants given is spent in running around and paying commission. Dealers take more than the government rate and that amount has to be paid upfront. Inferior quality equipment used to be given. Pumpsets of same brand are given at different locations by different banks and land development banks. By showing longer depths, cheating is done in pipes and while digging short depths labour payments are shown for deeper digging. Pumpsets were given without boring and fake payment were shown. All these accusations were accepted as unstarred question Number 2027 on 09-12-1983 in Rajya Sabha. After conducting various departmental and agency enquiries, the investigation was given to CBI. Six bank officers were dismissed in this case. In response to unstarred question Number 3246 dated 25-03-1983, they were accepted and once again accepted in response to unstarred question Number 958 dated 04-05-1989. Eight bank officers were suspended, whose names and addresses were informed. In that response, along with revealing the names and addresses, it was also informed that CBI had filed charge-sheets against 33 dealers. After that the case was suppressed and since then looting is continuing. Due to pressure from politicians and after distributing the commission, CBI closed further investigation of the case. Under this programme till now a loss of three thousand crore rupees has been incurred. Four thousand rupees on every boring and two thousand rupees on every pumpset have been charged more than the market price. Inferior quality goods were given, payments were forged. Lower castes and backward castes were most affected by this scam. This scandal was much bigger than the animal husbandry scandal. It is a big mystery why CBI closed the investigation on this case. National Committee of BJP Kisan Morcha expresses its serious concern over this issue and demands that CBI should reopen the case. In Bihar, this scandal is going on since 1980. Culprits should be arrested that because it is due to this scandal only that, politics in Bihar has been criminalised.

- ☐ There were more scandals than implementation of programmes initiated in the interest of farmers
- ☐ Urea and fodder scams are unpardonable
- ☐ Demand for a CBI enquiry into pumpset scandal.

**The Poor Farmers have to Wake Up to Economic Exploitation in Villages**

Poor farmers in villages are suffering the most because of corruption. Corruption of thoughts causes corruption of behaviour. With corruption of behaviour comes the corruption of values; corruption of values leads to straying off the path. When the path is lost, distortions creep in the culture. The vital juice that gives life to the nation comes from villages. Till the time sanctity is intact in the culture and values of villages, only then the nation will go in the right direction. Starting from the rule of Mughals up to British rule in India, only one thing has been done, that is to destroy the culture and values of villages slowly and steadily.

Foreign influence impacts urban life very fast, whereas it takes quite some time in rural areas. Rural population has respect for its culture, values and great people and they stay committed to them without seeking any rewards in any form or structure. Wealthy people who were interested in acquiring positions accepted all titles and positions even during the time of Mughals and the British. They thought that there was pride in accepting Islam and Christianity. Rural population had faced all sorts of hardships but they didn't give up their ancient path. The community of scavengers was always excommunicated, neglected and insulted by society. Even after having been treated as untouchables, they preferred staying as a part of the Hindu society to proselytising. Aren't such people worthy of respect?

Hindu society should have respected them and the atrocities committed upon them should have been stopped. Number one chair kept changing in the country, but number two chair was never changed. Kings had changed but the servants of the king remained the same. Riders had changed, but the move of horses didn't change. The sight of Mahatma Gandhi was focussed on villages, the impoverished and farmers. He saw the soul of India in their souls. The farmer leaders, starting from Patel to Choudhury Charan Singh, everybody was ever ready to fight to better the situation of farmers. Lohia and Deendayal used to talk about building an egalitarian society replete with social harmony and love for all in order to uplift the last man in the society. Their voice was echoed from all platforms in free India; however sadly it didn't yield favourable results. Programmes were designed in their name, slogans were shouted, announcements were made and propagations done over communication media. Reason was that the majority of votes were with them; 85 percent of the population lived in rural areas and 70 percent among them were farmers.

According to a survey conducted by the National Council of Applied Economic Research, if all the assets of bottom 20 percent of the population of India were weighed against the assets of Birla, the side of Birla would weigh more; 20 percent means around 19 crore of the population. If assumed that five persons constitute one family, it turns out to be roughly about 3.75 crore families. Farmers, villages and poor, where will they go? The population of whole of UP and Bihar wouldn't equal to Birla. Small farmers become marginal farmers and become landless. Land keeps getting divided. And after a certain limit, farmers become labourers. For example, according to agriculture census in 1951, farmers were 57.57 percent and by 1981 their population was reduced to 41.53. Agriculture labourers were 14.17 in 1951 and by 1981, their population increased to 25.16 percent, which proves that the population of farmers has come down and the population of labourers has increased. Reasons for it have to be studied. The implication is that one needs to go to the bottom of the rhymes and reasons causing such a bleak situation.

During the rule of British, the jobs of village craftsmen were taken away from them. All those people were employed in farming, due to which the burden has increased on agriculture. In America 4 percent, in Britain 2.8 percent and in Japan, 20.7 percent population is dependent on agriculture, whereas in India 69.7 percent; which means almost 70 percent are dependent on agriculture. Prosperity of the nation is dependent on the prosperity of nearly 70 percent of the population.

For the sake of votes, slogans were raised for their development. Feeling of nationality was propagated. In the name of land reforms, violent movements were launched. Hostilities were created. People for whom neither their ancestors nor they themselves were ever farmers, who never tilled the land, who never reared cattle, who could not differentiate millet from *jowar*, whose kids get educated from Russia and who live in big bungalows in the cities, they kept raising the slogans of land reforms. Tension between the villagers created a binary between the destitute and the Dalits. Here farm labourers were fighting and on the other hand, the prices of industrial products kept on rising. To divert the attention from inflation and economic exploitation, tensions were created in villages. Political, economic, administrative and industrial corruption kept brewing. Because of scandals involving animal husbandry, urea, Indira Awaas Yojana and Parliament and assembly, most of the farmers, impoverished people and villagers suffered the most. Whatever loss nation has incurred has been incurred by the poor, farmers and villagers who got a bolt from the blue. There is a quota permit in trade. Black money and black trade is there, in which commission for the government is included. On one side, grand palaces were built; people who used to go on foot started flying in aeroplanes; those who were unable to cover their body became billionaires. But poor farmers didn't have clothes to wear; in severe winters when an infant cried in the lap of her mother as she didn't have anything to cover her baby and give warmth to it, she would tear her saree and cover her baby. She herself would sleep naked just by wrapping a mat around her. How many of us saw this Bharat? How many could get to see ladies and men who live on only one pair of clothes? Women in the family of a farmer, who till about 10 to 20 acres of land, can't afford a soap bath at least once a month or wash clothes at least once a month. The future of their children remains bleak. On one side, it is secure future and safe life, on other side, it is total darkness and hopelessness. Until the time the urban, cultured people don't go and stay in the hutments of the poor, how will they get the real experience of life? Lord Rama for 14 years and Pandavas for 13 years roamed around in the forests and experienced the hardships along with the forest dwellers. They adopted their food, their attire, their language, etc. Rama, Krishna and Mahatma Gandhi succeeded because of their awareness of villages, farmers and the poor only. They have to be united to root out corruption. They have to be told that villages are getting developed because of corruption. People who talked about social justice have become rulers. By climbing the shoulders of lower castes and backward castes, they have reached the top. Majority of the population belonging to lower and backward castes lives in villages and hamlets. Farmers and villagers are like synonyms of lower and backward castes. The economic conditions of forward caste farmers who live in villages are much worse than the class four employees of cities. People with urban mentality think that farmers living in the rest of the country are having TV, fridge in the kitchen and scooter at the door like those of farmers from Haryana, Punjab, western UP and rural areas of Delhi. Even today there are such families in villages in which all the family members eat food in a single plate, turn by turn. "*Jaake pair na fate bewayi, so kya jaane peer parayi*" (Only the wearer knows where the shoe pinches). Chaudhury Charan Singh used to say that his son is the son of a farmer but not a farmer. When he used to tell the stories of helpless villagers, tears used to roll down his eyes. He had gone through the helplessness and pain of the villagers. Deendayalji had witnessed poverty. Gandhiji experienced the pain of the poor by living among them. Today those who have come into power in the name of caste are looting the same people ruthlessly. Ram Lakhan Singh Yadav, the accused in urea scandal and Lalu Prasad Yadav, the accused in animal husbanadry scandal, come from a community in which 95 percent are farmers and live in villages. Deva Gowda also comes from a poor family and is a farmer. By checking the price of diesel, he gave a gift to farmers. Today when inflation goes up, its burden falls the most on poor farmers of the villages. Villagers, farmers and the poor have to be awakened to fight against corruption, economic exploitation and foreign investment. They have to be told that the country wakes up if they wake up and the country also goes to sleep if they sleep off.

☐ The injustice meted out to the oppressed has to be furbished.

*BJP Samachar, 16-31 April, 1996*

☐

# 21
# The Struggle between the Divergent Cultures of India vis-á-vis Bharat

## The Feeling of Nationalism has to be Accorded Top Priority

It is not the question of any particular party, government, population, community or caste; instead, it is in front of the whole nation. They are not one or two questions but many types of questions. The perversions that have crept in have to be removed completely. New perversions and discrepancies are getting introduced to get rid of the existing perversions and discrepancies of varying nature. Poison can't be removed with poison. Generally, it is believed that poison is the remedy for poison. But poison acts against poison only when a person using it is aware of it. Any poison can't be destroyed by just any other poison. Poison has to be modified into a medicine. It is very difficult to have people who acquire that knowledge by doing research and experiments. The perversions and discrepancies created by foreigners in enslaved India were not removed; instead they were encouraged. Foreign rulers had their own culture and they made systems to rule over India based on that culture. It was against the Indian culture. Destroying Indian culture was their objective. If geography is like a body, then culture is like its soul. Religious and spiritual thinking are the soul. Life can't exist without the soul. Body can't stay without life. Foreign rulers tried to destroy the soul and life and establish their culture in place of it, due to which India is writhing in pain. They succeeded in creating a new class and new social order. Self-rule had come but our own culture didn't come back. To re-establish the national culture, everybody has to struggle with the desire for equality. In the world and especially in India, there is always one such class which imitates blindly. They are plagued with the nation that foreign culture, foreign civilisation and values are superior. They have no love for their own culture and traditions. They bowed in front of all the foreign rulers who had come and indulged in flattering them. Perversions have made inroads into their nature and in the character of that class. In the name of liberalisation and modernism, they accept slavery to foreign culture. Ram Manohar Lohia, the socialist thinker, once said in the Parliament that in India there are historians of two different ideologies. One considering cultural synthesis as the basis, is praising Indian liberal values and modernity and the other is looking upon it as cultural slavery. According to Lohia, cultural synthesis happened in India because of slavish mentality. If one lived with self-respect, one wouldn't have been winner or loser either. In front of Sikander, Porus didn't lose his self-respect. The influence of foreign culture is very clear in our economic, social, administrative and educational institutions. The nation is vexed by the culture of indulgence and consumerism. We became independent but we couldn't make new systems of our own. The loyalists of British rule were given the same respect in free India, which they were given during the British rule; those who suppressed the freedom movement, praised the British and worshipped Anglicism. They became the administrators of free India. It had become like Indian kings and foreign rule. As they had loyalty towards the queen, they became loyal to the throne. But in a democracy, the systems should be loyal to the people. Self-rule should have been built based on democracy but the servants of the people were made the rulers of the people. Wealth islands were built in the ocean of poverty. Privileges were made to send a few thousand people every year on to those islands. System has become more influential over the people. Suppressing the interests of people and gobbling up the major portion announced for the benefit of people became the routine of the system. Their capacity to digest was so strong that they could swallow the whole nation and digest it.

Because of democracy, rulers would either come on time or just before with vote boxes and go away. They may die untimely death, but administrators will be in their position till a certain age. They keep saying *"Koi nrip hoi, humme kya hani"* (one has nothing to do with the issue of one being in the seat of power). They and their chair are safe. Rulers keep changing and they keep changing, but the administrators have stayed there and will continue to stay there. Public is not the owner, instead they are owners of public. Even today, the farmers in villages are not respected; they don't get a respectable position in government offices or Secretariat. There is no respectable position for people using local language, local attire and local residence. There is a proverb in India, *"Gudadi mein lal chipa hota hai."* (a diamond will be hidden in the heap of dirt), but that is not the case anymore in India. In the heap of dirt, there is neither the diamond nor knowledge. Dayanand, Vivekananda, Ramkrishna Paramahansa, Samarth Guru Ramdas, Gandhi, Lohia, Deendayal were all *'gudadi ke lal'*. They were the inspiration and ideal of India. India worships idols. Idols of all these inspirational people were made and they have been worshipped. They were adorned with garlands and lamps were lit in front of them, but their ideals have been forgotten. Gautam Buddha was born and brought up in India but his ideals were followed in foreign countries. In India, his idols are worshipped but his ideals were given up. A tough duel is continuing in India between indigenous and foreign. On one side are people of India and on the other side are people of Bharat. Two nations were formed in one nation. There are two Delhis in Delhi. One is a Delhi of India Gate and Boat Club and the other is of rural and trans-Yamuna areas and of slums, which is Bharat.

When everybody fights by breaking the lines of dignity, it becomes a battle of righteousness. The battle for righteousness has to take place in India to establish dignity. The battle of righteousness should be fought in a democratic way. The battles between Ravan and Rama, Kans and Krishna, Kauravas and Pandavas, British and Gandhi were for righteousness. They were battles for establishing dignity. It was a battle between two cultures and values. Mahabharat was not a battle just for seeking princely power. It was fought to give a new meaning to social, economic, administrative, individual as well as family dignity and to establish it. The *Bhagvad Gita* became the guiding booking of that battle. Krishna was the hero. India was slowly getting divided into two parts. One is India and the other is Bharat. All the people influenced by foreign culture and values are becoming indulgent and consumerists are forming into one group. On the other side are villagers, farmers and the poor, who are getting united. The links of caste and community are weakening. There is nobody who is ready to listen to anybody; everybody is eager to tell. It has become difficult to differentiate between truth and falsehood. The ruling party is getting intermingled with opposition and vice versa. Those who raise slogans of the oppressed forget everything on becoming rulers. The Central Hall of Parliament is like a reception cell. Once when entered into that room, hell is not remembered at all. Yudhishthir had gone to hell before going to heaven and after seeing all his relatives and others suffering in hell, he just sat there itself. He dropped the idea of going to heaven. This is called the battle of righteousness. People who struggle for the sake of villages, the poor, the farmers, people who fight for the sake of the oppressed, the weak, the poor, the victims, lower castes, people who become representatives of the people to get them out of their treacherous life, when they reach Parliament and the Assemblies, they tend to enjoy the comforts of heaven. Those who talk about Marx develop vested interests. They all become one class and the character of the class becomes the same. Because of the common character, the interests of the class become the same. They forget about the pain, sorrow, neglect and humiliation of childhood—all things get erased from their memory. Struggle stays only till that time as they don't get to join in that class. They know that in villages people are getting divided into groups in the name of caste and community; people are still crying with pain and their bodies are being burnt without a coffin and people are getting swept away in the rivers; nonetheless they will be immersed in indulgence. The day their craving gets broken, then only their future and destiny will change. India will be transformed. The soul which is in the form of village, which is eclipsed by caste and community, will get liberated. When soul gets enlightened, the darkness gets dispelled. Culture, religion and human rights can't be seen in darkness. When the eclipse of caste and community is removed over the village-shaped soul, it will get liberated. When light enters into the soul, then darkness will get removed. Religion and culture and nationality can't be seen in darkness. Whoever gets caught in the hands of the blind, he doesn't want to leave them. There is a need to battle for righteousness to bring light into this darkness. The fight against British rule was the fight between Ravan and Rama. Gandhi, while chanting the name of Rama, was fighting for the sake of *Ramarajya* (rule of the Rama). When villagers, poor and farmers accepted him as their leader, they all joined him in his fight; it became a people's fight. Now, the fight of Dwapara is getting underway. Local rulers influenced by foreign culture and values are breaking all limits and dignity. Now the symptoms of people revolting against power are being seen. There is a need for rebellion in free India.

In India, especially in Bihar, saints and learned are getting imprisoned in caste. Saints and learned were not of any particular caste, community, religion or culture. They came to show the path to the whole world and for its welfare. Today in their name fanatics are created among the youth of their caste. Directionless, blind and goalless leaders are making the youth indulgent and pathless. By killing their souls, they are shown grand dreams of making them very powerful. Because of English education and culture, indigenous is getting destroyed. Unemployment, lack of work and lawlessness is increasing. With power, administration has become corrupt like a broker. After Independence, the drivers of India became the protectors of Englishness. The ghosts of English have started dancing in Indian clothes. Who are the culprits of this? Are the Central Government and the people who run the government responsible for this? There is a need for deep thinking on this issue. Rama, Krishna and Shiva were the trinity of India; they are and they will remain so. They are in every heart of the population and every particle of the nation. This is what Lohia, the socialist thinker, had said, "Today, the disciples of Rama and Krishna are making leaders by dividing the caste of Rama and Krishna. By wielding weapons and ammunition of the gods of three worlds, three macrocosms and three ages, they are resorting to gimmicks in their name." Why is this happening?

On political platforms where some actors have been worshipped, some politicians have started acting like actors. When leaders losing courage started taking the help of actors to gather crowds to entertain them, the ideals and principles got politically defeated. Did Gandhi, Lohia, Patel, Deendayal and Charan Singh take the help of any actors? Didn't they feel helplessness? They had willpower, they got strength because of penance. Keep telling their own point of view and keep walking on their own path, people started listening to them. At some point of time, they stopped and started moving along with them. Politics has lost the path and it has become a prostitute, a profession and a means for indulgence. Who made it so? Aren't the intellectuals of India aware of it? Don't the writers and journalists know this mystery? One has to have the moral courage to call a criminal a criminal. **From the womb of corrupt and indulgent society, morally courageous children can't be born.** They projected thieves as saints, prostitutes as ascetics, ill-mannered as good mannered, corrupt as visionary. Who are the people running such a system in free India? There are attempts to keep such people in power. People who indulge by taking foreign loans have made the country pauper. They try hard not to let the nationalists assume power and even if they come, they wish to let them stay in power for long because all their sins would be exposed and everybody will be unmasked. This is the secret which needs to be understood. All around there is one noise, *'Sarkari dhan ki loot hai, loot sake so loot, ant samay pachatavoge jab pad jayyega chot'* (public money is meant to be plundered, loot if you can; later on you may repent when you are out of power). Only villagers, farmers and the poor are not included in this loot. Their homes, lands and shrouds are getting looted. By raising slogans of supporting the lower caste, the exploited, the oppressed, and the victimised, people are coming into power and tend to forget the backward, but when removed from power, once again start holding rallies. See the thousand faces of them, see the boom of rallies, and see the magic of treasury loot. The self-respect of India is put to sleep. Its feelings of indigenous caste are suppressed. Slowly, India is waking up. Trying to know about itself, enchantment is getting cleared, armies are getting divided. The time for battle of righteousness has come; genuine is getting differentiated from the fake. In the flow of eternal and ancient, all indulgences, corruption, illusions and fear are going to be erased. India will reach its respectable position. Golden jubilee year will bring a new message altogether.

- ☐ The influence of foreign culture is very clear on India's economic, social, administrative and educational systems. Nation is suffering from indulgence and consumerist culture. We became independent but we couldn't make our own systems.
- ☐ The conflict is continuing in India. A tough fight is going on between the indigenous and foreign culture; on one side there are people of India and at the same time there are people belonging to Bharat on the other side.
- ☐ Slowly, India is waking up and trying to identify its true self. Infatuation and blind worship or xenocentric approach is slowly being consigned to the backburner.

*BJP Samachar, 16-31 October, 1998*

☐

# 22

# Nativity and Self-reliance are the Foundations for the Poor and the Farmers

Whenever the world faced social, religious, national or administrative troubles, some leader arose from villagers and from among the farmers and the impoverished to give direction to the nation and provide guidance to the world cowman Krishna, shepherd Christ and goat-keeper Prophet Mohammad had given a new direction to the world. While playing with children on the banks of River Yamuna, Krishna told them about the path of righteousness, taught them with local language, local attire, local food, local buildings, local culture and also local behaviour and local life. The public can be prepared for the battle of righteousness only through local faith and trust. This is the only natural route to a revolution. There are no hardships in the ideal which people naturally affiliate themselves to. The enjoyment of natural life comes only with the coordination of natural union and natural indulgence. Where there's lack of real self, it is futile to expect natural behaviour. Behaviour has to be very natural. The path of Krishna is very natural. Villagers grasp things very naturally. Their life is mingled with nature. Nature does her duty very naturally. Natural people are not tense about doing work, instead they enjoy it. This is the speciality of village life. Both Christ and Prophet Mohammad did the same. Even Lord Rama in India worked in a natural way. That's why he was called *Maryada Purushottam* (the person characterised with highest standards of all virtues and dignity). Dignity can't be there without being natural. He created faith in the life of locals very naturally. He wandered in the forest for 14 years and met the tribals in the forests. He adopted his life according to the life of tribals. He mingled with them and with their own feelings, their language, their attire, their food and their devotion. Rama mixed his life with the local lifestyle. If he had adopted the princely language, attire, food and culture of Ayodhya, he wouldn't have fostered so deep a trust among the locals, as he did. He tried to convert the kingdom of Rama into the kingdom of locals. He did localisation of *Ramarajya*. He did socialisation of the villages. He taught culture to the society. By doing nationalisation of culture, he unfurled the flag of righteousness. When the poor and the farmers of villages got united with the tribals and forest dwellers and joined the army of Rama, then only they could destroy Ravana. Ravana could only be assassinated by humans and monkeys. Many monkeys joined but humans were only two—Rama and his brother Lakshman. Where did those glorious, indulgent, reputed people go? The people living in cities didn't fight in that battle on the side of Rama. Even people from his own family, clan, didn't come. One should ponder over this. It was an army of monkeys and their leader was a human, who was the epitome of dignity. In that battle of righteousness, monkeys joined, but those people who enjoy power and princely comforts in Ayodhya didn't join. Monkeys mean, the army of poor farmers, villagers, meek and weak and the human being as God. When he became a God from a human being and succeeded to the throne, those who didn't join in the battle of righteousness surrounded him. When *Ramarajya* had been urbanised, the kind of problems Rama faced was known to everybody. Krishna living in the midst of the illiterates prepared them for the battle of righteousness. Balaram who held the plough in his hands was the leader of the farmers. Plough is symbolic of the farmers. Krishna had a disc in his hand which is a symbol of labourers. When the army of labourers and farmers started moving, the battle for righteousness took place and the dynasty of Kuru was destroyed. Their leader was Gopal. The word Gopal has two meanings. The word *'go'* is used for both cow and the earth. Thereby Gopal means both—the caretaker of cows and the caretaker of earth. The farmer is the caretaker of the earth. When troubles engulf the caretaker of the earth, God descends on earth. Glorious holders of power, princely men, owners of resources and wealth and those occupying posts turn away from righteousness and start adopting foreign culture, values, behaviour, thinking and mentality and enter a blind race, when deep troubles hover over farmers, the poor, and cowherds of villages. Listening to crying of the soul of these people, the eternal truth comes into consciousness to rescue the eternal truth. Who can keep a count on how many times Krishna ran? After hearing the cry of a helpless woman, Krishna ran to her aid. Krishna had done localisation of divinity. He spread godliness in local life. That vision and direction is not there in today's racist people, who obviously include authoritarians and selfish people and, who could not understand the eternal cycle. In India, there are many people still trying to bring momentum and consciousness in local life by emulating the characters of Rama, Krishna and Shiva. The life of the nation is hidden in the life of villagers. Momentum comes in the life of nation only if vitality is there in rural life.

Gandhi, Lohia, Deendayal were all travellers on that eternal and ancient path. Gandhi awakened the villagers, the poor, the farmers, the untouchables and the insulted. He brought faith in their minds and showed the path of respect. Villages, the poor and the farmers, woke up, the British rule had to end. Self-rule, indigenous self-reliance and self-dependence—these words mutated the minds of everybody. He showed the way to get rid of foreign slavery. He adopted in life the language, attire, food, culture and buildings of the locals. Indigenous people fought against foreigners and became victorious. But the unfortunate thing is that in the name of naturalisation, the people with foreign propensity sat in the seat of power. Bodywise they were Indian, but by mentality they were foreigners. Resources were those of an Indian but systems were those of the foreigners, government was Indian but culture was foreign. Institutions were Indian but education was foreign. Villagers were Indian but plans were foreign. Local culture and local values were erased slowly. Indians had caused more damage to Indians than the foreigners. The chanting of the names of Gandhi, Lohia and Deendayal continued but the path was not theirs. We were going after the traveller but deviating from the path shown by him. While moving behind the traveller who lost his path, India lost all its values and forgot its culture and disenfranchised from the path of nobility and righteousness. When everything was lost, how could spiritual knowledge stay? Even today, only in villages the soul of India is hidden. Righteousness is restricted to the houses of farmers only. Clouds of trouble hovering over the villagers, farmers and the poor is growing, danger is lurking. Gopal, the cowherd is getting destroyed. *Go-mata* or mother cow and mother earth are crying. It looks like somewhere in some farmer's home, God has descended on earth. When local language, local food, local attire, local culture, local values and local buildings are saved, the hymns will be saved. For spiritualistic nationalism and cultural unity should be protected and conserved the villager, the poor and the farmer by enduring great hardships. This is the call of this age.

*BJP Samachar*

□

## 23
# Where do We get Justice?

India is an agriculture-based country. The soul of India lives in villages. As many as 70 percent of people are farmers and 85 percent are villagers. It is unfortunate that in a democracy that nobody seeks the opinion of the majority. The majority who have maximum number of votes, are neglected and insulted. Media, newspapers and journalists have no time to interview them. As there are no transport and conveyance facilities, who takes pains to go to them? Nobody has any knowledge of the poor condition of villages in the country. During rains and floods, women, children, senior citizens have to use those pathetic roads and walking on foot becomes horrible. When they use bicycles for conveyance for some distance, they ride on the bicycles but at other times, bicycles ride over them. They have to carry the cycle on their shoulders. School buildings don't have roofs over them. In most of the buildings, which were constructed under government schemes, the roofs leak and seep. Unfortunately, the leaders who talk about the backwards, the lower castes and proletarians have got urbanised. As they stay closer to power they get influenced by urban culture and have only political motive in their eyes. Election Commission is also a symbol of that culture. Indian politics is imprisoned in the hands of the forward classes. Whether it is the Left Front who raises slogans of proletarians or the racists who raise the slogans of backward and lower castes, all are feudalistic and of urban character. They are authors of the destiny of India and architects of India's future. Election Commission seeks opinion only from those who are biased and elusive. Farmers' organisations are not consulted and aren't given time even when asked because farmers and villagers are considered illiterate and ignorant, as they only have knowledge of experience. How can justice be done when people holding important positions at the national level harbour hatred against a particular party, caste, individual and even group for that matter?

*Rashtriya Sahara, 24 May, 1999*

□

# 24
# Need for the Battle of Righteousness

Every year on this day there comes Lohia's death anniversary and gets over. He is remembered and people sing in praise of his policies. So-called disciples of him sing songs in his name and fulfil their duty. His disciples, who have gone on different paths will comment on his policies to fulfil their own vested interests. They try to justify the direction and nature of long-term, short-term and immediate problems. Today there are actors rather than leaders who wear the attire and talk, eat and speak like Gandhi, Lohia and Deendayal; can become good actors but can't be good leaders like them. It can be said that in today's time, there will be very few people who are as committed and sincere to their ideals and principles as Lohia and Deendayal had been. The so-called disciples of Lohia have to think over it.

The way there are Gandhians in government, abbey socialists and lower castes socialists have a similar tradition in all political parties. Nehru, Vinoba and Lohia—all three were travellers on this path. Government commentator of Gandhism was Nehru, commentator from abbey was Vinoba and commentator from lower caste was Lohia. The place where king, chief of abbey and trader sat was called throne. Lohia used to explain the connivance of Nehru, the king, Vinoba, the mahant (chief of abbey) and Birla, the trader. With flux and flow of time, the relations between individuals and positions kept changing. Nobody can become a chief of abbey by becoming a saint. Attempts had been started to combine the thrones of the king, the chief of abbey and the trader; communists and proponents of Nehruism are going to play major role in this. Nationalisation of industries and businesses is a part of this plan. Sitting on the throne for an entire life is the duty of the chief of abbey. Today the tradition of holding the highest post of any political party for one's life has started. Chief of an abbey holds the throne for whole life. Many so-called disciples of Lohia are busy in starting this tradition. The name of the party keeps changing but the chief remains the same. Path keeps changing but the sect remains the same. In the name of their ultimate duty, they are fulfilling their selfish interests. Lower-caste socialists are fighting against government socialists and socialists of abbey. Instead of kissing the feet of the chiefs of abbey, they are roaming in disguise, searching their own path and trying to make a long-term strategy in the immediate future.

For Indian socialism equal goal, equal knowledge, equality and harmony are essential life-giving chemicals. Similarly, self-rule, indigenous, self-reliance and self-dependence are its basic foundations. Are the disciples of Lohia trying to understand the detailed meaning of these words? Without understanding the gross and subtle, that is, the materialistic and spiritualistic meaning of these words, namely *sam* (equal) and *swa* (self), it is very difficult to understand the Indian socialist philosophy. These words are not of Lohia. These words originated from the streams of eternal and ancient Indian philosophy. Lohia had accepted that he got the meaning of *samta* from the *Gita* when he was in jail. How much devotion and attachment he had for the *Gita* and the *Upanishads* that only he would know. He never pretended about spirituality. He never humbugged about Hindutva. He never did any drama over nationality. All virtues were imbibed in him. There is a need to understand the philosophy of Hindu versus Hindu and Indo-Pak unity and Hindu versus Muslims.

First of all, we are Indians, after that only we may be Hindus or Muslims. The history of this country is a witness to the fact that there is no dearth of devotees of nation among Muslims. Even today, more than the Muslims of this country some of the Hindus by becoming authoritarians are opposing the spirit of nationalism. Muslim fundamentalism is growing because of Hindu fundamentalism and racism. Fundamentalism is in all castes and in all communities. In the name of liberalism, fundamentalism is getting promoted. All 'isms' related to Bhahmins, Thakurs, Bhoomihars, Yadavs, Kurmis, forwards, backwards, lower caste and Muslims are equally fatal elements for the nation. They are ready to battle for this. Fundamentalists of all castes and communities are stubbornly stuck to their point. Instead of accepting naturalisation, they seem inherently inclined to espouse the foreign. This fight between two ideologies is continuing even today. On the basis of caste and community, Indians consider Indians as their enemies, whereas they are not ashamed of accepting the slavery of foreigners. The disciples of Lohia have to think over it. The identity of the nation is in danger, and it is the duty of everybody to protect it. This is the battle for righteousness of Lohia. Efforts should be made to change the trend and nature. Having been in slavery for a long time, we couldn't be free from slave mentality. Whenever there was a battle for righteousness in India, nation, society, caste and dynasty, everything was divided. Truth prevails whcn the slogan of '*satyameva jayate*' (truth always prevails) is raised. Battle for righteousness has to be fought to ensure the primacy of truth. What is today's truth? Does racism prevail only in any one particular caste? Are the flames of rebellion and revenge raging in the minds of lower castes, backwards and the oppressed and unjustified ones? Isn't it a subject to be thought over after 50 years of Independence? Isn't the support of racism and communalism taken in unscrupulous manner to defend and protect dynasty and worship authoritarianism? Weren't political murders committed of talented, capable and nationalist people's leaders? Weren't we mute spectators when righteousness, values, culture, indigenous and self-respect were pulled down in Parliament? Didn't we dabble in indulgence, corruption, fear, and illusion? The disciples of Lohia who are supposed to fight against all these trends and nature, are going downhill on the path of degeneration. Lohia had talked about battle for righteousness and there is a need for that battle for righteousness. On his death anniversary, this is the tribute paid to him by his lower caste disciples.

*Rashtriya Sahara, 12 October, 2000*

□

# 25
# Where will the Farmer Go?

Since ancient times, development of India has been dependent on economic philosophy based on the economy of agriculture. Animal husbandry is the basic foundation of agriculture. Animal-based farming and equipment have been developed over time. Traditional agricultural technologies are being improved continuously through refurbishing them. Development was expedited in free India. Slogans were raised that India is an agrarian country and it lives in villages. More than 70 percent people are dependent on agriculture, which also includes the population of agriculture labour. Of them, about 60 percent of farmers till a land which is less than one hectare and 18 percent have land, less than two hectares. It has been proved by the statistics of Indian Government that 18 percent of the total farmers fall in the category of small and marginal farmers. All scholars, who have studied the village and agricultural economy, unanimously declared that it is not profitable to do agriculture on a land less than one hectare (2.5 acres). Judging from these parameters, 60 percent of farmers are non-profiting farmers. In *jamabandi* (settlement), the government document of revenue department says that many land settlements are of joint families. Land settlement is continuing from the time of grandparents and great-grandparents. It has not been divided. Some might be considered as small farmers based on those documents, but actually the owned land has been divided.

If physical and actual verification is done, one comes to see that around 9.5 percent farmers would have come into the category of marginal farmers. Given government statistics, the population of farmers is getting reduced continuously and the population of agriculture labourers is increasing in the same proportion. It becomes very clear from this that the children of farmers are becoming landless labourers by losing land due to which unemployment is increasing in villages. The population who does manual and agriculture labour is decreasing fast, whereas the pressure of people migrating from villages to urban areas is increasing continuously, due to which anti-social and foreign separatist elements are getting an opportunity. Distribution of land alone was not the only solution for land reforms. Agricultural reforms had to be done in a comprehensive manner, which couldn't be done. Land has been used to construct canals for agriculture. Many canals are left incomplete because of which, irrigation could not be done; thus whatever increase had to happen in agriculture output didn't occur. To improve the transport facilities, roads have been constructed for which a lot of fertile agricultural land has been destroyed. Land has been acquired for constructing roads; roads have been encroached upon. Why didn't police, engineers and district officials stop the encroachment? All the politicians, administrators, judiciary were travelling on that road and why didn't they pay attention to this? In Darbhanga, and even those engaged in land has been acquired for the construction of western Koshi canal, due to which thousands of farmer families have become landless and many more are going to be landless in future also. Whatever land has remained that will be acquired by NH 57. What will the children of farmers do? Water will come into the canal, but there won't be any land to irrigate. Farmers are weak, poor, unorganised and are caught in the quagmire of caste. There are no leaders, no actors, no administrators, no judges, no government to come to the rescue of farmers. Farmers are helpless and without any support.

*Hindustan, 15 May, 2005*

□

# 26
# Farmer: The Lifeline of Indian Culture

There is no leadership at the national level to raise voice in the interest of farmers. Whoever are there, they are professional politicians. They do politics in the name of farmers and engage in making deals. They keep misguiding farmers in the name of caste and exploit them physically, mentally and intellectually. All political parties set up farmers' wing and appoint all neglected party workers in them. Nobody is there to take care of the real farmers of real India. By making out the political farmers as lions in the circus, they keep misleading the people.

Today rearing of animals, such as cattle, sheep, goat, etc. is considered to be a demeaning profession. Agriculture is a culture; it is not just a profession. As long as culture of agriculture and values of villages are there, only till then Indian culture and indigenous values will be there. Only farmers are the lifeline of Indian culture, values, righteousness and tradition. Today they are dying. They are getting eliminated. They are made helpless and hopeless. Politician, whoever is in power and from whichever party he may be, he has no time for farmers. There is no feeling of respect for the farmer among politicians. The politicians who used to sing songs like "*Aavo, shramik, krishak, mazdooron inquilab ka nara do, shikshak, gurujan, buddhijeeviyon anubhav bhara sahara do*" (Workers, farmers and labourers, come and raise the slogans of freedom. Teachers, scholars and intellectuals lend support based on their experience). When they got the power, they got immersed in the comforts of power and in the vice of indulgence. Where did those dreams go and where did those slogans go? The politicians who adorn the crown of power, people of that caste enjoy watching the face of their leader and they start singing songs, like "*tu chhese badi hai mast mast*" (you are very interesting to look at).

Farmers of the whole country are crumbling under the mountain of troubles; all regional parties and regional leaders are ruling in the name of caste. Land of farmers is getting acquired forcefully under the Land Act at very low prices. Land is acquired through unscrupulous means. In Delhi, Haryana, and Punjab, thanks to Saheb Singh Verma, Ch. Devi Lal and Prakash Singh Badal, farmers are given proper compensation, but in Bihar, Uttar Pradesh and in the other states, land is being grabbed from farmers. In Bihar, land is taken for NH. 57 and the kind of atrocities and victimisation that is going on might not have happened even during the British rule. Apart from paying very low compensation, 10 percent commission is taken and farmers get tired of running from pillar to post to get that compensation.

*Hindustan, 20 February, 2007*

□

# 27

# Charan Singh, the Savior of Villages and the Backward

*Birthday Special*

23rd December comes every year and it will come this year also and this keeps happening. All days keep coming and going according to the cycle of time. Birth and death of every human being keep taking place in those seven days. There are twelve months, birth and death occur in those twelve months only. When at a particular point of time, planets and stars come together, at that time great people descend on earth. Choudhury Charan Singh was one of such great personalities. From childhood to old age, when memories come alive, he used to cry because of emotions. His language used to be the same whether it be while crossing through a village or writing about Boat Club. Flow of thoughts used to be same. The pain he had in his heart for the farmers of villages used to come out. He never hesitated to express his opinion, even though his own party people warned him against it. He had tremendous faith in his ideas. He didn't want to compromise his commitment with regard to decentralisation of rural economy, agriculture policy and political power. Gandhian philosophy had tremendous influence on him. He didn't know how to compromise. He used to put forward his opinion without any doubt, fear or inferiority complex. People used to say all sorts of things like countryside man, bucolic, unsophisticated, naïve villager, Jat and power hungry, etc. When he became the Prime Minister, a national-level newspaper published in its headlines *"Jatmara tab janiye jab Choudhury ho jaye"* (know that Jat is dead when Choudhury dies). It becomes clear with this what were the notions of urban and forward-class and caste people. The mentality of forward-caste and class hasn't changed much. Whatever drama they may do on getting motivated by political power and vested interest, yet the fact of the matter is that the element of inertia persists among them even today.

People do all sorts of things for the sake of political power, post, reputation, position and influence. Dr. Lohia has said, "Big people don't get caught even when they bungle lakhs and crores of rupees, but lower caste and backwards get caught even for 50 paise." Hunger for power is defined differently. People from big households get privileges to do whatever they want to do. The saying *"samarth ko dosh nahi gosain"* (the rich and the mighty aren't prone to accusations) is fulfilled. Indian society, howsoever generosity, it may boast of cruelty is hidden in its generosity. They exhibit equality but this element is clearly missing in their conduct with equality. Charan Singh was born in a village as an ordinary farmer's family. He reached the Red Fort in Delhi while growing up in the hutments of a village and walking in the midst of farm lands. By assuming the highest position in democracy, he became the Prime Minister. But it was not liked by the forward-caste and class people. First of all, he was a farmer and from the backward caste, who had become the Prime Minister with his language, attire, culture and values of a village. This must be his fault. Gandhian philosophy is not just an ideal and principle; instead it is a journey of life. Along with ideas and actions, it is a stream of behaviour. It is the real form of ideas and actions. It has transparency. Choudhury Charan Singh would say that the life of a human being should be homogeneous. The entire life is a stream. There shouldn't be any difference between private and public life. Public rule can't be there without public shame. Is this happening in today's politics, administration, business or even in society?

He confronted Pt. Nehru on the issue of cooperative farming. In the general session of the Congress, he opposed Nehru's proposal. It was not an ordinary matter. He was accused of being an opportunist. Some among those, who accused Charan Singh, got into power by walking on the same path on which Charan Singh used to go. The only difference was Choudhry Charan Singh was born in a poor backward family in a small village. That's why he was called an opportunist. Others were born in forward castes and class, so their opportunism was termed as idealism. To be born in a lower caste, backward caste or oppressed class means living a life of hell. They have to live by suppressing their self-respect and conscience. They have to remain dependent. They have to face the hardships of both defeat and suppression. They have to eat humble pie in all fields. When there is no aspiration, how can there be an ambition? In the social framework, their duty is to do hard work. Owners will reward them for their hard work. Owners have only name and they live with the support of that name. They have to do flattery even after having been talented enough. Dr. Lohia said that there will be two types of leaders among lower and backward castes—one is irritating and the other is sycophant. For the sake of power, people who like to enjoy privileges, wealthy and authoritarian society will make a temporary compromise with irritating leaders and at an opportune time, they will be thrown out. They make sycophants to flatter them and leave some of their leftovers for them. Sycophants consider the leftovers as great offerings. Choudhury Charan Singh kept fighting against such a system. He was neither irritating nor a sycophant. He was very talented and he was adored because of his talent. He followed that path which was followed by Gandhi, Ambedkar, Lohia and Deendayal. They had different forms but their nature was the same. There are parallels in their ideas, actions and behaviour. Even today Choudhury's fight is continuing. In some form or the other, someone or the other is continuing his fight.

Choudhury didn't give asylum to his caste people in the name of their caste or their children as political heirs either. He used to pay attention to his supporters than to his own son. He used to respect the heir of the ideology. While choosing people he used to give a lot of attention to their social, cultural and economic background. Writer has got the opportunity to be in his close proximity. On many occasions, he sent people from villages to be members of Rajya Sabha and Legislative Council, instead of people from wealthy houses. In 1980, the writer lost the election to Lok Sabha. All prominent leaders of the party were interested in sending a senior leader of the party as Rajya Sabha member. Choudhury didn't agree to that; he said, "Party doesn't need a rose flower; instead it requires an area of grains like wheat, millets and *jowar*." Without asking, he made the writer as the candidate for Rajya Sabha. The writer didn't get such respect ever again in his life. Late Karpoori Thakur, Ram Naresh Yadav, Choudhury Devi Lal and Meelamani Rautary, all became Chief Ministers in 1977 and they all belonged to backward caste and were farmers. All those leaders of Samajwadi and Lok Dal ideology, who were seen at national level, came up under the leadership of Choudhury Charan Singh after 1977. Choudhury Charan Singh picked all of them from the streets of villages and sent them to Rajpath of Delhi. After Lohia, Choudhury had selected 101 companions from the plains of Ganga and Yamuna, and from the heartland of India. All villagers, lower castes, backward castes and farmers were grateful to him. He passed away and the self-respect and respect for backwards at national level also left. Charan Singh had come to wake up everybody, He had woken up everybody and he himself slept off. Even today, lower castes and backward castes are politically exploited in the society. They are not respected but they get adjusted. They are not given credit but given posts. They are given officials but by giving a position they get exhibited. Choudhury Charan Singh didn't give asylum to the caste and dynasty, still he was termed as racist. He didn't protect his dynasty still he was called the promoter of dynasty politics. He never compromised on the principles for the sake of power but still he was called power greedy. He sacrificed, comfort, luxuries, privileges, wealth and means. Those who were imprisoned in the *chakravyuh* of caste and society and whose leaders are either directly or indirectly imprisoned by caste and family, they are credited as liberal and great. By the strength of promotion and propagation brass is turned into gold. Won't Mother India be kind to its children? The ideology of nationalism will be strong only when talented people from victimized, neglected, insulted, lower and backward castes are respected along with their indigenous values and culture. Their self-respect will be worshipped. Fight is on, many Charan Singh's have to come, the process will continue and in the end certainly a son from a hutment will be worshipped by becoming very talented.

*Hindustan, 23 December, 1999*

# 28
# The BJP has to Change the Face of the Society

The great sacrifice of Bihar just got over. Both nectar and poison have come out of this ocean churning. Fight is going on to consume the nectar, but nobody is ready to consume the poison. Nectar and poison both have to be consumed. Everybody has to volunteer to drink it by dividing between them, as some politicians because of their political ignorance, immaturity, personal ego and lack of experience just vomited out only poison. It was attempted to spread the poison of racism and communalism. Now it is necessary to curb both.

All the political parties and independents should introspect with an empty feeling. They should think seriously regarding what they gained or lost. In this election, there were mainly two pivotal points—one was the ruling Rashtriya Janata Dal coalition and the other, NDA, the main opposition. There was a drastic reduction in whatever was RJD alliance's strength. The RJD alone was short of almost one-third of seats, whereas the NDA's strength increased by one-third. There was one more alliance formed between the LJP and the Congress; it was against the RJD and the NDA coalitions. The LJP by modifying its older gangs contested the elections. The Congress got two seats less; lost by 20 percent. Public hasn't appreciated this alliance. Ram Vilas Paswan, the leader of LJP was emphasising making a Muslim Chief Minister and extending reservation to Muslims. But not even a single Muslim from his party could win the election. He was talking about social harmony and respect for extremely backward and lower castes while attacking the elements of racism and communalism. But he could win only in 29 constituencies. Both the parties of their alliance could manage to get only 39 seats. The other parties based on local situations and other reasons could manage to get a few seats; 17 independents got elected, but they all were having secret links with some or the other party. The workers of political parties worked to get those independents elected. I became the candidate of the Samyukta Socialist Party in 1967 due to non-Congress ideology. In 1974, during the agitation of Bihar, I tendered resignation for the first time. Emergency came, I had to face imprisonment; the 1977 storm had come and unfurled the victory flag of non-Congress ideology. At that time a team of youth was formed, who got the opportunity to enter into politics. Late Indira Gandhi was Indian; now Sonia Gandhi is of foreign origin. At that time many Muslim youth who were fighting continuously against Indira Gandhi, who were believers of Indian cultural values and traditions, are supporting Sonia Gandhi today. Majority couldn't be achieved even after the Congress, Lalu Prasad and Ram Vilas Pawan came together. Doesn't it mean that the voters of Bihar, specially from the lower and backward castes and even Muslim community haven't accepted their alliance? If the NDA and the LJP combined, it almost could reach the majority. Among the 29 MLAs of LJP, nine are Bhoomihars, seven Rajputs, four Yadavs and four Scheduled Castes and rest five are from different castes. Now the leader of the LJP should think, by looking at the pattern of his party, what kind of social equation can be formed? In his party, Yadavs account for 14 percent, and even among independents, the percentage of Yadavs is just 14 percent.

Three Muslims got elected to the NDA. The volunteers of the BJP lent good support even to those Muslim candidates. Even then, is BJP communal and LJP, which couldn't get a single Muslim elected, is liberal? All parties combined 50 Yadavs and 21 Muslims got elected. About half of those Yadavs are from RJD and rest are from different parties. Among the rest, 12 are from NDA. One-fourth of Yadavs are in NDA. Now all political analysts have to analyse the social pattern of election results. BJP was slightly successful in denting the base of RJD and Lalu Prasad Yadav. LJP and Congress worked to dent the base of NDA, but couldn't breach into the vote base of RJD. Instead by breaking into the voter base of NDA, it helped LJP and RJD. If it wasn't there, in the direct battle for righteousness between RJD and NDA, RJD would have been defeated and NDA would have got total majority. This game was also played under an international conspiracy. NDA too has to do some introspection. Because of social tensions and mutual mistrust, there was severe slowdown in Bihar. All parties were engaged in marching. Because of these speed breakers, politics has lost momentum and become very sluggish. There is a need to expand the social base. There is a need to form an expanded and extensive political base by bringing all, including lower castes, backwards castes, farmers, poor and forward classes into one fold. Today, in Bihar, there is a need for such leadership from lower and backward castes which the people from upper castes and classes will also accept with ease. Similarly, such a leader is required from upper castes, in whom the people from lower and backward castes can put their trust in. Both the parties of NDA, especially the BJP, had to change their dream. Without BJP transforming itself, the obstacles in the politics of nation and in Bihar could not be checked. Instead of blindly following fundamentalism, individualism and indulgent leaders of lower and backward castes, leadership has to be groomed from within. Nationalist and socialist thinker Lohia has said that in the absence of the power of principles, the power of majority becomes demonic. Whichever class has majority, the leadership has to be given to that class. This is the call of this age. It can't be said that people don't like the path of the BJP; but they don't have faith in the leadership of BJP. This time around, NDA has benefited by announcing Nitish Kumar the leader and by doing combined campaigning. However, every time some mistakes are getting repeated in the selection of candidates for elections. Public has more trust in local leaders; their personality will give more advantage during the election campaign. All the parties have to think in peace; everybody has to forego his ego. They have to learn to bend, leaving their stubbornness. By coming to a consensus, they have to work in tandem for the development of Bihar. RJD has been defeated but no party or coalition has turned out to be victorious. Feelings, aspirations and the message of the public has to be respected. This is the need of the hour.

*Hindustan, 10 March, 2005*

□

# 29
# Indulgence, Corruption, Terrorism and Violence

Indulgence, corruption, terrorism and violence have become more dominating. All these factors are in abundance in Bihar. Villagers, the poor and the farmers are desperate. Elections have come and the Assembly wasn't even formed, when it was dissolved. Elections were a story and now there is a need to understand, analyse the story behind the story. Once again preparations are going on for another election. Crores of rupees were spent and again crores of rupees are going to be spent, the burden of which will be borne by the common man. Crores of rupees are spent in conducting and managing elections. No individual is responsible for that. Whether they are independent candidates or candidates of political parties, they have to spend money from their own pocket. They have to arrange for money by some or the other means. If elections are held frequently, candidates have to take the help of capitalists; as a result, they become the protectors of the interests of capitalists. Often black money is used in election campaigns. When black money is used for election campaigns, how can the parliamentary democracy be free from corruption? This time whoever has won the election by collecting money from some or the other source, are confronted by a very serious problem—they couldn't become MLAs or could be called former MLAs.

How come it happened? Now the people of Bihar have to think about it. Who is responsible for this? What is there to worry about for leaders who are protected, reserved and safe? The people who have money and wealth in abundance, they are worried about how and where to spend that money? They can't spend that on public good. How can people sitting in peaceful and air-conditioned rooms know the experience of pain? It has become political fashion to talk about poor, weak, lower and backward castes. The more improved are the means of dialogue and communication, the more they have degraded. People read in newspapers and watch directly on TV channels, still, they close their eyes. In a democracy, public is the boss. When the boss closes his eyes and keeps watching the drama, who are going to reform? How shamelessly they talk on TV? They keep countering their own logic. They think all viewers and listeners are ignorant and idiots. But it is not so. Today, because of the improved communication facilities and because of education, political awareness has dawned upon people. Bihar has more political awareness. You may visit villages, streets, big cities and road crossings, wherever you go, you may come to hear political discussions taking place. Transformations and caste conversions also keep happening. Who doesn't know that Morarji Bhai was made Bhoomihar, Sardar Patel was made Kurmi, and Choudhury Charan Singh was made Yadav? All of them were leaders. Here even the incarnations of God are also imprisoned in various caste prisons. Irrespective of whether they are great men or saints, in Bihar they can't live outside of caste. Caste was made as the basis for elections. Politics has been made racial; criminalisation of caste and professionalisation of crime has been done. In Bihar, it is the rule of four pillars, namely profession, caste, politics and administration. Dr Lohia has said that in India it is very easy to change one's religion but keep getting grinded in the grindstone of caste. There is no way to get out of it. Will the youth be able to break these walls of caste prison by becoming rebels? If they can, Bihar will shine in the whole world.

During the time of Shri Babu, all Bhoomihars were seen with distrust in whatever party they were. But even the people of that caste were considered sympathetic to Babu. During the time of Vinoda Babu and Jagannath Mishra, the same notion was propagated about Brahmin society. During the time of Krishna Vallabh Sahay, people of his caste were also treated in a similar manner. During the time of Satyendra Babu, all the people belonging to his caste were treated in the same fashion. Today, during the rule of Lalu Prasad Yadav, Yadavs are also caught in a similar situation. To which ever party they may belong and however sincere and committed they may be, all are treated as second-class citizens. A Paswan, however he may oppose Ram Vilas Paswan, nobody is going to believe him. The people who are fighting for justice even after going through such insults are the people who are doing a true service to the nation. In Bihar, during the time of elections the colour of the caste spreads over everybody. Writer had gone through such a kind of experience and he is used to such a kind of treatment. People of the same caste consider them to be the enemies of the caste and people of the other castes consider them as outsiders. If it has to be told with complete sincerity and truth, in Bihar it is actually politics of caste only. God only knows how and when this will end. Congress Party has promoted racism and communalism the most. Robbers were told to rob without any fear and traders were told to stay awake. Before elections, they made Ram Vilas Paswan and Lalu fight against each other. Congress fought elections along with Ram Vilas, and openly challenged Lalu, conspiring against forming a government. When Nitish Kumar was about to form the government, then they got the Assembly dissolved. It is the strategy of the Congress that in Bihar important castes among backward caste keep fighting amongst themselves so that no leader could come into prominence. The Congress knows that if not today, tomorrow, Lalu will go deep into the quagmire because of his own reasons and get destroyed, being entangled in the cobwebs. If Nitish Kumar's leadership becomes prominent, then backward castes will get polarised. In Bihar, there are four prominent axes, namely forward castes, backward castes, Muslims and lower castes. Forward castes are unorganised. They are against Lalu but there is no unity among them.

There is a lack of unity, homogeneity and aggression. If they get to agree with each other and have a common goal, then there will be amazing results. Backward castes are in a majority, almost 54 percent. If there is an expanded unity among them, a new chapter may start. But they are also scattered in the name of caste. Under the leadership of late Karpoori Thakur, there was a strong unity. Ram Vilas is the leader of a particular lower caste and community. Muslims would like to share power, due to which they are being entertained by showing a film. Bihar is entangled in this *chakravyuh*. Along with loss of momentum, there is stagnation and social tension. Political marches are continuing. Everybody is gasping but nobody is able to progress. Because of urban values, professional character, indulgent mentality and hypocritical behaviour, the youth of Bihar are misguided. It's like an earthworm on the body of a snake. It can only try to dismount it. There is a need for social trust in Bihar. Bureaucracy and mafia is dominating the politics of Bihar. Politicians are becoming puppets in the hands of corrupt officers and social gangsters. All relief materials are getting looted and distributed amongst themselves. Even the investigators are keeping quiet after getting their share. Shroud is being sold, the logs in the cremation ground are sold, honour is getting looted, people, who are looting the honour, are made leaders. Facts and the truth are lying in front. Everybody is watching, everybody is understanding everybody. They are trying to cheat everybody. A very dangerous game is going on. Let farmers, labourers, proletariat, students, youngsters and elders come forward. By leaving attachment behind, if they get prepared for the battle of righteousness, then Bihar can become the best state in the world.

*Hindustan, 07 August, 2005*

□

# 30
# Politicisation of Reservation in the Reservation Politics

It is getting disintegrated. Polarisation is happening without pole. Pole keeps slipping and keeps changing its position. The differences between position-opposition, agitated-non-agitated are getting erased. Everybody is getting mixed up with everybody. The pole of all isms, opinions and paths has sunk the way the wheel of Karna's chariot sunk into the earth in Mahabharata. Similarly, the wheels of everybody's chariots have sunk. It was a quagmire made up of internal conflicts and contradictions. It was a question by Karna and he only has to give the answer to it. To be decanted is called losing momentum. Losing momentum is both destruction and death. Today politics is sunk in the quagmire of political parties. Everybody is questioning everybody and more difficult questions are popping up from everybody's answers. Nobody is able to give answers. There is no difference any more between logic, argument and sophism. Saint Kakubhushundi had answered the questions of Garud. The seeker was satisfied by the answers. *Gita* of Mahabharat is like Ganges of knowledge, a very great scripture. As it opens all glands, it is called Ganges of knowledge. *Gita* is full of questions and answers. Arjun, the seeker and Krishna, the one who gives answers, both of them stood in the midst of both warring sides, where nobody is in opposition to none. Both of them have their own vows. They are alternative sources. When all these sources get dried up, then quagmire only will be there.

To think in totality, a complete mind is required. Broken mind can't think in totality. When one thinks about the nation, then attention should be given to all castes, sub-castes, cultures, civilisations, communities and conduct and activities and also, all practices. The people who instituted the caste system did a liberal job. They controlled and limited the economic and social rights of the races they defeated. Unlike the other victors of the world, they didn't destroy them completely.

We have accepted democracy and adult franchise but social mentality remains feudalistic. Caste system is a system that strengthens the feudal system, without uprooting it completely it is very difficult to achieve the goals of national unity, integrity and social harmony. Without abolishing privileges, social equality can't be achieved. Among types of people, some are protected and safe; reserved and unsafe are living together in one country. There is worry about the future of the safe and protected, even reserved are agitating to get the protection and safety. But nobody is paying attention to those who are slaves and reserved. Who is going to place on the basis of reservation? For the kind of society, we want to form, we have to form such an organisation. The kind of legislature and executive we want to make, such an organisation and society has to be formed. Society is the centre of everything. According to the definition of the highest court, reservation can't be more than 50 percent. Those who consider this right, then they have to think why there is 60 to 70 percent reservation in some of the South Indian states? Why should it be supported? If it can be so much in South, then why is it illegal to demand the same? Isn't the whole country one? When lower castes are given reservation in promotions, then everybody supports it. Then why this privilege is not given to other backward castes (OBCs)? Why is that demand termed unfair? When is there reservation for women in municipalities, municipal corporations and village Panchayats? Then why isn't it right to give reservation for women in Assemblies and Parliament? Under reservation for women, women from lower caste and backward caste are given separate reservation and they are contesting elections on that basis, and everybody has accepted this. Why is it considered as a crime to demand the same kind of reservation for women from lower and backward castes in the Assembly and Parliament? All games are played just to garner votes. While the politics of uniting lower castes and forward caste is going on, at the same time at other places, attempts are going on to unite the lower castes and Muslims. While somebody is becoming a forward caste, at other times somebody is becoming a backward caste. How long can this logic of lower caste, backward caste, forward caste and non-forward caste continue? All these games have to be stopped. Today people of all castes, communities, classes and castes are well aware of their interests and also understand the secret behind the political games being played. They know the reason behind the political games of reservation. In the politics of reservation, they are playing the game of reservation politics. Everybody wants answers to all the questions. For the good of the nation, Indian culture and values, there is a need for cultural nationalism, spiritual equality and humanitarian love as well. If nationality is drenched in the essence of spirituality, then it strengthens the cultural nationalism.

*Aaj, 27 May, 1997*

□

# 31
# What Kind of Elections does Election Commission Want to Conduct?

This kind of situation arose for the first time in the Indian democracy. It was almost the same situation after the elections of 1989. Elections are conducted repeatedly and the pattern of results is almost the same every time. This time a new situation has come up. It is not clear in the Constitution what should be done in such a situation. Parliament comes into existence by the voting of voters. In democracy, the Assembly and Lok Sabha are formed by the elected representatives of the people. So voters are at the root of it. Until there is a system for free and fair voting, till then the outcome of the elections can't be fair. First, it is very essential that attention should be given to the safety and security of the voters. All these things are associated with the polling centres. United, powerful and influential castes or groups grab the votes of the weak and the meek. The power grants security to administrators of a particular caste and class; through the power of the state, administrators do all sorts of things to ensure that power stays on. Election Commission conducts election with the help these officers only. The members of Commission are also human beings. All human beings have some or the other weakness. Caste, community and selfish motives influence them also. Differences in opinions will certainly be there; percentages may differ. A decision taken by discretion should be transparent.

In India, elections are not getting conducted in a free, fair and sacred manner. After contesting elections from Panchayat to Parliament more than a dozen times, and being in politics for the last forty years, this writer has first-hand experience of it. The ruling party and the caste which influence the ruling party get all the protection. The groups, communities and castes which oppose the party in power are suppressed by the force of the ruling party. With protection from the ruling party, the minority opinion is converted to majority opinion. Fake voting happens and voters of opposition party are dragged out of the polling centres. Officers let people castes fake ballots in the ballot boxes in front of them. While counting, thousands of votes get tampered; they mix up fake ballots and count them too. The candidate and his supporters are thrown out of the counting station when they protest against it. Even after getting the certificate of election, they declare the winner as the loser and loser as the winner. To defeat the elected candidate, repolling takes place; sometimes re-polling is done more than thrice to get the losing candidate win the election and to defeat the elected candidate. Can this be called a true democracy? Will the free and fair election be like this? Will the Parliament and Assembly formed by such election be called as the true reflection of the public? Economic scandals are taking place because of election scandals. When the governments are formed through political and administrative scandals, then why can't economic scandals happen? Why can't it be so when *"Baap-beta dalal, tab bail ka daam barah anna"* (both father and son are brokers, then the price of the bull is 12 annas). All these ills are there in Bihar. Does the Election Commission have the power to stop all this? Is Election Commission itself unbiased? All these points are worth pondering over. They have to be debated.

More than 50 percent of the voters are extremely backward, weak, minorities, poor and meek. Minorities doesn't mean religious minorities alone. Where Muslims and Christians are in majority there the condition of Hindus is very pathetic; similarly where a particular caste of Hindus is in majority, there the condition of other castes is equivalent to minorities and in this all forward, backward and lower castes are included. At some places due to the fear of lower castes, even the forward classes are scared of casting their vote. Wherever one is dominant, there they tend to suppress others. But one has to give a thought to this that when in a Hindu society, some caste politically and socially exploits the minorities and other castes, then a big hue and cry is raised and immediately some party or the other goes to their rescue; but when people of Hindu society become, poor, weak and minorities and get exploited by the minorities, lower castes, etc., and when they are deprived of casting their vote, then why does no political party come forward to do justice to them? If at all, any party comes forward, then that party is stamped as communal. Aren't there political and social factors responsible for this? The Constitution of India has granted equal rights to every citizen of the country; then why do they get to have their rights? When forwards exploit others, then it is called atrocity and agitation is done against the exploiters by the exploited and it is called a fight for justice. But a weak and poor Hindu fights against the exploitation by Muslims or other communities, then why is it called communalism? And the other also becomes a reason for tension. What is the value of a ballot, is seen directly by the people. Mid-term elections of current Lok Sabha are taking place only because of one vote. Just one vote can change the fate and future of a whole nation. Because short by one vote, these mid-term polls are taking place. Common man is forced to bear the burden of thousands of crores of rupees. Maximum burden of this will fall on villagers, the poor and the farmers. The culprit has to be found out.

If the Constitution or any other thing causes hindrance in holding independent, free and fair elections, solution has to be worked out to remove them. Constitution is for the people; not the other way round. India is an agriculture-based country. 85 percent of the population lives in villages; 70 percent are dependent on agriculture; that is three-fourths of the voters are farmers living in villages. While deciding the voting time, their convenience has to be given priority. This time the protectors of Constitution have set September and October as the date for elections.

Many times elections were held in June and July in independent India, but never in the months of September and October. Holding elections during the *kharif* season when plantation will be at its peak, can only be termed as anti-farmer elections. Holding elections when administration is busy looking after the safety of flood affected, all political parties and organisations are busy in carrying various relief operations, is like rubbing salt over the wounds or like getting dresses made out of the shroud of the dead. There won't be any roads to access the polling centres, voters won't be able to reach the polling centres; they will not be given any protection or safety. Polling will be held in boats and ballot boxes of the opponents will be thrown into the flood waters. Nobody will come to know. Ballot papers will be dropped in the box, even without going to the polling stations. What can Election Commission do to avoid this? No records, no account; whatever the administration says, only that is right. What sort of elections does Election Commission want to hold? The elections conducted by Election Commission this time will remain as a black spot on the face of democracy in the history of India. Don't the President and Election Commission know that such a situation will arise because of no confidence? Aren't they aware of the strategy of the opposition? Being the protectors of the Constitution, can't they manage to run the Parliament for three more months? Can't they ask Atalji to seek a vote of confidence for the second time? What would go wrong by doing so? Annual Budget was passed; there was no threat to the financial crisis. The country wouldn't have fallen into abyss, if the government of Atalji continued for two or three more months? If Lok Sabha is in existence, then there can't be a gap of more than six months between the sessions, but when it is not in existence, then how can this rule be applicable? The Supreme Court would have explained this on its own. Highest court is the interpreter of the Constitution. Krishna had said that justice has to be defined, keeping in view the time, place and the conditions. Such a time has come in India's democracy. In case at this time, if such a calamity, either internal or external, arises because of which Emergency has to be declared in the country, won't it be recommended by this cabinet of ministers? In case the country has to attack any other country, won't this government be eligible to give orders to the Army for that? In case the approval of the Parliament is essential, then won't those formalities be completed by calling an emergency meeting of the dissolved Parliament? Or will they patiently keep watching the drama till the time elections get over and new Parliament comes into effect? Democracy is the most complicated and yet very beautiful system in the world. Opposition is also a part of the government. Interests of public and nation are above all. To think alike, by rising above feelings like hatred, jealousy, revenge, selfishness, is the basis of democracy. What does the duty of nation say? India has seen Emergency and experienced the atrocities committed during that time and has seen the way power got changed because of that. India has seen the leader of opposition presenting a sword to the Prime Minister in Parliament and also praising the Prime Minister. I have seen the minority government passing the annual budget with the consent of the whole house; has seen making amendments to the Constitution. Nation is superior; the people of the country are the bosses. Voters are the creators of Parliament and Assembly. Voters are bosses only for the sake, but in reality, they are the slaves of Election Commission, government and bureaucracy. When majority of the country will be reeling under the wrath of natural calamities such as floods, earthquakes, cyclones and storms, will the Constitution deprive the citizens of their right to vote? God comes down because of the farmer's call; this time also the same is going to happen. Elections have to be conducted only in the months of November and December. If Election Commission does not listen to it, then Nature and God will certainly listen to the call of the farmer. Going against the interests of the public and nation is like inviting treason. The President, Election Commission, the Supreme Court, all should come together and think over it.

*Aaj, 17 May, 1999*

□

# 32
# Karpoori Thakur had Given Self-respect to the Hearts of Thousands

If a lamp kept under the open sky keeps flickering in the midst of strong winds and cyclone, and keeps showing the path to lakhs of people with its light by piercing through darkness, then it is very natural for people to watch it dumbstruck. But this is true in the land of Bihar; for years this incident remained true. From birth till death, in spite of facing the wrath of political, social and economic cyclones, facing severe insult, neglect and ridicule, still a lamp left an unmitigated impression in the hearts of crores of people. It was none other than Karpoori Thakur.

He was certainly weak by wealth, caste and by land, but he was very harsh and pure. The influence of Karpoori Thakur was there on all castes, communities, classes of the society. He was a true warrior, who could speak for lower castes, backwards and the impoverished. He used to echo the voice of crores of people, who were classless, who were getting thrashed since thousands of years, who couldn't express their feelings and who were dying in suffocation. He was the voice of all these people. He didn't fight for just having power; instead, he wanted to show to crores of people that there is no monopoly over power of any one particular community, caste or race or individual. He fought all his life to generate hope and enthusiasm in the minds of crores of suppressed people and to leave an unmitigated impression on their minds. Who doesn't aspire to have power in politics? It is a different thing as some people born in wealthy families think that it is their birthright to have such an aspiration, whereas, it is not there for the poor and the oppressed. This is the inspiration that

Karpoori Thakur gave to everybody; that everybody should have the aspiration of getting into power. Unless lower castes and poor don't understand that power is the *kalpavriksh* (wish-fulfilling tree) and *kamadhenu* (wish-fulfilling cow) of this age and in the parliamentary democracy system, which fulfils their wishes, till then their fate can't be changed. As long as it is the rule of majority in a democracy, how can it be a crime to make the majority population partners in the ruling government or awaken the hunger for power among the majority population by creating that awareness among that majority population? As long as the majority of population remains weak, physically and mentally, till then, the democracy also remains paralysed. The society appears beautiful only when every part of it is beautiful. Karpoori Thakur took this fundamental ideology in inheritance from Lohia. Isn't it our ideal to make the society awake and conscious? As long as the majority of the nation stays paralysed, till then the nation also stays paralysed.

In a democracy, everybody should have participation in the state power and state treasury. As long as all classes of the society don't get represented equally, till then the feeling of equality doesn't come in the minds of the people. It's not sufficient to say that these people also have equal rights in this country. They give all their energy in building the nation but they don't get to enjoy even a small portion of the comforts. When they don't get the right value for their hard work, then the feeling of rebellion wakes up in his mind. How long will this continue that while some people work hard, the fruits of the hard work are enjoyed by someone else? Each one should get to enjoy the share of the comforts according to the hard work they put in into nation building, but why is it not happening so? When against such injustice and exploitation, a person like Karpoori Thakur raises his voice, then he is called a racist. After all, who is a racist? Are those handful of people who sit in the sky-kissing mansions and laugh loudly over the hard work of crores of people or are those people who become the spokesperson of these people and give voice to these voiceless people?

When the majority in society doesn't get the share in governance according to their number, then there will be some heat in their voice. Is it a crime to demand one's right? Karpoori Thakur used to ask this question and when he didn't get the response, then when he raised his voice against the of system very softly, on behalf of those crores of voiceless people, then these crores of minds got shaken. He wanted to give them the life of equality by bringing them out of the life of insult, neglect and ridicule. Whenever and wherever any atrocity is committed against any weak person, then one voice is raised against that atrocity; that voice used to be of Karpoori Thakur. That voice fell silent forever. For the sake of votes and politics, however may anybody talk, that is all only superficial talk. On the dais, everybody gives revolutionary talk against the system, but when they get off the dais, that behaviour doesn't stay with them. The reason for this is that an individual acquires only the values of that social and economic milieu in which he spends his life from birth to death. A person who always wears clean, white and costly clothes will never let a person wearing old, dirty and torn clothes come near him, however competitive he may be. Talented person only can identity another talented person. Don't analyse the leaders on the basis of their speeches on the stage; instead analyse them on the basis of the place they live in, the kind of food they eat and the company in which they move. This he learnt from Lohia.

Society can't be inspired by a leader who is very conservative, racist and pro-establishment by nature but talks anti-establishment. A leader is tested by the kind of people around him. Who will allow, not only in Patna but in the whole of Bihar, a person wearing torn, dirty, shabby and old clothes to sit next to him? Who will eat dry bread with *saag, sattu* by sitting next to him? Who is such a leader who will be seen mingling with them from within and without also. Karpoori Thakur was not just one leader but he was the leader of many leaders. He fought for giving leadership to those people who needed to be changed, to make them stand in the frontline of politics. He was fighting for this ideal of Lohia. He was not a leader of one term only; instead he became a leader after years of struggle, hard work, penance and with the blessings of lakhs of people. His voice was the voice of crores of people. He was the beat of crores of hearts. In today's politics, many people would like to come into politics on the basis of majority, but nobody allows them to be in the frontline of politics. Karpoori Thakur was against such politics. 'Learn to live with self-respect' was his basic teaching. Whatever break-ups he had done in politics, all were for self-respect. Without self-respect, an individual becomes almost lifeless. The society, individual and nation—who doesn't understand self-respect and self-dignity—is equivalent to a dead and non-living matter. He generated the feeling of self-respect in the minds of those crores of people who were treated like animals, because of which, he was treated as enemy number one by people who supported the establishment and exploitation. Today who are his enemy number one? Today there is an increasing trend of make-do socialists and many of them are victims of this trend.

Karpoori Thakur was not a rose flower, who would enhance the glow of the crown of the princely man sitting on the throne. He was ears of the wheat, which used to feed crores of people and mitigate their hunger. After him, there is a need for those people who would live on the ideology of Lohia, Charan Singh and Karpoori Thakur. Even if they have to encounter troubles for following this path, they have to keep this ideology alive on the strength of patience, courage, discretion and organisation. This ideology didn't develop in a day; instead, it has developed with years of penance, hard work and by the sacrifice of lakhs of people. If this ideology continues, then many leaders would come out of this ideology, but if this ideology dies down, then again for many years...

I pray to this great leader, friend, teacher and ideal while seeking his forgiveness that whatever he could accomplish when he was alive, that he should do it after his death. Keep guiding your colleagues who strayed off the path. You kept the torch of Gandhi, Lohia, J.P. and Charan Singh burning. Even after you have gone, keep that torch burning even in the midst of cyclones. By your inspiration someone or other will certainly come up, who by keeping the organisation and force built by you alive, will bring relief to the deep pain of Bihar, which knows from where that light comes out.

*Navbharat Times, Patna, 20 January, 1989*

□

# 33

# Today there is Neither Ruling Party, Nor Opposition

When speaking or listening, following the path of truth becomes a crime, the end of that society approaches fast. And when the institutions which build the character of a nation become visionless and directionless, then the nation gropes in the dark. In such a situation, one can get out of that darkness through a great battle only. The background has been prepared for such a great battle in India. Today both ruling party and opposition have to be weighed by keeping on the same side of the balance. Today there is neither a ruling party nor opposition. While a party is in opposition at some place, the same is the ruling party at another place. When opposition is integrated with ruling party and ruling party is integrated with opposition, then it has to be viewed with very subtle vision. By seeing the broader forms of a party, the character and its programme can be analysed, wherever that party is in power. If any organisation or a small institute is running under the leadership of any individual, then the nature of that individual can be understood by the functioning of that organisation. The broader picture is hidden under the subtle picture. When some small discrepancies are seen in the subtle picture, as the organisation acquires a broader picture, the discrepancies also keep growing bigger. If any individual is not clean while working in small institutions like municipal corporation, municipality or village Panchayat, how can he be clean when he is working at state or central level? If a party can't stay clean at state government level, how can it stay clean at the Centre?

A person who doesn't feel ashamed of stealing cucumbers, he wouldn't feel ashamed of stealing diamonds. If any individual can't upkeep the dignity of his own institution or can't observe democracy in his own party or organisation, that person can't give democracy to the nation. In other words, it can be said that if an individual can't observe the fundamental democratic principles in his own life, by no standards whatever can one claim oneself to be demöcrat. Today all over the world and specially in India, the influence of inferior and *Kalanemi* type of people is increasing. People with indulgent character can never be rebels.

If we judge all the political parties and its leaders through this parameter, we come to see where one stands. Leaders who appear to be democratic, socialist, liberal and sincere in their talks, in their actions, appear to be dictators, capitalists, fundamentalists, or those who do nastiest things for the sake of their family. The picture they form from the perspective of the commoners is not the same from the perspective of indulgent society. Indulgent society is caught in satisfying their desires and as a result, there is a lack in the vision of discretion. Society has the right to decide on how and what of an individual. An individual may draw a picture of himself as he likes, but what is his picture in the eyes of the society happens to be his real picture. Criticising the behaviour and qualities of others and condemning the actions of others and behaving in the same way and doing the same deeds has become the nature of today's politicians. Some selfish elements stay surrounded by them and keep boosting their ego. Because of their bloated egos, they don't get to see the truth.

Congress Party is in power but Congress alone was not in power; all opposition parties were also getting the opportunities to come to power. Even today, opposition parties are getting a chance to come into power in a roundabout manner. Congress revolves around one person. All the selfish elements keep coming together. It has become a platform, where people keep coming and going. What moral right does Congress have to criticise the government of opposition, which will criticise the discrepancies of the Congress Government? When dynasty and love for the son has become the basis of Congress Party, same dirt has gone down to the bottom. When the character of the leader is maligned, then the society would also imitate their leader. People who have become leaders by virtue of corruption, pretension, deceit, gimmicks and hypocrisy always prefer to be in the company of such people around them. A person of character and sincerity with the power of ethics can never indulge in flattery. A person who doesn't have the power of morals and ethics can never fight against injustice and immorality. Moral power can't be acquired without willpower. Willpower can't come with pretention. Today pretention has become the basis of politics. When a deed is sinful for others, how can it become righteous for the self? The bad and sinful deed of the Congress Party by which its government should have been ended, if opposition parties absorb the same bad deeds in them, what difference will be there between both the groups? When there is no difference between both the groups, what good is it doing to bring through change in power? Slowly, these fundamental questions are arising in the public mind.

After all, why should there be a change? There should be a clear-cut distinction between the Congress and the opposition, not only in their policies but also in individuals. A good individual of the Congress Party should be respected even in the opposition, but if opposition pays respect to a person from Congress who is unclean, then what will the world say? Nehru family is a victim of fascination for dynasty and son. Are the leaders of the opposition looking any different? In Nehru's family, one after the other someone is coming into power. This is dynasty politics and if the same thing happens in opposition, will democracy be there? Logic and knowledge is a double-edged sword. This blade, while tearing apart the opposition, also tears the person who is wielding it. Today, the mind of the common man is quite broadened. In independent India, they got many political trainings. Everybody wants to suppress the weak, poor, hopeless and destitute. The plundering castes are forcefully snatching the votes of these people all over the country. When Congress plunders, then it is called plundering of votes, but when opposition comes into power by doing the same, then it is not called so. The people who plunder keep arguing amongst themselves as to who is a brave plunderer. Everybody attempts to keep the weak dependent. The way they keep chanting the name of Rama, they keep chanting the name of the weak; but they don't want to raise his physical status. They all know that the day all these weak classes come together, then they will start ruling the country and the structure of the society will change completely. By any means, fundamental change shouldn't take place so that power may go into their hands. Players may change, but the game shouldn't change and furthermore, the playground may change, but players and the game shouldn't change. Players at will can change their sides and get laurels. The goal of politics has become that 'follow that policy by which one gets have the power by hook or crook.' Power is not required to implement a policy; instead policy is needed to get the power. In India, it is a time of transition; at this time philosophers and spiritualists should come forward. Even in this field, the trend of *Kalanemi* is highly prevalent. That's why in India, there is a need for a great war, where on all fronts, including political, economic, social, ethical, communal, religious, scientific, spiritual and administrative, one has to fight with the feeling of equality as against the trend of *Kalanemi*. The background to this has already been set. The ray of hope is hidden in the womb of hopelessness. With this belief that every time the light of hope comes out of hopelessness, this country moves forward and keeps the momentum going on. The present structure of ruling and opposition has to be destroyed; then only a new structure forms, which probably may have purity.

Everybody has to work equally for building a new age. The fascination for ruling party and opposition has to be given up for the sake of nation, society and humanity, and one should come forward by liberating oneself from all prejudices. This is the duty of hopelessness. When a ray of hope can be seen even in hopelessness, then people get inspired to move forward. In this age of hopelessness also, one has to keep working with hope. Whatever may be the present political and social structure, there are rays of hope even in hopelessness. This is the teaching of great men and the path shown by saints.

Today, what is needed is that all people of discretion, who are currently having different opinions should come together. People who are playing different games to cover up the sins, all those mysteries have to be exposed. As long as the curtains don't rise, till then the ray of hope can't be seen in hopelessness. When intellectual and wise people also accept the slavery of ruling power, then discretion keeps groping in the dark. It will be a great day for India when wise, intellectuals, philosophers and knowledgeable people get themselves freed from the slavery of the power.

The interest of nation is above all, but the interest of the humanity is even above the interest of the nation. The fight which is going to take place between sacrifice, truth and falsehood, righteousness and falsehood, selfishness and the ultimate, one has to join this fight by leaving fascination and illusion. Conch has to be blown to announce the great war to be fought to build a new India along with Gandhi, Lohia, and Jaya Prakash, by bringing together Marx and Lenin in which both ruling and opposition get intermingled. During this transition whoever fights against the institutions of power by becoming a rebel is worth worshipping.

Whoever starts a fight for justice and truth, all such people should get encouragement from all people only then the environment for building a new age will be created.

*Navbharat Times, 04 June, 1989*

□

# 34
# Disciples have Also Forgotten Lohia

23rd March comes and goes every year; many great people must have been born on 23 March, but in that list one more name gets added. Dr. Ram Manohar Lohia took birth on that day and a golden chapter was added in the history of India. Socialism gets a new direction and nationalism will have a new chapter. Social harmony and equality get a new vision. Principles and actions get a new explanation. People get to know about the abstract and gross form of politics; the secret about equal goals and equal intelligence gets revealed. Hindu versus Hindu and India versus Pakistan get a new basis. The knowledge of imprisonment of caste and birth will be cleared. Socialism gets the light of politics, economics and society; politics gets a multi-dimensional direction and the thought process gets started.

Human beings need not only bread, but also respect. Hunger gets mitigated by bread; however, the hunger of mind gets mitigated only through respect. Bread and respect are essential, if the people who are hungry of bread get respect only, and the people hungry of respect get bread, then both of them live with an inferiority complex and feel suffocated. That's why bread is needed, but along with respect. Bread without respect becomes slavery; respect without bread brings impoverishment. That's why both are required. Nation becomes strong only with respect and wealth. Lohia taught this to the backward and lower castes. He taught them to fight forever to get power. During his life-time, he nurtured not one, but many leaders. From village to the national level, today many leaders have acquired many reputed positions in Indian politics. The person who made them has passed away, but the people made by him have forgotten him. The path of Indian socialism has stopped at that level only, till where he paved it. The roads of socialism are getting broken and forests have come upon on those roads.

But one thing becomes highly visible, i.e. his disciples have put out name-plates after his name. Lohia has been forgotten but the name-plates of his name are shining bright. His disciples got the opportunity to run the governments in states. If they wished they could have implemented the policies of Lohia, but nobody tried to put into practice the idea of four-pillared government; nobody paid attention to give full rights to Panchayats and making Panchayats function as autonomous institutions. Giving full rights to Panchayats means giving power into the hands of villagers, farmers, lower castes and backward castes. Rights have to be equally divided based on the four lists, namely village list, district list, state list and central list made by the Constitution. Panchayats should have full control over government staff. Every five years elections to Panchayats should be held by the Election Commission on the lines of Assembly and Parliament elections. Why didn't it happen so? The reason is be it the forward classes or backward and lower classes, everybody wants to acquire power and run parliamentary dictatorship.

Lohia was in favour of giving 60 percent reservation to the backward castes, women, religious minorities and backwards in politics, business, government jobs and army as a way of special opportunities. Why did the disciples of Lohia forget this? They got busy in continuing the caste-based politics on coming to power. Lohia has said that 50 to 60 percent of the topmost leadership at national level has to be elected from lower castes based on pre-planned strategy. There is no need for going through legislation. It is better to do it as a utility. This can be done through a change in political leadership at the national level. By this it becomes very clear that while Lohia wanted to implement this through legislation, at the same time he wanted to build a social consensus over this through continued social and cultural movements.

If the change comes through social acceptance, there won't be any feelings of violence, hatred, revenge or reaction. But so-called leaders of smaller castes didn't implement these after getting into power and after gaining political strength. This is a complicated question, but Lohia had given an answer too. Lohia has said, "The political behaviour of smaller castes is very strange. Why do they become a part of this conspiracy willingly? This is beyond anybody's comprehension. One reason is very clear, although worse than the security given to animals, but without doubt, smaller castes do get much more security than whatever security upper castes get. Without it, they feel helpless." He further wrote, "Those who talk about abolishing caste system, when they get into power to protect that power and also with a view to worm back to power when they go out of power, they keep using caste unwarrantedly, not to eliminate the injustice meted out because of caste, system and not to uplift either one or other suppressed castes, but to maintain their supremacy, they keep using the fight against castes unwarrantedly."

The leaders of today have to be analysed by this parameter only. Special opportunities are meant to end the privileges slowly, and slowly make the ineligible as eligible; the way a swimmer teaches swimming to a non-swimmer, similarly by giving cooperation, protection and safety, the suppressed classes have to be brought into the pool of power to make them swim, giving an opportunity to a person standing at the bottom to come up. In the chronicle of history, Lohia had made a special arrangement for this. Whoever comes will go is the eternal and permanent truth of nature. Birth and death are cyclical. In the same manner, the centre of power in society has kept changing. Indian society has been divided into four classes, namely Brahmin, Kshatrya, Vaishya and Shudra. In current times, it is neither *Satyug* in India nor the distorted form of class system.

Today it is the caste system which has the ugly form of dividing society. The genius of India has been eclipsed because of the caste system, but the leaders of suppressed classes and administrative officers don't want to eliminate the caste system completely. When the caste system gets eliminated, then everybody will be freed from imprisonment. The scope will get broadened and a bigger personality is needed. Bigger personality requires talent, genius, scholarship, capability and eligibility. All these qualities can be acquired only through hard work, practice, penance and devotion. But these are not required to get leadership on the basis of caste. It is easy to generate jealousy through violence, reaction, revenge, anger and rebellion. People of all castes are almost following these methods only. People are engaged in racialisation of politics, criminalisation of caste and socialisation of crime. A competition is going on among all castes on this. Ways have to found to save the nation and society from this dangerous trend. That is why there is a need for the philosophy of Lohia; there can be other ways also.

Lohia had suggested a practical and pragmatic solution. He said that all political parties and organisations involved in economic programmes, on occasions of marriage, festivals, feasts and death, etc., socially have to move all castes towards this side and should attack on the caste system.

Today many disciples of Lohia are in different political parties and are in power. Fake and superficial debate is going on to stop unnecessary expenditure. Where is unnecessary expenditure, who is doing and how are they doing it? Profligacy is because of indulgence. Politicians, bureaucrats and businessmen, all the three of them want to drown the nation in the sea of indulgence. Nearly, 11 percent of population in the country are landless, who are called landless labourers or agricultural labourers; 69 percent of the land is less than a hectare and 15 percent land is between one or two hectares. Farmers who had land between one hectare and one-and-a-half acres are called marginal farmers. There is shortage of land on one side. At the same time in capital cities, like Delhi and other cities, mansions are built in two to three acres. Hundreds of acres were turned into cremation grounds, where memorials of political leaders have been built. In 1967, Lohia had given a programme to the coalition government, to construct residential complexes for ministers and construct multistorey building of one type in which all ministers would live. Residential offices should be built within the residential complexes and everybody should travel to their offices in one bus and all should leave together to their respective homes. Officers also should come to the headquarters at stipulated time and go back after work. This will bring work efficiency, punctuality and discipline. Secondly, the security which has to be set up at different residences can be arranged only at one place to save a lot of money. Thirdly, when everybody gets the same type of residence, then there is no scope for dissatisfaction to creep in; fourthly, transport expenditure will come down, fifthly, visitors get to meet all the ministers at one place only. Sixth, the biggest advantage is everybody will be in the surveillance of everybody. Everybody will see the visitors coming to meet any minister, because of which there will be a control over corruption automatically. Vision of equality would develop. Today buildings and vehicles have become indicators of prestige. The natural requirements are alike for all human beings. Because of buildings, vehicles, comforts and privileges, political unhappiness and rebellion are growing. If homogeneity and equality come in this, then purity will come in parliamentary democracy. Efforts should be made to control the expenses incurred in maintaining and decorating the residences.

Can't we be the rulers and leaders of nation by adopting a lifestyle like that of Gandhi? Can't we give freedom to earn and put limits on expenditure? Can't we build the nation by following the path of sacrifice? Take loan, spend on indulgences and keep making people mendicants. A beggar nation can never have self-respect and be respected. If money is short in the country and there is foreign pressure because of loans and there is influence of indulgence on the whole country, then can the whole nation take a vow to get liberated from this situation? If nation has the power to take the vow, then the path is very simple and easy. Rulers and administrators and staff should take a vow that for three years they will contribute half of their salary to the nation rebuilding fund, and next three years one-fourth of their salary will be contributed. If the ruling class takes such a vow, then the entire nation will take the vow. Lohia had initiated a discussion on 'Cap on Expenditure' in the

Parliament. But today the discussions are going on not putting a cap on expenditure but to increase the limit of expenditure. At the time Lohia explained with figures that by capping the expenditure every year, 15 lakh crores of rupees could be saved.

Lohia has left after showing the way. His disciples have lost the way, broken up and scattered away. But nation has to adopt that path. His disciples might have strayed off the path and are groping in the dark but his path is showing the light. Those were not only his ideas but it is the stream of Indian thought. Gandhi, Lohia, Deendayal, Charan Singh and Karpoori Thakur, all were the travellers of the same path. Many travellers, but the route was the same. Many visions, but direction was the same. On 23rd March, a crore of salutations to the nationalist, Indian socialist and father of society.

*Navbharat Times, New Delhi, 23 March, 2000*

□

# 35
# Why this Racism doesn't End?

Intellectual debate is going on racism, but it is not getting abolished. Even before and after Gandhi and Ambedkar, many great souls, saints and reformers came together to abolish it but the result has been zero. Even today the reality is that it is easy to change the religion, but it is not at all easy to change the caste. Many people got converted to other religions but they could never get freed from the stamp of their caste. Today caste system is still there in the society and is also assessing the personality of a person based on his birth. There is a need to think about ways to break this.

When under the leadership of Gandhi the whole nation woke up and jumped into the movement of independence, then powerful British had to run away. But while going they left their culture, values and mentality as inheritance to Indians. They developed the caste system in a new way. Feudal system got transformed into democracy but caste system couldn't be eliminated. The dominance of upper caste people continued in the administration. People having English education, commitment, culture and values have continued to hold administrative power. Native rulers had come to occupy the number one throne but number two position has remained with foreign-mentality people.

In the beginning, in independent India, there was not much spread of education among backward and lower caste people. As a result, their number was negligible in government jobs. Dr. Ambedkar knew this secret; even Mahatma Gandhi knew this. Mahatma Gandhi gave them the adult voting rights. In the world, movements were going on for a long time and many sacrifices had to be made to get the voting rights for women, non-white people, but in India, along with Independence, everybody got the voting rights and political equality was achieved.

Either because of the influence of Gandhi's ideology or because of pressure from Dr. Ambedkar, the principle of reservation was also accepted, although later on it was not implemented sincerely. If there was no reservation, not even a single MLA or MP would have come from lower caste society. Because of political partnership, their economic condition also started improving. Their children could see the cities, high schools and colleges and faced insults in educational institutions. The way reservations were given to lower castes, if other backward castes were also given reservation from the beginning, the map of India would have been different today. It hasn't happened so because people, who were ruling the country and people who dominated the administrative services for fifty years after Independence, were against the backward castes. Farmers and labourers are included in other backward castes (OBCs). Their population was almost 54 percent. Democracy is called the rule of 51 percent. They were deprived because, if they wake up and get united, then all the administrative services would go to villagers.

In spite of all these things, OBCs continued their fight. Then came the period of Dr. Lohia. He suggested a formula that OBCs, women, religious minorities, Scheduled Castes and Scheduled Tribes should be given minimum 60 percent reservation in government services, businesses and armed forces. Socialists raised slogans, Dr. Lohia *bandhe gaanth pichede, pave sou me saath* (Dr. Lohia united the backward castes and got 60 percent out of hundred). This had a major influence in the heartland of India. As the awareness kept increasing among lower castes and backward castes, their hunger for power started increasing. They started getting united and formed organisations. Based on castes, poles started forming among them also.

They started asking for 20 to 30 years after Independence leaders of which caste became Chief Ministers of various states, how many people of which caste were in the Central cabinet and top positions in the government services? How could there be dominance of a particular caste in states and at the Centre as well? How was the monopoly of a particular caste established, especially in states like Bihar and Uttar Pradesh, when a leader of particular caste became Chief Minister, all positions like Speaker of the Assembly, Chief Secretary, Director General of Police and Chairman of State Public Service Commission were occupied by people of the same caste? More than half of the people of the same caste became members of the ministerial cabinet. Through nominations, people belonging to some special caste were given priority for some important posts. Everybody was watching all this with their own eyes. But all this used to be done in the name of eligibility.

After many years the youth of lower castes and backward castes started asking the question that how come the selectors found people eligible only from amongst their own caste? Aren't there any eligible people in the other castes? Today the leaders of lower castes and backward caste want to follow the same policy. They also give the same old bad logic, that so far whoever got the opportunity, they all tried to see the eligibility, capability and talent in their own caste; if they do the same thing, what is so wrong in it? Are these privileges of caste only for feudalists, wealthy and prosperous classes? And for others is it a crime?

To eliminate racism, the caste system has to be eliminated. In India, the root of caste is not food habits, but it is the daughters. The caste system of food habits is almost removed. Nobody asks about the caste of anybody. Everybody eats and drinks together, but at the time of marriage, they give their daughters only in that caste where they were tied down on the basis of birth. Can this be broken? Of course, there are certain exceptions to it. But we know in middle and lower classes, how the people getting married outside their caste are tortured. Can't new rules and new programmes be developed? They can certainly be made. Some points are put forward for a thought.

Intercaste marriages have to be made mandatory for all the public privileges. In agriculture, jobs and businesses, 'one person, one employment' formula should be made into a law, which may enable decentralisation of power and everybody gets employment opportunity. Education system should be developed based on the formula—'king's child and child of a labourer should get same education'. Minimum and maximum income has to be fixed based on the formula 'not less than hundred and not more than thousand'. There should be freedom to earn money, but the policy of putting a cap on expenditure should be implemented. These are some formulae by implementing which a society of equality can be built. The ladder of the caste is standing erect, when that ladder gets cut, then the vision of social harmony and a healthy system can be actualised.

*Navbharat Times, 04 September, 2002*

□

# 36
# Better Light a Candle than Curse Darkness

When politics loses vision and direction, it gets influenced by individuals. When the influence of individuals increases, then the democracy of the party dies down. When democracy is lost in the party, then dictatorship starts showing its influence. Because of this trend the democracy in the country becomes weak.

Before Independence, there was feudal system based on the caste system in India. After that a system based on equality of votes was established in its place. In principle, we have accepted the ideal citizen equality, but in practice we haven't made it a part of our life. The feeling of commitment towards nation is very weak. The basic foundation of personal and social life is totally contrary to the ideal of nation building.

It was told that there is a freedom to vote and equality in every field of life because of which the feeling of equality kept growing strong. Today because of that, the fight for equality in social life has become very strong. Because of votes, the weaker classes of the society and the classes which were neglected in comparison to other classes have got a chance to get closer to power. As politics has become indulgent, so the youngsters are more influenced by trends of indulgence. The feelings of sacrifice and service have not awakened. A person from the lower caste who joined the privileged class, his hunger kept increasing and he was eager to do everything to satisfy his personal desires. It becomes easy to satisfy the desires and selfish interest with power. So the urge to grab power by hook or by crook or be able to stay closer to the circles of power has become intense. Vote has become a main pillar for that. When the chief of feudal system and upper caste fellow had seen that the vote is limiting his rights, then stealing of votes started. When robbing has started, those classes of society slowly woke up and started thinking, why are they stealing the votes? They were feeling incapable of protecting their power through natural and secret voting.

On the other hand, the influence of weaker classes of society was growing over Assembly and Parliament, because of which some progressive laws were made. Because of those laws, the established society got wounded. Votes were getting robbed only because of the wounds and in order to keep their power intact. As there was already monopoly of upper caste and members of the feudal system over the executive, they also became partners in robbing the votes as they also were shaken at this development. A sordid alliance has taken place between legislature and executive. When both of them came together, then the judiciary, which is the basis for truth and justice, also became weak.

To gain monopoly over power, monopoly over politics has become necessary. To have monopoly over politics, it has become necessary to have monopoly over political organisations, after all, political parties only send their candidates to contest in elections. So if there is monopoly over political parties, then they can make whoever they like as candidates for the election.

Till the time there is no candidate to their liking in sharing the power, they can't make the laws to their liking. Today dictatorship has become strong in the democratic system because of this only. Even though listening to the criticism of opposition with patience is the foundation of democracy, yet uprooting the parties criticising them has become the basic thinking of political parties. Those leaders who tend to have a different opinion in their own party and who seeks justice, and demand their share or demand to solve the issues in a democratic manner, those leaders are expelled from the party. They can never have democracy in their personal lives, in their organisation or in the country. Those who can't bring together people of their own party, then how can they keep the people of the country united? The major reason for this is thinking only of the self, doing only for self, living only for self, and drowning the self into the depth of self without caring for society or even for the country. To grab power, they criticise the people in power and the moment they get into power, they stick to the power in such a way that even after death they want to hold on to that.

Because of these ugly trends, attention was shifted away from the problems of weaker classes. These days discussions take place only on immediate problems; to suppress these problems new problems are created, which causes rage. It is easy to create instant rage as it gives instant benefit, but in the long run it causes a great loss to the country and society. It halts discussions on fundamental problems; as long as solutions are not found for fundamental problems, till then the country can't be full of life.

As long as there are privileges, till then the fight for special opportunities continues. Today all the political parties are involved in discussing immediate problems, wasting their time. We don't want leaders but policies. As long as the path is not right, nothing good will come out by following the traveller. The idea of direction will be known when we look at the path rather than the traveller. Today everybody thinks that if the top leaders are happy, their positions will be safe. Top leaders think that if they have the company of visionless, unethical, unprincipled, unidealistic people around them, then they will keep applauding them. Whoever they want, they keep promoting and demoting whosoever they want to.

Today it is very essential to control the seamless and open-ended ambitions of individuals and to strengthen the democratic systems within parties, the government and the country, some strong measures have to be taken. According to me, there should be a discussion on these issues:

- Whoever is the chief of a political party, he/she will not head the government and whoever holds positions in the party organisation will not join the government.

- The selection of candidates will be done by regional and central teams and the decision on who should join the ministerial cabinet also will be taken by the parliamentary board.
- Whether a minister is capable of being in the ministry or not will be decided by the parliamentary board on the basis of his/her performance.
- The government is responsible for implementing the programmes decided by the party and the announcements made in the election manifesto. If the government fails to do so, then the parliamentary board can reshuffle the Cabinet after consultations.
- Parliamentary board should not have more than one member from any one particular caste and the board should have sufficient representation of all sections of the society, including backward castes Harijans, tribals, women and minorities.
- Treating the policy statements and election manifesto prepared by the Janata Party based on the principles and ideals of Gandhi, Lohia and Jai Prakash Narayan to decentralise the political and economic powers during the 1977 elections as the basis, constructive, strong and time-bound programmes should be put in place. Then this question as to who will become the head of the government won't arise. As long as the path is not decided, till then there will always be a doubt whether we will reach the destination or not, even while following a good leader. The question of who is ahead and who is behind arises only when everybody is groping in darkness of visionless and directionless politics. When character, intention, commitment, ideals, principles, intelligence and generosity are neglected, then angst comes out from which the pest of racism takes birth, which destroys the society. Today everybody should get united to think about these serious issues. Writer is the state president of the Janata Party in Bihar.

*Navbharat Times, 29 August, 1988*

□

# 37
## Racism Growing Stronger

All around there is a dissent against racism, but racism is becoming much stronger. Only intellectual discussions are going on. To eliminate racism, a lot of efforts were put in at the level of principles, but still it has not been eliminated. One after the other, many great souls, saints and social reformers have tried to eliminate racism but with no result. Commentaries on scriptures have been written and were studied, but still the roots of racism remain very strong. From Gautam Buddha to Saint Kabir, and from Lord Krishna to Mahatma Gandhi, many people raised their voice against racism but couldn't abolish it. Dr. Ram Manohar Lohia and Pt Deendayal tried to break it in their own way, but couldn't break it. Contrary to their efforts, they were all imprisoned in various castes. It is very easy to change one's religion in this country, but it is not at all easy to change one's caste. History is a witness to it. People from Hindu religion have taken up other religions, but they couldn't get rid of their caste. Even after changing the religion, whatever status they were given in Hindu religion, the same status was given to them even in that new religion. Even after changing the religion, they still belonged to the Scheduled Castes/Tribes and Backward Castes only.

Racism takes birth because of caste. Caste is the by-product of the prevalent caste system. Caste system is determined according to birth. People born in so and so caste are considered to be very eligible. They are considered as scholars, the best, eligible and command respect even if they are idiots and inferior by their actions. People born in a majority society are considered ineligible based on their birth. Those castes which were considered as eligible because of their birth, the responsibility of governance, administration, defence and accounts were given to them, when the country was kept enslaved. Why had it happened? When eligible people were given responsible topmost positions and majority people were separated by saying that they were ineligible, then who was responsible for the slavery? Whoever was responsible, why didn't they accept the responsibility of defeat? It was a tragic irony that they while taking the credit for victory and for defeat they were blaming the common man. Even today the same custom is continuing. In the initial years, immediately after Independence, there was no spread of education among the lower caste and backward castes. That's why their number was negligible in government services. Dr. Ambedkar knew this secret and even Mahatma Gandhi also understood it. Scheduled Castes and Tribes were given administrative and political reservations based on the population, but it was not implemented sincerely. Intentions were not right. Because of the influence of Mahatma Gandhi's ideology and due to pressure and awareness created by Dr. Ambedkar, the formula of reservation was accepted. If there was no reservation not even a single person from lower and backward castes would have become an MLA or an MP. In the initial rounds, the MPs and MLAs of those classes were being used, but slowly as political and social awareness came in them, then they started demanding their rights. Strong and sharp leaders have come up from these classes also.

They started demanding respectful partnership in governance. They didn't like to live on charity. The feeling of self-respect has woken them up. Education started spreading fast. Because of the political partnership of power, their economic conditions improved. Their children could see cities, high schools and colleges. They faced insults in educational institutions. The writer also had a personal experience of this. Other backward castes also if given political and administrative reservations like the lower castes, the shape of India would have been very different today. It hasn't happened so, as whoever has dominated the administrative services and in whose hands the political power was, they were against the backward castes. Majority of the other backward castes are farmers and labourers, marginal farmers and agricultural labourers. They were very weak from the economic point of view but because of their population they were very strong. When the age of Dr. Ram Manohar Lohia came, he gave a formula that OBCs, women, religious minorities, Scheduled Castes and Scheduled Tribes should be given minimum 60 percent reservation in government services, businesses and armed forces. Socialists raised slogans, *"Dr. Lohia bandhe gaanth pichede, pave sou me saath"* (Dr. Lohia united the backward castes and got 60 percent out of a hundred). This had a major impact on states in the heartland of India. Among backward castes of states like UP, Bihar, MP and Maharashtra, there was a wave of awareness and euphoria.

Many leaders have come from the backward castes. It was a fortunate and good thing that many leaders of upper castes were leading this agitation. They worked as a supplementing and affiliated force and they expended themselves to the agitation. But it was so unfortunate that the leaders of backward castes forgot them. Dr. Lohia has given the formula of special opportunities to end the privileges enjoyed by people based on birth. At the time of the elections for the national committee of Sangathit Socialist Party, according to the formula of Lohia if lower caste people didn't get 60 percent representation, then the upper caste members used to vacate their places for the lower castes. The people who resigned were given membership as special invitees. They used to function as patrons and gave guidance, but directly on the stage they used to give opportunities to the backward caste only. If one had seen the Parliament from 1964 to 1968, then one would have known who was Dr. Lohia. He was himself in the Lok Sabha, but on the post of the leader of Parliament, he made leaders from backward caste like Maniram Bagadi, Ramsevak Yadav and Ravi Ray and made them sit in the front row. While answering the questions of journalists, he used to say that even if he sits at the back, his voice can be heard. However, the voice of leaders like Maniram Bagadi, Ramsevak Yadav and Ravi Ray can only be heard when they sit in the front row. That's the reason why he won the hearts of the backward castes.

But on Lohia's vision in Hindi- and Urdu-speaking states of India's heartland, the flag of communism would have been unfurled. Dr. Lohia, by stopping the progress of communism in the heartland of India, protected nationalist, cultural, indigenous, Gandhian and democratic systems. There is a need to know and understand this historic and social truth and facts. As the awareness among lower caste and backward castes increased, the hunger for leadership grew in them accordingly. They started forming organisations. To build the vote banks, everybody started playing their own games. Even lower castes and backward castes started understanding this secret; caste polls among them also started coming up.

The mentality of political parties can be assessed by the shape, structure and magnified influence of the political parties. The great revolutionary Lenin said that the kind of society you want to build, first build an organisation of the same structure. As Kabir said, *'Pandit baanche pothi lekha, Kabira baanche aakhan dekha'* (Learned tells what's written in the scriptures, but Kabir tells what he has seen). To eliminate racism, the caste system has to be eliminated. Even after marrying a Kushwaha, the daughter of Babu Jagjivan Ram remains a Scheduled Caste. The late Indira Gandhi, after marrying a Parsi, still remains a Hindu and a Brahmin. Why does it happen so? In India, the root of caste is not in the food habits but it is in daughters. The caste system in food habits has generally been removed. Nobody asks about the caste of anybody. Everybody eats and drinks together. But at the time of marriage, they give their daughters only in that caste where they are tied down on the basis of birth. Can this be broken? There are some exceptions, but we know in middle and lower classes how the people who get married outside their caste are tortured. Can't new rules and new programmes be developed? They can certainly be made. But the condition is political parties, society and Parliament have to take a vow that they will take strict action on these points:

- Intercaste marriages have to be made mandatory for all government privileges, agriculture, jobs and businesses.

- 'One person, one employment' formula should be made into a law, which may enable decentralisation of power and everybody gets employment opportunity.
- Education system should be developed based on the formula 'king's child and child of a labourer should get same education' because of same education, same education system and same educational institution, people can become equal citizens. Differences will be removed from childhood; if all children study in the school; then the level of education also will rise. System also will be maintained properly. Because of same education, the formula of equal opportunities can be implemented.
- Minimum and maximum income has to be fixed based on the formula, 'not less than hundred and not more than thousand'. There should be freedom to earn money, but the policy of putting a cap on expenditure should be implemented. This will help in saving the capital as this indigenous capital can be used in building the nation.

*Dainik Jagaran, 20 August, 2002*

□

# 38

# The Concluding Year of the Century Forecasts Something

Last year of the century is in currency. This century started way back in 1901. According to numerology, the total comes to 2. It ends in 2000. The sum of it also comes to 2. In these 100 years, what have we done, what have we seen, what have we gained and what have we lost? It is necessary to do this assessment. Through such analysis and review we get to know the facts correctly. As long as we don't get the facts right, we can't know the truth. If we don't know the truth, the future becomes very dark. We had seen the last phase of struggle for freedom from slavery. Struggle had started even much before but the common goal and common awareness could not be formed. Under the leadership of Mahatma Gandhi, common goal and common awareness formed. Under foreign rule, there was no welfare of the country and everybody came together to get rid of foreign rule. Nation had awakened; the whole nation had woken up and the powerful British had to quit the country.

It has been dreamt about bringing life to villages by evolving good programmes and formulating a show of schemes. Farmers in villages were hoping for a good life ahead. English had gone but they left behind their ways of conduct. The bureaucrats, the loyalists of the British, who cooperated with the British to suppress the freedom struggle, remained in their own position even after so many years of Independence. They made an agreement with Gandhi's principles with the ruling system of the British. Principle has been lost, system has become dominant and influential. English-loyal bureaucrats have started making

Englishness very powerful and bureaucracy started ruling over the democracy. Gandhi's photo has been put up, but the ideals, principles, soul and intentions have been murdered. It is called hypocrisy. In India, the hypocritical form of democracy is in practice. Are we able to liberate the democracy of India from this hypocrisy?

In a democratic system, ministers are the rulers. But ministers are only the spokespersons of their ministries. They announce the programmes prepared by bureaucrats. The put curtains over the sins of bureaucrats. The criticism against the ministry is considered as criticism against the minister. Ministers give the answers, but ministers give only those answers that are prepared by the bureaucrats. But the truth is that in most of the cases, ministers keep justifying the facts hidden by the ministries and keep taking the responsibility of others. It is called ministry but they are separate; all ministries put together is called Secretariat. That means, in the group of secretaries, minister becomes the target for criticism. Minister is put in the cage on accusations of corruption but those people who keep moving like a crocodile in the pond of corruption keep enjoying. The minister who wants to turn the power in favour of the weak and poor villagers will be thrown out. It is essential that the minister should be the supporter of privileges, enjoy the comforts and work as a supplementing agent of the system.

This century had witnessed all the isms. It had also seen different power structures and combined power structures too. The bureaucrats and privileged people are eating away more than 90 percent of the nation's income and on top of it; they sit on the chests of people and grind them over. Ninety percent of the nation's income is eaten by bureaucrats and 5 percent of the share is eaten by municipal corporations and legislatures, whereas rest of the people are just living on the remaining 5 percent. This is the actual economic condition. Aren't the ruling party and the government responsible for this? Every day, noises are created in the Parliament to increase the privileges of the privilege-loving groups. Schemes are going on in the name of poor, farmers and villagers; foreign debt is spent in their name like water. But still they don't even get to have 20 percent of that. There are many such schemes in which total 100 percent is spent at top level only. Villagers and farmers are sent to jail for stealing 50 or 100 rupees, whereas people at Secretariat gobble up hundreds and thousands of crores of rupees and sit in respectable positions. Thousands of cases have been lying pending for a long time. The accused in the corruption cases have either retired or even died in a number of cases also, but the file has been stuck in the cycle of corrupt system.

What are the reasons for such a pathetic condition? It is primarily because of the network of bureaucracy spread all over the world. It has been nationalised and globalised. Whoever tries to attack their system will meet an untimely death, but can't shake it even slightly. If the system of Secretariat wants it can change the chair of ministry, but ministry can't change the secretariat. Through the rule of village (*gram-swaraj*), power has to be decentralised, through decentralised dispensation, the responsibility of village and agriculture development should be delegated to Panchayats, to lighten the burden of secretariats. Due to the weight of files, the roofs of secretariat are cracking. Villagers should be made partners in governance. The funds given to MPs and MLAs should directly go to village Panchayats. Panchayat schemes should be formulated and implemented. They should only be given assistance in finance management and technical support.

Schemes should be developed, based on ground reality and practical knowledge. There is a need for localisation of Planning Commission. The prototype of the plans should be developed in villages and should come from bottom to top. Right now plans go from top to bottom. Development tree should grow from the soil towards sky and the water from the sky should reach the roots of that tree. There is a need to develop village plans, district plans, state plans and Central plans based on the ground realities. The bureaucracy of today doesn't have the experience of villages because there is no representation of people from villages in the administrative services of India. People from urban areas and from rich families dominate the Indian administrative system, who can't empathise with the pain of the villagers. How can those who haven't seen directly the problems faced by farmers give solutions to thier problems? You meet people occupying top positions in animal husbandry without having never reared any animals and who don't even know the difference between a cow and buffalo. People who never cultivated green vegetables or any other crop like sugarcane, maize, wheat and rice are making plans for agriculture. They go on foreign tours to know about developing prototypes of plans for India. Villagers have knowledge about the flow of rivers, in what direction the rivers flow in villages, how and why floods come, what should be the route to divert the flood waters and how to remove flood water, etc. but the plans of the schemes are made on paper. On maps, all the rivers look the same. Right now the western Koshi canal is under construction. Let anybody go and investigate it. For good construction, plans should be made by experts. Then only the idea of village rule will be realised.

The battle of Mahabharata is raging all over the world. Slowly, the population of the world is getting divided into two parts. One side consists of modern materialists and scientists, who want to destroy the seeds of natural and ancient wealth through materialistic wealth. They don't like multi-coloured, multi-quality and multi-purpose seeds; they prefer uni-coloured seeds and those seeds which give fruits according to their intelligence. These people by hybridising all seeds and species of the whole world want to destroy their fundamental qualities and shape. On the other side are people who believe in natural wealth, who want to preserve and conserve the natural and ancient wealth. Natural wealth has many qualities; the cycle of crops from seeds and seeds from crops is continuing. Farmers can be the owners of crops and seeds independently. They keep changing the patterns. The people of materialistic wealth want to make all the people in the world into slaves. From their seeds, crops can be grown but seeds can't be made from the crops.

A duel is going on between high-tech and traditional tech. High-tech people through their technology want to destroy all traditional technologies of the world. In every country based on thousands of years of geographical, natural, economic, cultural and social conditions, people have developed their own technologies. In the name of high-tech, attempts are going on to end the traditional technologies based on experience, behaviour, trial and error, and wisdom. It is not only in India, but all the countries of the world are facing the same question. While high-tech is getting globalised and liberalised, the traditional tech is getting homogenised at global level. Some people can be bought with the pressure of the capital, but the eternal and ancient stream of any nation can't be purchased. In the concluding year of the century, everybody should think about it. India's role will be that of a frontrunner. It is a chronic ailment, so the treatment will continue for a long time, the medicine will be very bitter. This battle can only be won with strong determination, temperamental balance, humble approach and balanced talks. All the people let disease grow and all the people spread the poison, but the treatment has to be given by the present time. Past is past but whatever is today, that is the present condition.

*Aaryavarta, Patna, 30 June, 2000*

□

# 39

# Only with the Power of Lord Shiva the Construction of a New Society is Possible

Bihar has been subjected to division; rest of the Bihar is not Bihar anymore. Today central Bihar, north-eastern Bihar and north Bihar are looking separate. Whole of north Bihar is also not united. Jharkhand had to be separated long ago. Though delayed, at least the wish of those people was fulfilled. As per the wish, they got their own state, but they need strong determination, willpower for the development of the state. The business of the people who did politics in the name of Jharkhand has closed down. There is a need to think about how many leaders have worked for the agitation of Jharkhand from the beginning till date and how many have ditched the agitation? Now slogans are raised on the issue that the Chief Minister and the Governor of Jharkhand should be from Adivasi (tribal) community. Scheduled Caste and Tribes have to be differentiated. Whoever is living there for years, they are all tribals. There is a difference between tribals and the domiciles of Jharkhand. Slowly, this fire is also smoldering; it will be stoked further. Who are tribals? What is their identity? Who are real tribals? The fight between fake and original tribals has started already. The fight between Santhal Pargana and Chhota Nagpur has started. Will any good happen to that new state by this fight? What is the mystery behind it? This will be cleared slowly. It was the rule of Lalu over whole of Bihar. With utter arrogance, by beating the chest, Lalu Prasad was ruling the state. All the people who contested the elections against him by forming a front and individually as well, have failed to defeat him. Whether it is helplessness or strong desire to be in power, Congress was with Lalu and it still will be with him. Both of them will be dancing together on the stage of power and will be abusing each other off the stage. The people of indulgence don't break up easily. They know that if they break up, they will be finished. They are experts in abusing each other, fighting amongst themselves and being angry at each other. It is the nature of indulgent people to challenge others on the dais and flatter them in the background. They keep devising new formulae for this. Behaving according to opportunity is the history of indulgent people. It is the same story of the people who go along with them. The poison of racism is spreading all around. Some are made leaders of Yadavs and some others are made leaders of Brahmins. Similarly, different people are made leaders of Bhoomihar, Kushwah, lower castes, backward castes, tribals, minorities and all other castes. All are called racists and everybody keeps challenging others. This has psychological influence. Whenever a person of some caste calls the other person as leader of some caste and as a racist, then naturally the common man gets misguided and starts believing that so and so leader is their saviour and protector, even if that person of their caste is corrupt, characterless, and a persecutor. Whenever anybody gets a chance to select somebody from their caste, then they gather all the bad characters of their caste and assassinate good, talented and eligible people. No racist leader becomes a leader on his own, instead he is made the leader of his caste by the leaders of other castes. The influence of caste on Bihar politics is not an issue of recent times. In the politics of Congress, a fight used to go on between Babu Sri Krishna Singh and Anugrah Singh; to some extent the influence of which can be seen even today in some parts of Bihar. Writer became an MLA in 1967; from then onwards he is a witness to the *chakravyuh* of racism and sufferer of the caste politics.

Yadavs may get elected from any party but it used to be said that they came by the grace of Ramlakhan Babu. Similarly, whichever Rajput or Bhoomihar wins the election, it was said that it was because of Chhote Saheb alias Satyendra Babu and because of late Mahesh Babu. Although the truth is entirely different. In 1967, the Samajwadi (socialist) movement showed its impact. All socialists, overcoming the social, economic hurdles got elected with the support of poor, weak, lower castes and backward castes. The evidence to this was that in 1977 when there was a fight for leadership between Karpoori Thakur and Satyendra Babu, then most of the Rajput MLAs supported Karpoori Thakur. In 1968 when there was a fight for party leadership between late Karpoori Thakur and late B.P. Mandal, on whose name the Mandal Commission became very famous, at that time the majority of Yadav MLAs supported Karpoori Thakur. The writer had to bear the insults in his assembly constituency Kewati, as he supported Karpoori. Very few people had to face such an experience. In the same way, the kind of insults faced by the upper caste socialist leaders in north Bihar, only they knew. They were subjected to such a severe pain that they had to face social boycott. Dr. Vaidnath Jha in Benishatty of Madhubani and Kapil Dev Singh in Patna are alive to narrate those stories. Like that, there were so many leaders who sacrificed everything for this movement of social transformation, but today, they are leading a life of anonymity. In present-day social revolution, there are many such people whose ancestors had insulted the social revolutionaries of that time; it can't be talked about. All lower caste and backward caste people should express their gratitude to those upper caste people who sacrificed their lives for this cause. Many leaders of lower and backward castes are enjoying over the sacrifices of these people while there was not even an iota of their contribution. In those days, the people used to do social and economic revolution to bring equality in the society, whereas today people shout slogans to enjoy power.

Why are there so many extremist and violent incidents taking place in central Bihar? What is the reason for it? Is it only because of social exploitation? Researchers of social science if they analyse the situation based on psychology along with social and economic reasons, then they will get to know the truth. They should conduct a serious investigation on the way elections are conducted in parliamentary constituencies, like Aurangabad, Vikram Ganj, Gaya, Jahanabad and Arrah. When truth gets revealed, the kind of games played during the election, starting from 1952 to 1972, then everybody will be shocked. To know the way opposition used to get suppressed, one has to contact the veteran leaders of that place. With the support of ruling Congress Party, on ground strength and caste protection given by administration, the lower castes, backward castes and poor were suppressed. Many among Ram Ekbal Singh, Ram Avadesh Singh, Tulsi Singh, Ram Sakal Singh, Latafat Hussain, Brijbihari Choudhry, Upendra Verma, Jagdev Prasad, Prof. Rampyare Singh, Avadh Singh, Parashuram Singh, Chandradev Prasad Varma, Mundrika Singh, Sachhidanand Singh and Sarayu Singh are still alive but many more became martyrs. They all belonged to ordinary families. Late Keshav Shastri was born in a Bhoomihar family; ancestors of the writer consider him as the saviour of lower castes and backward castes. But when asked about it, Bhagawati Devi and Eshwar Das have revealed how much they were tortured. They remained as stories about the socialists who were born in upper castes but still lifted the talented people from among the lower and backward castes on their shoulders. During elections how people from weak, poor and backward castes were stopped from casting their vote, their houses were burnt, they were persecuted, they were not allowed to do labour work, their women were ill-treated and harassed barbarically—all this became a narrative which has been lost in history. With the protection of power, votes used to be looted. It is true that political awareness had come much before among the backward castes, who had land and who were in majority. People from Yadav, Kurmi and Kushwaha castes came forward and used to fight, as they had become united. More and more political awareness started coming in them along with social awareness. In Congress, Varichand Patel, Mrs. Sumitra Devi, Sahadev Mahanti, Babu Devsharan Singh, Mungeri Lal, Quayum Ansari and Ramlakhan Yadav, 'the lion of Bihar', by coming together, started uniting all lower caste and backward caste people. Babu Krishna Vallabh Sahay used to give political protection. Year 1966 was considered as the red hot year in the history of Bihar. In Gandhi Maidan along with a conference of Yadavs, a conference of backward castes also was organised.

Sahay inaugurated the conference as the Chief Minister of the state. Everybody climbed on to the same stage and started raising slogans from the stage on how to bring the backward caste people to Patna. Socialists were already heated like the red hot iron and it was further strengthened by the heat generated by Congress. Elections were held in 1967 on an understanding within the opposition and there came a change in power. For the first time, the structure of Bihar Assembly looked different. The youth from lower caste, backward caste and forward class had entered the Assembly. Social transformation had happened. There was a considerable increase in the number of backward castes. Socialists became a part of the government along with communists, Jana Sangh and the party of Raja Kamakhya Narayan Singh. Mahamaya Babu was made the Chief Minister. Why and how Karpooriji was stopped from becoming the Chief Minister was a mysterious story. Karpooriji's leadership had come up. The vision, direction and social philosophy of Dr. Ram Monohar Lohia has totally changed Bihar. Lower castes, backward castes and the poor will never be free from the debt of Ram Manohar Lohia. But it is a tragedy that they all forgot about Dr. Lohia; there are still some people but they are also gradually forgetting him. The way a priest needs some or the other idol, similarly political parties always need name and a photo of some or the other great leader, whether they may have respect towards that person or not.

Today north Bihar is peaceful and vis-á-vis the rest of Bihar, it is still peaceful. Extremism and terrorism are there in some districts of north-western Bihar but not like-central Bihar and Jharkhand areas. Political exploitation is also going on there, but it was not so hard because of social exploitation and the power of land. Since the time there was an attempt to give the hue of caste to politics, there started some tension. There was a time when from Bagah to Kishanganj at least 10, 12 Congress MLAs from Brahmin community used to go to the Assembly, but today only one or two would get to the Assembly. One has to find out the reason for this. There are many such Assembly seats, where starting from 1952 up to 1990, non-Brahmins couldn't win. But today backward castes and Muslims are winning these seats. There is a need to think over this. Democracy will not be stronger if any of the castes is marginalised. Intoxicated by power and with the support of rule of law, if the democratic rights of people are snatched away, sooner or later there will certainly be a rebellion and explosion. All communities, castes and political parties have to learn this lesson.

Today whatever may be the strength of lower castes, backward castes and extremely backward caste, MLAs in the Legislative Council and Assembly, that much representation was not there ever before. This change happened since 1977. Their strength has increased in Lok Sabha and Rajya Sabha because of Bihar and Uttar Pradesh. A study has to be done to find out the reasons by which their strength has increased. In the ministerial cabinet of Bihar, a particular caste used to have one-third strength, lower and backward castes used to have a representation for namesake and the way various things are exhibited in a circus. The way scratches on the stone remain permanent, in a similar fashion, the election of Harlakhi of Madhubani district left a permanent blot on the democratic system. Still north Bihar maintained its peace. For the last five to seven years, some leaders are trying to create unrest in north Bihar. They are doing the politics of weapons with the support of black money, provoking racial fanatics. They are involved in earning money through extortion, contracting and liquor business, due to which they are terrorising people with kidnapping, murders and terrorism. They are getting protection from leaders at national level in the name of caste. They get secret money from different means and use that money to provoke anti-social and unemployed youth of their caste. Mithilanchal is the most peace-loving region. The impact of political fights does not reflect in social life. The kind of tactics used by some external leaders to continue their dominance are going to cause some sort of explosion in Mithilanchal. To take revenge, if all the lower castes, backward castes of Mithilanchal come together and adopt the politics of violence, then Mithilanchal will also burn like central Bihar. The cycle of history gets repeated and continues to do so. *Satyug*, *Tretayug*, *Dwaparayug* and *Kaliyug* keep coming in a cyclic order. Whoever is sleeping will wake up, the slave becomes a freeman, a servant becomes an owner. This has to be accepted naturally. In 1977, the way Karpoori Thakur was insulted, nature is punishing Bihar for that sin. At that time they couldn't accept Karpoori Thakur, a well-educated, humble, scholarly, wise and generous leader from backward caste; today people are forced to accept a leader like Lalu.

At that time if they had accepted him with a natural feeling, then today the situation which they are accepting with fear wouldn't have come. A lot is still remaining in the rest of Bihar. By searching for those remains, their faults have to be refurbished. If the people of central Bihar and Mithilanchal accept the social change, then Bihar will become the path-breaker to the world. They have to choose between Kans and Krishna, Ravan and Valmiki, and Babar and Akbar. All the liberals of the whole society should come together to build a new society. Writer had the experience of suffering in the hands of his own caste and other castes. In 1980, in Darbhanga Lok Sabha election, how I got defeated, I experienced them both.

In 1996, 1998 and 1999, by contesting election from Madhubani, I gained experience of both winning and losing. Author has seen the game of racial, religious and communalism. Lalu was my disciple; today he is a close family relative, still the amount of suffering I experienced under his regime is beyond description. A nation is based on the foundation of courage, bravery, humility, generosity and strong determination. There is a feeling of revenge in the minds of lower caste, backward caste and of course, the poor. They are very angry because of the feeling of revenge. Like Lord Shiva pacified angry Kali, can't we become a corpse for some time?

Only that society can create a new age which is equipped with the power of Shiva to pacify Goddess Kali.

*Aryavarta, Patna, 10 September, 2000*

□

# 40

## The Moving Narrative of a Poor Farmer and Soil

Too many great leaders emerged during the freedom struggle. All of them were talented and capable leaders of their time. The way sun being in the midst of planets and stars while lighting up on its own, lights up the planets and stars around, similarly Mahatma Gandhi used to enlighten all other leaders. Many scholars and learned people coming from the fields of politics, economics, culture, religion, spiritualism, science, literature and psychology used to hang around him all the time along with the experts of legislature. Because of the vision and direction of Gandhi, they all worked very sincerely with full determination and brought freedom to the country with true devotion, dedication and commitment and worked towards building up a new nation. A change in power had come; India got political freedom. Every adult citizen got the right to vote. India was supposed to set its direction based on socialist ideology, but an illusion had crept in that. Other ideologies started showing their influence on indigenousness. Political activists, the soldiers of freedom struggle, workers engaged in various activities at village level and talented people born in ordinary families or those hailing from modest backgrounds were slowly pushed to the margins. The influence of people holding high positions in government services steadily increased. An internal fight began to end the dominance of people who were sincerely connected with Indian values, culture, ideology, principles and traditions. The indigenous were defeated in India at the hands of Indians only, and the Englishness became victorious. Englishness totally influenced the entire administration. Feeling of inferiority and lowliness towards people living and working in villages was created in the minds of people with English mentality. Those English-cultured people started considering them as rulers and the villagers as the ruled and with the feeling of king and the subjects, their mentality became very narrow. They always tried to suppress the rural people. Had Panchayati Raj been established as per the idea of village rule of Mahatma Gandhi, then power would have been devolved from their hands as all administrative powers were in their hands. If the power would have gone into the hands of villagers due to village rule, then the power of top officials would have been divided. Rural people are illiterate, cultureless, weak, meek and ignorant, suffering from such prejudiced opinion how can rulers allow the power to get transferred to the backward and lower caste people who were ruled over since ages? Mughals and British were outsiders. People who worked as slaves to outsiders, how can they bow in front of their own country people? According to them, it is better to be slaves of outsiders than being slaves to rural, lower caste, backward caste, poor and week indigenous people. While villagers and farmers only protected the Indian culture, values and traditions and religion, political slavery was accepted by the rural people out of compulsion, but they didn't accept cultural slavery. They had accepted the Mughals and the British as their rulers but they didn't accept to sit next to them and eat together. Because of the caste system, the scavengers and 'doms' were considered as lowest caste and they used to be kept on the outskirts of villages and banned from taking water from ponds and wells, and were not allowed in the temples. Great were those people and they have to be respected and worshipped, as they bore all the insults and ridicule of the Hindu society, but they didn't accept the slavery of Mughal or British culture. They accepted to eat the leftovers of the Hindu society, but they didn't agree to drink water from the Mughals or from the British. Shouldn't Indians bow to their patience and worship them? On the other side, people who were holding high positions, always accepted the slavery of foreign culture, values and power happily. History is a witness to the fact that they surrendered everything for the sake of their post, reputation, respect, wealth and comforts.

In independent India, people, who were considered to be illiterate, ignorant, uneducated, bucolic and uncultured, were absorbed by indigenous as well as traditional professions. The family grew bigger of the people who used to live by engaging themselves in small and petty trades and their businesses also grew in the same proportion. The farmlands of farmers kept dividing, still they didn't give up their farming. They didn't go bankrupt; they didn't go to anybody seeking to acquire their business or farming. They didn't go begging to foreign or Indian company. They were full of zeal and they still are and they will remain so in future too. They have self-respect and they will be so in future too. In spite of all this, they are still illiterate, ignorant countrymen.

There was a craze for nationalisation. By colluding, through surreptitious dealings and through tie-ups, they started the process of acquisition. Its management was given to retired officers, IAS officers and great scholars and intellectuals. Public sector undertakings were established. Slogans were raised and hopes were aroused. The map of heaven was drawn. That was a time, when everybody was fascinated by Pt. Nehru. Everybody became crazy over slogans of socialism, communism and liberalism. The management was given to so-called rationalists. Great scholars had occupied all high positions of governance, administration and management, etc. but whatever happened isn't hidden from anyone. All public sector undertakings ran into losses. The condition of undertakings run on government grants is very serious. Who ate up the grant money? Where did the knowledge of management go? Who looted those assets? Who is responsible for this? Today all those units are being handed over to private people. The bureaucrats, who are very proud of their intelligence, education, skills, expertise, experience, capability and administrative management, should be asked as to why did such a situation arise? What is the reason? What happened to all those undertakings which were given grants? Most of the undertakings were already under the management of private people. They became sick; that's why they were taken over by government. But there was no improvement in their condition. Who is responsible for this? Scholars were sitting in high positions of management. The leaders of labour unions are supporters of socialist and communist principles. Are those leaders of labour unions not responsible for this sorry situation? The economic policy of the country had gone wrong at the time of Independence only. By nationalisation, all favoured officers were given high posts in those undertakings. After retirement, they were encouraged politically. By establishing various institutions such as commissions, societies, trusts, etc., they were appointed to take independent decisions related to management. They were allowed to go on foreign tours. They started going on foreign tours on the pretext of participating in conferences, to learn and gain experience, for training, to understand process of management, establishment, etc. The amount spent in the management of these undertakings was many times higher than the amount spent on management of private sector units. Government took over the banks. Ruling party handed over the treasury of banks to the capitalists dedicated to the nation. As long as banks were under private sector, till then how much money of the private got lost? How many scandals happened after nationalisation? How much money was owed by which industrial house? An alliance was struck between king, businessman and bureaucrats and the three started looting together. Who doesn't know the criteria followed to appoint officers in high posts in public undertakings? Public might remember the scandal of Nagar; by favouring them, all their favourite people used to be given appointments. These questions have to be put to those people who are playing the role of opposition. How much money was owed to farmers and the poor and how much money was owed by big industrial houses? Are these managers not responsible for the debts? Politicians are getting imprisoned for scandals of 100 and 200 crores, but the people who gobble up lakhs of crores are getting protected by various means.

There is no need to listen to the story of the journey from Pt. Nehru to Manmohan Singh. A process has been started under a well-hatched conspiracy. In the name of socialism, public sector undertakings were established because once they fail, then doors can be opened to foreign investors. Dr. Lohia used to say that the first Prime Minister of independent India was the last Viceroy of British rule. Why was an open invitation given to foreign investors in India and who gave it? All conspiring bureaucrats have established either direct or indirect contact with foreign companies. Reservation has been implemented in all government departments and undertakings and its proportion keeps increasing. Employment opportunities keep reducing. Reservations will not be implemented in private sector. Whoever is benefited by reservation, their children will be deprived. All the business done through indigenous and traditional technology is in the hands of lower castes and backward castes. As modernisation kept increasing, their employment was snatched away. The cottage and village industries of villagers were shutting down. In the first round, all big indigenous industrial houses took away the business of villagers. Now their business is snatched away by foreign industrialists. Big fish is swallowing the small fish. Tata had taken away the jobs of lakhs of ironsmiths of villages and Bata had taken away lakhs of jobs of cobblers. Now the clouds of troubles are hovering over them. At that time, so-called Indian intellectuals, economists, industrialists and businessmen were singing in tune with each other; today they are all writhing in pain. This is the brief story of economic journey starting from Nehru to Manmohan Singh, of bureaucrats and their vested interests. There may be a few exceptions. One independent commission should carry out general investigation to find out what are the assets of people working in managerial positions in public sector undertakings. In the name of NRIs, whose money is coming to India? In India, the poor, villagers, farmers and the weak have always loved their motherland and respected it and sacrificed their lives for its protection. Even today, it is the chest of their children that is receiving the bullets.

With their blood, the history of India's sacrifice and accomplishments has been written. Their ancestors had done the same thing since ancient times and they are continuing the same even today.

The rulers of India have to accept this stark reality. It can be done by creating national awareness; government can't do it all alone. Today the accused is acting like a security guard. Creating a web of illusion, in the administrative system, the children of those whom they had favoured are sitting.

Efforts to reform are going on. Along with duel and internal fights, opposition and internal conflicts are continuing. This is Mahabharata.

There is a need to lift the *Gandiva* with direction, vision and determination and without any compassion.

It is essential to understand the truth and facts. This is the compassionate story of village, villagers and the poor.

*Aryavarta, Patna, 21 December, 2000*

□

## 41

# The Great Deception has been Proved Once Again

Who is the sinner—he who steals justice or the one who while searching for justice breaks the glass of obstruction? Currently, this is the question facing India. Instead of 1989 if we review from 1977, the prevalence of deceit, pretentions, tampering and cheating in the ocean of experimental politics can be seen very clearly. There are more discussions on vote of confidence rather than the no-confidence vote. What is the reason for this? Why were the orders to bring the confidence vote given time and again? Government gets dissolved not because of the no-confidence motion brought in by the opposition, rather because of the cheating done by the supporting parties. Why did it happen so? Is this kind of conduct in a democratic system considered right? Attention was not given to the reputation, respect and interest of the nation. By keeping personal reasons and interests above all, defections took place by crossing all the boundaries of rules, ethics, traditions and standards; money and posts have been distributed. Cases were put up in courts which are still going on. People who have voted at personal level by breaking the party discipline were patronised. Knowing all these things, journalists, writers and intellectuals of the country have supported those people and described them as progressive and great. By chanting their names, they have misguided the public. The winds of negative politics divided the voters in the name of caste and community. All sort of wrong things were done to hide their personal corrupt practices. Isn't the public aware of these things? The biggest change had come in 1977; such a huge public agitation didn't take place since 1942. That agitation was against foreign rule, culture, values and administration to get Independence, self-rule, self-reliance, self-respect. The agitation of 1974 was against indulgence, fear and corruption of the indigenous rule. All democratic forces came together to fight against the indigenous dictatorship. Under the leadership of Congress, a non-Congress government was formed. There was influence and pressure from Congress; the Janata Government got divided. Government was dissolved ahead of its term and mid-term elections were held. Congress Party supported the Government of Choudhury Charan Singh. It had given its support in writing to the President; even before the vote of confidence would have taken place on the floor of the house, the Congress Party withdrew its support and Charan Singh's Government couldn't stay. The reasons were curtained. Charan Singh made village-oriented economic policies. Priority was given to agriculture and budgetary allocation was made for that. Inflation was steadied and the prices of daily-use commodities came down and the common man felt some relief. This was not appreciated by the indulgent, corrupt and profit-oriented people, so they brought the government down. Indira Gandhi was arrested and was sent to jail. Charan Singh got her arrested. Indira took him into confidence; ordinary farmers from village trusted her and Janata Party got divided. There was tension even within the party.

Why the Congress Party deceived was an open secret even then the people of the country were misled. The party which deceived through vote of confidence was placed in the seat of power.

In 1990, Congress Party extended its support to Chandrasekhar Government, voted in favour of Chandrasekhar Government during vote of confidence and then, immediately after the budget session, withdrew its support and once again brought down the government. In 1991, mid-term elections were held. Congress formed the government during the rule of Janata Dal also. There were internal tensions; there were trends of dictatorship in Janata Dal and people from within the party were getting insulted. In spite of all this, they didn't reach to the point of separation, until Congress supported the division. Everybody left the Congress and joined the Janata Dal, driven by their personal interests. They enjoyed the power while in Congress and as they didn't get share in power, they left the Congress. It was not the case in 1990.

Chandrasekhar was a socialist and even in Congress he remained an agitator. Some people were kicked out of the Congress, whereas Chandrasekhar kicked Congress and quit. He ventured the risk for the sake of change and left Congress. Whatever happened to Charan Singh, the same thing happened in case of Chandrasekhar also. In 1996, Deve Gowda became the Prime Minister; he also became the target of betrayal. In 1998, for the first time under the leadership of non-Congress leader, a non-Congress government was formed. This government didn't have the support of Congress and Left Front. Congress and Left Front parties were always allies. Congress and Left Front parties always remained partners in sharing of power and comforts but outwardly they kept fighting with each other. Vajpayee Government was betrayed and Congress has a hand in that too. They had a secret alliance with Jayalalitha and she was caught in a pretentious trap. They showed an illusionary alternative that was going to come after the fall of Vajpayee Government. A game of illusion was going on in Hastinapur; this time also the illusion showed its magic. '*Maya mahathagani, hum jaani*' (illusion is a great deceiver, we know that), saint Kabir used to sing this song. The teachings of saints are true always. At the time of voting on vote of confidence, the elusive form of 'Amma' (Jayalalitha) became clear. Even in this also, the game of betrayal was hidden. Jayalalitha was also deceived; she deceived Atalji. In this game of betrayals and counter betrayals, public was deceived. It was the moral responsibility of the people who contested elections together by forming a united front that they shouldn't deceive the leadership. The betrayal done to Atalji was in real sense a betrayal of the public who voted for the candidates of those parties because of Atalji. Left Front and Congress traded various allegations against each other before the elections.

But both of them got united and became partners in bringing down the Vajpayee Government. This was also a betrayal of voters. Laluji supported Congress and Congress supported Lalu. They reciprocated each other during the Bofors and fodder scams. Mulayam Singh didn't cause any internal injury to his voters. In the battle between insiders and outsiders, he didn't support outsiders. Mulayam Singh was also one of those socialist leaders who followed the path shown by Lohia. Prior to the non-Congress strategy of Lohia, he followed the strategy of equal distance. In spite of this in comparison to Jana Sangh, he used to consider Congress as more communal and dangerous. He used to consider Congress as poisonous as a two-tongued snake. He used to compare it with a powerful enemy and a weak enemy. If he had to choose between the Congress and Jana Sangh, he would have preferred to go with Jana Sangh rather than Congress. When it came to nationalism and language, then he used to be more close to Jana Sangh. Re-establishing the ubiquitous presence of indigenous elements by eliminating foreign attire, foreign food, foreign language, foreign culture and foreign values was his objective. Putting a foreigner at the helm of the nation, isn't it playing with the country? Mulayam Singh did the same thing which Lohia would have done if he was alive. The pride of the nation and respect will be above power, selfishness, position and money. People will try to protect it even by sacrificing their lives.

Chandrasekhar suffered the betrayal of Congress; given that, what could anybody expect from him. He did according to that only. Nation would remain grateful to both of them. One may or not get power but in the pages of history, these two names will remain indelible.

Congress had betrayed Vallabhbhai Patel after Independence; didn't allow him to be the leader even after having majority. Congress also caused an internal attack to Lal Bahadur Shastri in a foreign country, and the whole world knows what was done to Shastri. What has happened to Charan Singh, Chandrasekhar, Deve Gowda and Gujral was all known to everybody. The question that comes to everybody's mind is as to why Congress always ditched and played false with those leaders coming from an ordinary and humble background? The episode of Choudhury Devi Lal was linked with the episode of Chandrasekhar; the story of a farmer was hidden in this also. The class character of Congress was the character of upper-class feudalist. Where power is considered as a gamble, ethics and righteousness are of no value to them. In this very Hastinapur, Shakuni, who was throwing dice on behalf of Duryodhan, had tricked Yudhishthir to bet on his wife also and won the game. In front of the full court, the daughter-in-law of the clan was disrobed. Congress is busy playing the same game even today. Congress preys upon the farmer and rural leaders through attacks, internal attacks, counter attacks and ditching. For the first time Mulayam Singh could escape being a victim. People who played the game of attack and ditching were caught in their own web of deceit and stratagem. Ashwatthama used the *brahmastra* on Arjun but as it misfired, Ashwatthama had to lose the precious stone off his forehead. Bearing a wound on his forehead, the undying Ashwatthama had to roam around, writhing in pain. By abusing the verdict of the public—the *brahmastra* of democracy, the opposition got scattered. Congress, having lost a guide like Mahatma Gandhi, will roam around in pain while bearing wound of a foreign leader. Congress was coming into power walking over the corpses. After Independence, it came into power over the corpses of Bapu, Lal Bahadur Shastri, Indira Gandhi and Rajiv Gandhi. It came into power while dancing over thousands of corpses in Delhi; Congress can't do anything without a corpse and shroud. Through the strategy of ditching, it was playing the game of dice with power. It was for the first time that the Congress was defeated by its own dice. Many people were involved in this game. Some faces are yet to be unmasked. The public of this great India will certainly unmask all those faces this time around. The sacrifice of thousands of children will not go waste. Self-rule, Indianness, self-dependence and self-reliance will be protected with self-respect. India will wake up and it will undergo the success of transformation as never before.

*Aryavarta, Patna, 07 May, 1999*

□

# 42
# Right Representation Forms the Basis of Equality

The discussion on constituting a commission to decide upon the Constitution picked up momentum. Everybody including jurists, constitutional experts, politicians and journalists started discussing it, arguing in favour and against it. Everybody talked about Constitution and everybody knew the meaning of Constitution. But there is a need to understand the subtle, detailed and spiritual meaning of that word. In Hindi, the word '*sam*' itself has an extensive meaning. The meaning that emerges when all words such as '*samata*', '*samanta*', '*samrasta*', '*samrupata*', '*samadrishti*' and '*samabodh*' are combined, is called '*sham*'. '*Sham vidhan*' means such a legislation in which all these attributes are there. The opposite of '*samata*' (equality) is discrepancy. The discrepancies have to be found out. Equality comes when discrepancies are eliminated. Similarly, discrepancies disappear when equality comes. Discrepancies remain in their subtle form. Inner conflicts and inner battles keep appearing and develop and with time, get destroyed. Once again the process starts. No ideology, vision, principle and ideal remain permanent and eternal. Change is the rule of nature. According to the rule of nature, the cycle of time rotates. According to the cycle of time, all things keep changing. Because of inner battles, internal conflicts crop up. The ocean waves rise and fall and break down by hitting the shores. This order continues. There is water in human body; to get affected by cold and heat is its nature. Desires are like waves which can't be annihilated. Similarly, internal conflicts will be there for all legislatures, but amendments keep happening to keep the feeling of equality intact. If the proportion of spices is more than the quantum of chicken, obviously the natural taste of chicken is lost. In the same way, if the proportion of amendments are more, then it is natural that the roots will be extinct. One amendment will go against the other amendment. The interpreters influenced by the character of their class, mentality, beliefs and ideology have their prejudices and biases. As long as they are affected by some such entities, till then the feeling of equality can't come. A beautiful explanation was given in *Gita* for equality. Can a society of equality be established by the current Constitution? Can all the discrepancies be removed? Will all the citizens be treated equal? Does the feeling of equality there in the fundamental rights? Is there an equal legislation and code of conduct for all citizens? Can a society of equality be built when there are privileges and discretion? Can talent be developed among people availing of special opportunities and reservation? Can social and administrative equality be envisaged when there are economic inequalities? Can political equality come when there are social and administrative inequalities? Can equality come without totality? There is a need to think seriously on all these issues. It is not possible through amendments.

Blind support and blind opposition are the major obstacles in the path of equality. Obstacle is more dangerous than opposition. That is the notion with regard to the Constitution. An amendment was made in its preamble. Why was an amendment made in the preamble which was unanimously accepted by the Constituent Assembly? Was the vote of majority abused for political advantage of the self? Can the goal be achieved just by rewriting some words? One has to act accordingly. Parliament wasn't like a Parliament. *Sansad* (Parliament) is formed by the union of '*san*' and '*sad*'. Now the difference has been erased between '*sad*' and '*asad*'. Is '*sansad*' a '*sansad*' in the real sense? Amendments and restructuring get done. The government doesn't get amended; instead it gets restructured. Similarly, there is a need for restructuring the Constitution. There is no need to panic to restructure the Constitution. It is natural for realists to get panicky, but even so-called socialists and communists who call themselves revolutionists panick; then, who are called realists? When the process of restructuring starts, it will take some time. First of all, a prototype will be made, then there will be discussions over it. Will there be a discussion in the Parliament? Whether the discussion in the Parliament is successful or not, the discussion on the streets will be successful. Today it is essential; it has to be discussed extensively. The Constitution has to be restructured by the institution formed through adult voting. One shouldn't go after the ideas of the cream of the society; cream is hidden in the milk. Cream will come out through churning. The process of social churning is going on, but nobody is ready to drink the poison. There is political, social, administrative, intellectual, educational and economic awareness in the society. All sorts of internal conflicts have come up. There is a need to sort them out; that's why there is a need for restructuring the Constitution.

The fight among the executive, the legislature and the judiciary is at its peak. The fight is causing delay and loss of momentum is seen. There is a need to interpret the relationship between state and the union. There is a need for interpretation of relationship between states, local institutions and Panchayati Raj institutions. There is a need for explanation of decentralisation of administrative rights. There should be a provision to strengthen the lowest unit of administration. Provisions also should be made to ensure the partnership and participation of public in a democracy. Provision is needed to ensure political, administrative and economic decentralisation. By becoming autonomous and self-reliant, educational institutions should perform educational activities; a provision should be made to that effect. Education should not be just for profession; instead it should contribute in building the character of the nation. There should be minimal interference of state and self-governance should be established on the basis of self-rule. There is a need for making provisions in the Constitution to eliminate individualism, dynasty, democratic dictatorship, racism and communalism. The character of all political parties and all such other institutions and organisations should be democratic, and there should be a provision in the Constitution for this. The right to conduct elections should be held regularly for all such institutions and should be given to the Election Commission. Political organisations have to be constituted in a democratic manner; such a provision should be there in the Constitution. Many such ailments are bothering the democratic system and they can't be treated with amendments. That's why there is a need for restructuring the Constitution.

In India, there are many types of citizens—secured, protected, reserved and neglected are four main types of citizens. The dominance and influence of secured and protected is there for a long time. The neglected are struggling to get their identity and dominance. Majority of the country's population is neglected. The minority is ruling over the majority. Villages, villagers and farmers are neglected. Citizens are divided into two classes. One class is dependent and the other is the provider. The ruling of a few people, ruled by few people and for a few people. **The Constitution has to be restructured from the perspective of spirituality, society, culture and religion.** The Constitution should be such as may help in establishing a society of equality. It should bring goodwill and cooperation. It should strengthen nationalism, self-rule, self-governance, self-respect and self-reliance. It should eradicate all discrepancies and bring equality. A system should be in place to ensure that all classes are respected. The people on lower rungs should be able to reach the top naturally without any obstacles. The system should free the nation from the imprisonment of birth, caste and womb. Many talented people today are leading a life of destitution, rejection, negligence and ridicule; they are like diamonds in the rough. They are living in slums, whereas many people because of wealth, privileges, means and by the grace of God, are exerting dominance.

The sun of talent has to be liberated from eclipse. There is no point in taking the name of Chanakya; instead Chanakya has to be searched for. Dandi Swami will be found only when one looks for him. Saint Virjanand only can bring up Saint Dayanand. Samarth Ramdas only can bring Shivaji, Only Ramakrishna Paramahansa has the ability to bring Swami

Vivekananda. Only Gandhi, Lohia and Deendayal can dream of nation's reconstruction. The objective of rebuilding a nation is hidden in the restructuring of the Constitution. There is a need for comprehensive thinking along with restructuring and rebuilding. This is the call of this age and this is the nation's duty.

*Aryavarta, Patna, 14 May, 1998*

□

# 43
# Is it Rright to Tax the Income from Agriculture?

Serious discussions are going on to levy tax on agricultural income. Urban-based economists influenced by prejudices and bias can't understand the importance of agriculture. Attempts are going on to impose the economics of Western countries on India. Lesser the population that depends on agriculture, wealthier will be these countries. So much poorer will be those countries where more people depend on agriculture. Almost unanimous is the opinion of all economists and agriculture experts of the world in this regard. When cottage industries are combined with agriculture, then people dependent on agriculture can prosper. The economic policy will be different in the countries which are focusing on industrial development. People dependent on agriculture don't have work throughout the year. When they are fee from agriculture, they produce through cottage industries. If they engage in cottage industries, they can have income from both sides. All the families are involved in producing things; that's why it is called family industry or cottage industry, where there is a minimum or no labour required from outside. Animal husbandry is an industry linked to agriculture. India's agriculture is animal dependent. Modern and scientific agriculture needs machinery. Because of mechanisation of agriculture where the output has increased, it also increases the cost of production. Machines require diesel, mobil-oil and other equipment, which are produced by big industries. Indian agriculture is becoming dependent on those industries. As long as agriculture used to be done through animals, investment used to be very low. All farm equipment used to be manufacturing in villages only, due to which there used to be cottage industries for manufacturing farm equipment in villages. Gradually, those cottage industries were shut down and all those people engaged in cottage industries became unemployed. Indian economy was based on manual labour. Less land, less investment. More manual labour used to be the basis of that economy. They used to live by working together and consuming together. Gandhi and all others who followed Gandhi have advocated continuance of this policy only. It was the bad luck of the country that people used to take the name of Gandhi and sing praises of Gandhi but policies were made against his principles. The country is experiencing the ills of those policies. Instead of infusing strength in agriculture through industrial profits, attempts are going on to pay for industrial losses through agriculture. In this context, they are planning to tax the agriculture income. This proposal is brought by those economists, who are looting the world through capitalism, feudalism and unconventional business. 55 percent of the total world's income is consumed by 5 percent of Americans. Unfortunately, some Marxists have become victims of this trap of illusion. Marx had talked about proletarians. The Hindi meaning of proletarian is 'the one who lost everything'. Not only loser of wealth but also lost body and mind; hopeless and destitute. It is an irony that the leadership of political parties that talk about proletarians is in the hands of urbanised, upper middle class and connected with industrial labour unions. Indian political class character is feudalistic and urbanised. As a result agriculture and villages are continuously neglected. For this villagers, farmers and labourers are also to be blamed. The ghosts of caste and community ride on the heads. They don't have the unity of class. In all other professions, they are aware of their class; that's why they get united. Even if they belong to different parties, they still fight together for the benefit of their class. Even those who fight for different political parties very sincerely during elections come together to fight for the interest of the class. All political parties keep dividing the farmers. Without having a flag, they can't fight as a group.

This is the reason why people are planning to levy tax on the income of this unorganised, helpless, majority group. When so-called liberals, Marxists and nationalists come together, then the bleak future of farmers, the poor and the villagers can be seen very clearly.

Why is economics called a science? The meaning of science is to analyse the multi-dimensional influence, identify its momentum, direction and structure. **Economics has multi-dimensional effect on human life. That's the reason why economy, righteous duty, desires and liberation are made into sciences.** All education is included in these four. **The political, social, administrative, religious and spiritual form of economics has to be understood.** All aspects, such as how to control it and what are the impacts on country, time, and social and economic conditions have to be given a serious thought. A legislation has to be made to accomplish desires, righteousness and salvation through economy. Why did the need to study it seriously arise in India? Have the people involved in agriculture become so rich that income-tax has to be collected on their income? Have their conditions improved so much that they have become very rich? How is it investigated? Which agency has to investigate? According to the government figures, when the population of income tax-payers has increased, then how come there is a drop in the tax collection amount? The expenditure on collection of tax is increasing. Income-tax officials are considered to be very scrupulous and pious. All those people in India, who earn income through production, by providing services are dishonest and thieves; only income-tax officials are honest and sincere. The amount of authority given to them was not given to any other officer of any other department.

Till three to four generations ago, farmers used to be in a joint family. Now those families have been separated. Still there are some fortunate families which are living as one unit. Who are prosperous peasants and who are called prosperous peasants? Farmers of south Haryana are poorer than the farmers of north Haryana. Commercial and industrial farm houses are different. They have formed research centres. There is no delimitation act on the lands of sugarcane mill-owners. They own hundreds of acres of land. Big industrial houses have farms where farming is done. There too the delimitation act is not applied. In Delhi, in the name of cremation ground, hundreds of acres of land has been given to construct memorials of many political leaders. About 50 percent of the farmers out of a total 70 percent don't have that much land for farming, which is there within the compound of a bungalow of a political leader and an officer. Fifty percent of farmers in the country don't have that much annual savings which an MP or an MLA gets per day or the President and Chief Justice of India gets per day along with other privileges. The amount spent on a day's salary and other privileges of university teachers, almost 40 to 45 percent of farmers are unable to earn that much earning in the whole year. The amount spent on one day's salary of high school and primary school teachers, the families of children studying in those schools fail to have that much amount of annual savings.

Giving a logic that government servants are getting tired of paying income-tax and wealthy peasants are enjoying life is a cruelty and ridiculing of humanity. Government servants get bonus for non-productive labour. What is produced in government offices? What is the benefit of that? Even then bonus is given. How is it justified? When there is inflation, dearness allowance gets increased, but when prices come down, then why is it not reduced? When the prices of agriculture produce are increased, then a big hue and cry is made and it becomes a major news.

*Aryavarta, 23 June, 1999*

□

# 44

# The Incidence of Flood is a Common Phenomenon in Bihar Sans Remedies in Place

Bihar gets flooded every year and it is a usual episode, and people keep suffering from it. In Bihar, the floods don't come in one way only; it has different routes, directions and stages. The floods which come in rivers sometimes come in time and recede back in time, but sometimes they come before time and sometimes untimely. While it destroys many people, still it makes some people very rich. Many homes keep crying, while some homes have a song on their lips. Who can listen to the story of floods? The writer was born in a place in Bihar which is always affected by floods. It is both the maternal and in-law's house of floods. Sometimes floods come and recede away very fast but at other times, it just stays there for almost till the time of Dussehra. May be God also doesn't know how people who are affected by floods live for four to five months. All means of transport are disrupted. Villages are surrounded by flood waters. Only on boats people go out, but boats will not be there for everybody. If there is any small mound, embankment or some highland, all the men of the village go there to attend to Nature's call. The boatmen operate the boats only on scheduled timings in the morning and evening. Who will know the problems of children, women, patients and elders? Youngsters and abled sometimes control their urge for eight to ten hours. Sometimes people relieve their urge by standing in knee-deep waters and mud; sometimes sit on the tree branches and relieve their urge. Due to lack of water, they eat raw and uncooked food. Stomach gets upset but they can't get the medicines. There is no place left to get good sleep. Newly-wed brides will have a hell of a life; pregnant ladies with full-term pregnancy sometimes die during labour itself and even newborns also die. There is no land available to cremate or bury the dead. The corpses without shrouds are given away to flood waters. It may appear that narration of the writer is full of lies but the reality is much more horrifying. Officers and politicians living in grand mansions may not even understand their plight, but only those who experience and who endure the hardships will realise what it is to live in floods.

There is no solitary type of floods in Bihar; there is a story hidden in the floods of Bihar. In the face of the flood of corruption, natural floods are very small. In the flood of corruption, murders, kidnappings and plundering floods of the whole world get mingled. In the flood of racism, communalism and smuggling, floods of whole cosmos get drowned. Even God can't get to the bottom of these floods. Bihar, drowned in the floods of indulgence, doesn't even know what the floods of rain are like? People drowned in floods are called upon to reach Gandhi Maidan of Patna. Election Commission is telling them to cast their vote. Election Commission is helpless whether people are in a position to go to polling booths or not, whether election officers could reach the polling station or not, whether ballot papers and ballot boxes reach the polling booths or not, whether voters are alive or dead to cast votes, they have to conduct the elections as per the fake interpretation of the Constitution. Because of elections a major flood of corruption is in the offing. Roads get repaired; mud is not going to be available anywhere; it will be brought from outside. Bricks will be carried out of kilns, boats will be arranged, in the name of election management. Crores of rupees go into corruption in flood-affected areas. Rural voters, farmers and labourers are left out. Only with the votes of urban people and roadside scoundrels, the Lok Sabha gets constituted. Villagers, farmers and agriculture labourers are like insects; otherwise also, where is the place for these people in the current system of Parliament. Who is there to bother about them in the political and administrative system? The way *'baba naam kevalam'* and *'hare ke hari naam'* are chanted their names also are chanted. Racial conferences are held for votes' sake, but farmers' conferences or agricultural labourers' conferences are not held. Conferences of minorities and lower castes can be organised for votes but conference of backward classes can't be organised. There are groups of castes, there are many groups in lower castes, even among minorities there are many castes. Many conferences are being held for these castes also. There are many castes in backward classes also and conference are taking place for these castes but not even a single conference is organised for the entire backward class. In Patna, every day such conferences are taking place. There is no room left on the wall to paste the posters; they are pasting posters over posters. New political parties are being founded. The way new shoots come out of bamboo during rains, in the same manner new shoots are coming out of various political parties. This is also a kind of flood which is going to be very dangerous as it will bring a lot of destruction. Money is required to organise these rallies, and the money is collected by government officers, contractors, businessmen, MLAs, MPs and people who smuggle goods from quota. All this burden has to be borne by villagers, farmers, minorities, weak, meek of the society and labourers. Because of elections at the time of floods, there is a flood of conferences also. The howls and cries of flood victims get drowned in the flood of elections. Just for a short time, the floods of rain make the ground even by covering the high and low areas of the ground. By making the ground even, it brings equality, however short the duration may be. But these caste conferences bring the floods of fury and rage of discrepancies, hatred and destruction. The society is burning in that rage and whole of Bihar is wriggling in those flames.

The whole of Bihar is drowned in the floods of indulgence, fear, corruption and hunger. There is a race going on to make caste leaders. Politicians who are promoting racism and racial fanatics are accusing the other leaders as racists from stage. By showing false dreams to the unemployed youth of their respective caste, they are making them violent. There is shortage of water but liquor flows in abundance. Meat, alcohol, chicken and all other things that go along with these are needed by them. They need money for this and that much money can't come through natural means. Whatever benefits have come through the MP or MLA funds, they have caused losses many times more to the society. Political volunteers have become contractors and commission agents. They have become sycophants and blind followers of politicians. Their character and nature are lost. As the character changed, their faces also changed. Their only duty is to arrange comforts, means and resources for their leaders. Is it only these people who are taking advantage and who are bad characters, opportunists, cunning and manipulators? Sincere, committed and talented party workers are pushed to the borders. Votes get looted and are looted. For this arms and money is needed, for which some compromises have to be made and whoever is good in doing so is considered a committed volunteer. Isn't this flood of distortion more horrifying than the natural flood? Isn't the influence of distortion more dangerous than the influence of culture? During floods, waters of many small rivers get mixed with the water of a bigger river, similarly during the time of elections, leaders of small castes and groups are very eager to join some big party. Their basis is not service to the community and good conduct; instead it is the strength of their caste backing them. By setting the caste equations, they want to do good for the nation. Administration is divided by caste. For leaders of particular caste, officers of that caste extend all sorts of support. They extend their support to those leaders in proportion to the benefits they are going to get in return.

The relief fund comes from the Centre for flood victims. The fund goes to the blocks via the districts, funds come and go, get distributed, all things are done on paper. One bag of wheat, one bag of bengal gram, two hundred rupees, one saree and one *dhoti* get distributed. It is very difficult to identify, who is receiving and who is distributing. The relief money given to the flood victims comes back in the same route. In Bihar, everything is done through various departments and officers are the main people who do all these things. *'Baap-beta dalal, bail ka daam barah anna.'* There is no hassle of commission in administrative operations. Top people take their commission in the beginning itself. Same procedure is followed till the bottom. This process of keeping their commission had started from the time of Jagannath Mishra's regime. Lalu received this secret from him only. Even today it is continuing. Last year, wherever roads, embankments and safety embankments were broken, they all are still in the same condition. The repair work was stopped in between. All payments were done because soil was eroded in the flood waters, bridges and small culverts were started during the rainy season, diversions were made, all those were washed out in flood waters. Floods come and wash away corruption. Floods sanctify all the officers, leaders in power and their sycophants. Hey, leaders of castes, voters, farmers, labourers and the people of Bihar, light the lamps and worship, put flowers, chant slogans of victory to floods which clean up the corrupt. The way a flood brings soil along with it and fills all the ditches and goes away, in the same manner, it covers up with mud, the corruption of all officers, contractors and politicians. People of Bihar and flood-affected of the country hail the Election Commission; reason? Whether you live or die, but in the name of democracy, you should vote even if you are dead. Elections are also a type of floods as it also away a lot of bad deeds. See the floods of Bihar and see the magic of money looting.

*Aryavarta, Patna, 14 July, 1999*

□

# 45

# The Dream of *Ramrajya* will be Fulfilled only with Local Governance

*Ramrajya*, the dream of Mahatma Gandhi, can only be realised through local governance. The objective of self-rule and self-reliance can be achieved only through local governance. Self-respect can be protected through self-rule and self-reliance. Through local governance, villagers, the poor and farmers can be made partners in democracy. The training in democratic system can be obtained through self-ruling of village councils and local institutions. The meaning of Gandhi's *Ramrajya* and local governance meant localisation of power in order to limit it. In a feudalistic society and under the British rule, the administration remained feudalistic only. Because of racism and feudalism, the majority of village population was kept away from power. As a result, they led a hopeless life. They didn't have a sense of belonging to the nation. Nobody was there to bother about them. Because of caste system, majority of people were treated as ineligible, inferior and untouchable. People who performed labour were considered to be lower. Gandhi tried to remove that inferiority feeling from their minds through *Ramrajya* and local governance. He convinced them that in free India, power will be localised. Power means complete decentralisation of all sorts of power including political, economic and administrative power. In a feudalistic system, absolute power rested with the dictator. The basis of dictatorship is individualism. In a decentralised system, everybody has partnership in power. On the basis of cooperation, consensus, goodwill and coordination, governance is done in a collective manner. The basis of collective thinking will be very extensive and because of which there will be momentum in society. Due to momentum, the society gets vitality. In a democracy, if people are full of life, then the system acquires momentum. As the system gets speeded up, development activities also pick up speed. In India, people have become lifeless and the system has become lethargic. Because of lethargy, the dominance of administrators with personal interests has increased. Instead of being the centres of service and welfare, they have become centres of indulgence and luxury. Democracy was turned on its head. India, instead of becoming democratic, has been entangled in the system of systems. The system has become overpowering and dominating. India is caught in the web of the system. The burden of the system has fallen so much over people that it is on the verge of a breakdown. Democracy in India is almost dying. The disciples of Gandhi have assassinated the ideals of Gandhi.

Dr. Lohia, the nationalist thinker of Indian socialism, had visualised a four-pillar governance. His vision was that the entire governance should be erected on four pillars. All four of them should be independent and autonomous. Their rights should be defined and enlisted in the Constitution. The percentage of national income should be divided equally among all four pillars according to the provisions made in the Constitution. There shouldn't be any interference in anybody's rights. The governance, standing on these four pillars, will work autonomously following the provisions and rules defined by the Constitution. Village, district, state and Centre are the four pillars of his conception. More emphasis was given to local governance. Panchayat is the primary school of democracy. If the education at primary school is very good and pupils are taught discipline, then in future students will become responsible citizens. If the foundation at the primary school is weak, then students will remain weak forever. Similarly, in a democratic system, village will be the primary base. Local energy, local consciousness, local feelings and local life can be seen directly in village Panchayats. The life of a nation is in the life in a village. When villages become lifeless, then the momentum of the nation gets lost. The soul of India is in villagers; the soul of villages is in agriculture, the soul of agriculture is in farmers. There is a strong link between villages, farmers, cottage industries and handicrafts. Village Panchayat is a small unit of Parliament. Gandhi had dreamt of self-rule of villages through Panchayats. Lohia tried to give a proper shape to this dream. Ideas are formless; through programmes they can be given a form and shape. Lohia had given concrete shape to Gandhi's ideology. He presented a clear picture of decentralisation of power and governance. When total governance, administration and the whole system stands on these four pillars, then all administrative officers will work under the authority of that particular pillar.

People born in the feudalist society and brought up with caste ego, will never accept to work under their authority. When IAS and IPS officers start working under district heads, then the respect for local culture, local attire, local values and local languages, etc. will grow. Unfortunately, the disciples of Gandhi who kept singing his encomium have now forgotten all about his philosophy. Similarly, the disciples of Lohia, when they got an opportunity to rule, they became indulgent and forgot Lohia's philosophy and started groping in the thick darkness of indulgence, corruption, individualism and racism. In Bihar, one individual was born who was like a diamond in the rough and had potential to be the savoiur of the poor. He was the personification of sacrifice, humility, generosity and penance. He implemented the philosophy of Lohia, but couldn't get time to complete it. He didn't get the total support of society—he was Mahatma Karpoori Thakur.

Deendayal Upadhyaya, the thinker of cultural nationalism and integral humanism philosophy has given a philosophy of social harmony. He suggested worshipping the impoverished as God. He emphasised on decentralisation and told about getting social equality through love and affection. He emphasised to look for diamonds indigenously by internalising that. Local culture is at the root of cultural nationalism. At present in UP, Kalyan Singh the disciple of Deendayal is in power. He started a bold initiative of decentralising the political, administrative and economic powers. This is a movement and a struggle. It is a campaign started against the people with vested interests. The government staff working in Panchayats is brought under Panchayats. The case was taken to the Supreme Court. The Supreme Court in its historical judgement upheld the decision of the state. The head of the block Panchayat should have the right to give confidential reports of all the district officers including Block Development Officer, and block level officers and staff in their character register. Similarly, the character register of all district-level officers including District Collector and all district-level executive officers should be under the control of the chairmen of the district Panchayat. The payment of salary and other allowances of all block-level officers who work in the field should be given in consultation with the head of the village. Kalyan Singh has taken up a major social harmony campaign. Why are the government workers not ready to work under the lower caste and illiterate people? What is the reason for this? Teachers in schools, Panchayat servants and staff, C.I workers, etc., all of them work in Panchayats. Who will supervise them? Wherever they work, if they are under the supervision of people's representatives of that place, then what's wrong in it? How is it going to cause any problem? Author has the experience of being a Panchayat president at village, block and district levels. In the current scenario, the servant rides on the back of the owner. Kalyan Singh has tried to put the owner on a horseback. The MLAs who are opposing Kalyan Singh for this initiative are the patrons of feudalism and racism based on the birth of a person. What is the meaning of social harmony? When discrepancies go away, equality will come. When ground becomes even, then when water is poured on one side and whole ground gets irrigated. Proper irrigation is not possible on an uneven ground. When there are political and administrative discrepancies, then social and economic equality can't be achieved. As long as there is no equality in these aspects, till then cultural equality can't be achieved. Till then, imagining about cultural nationalism is like groping in the dark. Preparations are going on in the country for the battle of righteousness. Delegating rights to Panchayats and empowering farmers is like infusing life in the nation. Today, who all are becoming martyrs in Kargil and also while protecting the borders of the country? When the chest of farmers and villagers gets broadened, then the borders of the country also stay broad. If their chests shrink, the borders also shrink. Kalyan Singh should bring a law to establish a farmers' Panchayat or farmers' Parliament in every district. Officers of the committee of agriculture market, registry office, revenue department and forest department should be brought under farmers' Panchayat. Government servants are called public servants, but they think that they are public rulers rather than being public servants. This is a battle of public rulers versus public servants. It is also certain that the government servants of all castes are against this movement. Villagers and farmers should open their eyes and realise that nothing good is going to happen just by singing praises of Gandhi, Lohia and Deendayal. Their ideals have to be given a concrete shape. All women, lower castes, backward castes, villagers, farmers and artisans have to come together in this struggle. But it is a misfortune of India that the society divided by the caste system is cutting its own limbs and offering them as oblations in the sacred fire. Is this movement for the upliftment of any particular caste? If not, then the rural population of the whole country has to take part in this agitation. Whatever steps have been taken to protect the self-respect and respect of the farmers are worth praising, commendable and should be followed by all. The movement which started at the confluence of Ganges, Yamuna and Saraswati will definitely show its colour.

*Aryavarta, Patna, 28 July, 1999*

□

## 46

# What does Bihar Want?

Mere utterance of Bihar's name causes commotion, tingling and prickling in people. They start comparing the Bihar of earlier times and the current situation in Bihar. At some point of time, Bihar used to be the centre of peace, comfort, harmony, learning and courage. But today the same Bihar has become a synonym with terrorism, lawlessness, violence, vulgarity and arrogance. Where so many great people took birth and gave the message of humanity to the world, today in that place kidnappers, extortionists, criminals and terrorists are roaming without any fear. The place which used to spread the light of spirituality of knowledge and learning, today it is overcast with dark clouds of ignorance and illiteracy. A place where once even parrots used to hold discussions on scriptures, there today people are deprived of basic literacy. Arms and ammunition have taken the place of scriptures. A cache of illegal arms will be available any time. Law and order have become deaf, dumb and blind. Where the socialist and communist revolutions used to echo, today is experiencing the explosions of racism and communalism. Where there used to be continuous struggle against corruption, power, administration and social exploitation, today a fair of sycophancy is going on. Where a continuous ideological battle used to go on between ideals and principles, there a battle of sycophancy is going on between the power-greedy and selfish people. A place which used to have platoons of people working against the power, where eligible, committed, fearless and talented administrative officers used to function, there the population of spurious characters, sycophants and scamsters is continuously increasing. Downfall has taken the place of development. Going on the path of degradation, it is soon going to be destroyed. Deterioration is happening in all fields. After all, why is it happening so? Who is responsible for this downfall? Is there no way of getting out of this quagmire? Is it a gift of a particular caste, community, or a political party or a leader? Without knowing the cause, no ailment can be treated. If the cause is removed, ailment will be cured. That's why there is a need to find out the root cause of the problem and uproot it completely.

Since Independence, Bihar had been on the path of destruction. The court of Delhi needed sycophancy and Bihar was a university of sycophancy. Working in the interest of Bihar was not their duty; their duty was only to stay in power by flattering the Delhi court. Self-respect of Bihar is dead and the leaders of Bihar have killed the soul of Bihar. Earlier there was no social consciousness because of which there was no political consciousness. Social exploitation was going on due to economic disparities. Whoever had power were realists; they didn't need any change. Socialists and communists were the people who wanted change. Communists were agitating to end the class disparities and economic change and class struggle was started because of this and consciousness had come. Because of class struggle, class hatred had increased. Leadership was in the hands of higher castes. Socialists in the initial days used to fight under the wings of Marxists. Gradually, two ideologies have come up on socialists and internal fights have started between Marxists and Gandhians, which resulted in a separate socialist ideology under the leadership of Dr. Lohia and came to be known as the ideology of Indian socialism. A scientific thought was given on the Indian caste system. In Marxian scientific socialism, there was no place for discrepancies in caste system. Only economics was given importance. They felt that social equality can be achieved once economic discrepancies are eliminated. Lohia had given a new dimension to it and brought freshness in the flow of thought. He brought class and caste together. Due to the momentum, caste keeps becoming class in due course of time. When momentum gets lost in the class, it becomes static and becomes a caste. Life means consciousness and inertia is death. As long as the process of caste becoming a class was going on, India remained powerful, but the moment this process stopped, since then inertia had set in the society and India has become poor and weak. This philosophy of Lohia had shaken the lower castes and backward castes of Bihar and brought new consciousness among them. Exploitation of class was getting protection from the castes system. After Independence, power had gone into the hands of those, who has social, economic, administrative and land power. All powers had accumulated at one pace. After getting the power, they became fanatics due to the intoxication of lordship. Feudalists got the protection of power. It is quite easy to think what will happen when the feudalists become dictators and when they get the protection of power? Humanity will not be there; even wild animals also shy away from their cruelty. That's what had happened in Bihar. People of one particular caste claimed monopoly over power in Bihar, though they are fewer in number but still they dominated Bihar. In those days, backwards and lower castes lacked education, wealth and awareness, and they there was no unity amongst them. Where Marxists generated class consciousness through class struggles, the supporters of Lohia, by starting an economic and social revolution, created hunger for social equality. A movement for partnership and participation in power started. Now they don't need partnership and participation power, but the leadership of power.

People who racialised politics thought that their dominance will continue to be there forever, but this was the downfall of politics. In the name of caste, fanatics, criminals, extremists and violent people and corrupt have started coming to the fore. The python of the caste started swallowing all the good people of its own caste. Like a snake, politics also started devouring its own people. Whatever had to happen has happened. Due to politics of caste, politics has been criminalised and crimes have been racialised. Whole society was suffering in the hell of politics, votes were snatched or votes were cast using power. Administration became corrupt and all these misdeeds were done in the name of caste. Hindu fundamentalism strengthened Muslim communalism. Hindu communalists raised the slogans that votes and daughters were being given in the same caste, while Muslim communalists shouted slogans that votes and daughters should be given in the same community. A few people raised these slogans for everything. Ideals, principles and ideology were left out. Each caste started making its own heroes. They started converting the unemployed and weak youth of their caste into gamblers, alcoholics, criminals and corrupt. They needed money for this and started looting the state treasury and looting was institutionalised. Some such agencies have been founded which started looting money in groups. Cooperative societies started converting individual looting into cooperative looting. Various private institutions were founded and started giving government grants to these institutions. Government treasury was looted to please teachers, principals, *maulwis* and government staff. Development was blocked by looting the foreign loans, grants and cooperation. A class of looters was formed which started working beyond caste, community, religion and political party. To strengthen the culture of indulgence, groups of corrupt people were formed. Democracy was dead, whereas groupism, violence, corruption and racism have survived. While belonging to different political parties, they have worked for their own caste. Played the games of opportunism and played internal politics to make the same caste candidate of opposition party get elected by defeating their own party candidate. In spite of all these misdeeds, they were receiving the respect of their own party and society. Did Marx, Gandhi, Lohia and Deendayal ever think of such a society and individuals? All social scientists, economists and researchers should go to Bihar and carry out studies. Whatever is found in Bihar will be found all over the country; whatever is not found in Bihar will not be found anywhere in the country.

The seeds of present are hidden in the past and the seeds of future are hidden in the present. Whatever deterioration and degradation is happening in Bihar, those seeds were hidden in the past. Whoever had sown these seeds in the past, those people were threatened by the plants that germinated from those seeds sown by them. All seeds haven't sprouted yet. Lalu Prasad is the combined photocopy of all those; he is the photocopy of the past. The future can be predicted from this itself. Lalu, who got elected from north Bihar was disappointed by the results of Patna and burst upon the paramilitary forces in north Bihar. Whatever had to happen has happened and whatever shouldn't happen that too happened. Do these politicians have the courage to tell the truth? Do they have the power to fight against the corrupts in the caste and criminals? People who are used to enjoying the comforts of power, position and reputation from people of their caste who are in the government don't hesitate to draw same benefits from the people of opposition party when they come into power. There is a need to liberate Bihar from counter-revolution, counter-violence, reaction and counter-attack. The feeling of nationalism can be strengthened only by creating awareness about social and cultural consciousness. The darkness can be driven away with the strength of righteousness and spirituality. The seeds of hatred can be removed only through cultural cooperation, social harmony, communal goodwill and generosity. There is intensity in speech but there is no affection in the heart. There should be a feeling of affection to have a vision of equality; there should be the courage to lift the weak on one's shoulders. One has to have a liberal vision to bring everybody into the mainstream of nationalism and bring everybody together with respect. For the sake of votes, fundamentalism of racism and communalism has been promoted and made like imperialism. Racial imperialism has become more dangerous than political imperialism. People who talk about culture and values are also bowing to racism. There is a need for nectar to neutralise the effects of poison. While trying to cut the feeling of caste within caste itself, the poison of racism is spreading in the whole society. There is a need for atonement not only by individuals but the entire society. There is need to develop the strength to burn out all the disorders through repentance. There should be strength and determination to structure the organisation and government according to the will of the society. So-called socialists and Marxists have contributed enough to destroy Lalu Prasad and Bihar, because of which they themselves are scattered away and becoming extinct. Whatever they couldn't do that Congress Party has done. A lot of experiments have been done in Bihar. Bihar has seen all isms. Racism is devouring all isms. Sycophants and people who revolve around power are progressing. Bihar has to be liberated from all these things. Bihar is wriggling with intolerable pain for its transformation and crying with internal pain. Explosions are taking place, one after the other. Holi is being played with blood. Bihar is in search of a solution to all these ills. The seeds of all these things are hidden in that soil only and their rejection is also hidden in the same soil. There is a need for people to identify them. The people of Bihar have understood everything. The future will tell what collective efforts are taken by the people of Bihar. Bihar will become the Bihar of love, affection, goodwill, peace and compassion.

*Aryavarta, Patna, 25 April, 1998*

□

# 47
# Bihar was Good but Became Very Bad

Bihar used to be good and it didn't become bad in a day. Leaders have started promoting castes for the sake of vote banks and everything started going down for the worse. Somebody supported corruption a little bit and some others caused a lot of damage to the virtues of Bihar in order to acquire power. Hukmdev Narayan Yadav, who had been a co-partner in the political process of turning the nectar into poison has in a way accepted his crime in the court of *Aryavarta* readers through this article. He said all those things which can be told and there are some untold which can't be told, they can only be understood.

Bihar has been the point of discussion for the past so many years. But from the time Lalu Prasad has come into power, it has been discussed even more. More than Lalu, his blind opponents have made Bihar a topic of discussion. Bihar, suffering from corruption, administrative failure, extremism and terrorism is crying for help. Are all these ills a result of one party's rule for one year or one day? Is one party, one leader and one organisation responsible for this? Are land disputes, economic disparities and class specific struggles the only reason for it? Is racism dissolved in the blood of Bihar politicians? People looking for answers to all these questions are trying to give solutions without looking for the right reasons. If there is racism in Bihar and if people are influenced by it, then why did it send most of the outsiders as MPs? Why did no other state in India get such an opportunity? Not only sent to Parliament but also outsiders were made ministers from the quota in Bihar. Is any other state capable of displaying such generosity and nationality?

How could late Ashok Mehta, late Acharya Kripalani, late Madhu Limaye, George Fernandes, Ravindra Verma, Younis Salami, Sharad Yadav and Indra Kumar Gujral be made representatives of Bihar? Mufti Mohammad Sayeed had come to contest from Bihar, but just by coincidence got defeated. How could famous journalist M.J. Akbar get elected from Bihar? People who accuse have to give answers to these questions. George Fernandes and Ravindra Kumar Verma was given ministerial berths from Bihar quota, while in that same Lok Sabha, in 1977, people like Babu Satyendra Narayan Singh, Shyam Nandan Mishra, late Ramanand Tiwari and late Karpoori Thakur were present from the same party.

### The Tradition of Bihar

Worshipping the national-level talents has been the tradition of Bihar. Can the victory of Ashok Mehta from Bhoomihar stronghold, Acharya Kripalani from Yadav-Rajput stronghold, Madhu Limaye and George Fernandes from Rajput, Yadav and Bhoomihar stronghold and Ravindra Verma from the stronghold of backward be called caste politics? The great leaders of Yadavs were getting elected from Madhepur and Madhopur remained the pole for Yadav politics. But still, Sharad Yadav, who otherwise belongs to Madhya Pradesh and who can never compete with those great leaders of that place, got elected twice from Madhepur and sat in the front row of the Lok Sabha by getting the national leadership. Does it not speak of regionalism, racism and fundamentalism? Late Mahesh Babu, the leader of Bhoomihar, got defeated by Mahamaya Babu. Similarly, Krishnakant Babu, who was considered as the pillar of Bhoomihar, got defeated by Mahamaya Babu in Goraiyya Kothi.

No other state has made so many leaders of different castes into Chief Ministers as did Bihar. Continuously for three terms, Babu Krishna Singh was made the Chief Minister. According to 1991 Census, the population of Bhoomihar was 2.5 to 3 percent of the total population. Is it possible for 3 percent population to make a leader Chief Minister for three terms? Five people of Brahmin community became Chief Ministers in which two are still alive. The population of Brahmins according to the same census was 5 percent. Could five people have become Chief Ministers on the caste strength of 5 percent? Three people from Rajput caste have become Chief Ministers among them one is still alive. Rajputs are 4 to 5 percent of the total population. Three people from Yadav caste have become Chief Ministers among them two have died and one is still alive. Yadavs are 11 percent of total population. Once a Muslim became Chief Minister who is still alive. Muslims are 12 percent of total population. Two times Kamakhyas have become Chief Ministers who are of 1.5 percent of population. Both of them have died. Twice from Scheduled Caste have become Chief Ministers and one was from the caste of cobblers and other was from Dusadh caste. All Scheduled Castes put together are 14 percent in which cobblers and Dusadh are of 5 and 6 percent respectively. Late Bhola Paswan Shastri died and Ramsundar Das is still alive. Once for three days a person from Kushwaha caste became the Chief Minister. Once one person who was very poor, weak and backward among the backward castes became Chief Minister twice and Deputy Chief Minister once; he was late Karpoori Thakur, whose caste has no population in Bihar.

### Facts to be Borne in Mind

Dhanik Lal Mandal, who belonged to the backward caste which has 2 percent population was made the Speaker of the Legislative Assembly. I am recollecting this fact because young politicians, party workers, writers and journalists don't know the history of Bihar properly. In the Sanghathit Socialist Party, which struggled to bring social harmony, had leaders belonging to higher castes in the front row. The kind of insults and ridicule they faced while supporting late Karpoori Thakur in leading the socialist struggle was not even faced by the lower castes and backwards castes. These upper caste leaders who lifted backward caste leaders on their shoulders are to be revered and their debt can never be repaid. People from upper castes were among the communist leaders, who led the struggle of land reforms and proletariat. Even the number of landlords was more than those castes in the struggle.

## Why was this Degradation?

After all, why did it degrade? What was the reason for it? This can be a topic for research. On one side, while class hatred was being spread around, on another side, in order to protect their wealth and political power, caste feelings were getting intensified. Based on capability, eligibility and generosity an individual could reach the peak of political power, but some leaders of inferior level gave it the shape of racist power. Whoever got into power, people of that caste started considering themselves as the ruling caste. The administration got full support from the rule of the ruling caste. The juice which gave happiness, that juice itself turned into poison. In long-term politics, those castes are suffering from the ill-effects of past and they have to face it. In the beginning, the axis of power was Congress Party. The struggle of Bhoomihar and Rajputs was continuing and the Congress politics was divided between these two axes. Then the Brahmin pole came up. Then between Brahmin and Rajput, the fight for political power continued. Both factions started encouraging lower castes, backward castes, women and Muslims of their respective factions. During the same time, Krishna Vallabh Babu formed a front with backward Hindus, Muslims and lower castes. The strength of the numbers went in favour of him and he got into power. Ramlakan Babu, Varishandra Patel, Dev Sharan Singh, Sumitra Devi and Mungeri Lal were brought into the front row. Muslims, Yadavs, Kushwaha, Kurmi and lower castes got a chance to come forward. The backward castes of Hindu society gave respect to Muslim, Quyum Ansari, who wasn't given votes by the upper caste Muslims.

The backward castes within Congress were getting united. At Gandhi Maidan in Patna, under the leadership of Krishna Vallabh Babu, a huge rally of backward classes was organised. At the time of Yadav rally, polarisation of backward caste had started. Around the same period, suppression of politics also started. People who were about to lose power in Congress started hurling fire at Krishna Vallabh Babu. Student agitation had begun; inflation increased. All the opposition fought together. Many students were killed in police shooting. A heavy lathi-charge took place. Karpoori Thakur, Ramanand Tiwari and other socialist and communist leaders were heavily lathi-charged and curfew was imposed. Elections were held in 1967 and all opposition parties fought the elections with an understanding. A change in power had come. Congress people openly worked against Congressmen.

### Yadav-Kurmi-Kushwaha

For the first time in 1967, many MLAs from Yadav, Kurmi and Kushwaha community reached Assembly by winning elections. Many talented and influential leaders from backward castes shone and their reputation grew high among their respective castes. Many among them became deputy Chief Minister, ministers and Speaker of the Assembly. The suppressed had come out, tearing up the thick cover. Backward caste got a proletarian leader. The fight for social and economic equality was intensified. Under the leadership of late Bindeshwar Mandal that rebellion took place and with the support of Congress, they formed the government and the politics of secession and alliances started. Leaving out the principles, only politics of power had started, Congress and opposition, both, joined the race for power. The struggle for economic disparities, administrative corruption and problems of public slowly got weakened. Social struggle for the sake of power intensified and caste politics made its presence felt. In the political churning, where once nectar was released, there poison had come out. When the people who drank nectar started spreading poison, then it spread poison all over.

### Crime and Corruption

Racialisation of politics and criminalisation of caste and corrupting the administration started. During the rule of Jagannath Mishra, the earlier history of steel fodder, and Chirkunda scandals were suppressed but new scandals started getting exposed. What all happened though by the grace of God, 1977 came and a change in ruling power happened. The suppressed class stood up by thumping their chest. The flames of hatred came out in revenge. The flames of extremism, humanity, nobleness and generosity became ash and Lalu Prasad entered during that extremism. Petrol was poured in the burning fire. Whatever fire was ignited by Jagannath Mishra, Lalu expanded that fire. As long as talent was worshipped in the Congress, till then the path was right. When racism, criminalisation, corruption and unethical practices entered in the Congress, then along with Congress, in all other parties, the same thought process started.

People leaving Congress once again started coming into power with the support of non-Congress parties. The strategy of non-Congress ended all ideologies. Blind opposition and blind following are equally dangerous. Non-Congress strategy was started under the leadership of Congress. Jagannath Mishra and Laluji joined hands but the whole society was left divided.

Bihar today is on the verge of explosion. The struggle for caste domination and monopoly is continuing. Not domination but monopoly is wanted; not equality, slavery is wanted. In the name of equality, while one class is spreading hatred, social violence, counter-violence, intensifying the bloody struggle, the other class is searching for slavery in the name of equality and empowerment.

Social equation is not a formless formula; rather it has a form of lifestyle. It comes with practice rather than preaching. It comes with behaviour rather than with ideology. It comes with character rather than with thinking. Somebody should gather noble people.

*Aryavarta, Patna, 02 July, 1997*

□

# 48

# Reservation is not a Solution

Every cultural masses at large tend to look for the seeds of present in the past. People of all countries, societies, races and religions look for the context of events happening at present in the womb of the past. Events keep happening the same way, but place and people keep changing and shape, colour, form and modes keep changing. *Mahabharata* of India is such an epic, which has everything. Characters, good sons and bad sons, everybody is there at one place. You get to see all sorts of warriors like *rathi, adhiradhi, maharadhi* and *saradhi*. Epic *Mahabharata* is eternal and ancient; it has both external and internal stories. It is the story of internal as well as external battles. It enables you to see the opposition, obstacles and internal conflicts, etc. directly. Today's India has entered into that same *Dwaparyug*. In this *Kaliyug*, it appears as if the phase of *Dwapara* is going on. All including dynasty, race, society, group, community, culture and civilisation are getting divided and disintegrated. Polarisation is happening without any pole. Pole is shifting away and place is getting shifted and place is changing. The difference between ruling party, opposition and agitation are getting erased. Everybody is getting mixed up with each other. The axis of all isms, opinions and paths have been sunk the way the wheel of Karna had sunk in *Mahabharata*. Karna's wheel was sunk in the quagmire formed because of internal conflicts and internal fights. It was the question asked by Karna and he only had to give the answer to that question. The answer to every question is coming back as a more complicated question, which Karna couldn't answer. Being unanswerable can be called losing momentum; losing momentum is both death and destruction. Today's politics have sunk in the quagmire of political parties. Everybody is questioning and nobody is in a position to answer the tough questions that are arising from the answers given by everybody. Saint Kakabhushandi could give the answer, the querist was satisfied by the answer. *Gita* of Mahabharata is the Ganges of knowledge and very sacred. As it has the essence of all texts it is called the Ganges of knowledge. Whether there are questions or answers, everything is there in *Gita*. Querist Arjun and answerer Krishna, both of them stood in the midst of two warring parties where both parties faced each other. Nobody was in opposition to anybody. Both of them had their own vows and determinations. They hadn't come to fight for an alternative. Today in the quagmire of parties, search is on for an alternative. Excited Arjun went on asking complicated questions, one after the other, Lord Krishna went on giving answers with a cool and composed demeanour. In the end he said, "Do you have any questions still left? I have answered all your questions; now do whatever you want to do. Fight if you feel like fighting; if you want to go on whatever path is shown to you, otherwise do whatever you feel like doing. You have to take the decision and you have to walk on the path." Today there is no such composure, courage, bravery, generosity, patience and vastness. It is considered right to pose questions anywhere. Don't ask questions mean don't be curious. Whoever follows with closed eye becomes either Dhritarashtra or Gandhari. Logic is the basis of democracy. Debates, dialogues, seminars, thinking and introspection are considered to be the means for intellectual development. Introspection, self-thinking and self-composure are said to be the sources that grant divinity. When all these sources get dried up, then only quagmire will be left.

A complete brain is required to think comprehensively and in totality. Comprehensive thinking is not possible with a divided mind. When we think about the nation, then attention should be given to all castes, sub-castes, cultures, civilisations, communities, conduct and activities and also all practices. The people who instituted the caste system did a liberal job. They controlled and limited the economic and social rights of the races they defeated. Unlike the other victorious people of the world, they didn't destroy them completely. We have accepted democracy and adult franchise rights but social mentality remains feudalistic. Caste system is a system that strengthens the feudal system; without uprooting it completely it is very difficult to achieve the goals of national unity, integrity and social harmony. Without abolishing privileges, social equality can't be achieved.

Equality can't be achieved without putting an end to privileges. Different types of people are protected, safe, reserved and unsafe but are living together in one country. There is no worry about the future of safe and protected; even reserved are agitating to get the protection and safety. But nobody is paying attention to those who are slaves and unreserved.

Reservation is not a solution. The struggle is actually between special opportunities and privileges. As long as there was no reservation, till then no eligible person came to be seen among lower and backward castes. Today all political parties are seeing eligible people among these castes. Wherever the law is implemented, there are helpless to follow the law. But where the law is not implemented, there once again they can't see any eligible person among those castes. Why don't political parties elect people from lower and backward castes to the topmost posts in their political organisations? When the Constitution gets amended then women will be made contestants in 33 percent of reserved constituencies. They will get eligible women candidates, but who will give them the positions in political organisation on the basis of reservation?

The kind of society we want to build, we have to form such an organisation. Society is the centre of everything. In all fields, people come from the society only. Political parties make candidates for Assembly. Their organisations have to be democratic, transparent, balanced and harmonious. Just a look at the structure of any political organisation should reflect national unity, integrity, generosity, harmony and solidarity. Even an illiterate and ignorant can understand by just looking at the structure.

According the definition of the highest court, reservation can't be more than 50 percent. Those who consider this right then they have to think why there is 60 to 70 percent reservation in some of the south Indian states? Why should it be supported? If it can be so much in south, then why is it illegal to demand the same? Isn't the whole country one? When lower castes are given reservation in promotions, then everybody supports it. Then why this privilege is not given to other backward castes (OBCs)? Why that demand is termed unfair? The basis for reservation should be same everywhere. Based on a policy prepared with a broad perspective reservation, should be implemented with transparency all over the country. It is alright to give reservation at the time of entrance examination, but every time promotion based on reservation is not right from the human perspective. Reservation should not be given only in government offices and elected institutions, instead it should be given in all organisations and institutions, including political organisations.

Making provisions for reservations in education and educational institutions is like posing obstacles in the path of talent and capability. All upper castes have committed the crime of depriving the lower castes of getting education. Today while repeating the same crime through reservation, depriving the talented children belonging to upper caste from getting admission in educational institutions will be a serious offence. All these games are being played out for getting the votes.

Somewhere while the politics of uniting lower castes and forward castes are going on, at other places, attempts are being made to unite lower castes and Muslims. While somebody is becoming a forward caste, at other times somebody is becoming a backward caste. How long this logic of lower caste, backward caste, forward caste and non-forward caste will continue? All these games have to be stopped. Today people of all castes, communities, classes and castes are well aware of their interests and also understand the secret behind the political games played. They know the reason behind the political games of reservation. In the politics of reservation, they are playing the game of reservation politics.

Everybody wants answers to all such questions. For the good of the nation, Indian culture and values, there is a need for cultural nationalism and spiritual equality and humanitarian love as well. If nationality is drenched with the essence of spirituality, then it strengthens the cultural nationalism. India is surrounded and is looking for right answers. It is waiting for the right time.

*Aryavarta, Patna, 02 July, 1997*

□

# 49
# Man Slaughterer are More Callous than Wild Animals

In Bihar, the incidents of human killings keep happening. Sometimes, the wild animals show compassion towards children. But the killers in Bihar are even more callous than wild preying animals. Such incidents have become so regular that people don't even pay attention to them. They kill so gruesomely it appears as if there was no humanity left on earth. Why is this process of killing going on? Who is responsible for this? What can be done to stop this? Solutions to the problem have to be found out. These incidents mostly happen in central Bihar. These murders are spreading to north Bihar also. The situation in south Bihar is also somewhat similar to central Bihar. The economic framework in these three regions of Bihar is different from each other and even caste balance is different from each other. Wherever there is dominance of Bhoomihar and Rajput among upper castes, such incidents keep happening.

Times have changed. *Zamindari* has been a thing of the part. In democracy, it is the rule of votes. Society is lacking citizen consciousness due to lack of education. By coaxing and bribing, illiterate people are made blind followers. Slowly, they are also becoming aware and education is being imparted to them. The children of tribals, lower and backward castes have started attending schools. As there are no employment opportunities, people are migrating to Delhi, Punjab and Haryana and to other cities in the state. They get relief from the suffocating environment of villages and have started breathing fresh air in these big cities. The lure for better food, clothes, houses and other means has increased among them. They have started taking up government jobs; started doing jobs and also businesses. Along with citizen consciousness, they have come to know about self-respect. They understand the value; of vote, because of vote they are getting opportunities to progress in society. Leaders have come up among them. These leaders, to fulfil their selfish motives, started spreading the poison of racism among them. Slowly, the struggle has grown big.

Due to the communist movement, where the land struggle has become very severe, at such a place, thanks to Ram Manohar Lohia, the socialist movement has become very intense. Due to economic and social struggles, political agitation has also become very severe. In 1967, due non-Congress ideology, there was a change in government in which communists and socialists became the major partners. Where socialist leaders, like late Karpoori Thakur, Ramanand Tiwari and Kapildev Singh assumed power, there communist leaders like Indradeep Singh came to power. Jana Sangh and Janata Party of late Kamakhya Narayan Singh was also part of the same government. The talent of late Karpoori Thakur started spreading and reached its peak in 1977. If the talent of Karpoori Thakur didn't get the support of respected Kailashpathi Singh, a leader who was considered to be the main pillar of Jana Sangh in 1967, his talent would have been eclipsed once again as had been the case in 1967. Even after being the leader of the major party within the coalition government, he wasn't allowed to be the Chief Minister. The essence of the story is that in Bihar, due to economic, social, political and ideological struggles, individual awareness had dawned upon the masses. As the political awareness increased among lower and backward castes, their struggle for votes kept intensifying.

Political suppression was less in north Bihar. Fight was going on against social oppression; movement was going on in north Bihar against wearing the scared thread, observing rituals and Brahminism. Leaders of backward castes, like Late Akshyayvrat Roy, Veer Chand Patel, Bhupendra Narayan Mandal and Karpoori Thakur had come from north Bihar. During the time of Jagannath Mishra, north Bihar became the place for power struggle.

The alliance between communists and socialists happened because of racism. Due to insatiable avarice for power in racism, they both came together and led to their separation and of course, got divided into different factions. They became different interpreters and commentators. To fulfil their personal interest and to satisfy their own indulgences, they started making groups and it continued so. *'dil ke tukde hazaar huye, koi yahan gira koi vaha gira'* (the heart is broken into thousand pieces and some fell here and some fell there) has proven true. Even after getting to rule, they couldn't implement land reforms properly.

By raising slogans of distorted land reforms, communists have created unrest among villagers. They started taking commission from the contractors and monthly commission from government officers besides tax from landowners. They have started exploiting worse than *zamindars*. Whoever got trapped in their trap, started losing everything. They lost respect, self-respect, citizen rights, everything. Everybody was living with fear and under terror. The situation of both supporters and opponents was the same. Racial armies were formed and bloody struggles kept happening. Slowly, politics was criminalized. While individualists and communists killed the poor by using them as pawns, on the other hand private armies were fighting in the name of protection of landlords. Landlords were getting robbed both by the extremists and by the protective army of the landlords. Government was robbing in its own way. Whatever grants came for health, education construction of roads, rural development, irrigation and Jawahar Yojana, everything was distributed as in the proverbial story of monkey distribution. All extremists, officers and leaders in power ate away all the money.

Farmers were frustrated with inflation and increased investment in agriculture. They did not get right prices for their crops. All irrigation schemes were incomplete in central and south Bihar. During the time of Krishna Babu and Anugrah Babu, people, because of ignorance and under the influence of racial fanatics, whatever aggression and arrogance was displayed due to the protection they got from the ruling party, poor and innocent people suffered from the ill-effects of those acts.

Telling the story of Lalu Prasad is like licking the dirt with one's own tongue. Today in Bihar, the government is like what happens after crossing the limits of lowliness reached due to the desire for indulgence, greed of dissatisfied mind and unrest of soul. People keep illegal weapons and move with platoons of private army and have become accused in hundreds of crimes. By thrusting arms in the hands of unemployed youth of their caste, they are making them characterless and criminals, thereby spreading the fanatics of racism.

People who follow the leaders and raise slogans are bleeding to death and leaders, walking over their dead bodies, keep shaking hands with each other or partying by spending the secret money. They keep gritting their share from each other; keep having fun. Politicians are responsible for whatever killings are happening; truth will come out at sooner or later.

Whosoever people are worshipping like gods, their demonic form will come out and their crimes will be exposed. Bihar is howling and crying. To reduce the influence of one caste, some other caste is getting encouragement. Politics is dancing like Mahakali. Now to stop the strides of Mahakali, an individual with Lord Shiva's personality is required. The day Bihar turns itself on and gets ready for the battle of righteousness after getting liberated from all illusions that day the direction and state of whole nation will change. Bihar needs a chance to look at itself in the light from within.

*Aryavarta, Patna, 29 December, 1997*

□

# 50
# How Long will this Loot Continue?

The organised class is dominating and influencing the politics of the country. The influence of people with selfish motives is more on the government. Besides being organised and talkative, they are also intellectuals. Being urban-cultured they have influence over media channels. They keep fighting unitedly for their salaries and allowances. They have influence over administration.

People in the government administrative services always keep threatening the government. If the government doesn't listen to their demands, they go on strike. During the strike, they don't get divided into caste, community and ideology. They fight in unison. Different workers' unions come to an understanding and all come together. Organised class for the interest and benefit of their class, forget everything. The way workers of government and non-government sectors are organised, similarly the members of legislature also become an organised class. Members of Assembly and Parliament unitedly keep fighting for their comforts and privileges.

Almost 85 percent of people live in villages; 70 percent are dependent on agriculture. Nobody thinks about their comfort and privileges. The population working in government and non-government services is not more than 5 percent of the total population, which includes members of Legislature, i.e. both Parliament and Assembly and employees of Legislature, etc. Everything is done to bring prosperity in the life of 5 percent population. In democracy, there are two types of representatives, one is appointed and the other is elected. Both appointed and elected are said to be servants of the public. But this is very tragic, surprising and shameful that while serving the servants and representatives, the owner is losing everything including bread, clothes and even a roof over his head. The entire burden is put on those people. Various consumable items are imported from foreign countries, and the homes of those 5 percent are decorated with various conveniences and means. Two types of laws are made; one is for the people of India and the other is for the residents of Bharat.

The real India lives in villages; somebody should conduct a survey or an economic and social science institute do a survey by itself to find out how much diesel and petrol is consumed by agriculture and related activities and publish those truths and facts. Being a farmer, the author knows that petrol is not used for agricultural activities. It can't be said for sure but petrol may be used in agricultural research centres. Less than 0.5 percent of farmers might be using petrol for their private vehicles. Even in that, people coming from other professions also might be included. Vehicles of government and private companies keep running and petrol is consumed like water. The prices of petrol keep increasing and in metros the population of petrol-consuming vehicles keeps increasing. Smoke and noise keep growing. Government vehicles are increasing. The figures for petrol and diesel consumed by the vehicles of Central and State Government in the last 10 years should be made available. The author estimates that the government consumes one-third of the oil which include government departments, semi-government institutions, public sector undertakings, and vehicles of MPs and MLAs.

In 1967, the author became an MLA and at such a time there used to be around 10 to 20 cars in the Vidhan Sabha premises. Even very senior leaders used to go on foot or by rickshaw. Today in the same complex of Vidhan Sabha, space is not available for parking cars. Hardly would there be any MLA who does not have a car. In 1977 when the author came to the Lok Sabha, at that time, where the statue of Bapu is erected today, only a few cars used to be parked there and in the parking space at the back, only 25 to 50 cars used to be there. Today, the parking space has increased 10 times, yet, one doesn't get space to park the car. In the ministry, the vehicles meant for government officers and ministers have gone up. In the ocean of poverty a few islands of wealth are made and grand mansions are built on those islands. Farmers, people of lower classes and lower middle classes are dying; only upper middle class and upper class are enjoying life. On one hand, people are yearning for water and praying to the rain gods for water, on the other hand, a wealthy person is singing the song *'Jhoom barabar jhoom sharabi'*. How did the inflation affect those in power, like rulers, administrators, organised rich class, commission agents, big businessmen, and industrialists? The shops selling consumer items are increasing; luxury items are stacked up. Writer has seen with his own eyes some bathrooms contain so many luxury items that the total assets of one family of lower 20 percent of the population will not be equivalent to those items. The value of petrol consumed by them in one day, a family may not earn that much in one year. Those people who haven't seen such poverty and who were not born in such a society, how can they know this truth? Whoever is born in that society and has experienced that impoverishment also after getting power, forgets all about it. People like Karpoori Thakur and Charan Singh are very rare to remember such things. People who follow the path of Deendayal and Lal Bahadur Shastri are to be seen as exceptions. How is it going to cause any great loss to the country if petrol imports are stopped and all private vehicles are banned? If petrol imports are banned, then the import of all cars that run on petrol will be stopped. If their imports are banned, it will do good to the country. The burden of debt will be reduced; all types of pollution will be reduced. But the problem is how can these 0.5 or one percent people be made angry? Who can make the foreign powers angry? A habit of enjoying by taking debt has been created. Whatever petrol is produced in the country, why can't we spend less than that? If we take such a vow, oil prices will come down drastically. Big cars can be given to ministers and government officers and all other staff should go to offices in them only and in the evening, they should go back home in the same vehicles. Does it reduce their prestige if they travel together? Government vehicles are used carelessly. They are used for family purposes. Government vehicles are used on family occasions like marriages, death ceremonies, etc. Everybody knows it and everybody sees it but nobody wants to talk about it. This is called vested interest. Our thinking is not nationalistic; we are getting sunk in the quagmire of corruption and indulgence culture. The expenditure on vehicles of industrialists and other big officials of the company is borne by the company. But it will necessarily have its cascading effect on others. After all, in the end, this burden falls on the farmers and poor people of the country. How long will this loot continue?

MLAs, MPs and government servants, by making vehement demands and by making a hue and cry, get their salary and allowances hiked. On an average, an MP and an MLA gets around rupees 18000 per month, excluding the expenditure involving facilities like residence, transport, telephone, etc. These apart there are certain privileges and secret sources of income which is separate. Officers like IAS and IPS may get around 25 to 30 thousand rupees per month as salary and allowances. Allowances paid are many times higher than salary. More water in lentil soup. Government servants and staff get pension based on their salary. MLAs and MPs get pension more than their salary. If the salary of an MP is 1500 rupees per month, then the salary of the peon should not be less than 2000 rupees. This is what the Pay Commission says, "If an MP gets 1500 rupees and a peon who works under him gets 2000 rupees, then how is it logical? This is one aspect; there is another aspect to it, knowing which is very surprising as well as it will make one very happy. According to the salary, as per prescribed rules, allowances and pension are given to all government servants. Whereas for people's representatives, there is no proportion between salary and allowances and there are no prescribed rules for pension. Sometimes pension can be four times the salary. Freedom fighters and retired government servants keep receiving the freedom fighters' honorarium and pension respectively even while being members of the Assembly or Parliament. Former members of Parliament and Assembly keep receiving pension from all three sources and sometimes from four sources also. Who must have seen such a blind law and disparity causing law? The expenditure incurred on security is separate. One-third of the reserved forces is engaged in security duties of VIPs. They get railway and bus privileges and also conveyance allowance. They travel by train or bus but claim the car allowance. Visitors who have gone to Central Hall of Parliament must have seen the food facilities, such as meals, hot beverages and cold beverages, milk and milk products available on subsidised rates. Where does one get to eat stomach-full vegetarian meals for six rupees and non-vegetarian meal for 15 rupees? That is not known but it is available in the Parliament. Where does one get two pieces of butter toast for 90 paise and milk coffee for one rupee? If all the poor people of India become MPs or guests of MPs, then they would get to eat the cheapest meals, snacks and other food items. Readers who must have seen the residences of ministers, MLAs, top officials of state governments, businessmen, industrialists in various state capitals, the amount of land which is there in the compound of those residences even that much land is not there with marginal farmers either for farming or for their residence. The amount of land which is there in the compound of all heads of the government departments at district headquarters, that much land is not there with small farmers. As far as Delhi is concerned, it is a different case altogether. The residence of President is almost equal to the whole of a village. India Gate is equal to a Panchayat. Prime Minister's residence is equal to a street. The amount of land on which the residences of ministers, senior MPs, top officials, businessmen and industrialists are built, on that much land thousands of families can live in houses constructed by cooperative housing societies. In those residences of district, state and Central Government, farming is done by spending government money. The produce is taken by the people living in those bungalows. Among the 40 percent farmers, 70 percent farmers don't have land comparable to one such bungalow. Memorials are built on hundreds of acres. This is called social justice and land reform and proletarian revolution—18 acres for one living family and hundreds of acres for the dead. Personal vehicles are run by government's or supporter's petrol, but the car allowance is personal. Commercial discussions take place over telephones and bills are paid by the Assembly or Parliament. As the case may be, air travel is done for personal reasons but fare is borne by the institutions concerned.

Great are the poor farmers, lower castes and backward castes and the proletariat who are bearing the burden of all these expenses. The burden of the privileges of these 5 percent population is borne by the people of low level. When they grow unconscious, then they are given an intoxicating dose of caste, community, religion and sect. The top has become so heavy that the bottom is unable to put up with its weight. It is trembling; nobody can tell when this structure will collapse. When earth fails to carry the weight, then nature causes earthquakes. In the same way, when the burden at the top increases and when bottom fails to carry the weight of expenditure of the top, then internal war or blood revolution takes place. Terrorism pervades all around. There is political lawlessness everywhere. Aggression and indignity is dancing all around. Who bears the brunt of growing oil prices? And on whomsoever it falls, don't they revolt? Left Front and people for social justice are vocally demonstrating their opposition, taking protest marches on to the streets, but enjoying taking a dip in the ocean of bliss while sitting in airconditioned rooms. Double talk, double conduct and double characters and like a two-tongued animal spreading poison in the nation. These have to be eliminated.

Plenty of ailments and variety of reasons—remedies have to be found out. People are suggesting them, but it is unfortunate that nobody has paid attention to them. Now the time has come, in a scenario when awareness is coming in the nation, the whole nation has to think with total consciousness. There are some solutions which can be given a thought. Minimum and maximum income levels have to be fixed; the difference shouldn't be more than 1 : 20. Upper limit on expenditure should be fixed; if expenditure crosses the limit, tax should be levied on it in multiples of the amount spent. There should be equally fixed rules for giving salary, allowances and pension to all those drawing pension from government treasury. Whoever wants to avail can avail. Once retired from IAS, IPS and judiciary services, people shouldn't take up any appointments in any government, semi-government or non-government institutions even if those positions are without salary and should not be on positions of advisors, etc. Age limit should be decided equally for politics and administration, both. There is a continuity in administrative services, whereas in politics it is not there. So taking this point into consideration age limit should be fixed—not more than two terms or 10 years. Nobody should continue to hold the post of Prime Minister or even Chief Minister for that matter. Three terms or not more than 15 years—nobody should hold ministerial berth. No one should contest elections or be a member of any House for more than three terms or 15 years. From Panchayat to Parliament, people should become members of any House within a fixed age limit in different ways. Whoever is in political party or organisation shouldn't be in government. If convicted for corruption or under any such allegation involving moral turpitude, they should be barred for lifetime. All MLAs, MPs and ministers should get equal privileges and privileges like salary, residential and other allowances should be the same. A residential complex should be built for all the ministers and they should live there only. In one vehicle they all should go to their respective offices and come back at the same time in the same vehicle. The expenditure on security will be reduced and it will give convenience to the citizens who call on them. A mandatory condition should be made for all MLAs, MPs and people working in administrative services and using such official vehicles for personal use is to be treated as a malpractice. A model code of conduct should be put in place for all public servants and people in administrative services—whoever fails to follow that will be thrown out for life from those services.

MLAs, MPs and members of any elected institutions should not become members on Board of Directors of any company. If elected and appointed representatives work in cooperation, then social harmony will come automatically. There are resources, means, eligibility, wealth, labour, culture, values and organisations in India; only things lacking are the will to build the nation, ethics and character, dedication and commitment towards nationality and culture. Everybody has to be woken up. By strengthening the bottom, the top has to be made strong. If farmers and villages gain strength, then nation becomes strong automatically. Would all of us like to think over this?

*Aryavarta, Patna, 24 September, 1997*

□

# 51
# Skilled and Capable Human Beings

Only just a few people the world over and particularly in India are secure. A few more people are protected. In the same way, a few people are reserved while a great many more people are unprotected. Those who are secure, they don't have the fear of future as they will be safe somewhere and somehow. System was made in such a way that there won't be any danger to their safety. In ancient India, there used to be a principle of different phases or stages (*ashrama dharma*), in which life was divided into four stages. Each and every individual would lead a life according to that. There is no relaxation of any sort in that—*brahmacharya* (celibacy), *grihasta* (stage of householder), *vanaprastha* (stage of forest dweller), and *sanyasi* (stage of renunciation). Considering the life expectancy to be a 100 years, the age has been divided into four equal parts procedures of conduct, thinking and practices have been prescribed for each of the four stages. Anybody could be a passenger of that path. Everybody has the equal right to get education, knowledge and experience. There were opportunities to acquire power through penance, practice and devotion. That was *Satyug*. An individual was not worshipped by either caste, creed, wealth or on any other basis. Individuals used to be worshipped based on education, knowledge, intelligence and character. The society of equality can be called *Satyug*. In that age, none was safe or unsafe and in the same none was reserved. Everybody was safe and protected. Whole society and rules were run based on the same *ashram dharma*.

This system was distorted when this *ashram* was converted into caste system (*varna ashram*). Brahmin, Kashtriya, Vaishya and Shudra, four castes were evolved. The system was formed on the basis of four means, namely education, power, wealth and service. All the four are important means. It was said that people who got education were Brahmins, who got physical power were Kshatriyas, who got wealth were Vaishyas, and those who sacrificed and served were Shudras. Everybody was given opportunity to go or come into these four compartments. Anybody could become Brahmin, Kshyatriya, Vaishya or Shudra. Brahmin was a position which was given to anybody after acquiring the prescribed eligibility. There used to be momentum; being in motion; inertia never used to set in the society. Everybody was given equal opportunity to rise up in society and because of which everybody used to try to rise up. People used to do penance and practice to become a Brahmin. The stage of studentship was converted into Brahmin. For happiness and prosperity in family life, wealth is needed; wealth is acquired through agriculture and business. Physical power is needed to control those who couldn't put in hard work. To acquire power, they used to do physical and mental labour. Society used to give them protection and they used to offer physical and spiritual services. Servant was also given equal status. In place of *sanyas ashram*, Shudra caste had come. Earlier every individual used to be by himself Brahmin, Kshatriya Vaishya and Shudra; self-reliant and self-dependent. Afterwards they became dependent on others for services, protection and wealth.

With the passage of time, there came divisions in the caste system. Offshoots started coming in Brahmin, Kshatriya, Vaishya and Shudras. On the basis of knowledge and action, two sects formed among Brahmins—those who followed the path of knowledge and those who performed rituals; then offshoots came in those also. Many sects have come in pursuit of knowledge as well as in performing rituals. They used to get positions based on these factors. The same became castes afterwards. *Varna ashram* has become caste system. There were no offshoots in *brahmacharya,* but Brahmins started having offshoots. Offshoots started coming from all the offshoots. Even Kshatriyas were divided; whatever department of protection they got they were given positions accordingly. Based on the position, they started getting the posts. Positions took the shape of clan. Offshoots came in trade, agriculture and animal husbandry. People of these professions were given positions based on that proposition. Based on these positions, castes kept forming. People who were engaged in trade, agriculture and animal husbandry started taking up different businesses and accordingly they started getting positions. Castes such as blacksmith, cobbler, goldsmith, oil maker, cook, potter, etc., came because of their professions. People engaged in a specific profession belonged to one caste. As Kshatriyas and Vaishayas entered *grihasth ashram* many castes formed. When positions and posts were determined by birth, castes system was developed. Economic basis had been lost; the web of caste spread so wide that the whole society got trapped in that. With the objective of acquiring expertise and capability in a particular profession, families of a particular profession continued to pursue the same profession. Professional families have institutions that impart technical knowledge. Experience used to be the basis for capability and expertise. The knowledge gained through experience was considered to be superior in India. Seekers used to gain knowledge through experience. Similarly, in every profession people used to gain knowledge through experience. They used to become famous on the basis of their expertise and capability; their goods used to get sold in villages. Society used to give protection to every professional. All were formed, based on security. They also used to get protection and safety from the society. In this way, based on the place of profession and subtle divisions many classes kept forming. Since the tine activity was linked to birthright, since that time diligence, talent and capability started deteriorating and darkness of ignorance and lack of energy started spreading and worshipping or insulting an individual based on his birth started. Based on birth, they used to get position and post. The whole society was imprisoned because of birth in the prison of 'caste and womb'.

As long as there was *ashram vyavastha,* there was peace in the society and it was well organised. Every individual was a Brahmin, Kshatriya, Vaishya or Shudra. There was no discrimination among human beings. Human qualities were worshipped. Based on gender, human beings were not discriminated as men and women. Everybody was safe and protected by everybody. There was a feeling of equality. There was generosity and goodwill. All were tied by the same string. All were citizens and rulers at the same time. Today in India and in the world as well, eligibility, capability and talent are imprisoned in the hands of a few. They have monopoly over wealth, sources and reign and also over industry and production. As long as there was decentralisation in India, there was peace. Few people by forming into groups and gangs, made themselves secure. People protected by these groups started hailing them. People who got security, protection and privileges started dominating the society. In a democracy, everybody gets an opportunity to be a partner in power. In democracy, there is no room for privileges. Where there is equality and harmony, discrepancies and privileges can't stay. In independent India, where, on one hand, issues like equality, harmony, independence and nationality were picking up fast, poor, weak, neglected and ridiculed people of the society were also rising, on the other. As the lower castes started coming up, they started attacking privileges. The character and mentality of political parties was feudalistic and the privileges acquired because of caste at the time of birth had become very important. The conscious, unconscious and subconscious minds were influenced by vices and the organisation of political parties also became like that only. Because of all these complexes, fights between privileges and special opportunities started. If everybody gets equal opportunities, privileges will go. Secured and protected people may quit their stubbornness. The day this feeling goes away from their minds, that day the fight for special opportunities and reservation would go away. As people who got reservations, unprotected people getting special opportunities began to suffer from counter-violence in India. They want to do injustice. Injustice can't be refurbished by injustice and falsehood can't be refurbished by falsehood. To transform India, justice and battle for righteousness are required and whose seeds are hidden in the womb of ancient India. We have to find modernity in our antiquity. Ever antique and ever modern is called eternal.

The fire of political counter-violence is burning intensely. We have to look for nectar in our antiquity, culture and standards.

We have become both blind believers as well as blind non-believers. Blind non-belief is as dangerous as non-belief. On the one hand, we are running after Western culture with belief and on the other, we have become blind non-believers of ancient Indian culture. We have damaged our face because of imitation. We are running after that culture of indulgence in which our saints, sages and reformists saw seeds of hopelessness. We have become directionless as we have lost our vision. We are trying to find solutions through the ruling power. Individual power, social power, righteous power and spiritual power are considered superior. People who talk about equality start sowing seeds of disparities as they get into power. People who regard Gandhi, forget about Gandhi; people who followed Lohia, have forgotten Lohia. Do the followers of Deendayal remember his principles? Their time of testing is going to come. Ruling power should be combined with power of righteousness, spiritual power and power of ethics. Can we do this with the battle of righteousness? Time has come to think about the duty of the ruler, the duty of wealth and duty of action. When righteousness is put under the control of ruling power, then righteousness becomes impotent and ruling power becomes demonic. When both power of ruling and power of righteousness cooperate with each other, then only a path of welfare will be found. The way *ashram dharma* was converted into *varna ashram* and *varna ashram* has been converted to caste system similarly, democracy was adulterated with individualism, dictatorship, dynasty politics and racism. Democracy can be protected by a dignified personality. Today there should be interest in agitation, affection towards indigenous, respect, pride about Indian culture, civilisation, standards, righteousness and nation. If India gets transformed and is able to remove layers of dirt, then it will shine like a bright sun. It will take the position of universal teacher. Before becoming a guide to the world it has to remove all distortions from within. The real nature will shine once the distortions are removed. Then only the meaning of solidarity will be understood. For this great action, India has to get ready. It requires a battle of righteousness.

*Aryavarta, Patna*

□

## 52
## Need to Overcome the Shortcomings

All over the world, subtle conflicts are appearing among races, religions, gender and economies. The human race has divided the society into different forms on this basis only. As the broad thinking-based humanity is getting shrunk, human heart is also getting shrunk and has started dividing the human communities into small boundaries to give an expansive shape of orderly development, happening. Not only since ancient times, but since time immemorial, 101 great human beings have taken birth. Attempts have continued to give a broad form to human race. To give an expansive and majestic form to human race, the mind and heart of the human being has to be broad and majestic but so far, those efforts have not borne fruit. While on one hand, attempts are going on to bring whole humanity under one righteousness and one organisation, on the other, attempts are going on to divide humanity on the basis of castes, communities, gender, nation and region. This internal battles are going on even today. People who followed the path of love, compassion and sacrifice have always tried to make society very broad, vast and majestic. On the other hand, people with the nature of hatred, violence and indulgence are continuously trying to divide the humanity into small pieces. The fight between these two tendencies is going on continuously. Human groups are fighting with each other but in reality, this is a fight between two tendencies. This is eternal and still continues. People working towards broadness and macrocosm gave the vision of human welfare and universal brotherhood, but on the other hand, people who wanted to break humanity, raise the slogans of welfare and religion. If both sides are talking about righteousness and welfare, then what is the truth? This can be decided by only that person who is unbiased. The unbiased can undertale influential initiatives only when he has ethical, moral, spiritual and physical power with him. If unbiased is weak, then he will be crushed between the two sides.

Today the slogans of human welfare and religion are at their peak. All games are being played in the name of religion. Both sides are defining religion. All are taking the name of God and explaining the form, attributes and types of God. What is true is the topic of investigation. The vision of the both is same, and tendencies also are same. Ideologies of the both are same and the conscience is also same. Their objectives are same and their determination to achieve their objective too is same. When both of them have the same vow, then they can't be alternatives to each other, but the opposition to their determination is considered an alternative. The direction also is same for both sides and the direction is to get power by any means. Two demons, Shumbh and Nishumbh, are fighting to get the beautiful lady called power. As that beautiful lady is abstract, broad and vast, there are a number of people on each side. Whoever wants to enjoy themselves the comforts of power, joins one of these two groups. Some people are in both the parties knowingly, while most people are in their party in an unconscious state, impulsively and in a fit of change. Whoever says that both these parties as cheats and darkness, they will be pushed into the corner. While one is a buffalo dung, the other is cow dung. One is saying cow dung is sacred than buffalo dung; but nobody is listening to the person who is saying that after all both are dung only. If we analyse with this perspective, then it becomes very clear that whoever is shouting the slogan of religion is going on the path of falsehood, because every businessman will promote his goods by claiming that they are the best, even if they are inferior quality goods inside a shining box. This is the age of commercial promotion. Through the channels of advertising, they influence the minds of the people. The minds of people get influenced very fast in the flow of arousing feelings. Today the people fighting in the name of religion, also through these advertising channels, try to prove themselves as upholders of religion. Whatever may be the case, a few people knowingly follow the path of falsehood by raising the slogan of religion and are talking about protecting their religion. But those people who call these people hypocrites also don't know what is religion. Reality is that both the sides are just talking and neither know the nature of religion. Those who consider themselves as interpreters of religion, they also don't know the nature of religion. Whoever knows, they are keeping quiet; even if they want to speak, their voice is suppressed in the cacophony of advertising channels. The way the voice of Yudhishtir was drowned in the sound of Krishna's conch, but at that time, the objective Krishna was different to what it is today.

This is also an issue of subtlety and the ideology of both can be combined mutually very easily. This has to be thought over very seriously. Only one formula is the leader of both sides. All of them are pious no matter who applauds them and becomes partners in acquiring power. All the opponents are sinners. There is no concern about the person's actions, thoughts, colour, creed, lifestyle, etc.; they are pious if they follow them and keep hailing them, even if they had opposed them continuously earlier. In this second, he is an opponent and the next second, he is in the same party; in this second, he is a sinner and the next second, he is very pious. Let alone the flow of Ganges even God himself might take some time to take all these people of falsehood to his abode. But these people are superior to God—just in a second they lift a very inferior person and include him among the people who hail them and associate them with their gang. The leaders of both sides keep meeting over lunch, dinner coffee snacks and what not and at many places to exchange notes. They keep opposing each other just to appear that they are alternatives to each other. May be the *Kalanemi* of Ramayana also would get defeated by these people. He was caught by the great Hanuman, but these people are capable of enchanting even Hanuman by offering him a sweetmeat. They just join hands for the sake of power and go separate ways next second for the sake of principles. Whether it is a Rama temple or Babri mosque, both the sides get divided into so many sides and keep playing games. If that is the thing, then why don't they get separated in the name of Rama and Rahim? The people are shouting slogans that both Rama and Rahim are one; both of them want to maintain the existence of both temple and mosque, while the villains have the chance to continue their games. This game is going on all over the world. This is an auspicious event that the people of Russia have experienced the truth and the person who made it happen, joined in that light of truth. It appears like this is going to happen in all the countries. When the process of disintegration starts, it only stops after reaching its goal. Who are separatists, terrorists and nationalists? They are all Shumbhs and Nishumbhs who are trying to get the beautiful lady called power. Rulers and administrators have encouraged these elements for their selfish interests and now they are blaming those elements. Why do they panic when those people, instead of staying as their supporters, try to acquire power by the strength of those very means? Indians, who swim on the waves of religious feelings, get ditched the most. The interpreters of religion have fled as the chiefs of abbeys who protect the religion also get attracted to the beautiful lady of power. When a saint comes out of the fire of penance, he also needs coolness; instead of looking for that coolness from within, they look for it in the corridors of power. This is also an ancient stream. It is the speciality of Indian philosophy that everybody gets something to justify his argument. They may or may not know in what context that logic was given in the scriptures, but still they keep citing that precedent. Generally, who has that much knowledge to analyse this. Those who can analyse themselves give it a shape of logic by putting it over the edge of misplaced logic. The whole world is caught in this odd situation. Some individual on the basis of spiritual consciousness can become a guide. But in this age of electricity whether he will be proved relevant or influential is anybody's guess.

Today there is a need to put an end to all such tendencies as caste, creed, gender, form, colour, nation, language and region which have caused grave destruction by starting a vigorous dance and continuously drinking the blood of humanity. People who are pursuing this path should proceed with this perspective. Then only the whole of humanity will come under one organisation for the sake of world welfare. Only then the expanded and majestic form will be acquired.

*Aryavarta, Patna, 21 April, 1995*

□

# 53
# Why and What Type of Presidential System?

Once again this discussion has caught the attention that in India, the presidential system of ruling should be implemented. Be it in restaurants, hotels, railway stations or bus stands, everybody is discussing the same issue. People keep discussing the pros and cons of the system, but nobody discusses aspects like why should presidential system, for whose sake, who should implement and how it should be implemented, what is the purpose of such a system, which other countries have such a system, whether there is peace and is it a good system? It is not just about presidential system; according to political experts, whatever ruling systems have been explained by them are existing in some country or the other and their different forms also can be seen. Similarly, whatever economic systems have been described, they are also existing somewhere or the other. It is the fortune of the 20th century that all economic and political systems are existing at the same time. It is also an issue for thinking that why did all these systems fail to strengthen the feelings of peace, compassion, comfort and brotherhood? Why is it happening so?

There will be a formula to run any system. Formula can also be called a secret. System is put in place on the basis of formula. Initiatives are taken based on the system. To manage the initiatives, there will be a process. If the system isn't put according to the formula, the direction, initiatives and processes will not be proper. The formula of democracy is—it is by the people, of the people and for the people—the ruling system.

The administrative system should have been developed, based on this formula. That is the reason why it is said that the democratic ruling system is the best and the most complicated ruling system of the world. It is considered to be the best because in this system, people get the training to rule the country. When public awareness, public consciousness, public cooperation and public participation is not there, the soul of democracy dies. Instead of people, individuals get to be worshipped. That is why democratic India has seen all things like individualism, dynasty, groupism, racism, communalism, lawlessness and dictatorship, etc. Even we have seen corruption and democratic dictatorship. What didn't happen on the strength of majority in the Indian Parliament? This is only a proverb that in a democracy, the opposition is a part of government. Reality is very far from it. Leave alone the opposition, to shut up the opponents in their own party, what all the games they play. Everything, including the people, the schemes, the processes will remain the same; only the system will change. The whole world has to change completely. Cooperation among political, cultural, administrative, social, economic system is called for. There should be harmony and solidarity among them.

The President will be an individual; even today it is people that run the entire machinery. As long as the interest and will of the individual is not controlled and put within limits, no system will be successful. In America, there is a provision that a person can't be the President for more than two terms. But for the sake of a particular person, if the provisions are changed, the element of sanctity will be lost. Whosoever we are thinking to be the greatest, highly intelligent and most brilliant, there may be some other person much more talented than this person and might be hiding somewhere. Democracy provides an opportunity, but if the opportunities are stopped, democracy can't have life and momentum. If we make a provision that no person can be a Prime Minister or minister for more than two terms or 10 years, no person can be a member of any institution for more than three terms or 15 years. Institutions, such as Panchayat, local institutions, universities, assembly and Parliament are different units.

No individual can contest in elections for any institution. By getting training in Panchayats, by the time an individual reaches either the Assembly or the Parliament, then harmony, cooperation will be more in his behaviour, thinking and actions. Here when a person assumes some position, he will be there in that post forever. Provisions and legislature are meant to be implemented for a lifetime. It shouldn't be like a person holding a post for two or three terms and then leaves that post for some time and once again comes to take the post for another two or three terms. This kind of explanation promotes individualism, groupism, selfishness, etc. Similarly, there is the issue of age in administrative services. An individual retires after the age of 55 years or 60 years, but in politics there is no age limit. After taking retirement from administrative services, they enter into politics. An individual who has dedicated his entire life to a party, organisation or society is left behind, but a person who enjoyed the privileges, comforts of government service joins politics to enjoy the comfort of power. Volunteers who keep agitating against administration, have to accept the leadership of the administrative officer. Here the whole formula of democracy breaks down and conspiracy comes enters the system. Will the presidential system be able to stop this?

The form of ruling can be seen from the shape of the organisation. Control over organisation should be there so that it can be used to form the government. Congress has set the precedence of having one head for both the government and party organisation. The formula of democracy was broken down. When both government and organisation is under the control of the same individual and his group, then the chance of new talent rising will be lost. No person should hold any position in an organisation for more than two or three terms; then the process of transformation will begin. New people will get the opportunity to lead the organisation. This is not the only question of worry that there will be a danger of holding elections time and again for an Assembly or the Parliament as the ruling party comes into a minority either due the defection of members or due to divisions within the party. This danger will be there and amendment can't be made to the effect to let governments keep changing but the Parliament will run its full term. Whatever is the national policy, that can't be changed. There is no national policy for India; it is the policy of political parties. At the time of freedom struggle, whatever issues we were fighting for, all those issues are slowly getting lost. There is a need for a national policy and consensus on it.

Some people are avoiding a discussion on presidential system, because they doubt the intentions of those people who want to discuss this. They suspect that, people being scared by the increasing strength of lower castes, backward castes, poor and minorities, want to impose the rule of upper castes and capitalists through the presidential system. But what is there to be scared of? Based on adult franchise rights, the President at the Centre and Governors at the state level will be elected. This will incur costs. If MPs and MLAs jointly elect the President and Governors, then also whichever party is in majority, the President and Governors will come from that party only. Even then the point to be thought over is that lower castes, backward castes and minorities fear that, considering the nature of these political parties, they cannot see anything beneficial to them. How to clear their doubts is to be thought over? One more idea is that an election committee should be constituted for this purpose. Village Panchayat, village council, district council, local institutions, university staff, lecturers and members of the Bar Council will be made voters of the electoral council. There can be direct and indirect cooperation also. The process of election can be decided later but first of all, there should be a serious debate on the utility of the presidential system and along with that one has to discuss as to how to make the parliamentary democratic system lively, and make it work in the interests of people. No system can work in the interest of people as long as desires, inclinations, tendencies and nature of individuals are not controlled and set within limits. This needs rules and regulations and if possible, there should be constitutional provisions for that. As long as there is no cooperation among formulae, systems, thoughts and actions, till then nothing can be achieved by changing the system, plans and processes.

*Aryavarta, Patna, 16 May, 1995*

□

# 54

# Need for Land Reforms in the Right Sense

The slogans of land reforms are going on very fervently; government is also promoting very seriously. It is considered that land reforms mean redistributing the land only. The movement of land donation was started by Vinoba Bhave who took the land in donation and distributed it among the landless. An evaluation should be done to assess that during this movement, how much land was given to any institute, how much grant was given by the government, how much did it cost per acre and how much land was good for agriculture, how much land was fallow and how much was waste land? Distribution of land was considered as the only objective of land reforms. Why to talk about socialists and communists, even in Congress, those people who were considered progressive were talking of land distribution in the name of land reforms. There are many among them who don't have any connection with land. They had never gone to the ground, never did farming under different weather conditions like rains, winter and summer. They don't know the problems involved in agriculture. The leaders of political parties never bothered about agriculture. They were discussing their revolution in coffee houses, restaurants and at seminars and conferences. They had this notion that the centralisation of land and the system of *zamindari* was the reason for impoverishment and disparity. This was indeed one reason, but it was not the only reason. In addition to agriculture, many people had other sources of income. They never depended on agriculture for income. Farmers, who do farming on 10, 20, even 50 acres of land couldn't afford to give good clothes, nourishing food to their family or give education and comforts of life to their children. If we do an assessment of the amount of labour the family members put on their farm, it can be said that they are like agricultural labourers working on their own farm. The only difference is that they don't work for others, but their standard of living is equal to that of agricultural labourers. A few farmers in places like Vaishali, Muzaffarpur, Samastipur and Nalanda districts of Bihar and in states like Haryana, Punjab, West Bengal and Uttar Pradesh where they have irrigation system and other means of income may not understand this. The fertility of land is so much that the yield will be more than expectation and agriculture is not dependent on rains. They have water in their hands; they can give water according to the needs of the crop. Land was consolidated before delimitation began. There is a road to get the tractor on to the farm. Farmers have land at one place. There are a greater number of private wells, sufficient supply of electricity and facility of marketing. Where such systems are in place, there are no agitations for land and no land disputes. The politicians of that region were connected with agriculture. Pratap Singh Kairon, Charan Singh, Rao Virendra Singh, Choudhury Devi Lal or Chaudhary Bansi Lal, all were farmers. Even if they are leaders of Jat, Ahir, Gujar, Kurmi, Kushwaha, or Brahmins, Thakur, Bhoomihar, Muslims and Scheduled Castes, still they were all farmers. So they know the pain of farmers. In states like eastern UP, West Bengal, Orissa and Andhra Pradesh land settlement wasn't done. For the development of agriculture, the system like irrigation, electricity wasn't set in place and farm equipment wasn't made available; and farmers were not given any training. Wherever emphasis was given on agricultural development, in all these places land reforms had been done and leaders came up from among farmers. There was no influence of communists in these places. Racial tensions and violent incidents were almost nil. Even if there were some incidents, they were not because of land-related problems. The movement of sharecropping was not there. Where the leaders have come from outside, influenced by the socialism and communism of Europe and Russia, who used to acquire the means of indulgence through politics and business and whose children were in high posts in government, they ran a fake agitation for land reforms. Consolidation of land was left incomplete and it couldn't be completed ever. Red tapism, corruption kept increasing and the benefits were enjoyed by officers and politicians. Irrigation projects became endless pits, the projects went on forever and still remain incomplete. Even before getting water, guest houses and buildings were built. Officers and staff were given appointments on the basis of caste. Whoever came into power he put people of his caste on these posts. Irrigation didn't happen, land was gone, canals lay unused, government money was spent. Ghosts started living in residential complexes, guest houses and in office buildings. Even then, government money was spent. The irrigation of projects of north Gandak and Koshi rivers are proof of this. Irrigation was considered a part of land reform, but no revolution took place. No violent actions were taken against corrupt people. Farmers have been robbed and people of Bihar kept collapsing under the weight of taxes levied because of these projects. The mansions of officers, politicians and contractors were built in cities. Half of the new houses in all cities are a gift of irrigation projects. Nobody stood against these things. One should search for answers to this; all will be found attached to the same tree. They were resting under the branches of the banyan tree of caste and keep resting in future too. If they looked for solutions when treating irrigation projects as part of land reforms, had they constructed sluice gates and small embankments wherever required on small rivulets of north Bihar, farmers would have been happy and prosperous by now. But why didn't it happen so?

Transport, electricity and marketing are also very essential for agriculture. Why didn't they consider this as a part of land reforms? Everybody is aware of the electricity problem. Only villagers know the trouble in reaching electricity up to their village. People living in central and north Bihar or who visit these places would certainly know, but people living in Patna and other places, how could they know? When they get all the supplies such as grain, vegetables, dairy products, *ghee*, butter, oil and other valuable food items free of cost from contractors and officers, then how can they know about market prices? Their foreign-breed cattle are making the white revolution successful by eating fodder free of cost. Their children are surfing in the ocean of milk. They are raising slogans of land reforms; distribute land and snatch land. They were given a piece of land which they couldn't keep; there was no additional land left after delimitation. *Zamindars* kept selling that land at a very low rate, like peanuts. Lower caste and backward caste people kept purchasing that land. The ownership of land changed hands. On paper, *zamindars* were still the owners of that land. Government wants to snatch the land from them, but the reality is that most of the land is under the control of small farmers. Those who purchased the land and are tilling it are also small and marginal farmers. Today you don't get a single boy who has five acres of land. In Bihar when families look for grooms having 10-15 acres of land for their daughters, then three cans of kerosene get burnt. Those who have some extra land, they sell it and invest in business. They have started some other business; migrated to cities. Their children got into high posts. Marxists and IAS officers jointly want to push this peaceful Bihar towards civil war. No voice is raised against inflation, wasteful expenditure, corruption and foreign investment. They don't want this agitation to be strong because most people live in villages and are suffering due to inflation, wasteful expenditure, corruption and foreign investment. They will be made the biggest consumers of consumer goods. Let them not get to see this and let them be engaged in land struggles so that the economic, administrative and political looters get time to loot with ease. When land has already gone into the hands of backwards and they are farming that land already, then what is the meaning of land reform? Right now, being blind, the Government of Bihar, which is caught in the grip of Marxists and might not be understanding this, but in the due course it has to face the consequences of this. It is mistaking the counter-revolution for revolution. What is needed is reforms in agriculture rather than land reforms. The more the land gets divided, the more disastrous it will be. All agriculturists and economists are saying the same thing. Late Charan Singh used to say that farming on a land less than 2.5 acres is disastrous. He discussed in detail all this in his book titled *Bharat ki*

*Bhayavah Arthniti Karan and Nidan* (*India's Horrifying Economic Policy—Reasons and Solutions*). The socialists and communists of Bihar should think about this. Being free from prejudices, they should look for solutions to this problem. The structure, character and nature of all political parties have changed. Observe the flow of times and change the flow of society in accordance with changing times. Delimitation act was made in the name of land reforms. Delimitation of land is delimitation of income. Land can increase the yield only to a certain extent; after that limit the yield will only decrease. This is an eternal rule. There is scope to increase income limitlessly in business and industry. A limit is set for the income of farmers. Limit on the income means limit on expenditure. When limits are set for the income and expenditure of farmers, then why can't it be done for other classes. Politicians, businessmen, industrialists, contractors and officers take the capital of the country to foreign countries. They get different types of discounts and privileges, but farmers remain bounded by the limits. The education and other things of farmer's children will happen only within those limits, whereas children of others have full freedom to develop their personality. One has to run within the boundary of the circle and the other has limitless area to explore. When there is a competition, who will win? The children of farmers lag behind and keep lagging behind forever. If the act of delimitation is made, it should be made in totality. '*Samvidhan*' means equality of law. Today efforts are going on to bring equality using a lopsided law. The slogan of land reforms is incomplete and one sided. Racial fight strengthens racism; it strengthens reactionary forces. It proves the proverbial story of Betaal and the tree. Nation wants to take a new turn; there is a need for comprehensive reforms. Land reforms should be done along with political, economic, administrative, industrial, organisational and character reforms. Then only nationality, harmony, unity, integrity and humanity can be protected. Whole nation has to think about it. Even when we are not here, this nation, culture and land will continue to exist.

*Aryavarta, Patna, 05 September, 1995*

□

# 55
# Criminal Culture in Politics

Here, there and everywhere, discussions on politics keep going on. Politics influences everybody. People are vexed with the dirt and sordid episodes of politics. The general perception about politics is that it has gone into the hands of criminals. What is the root cause of it, nobody thinks about this. The intellectuals of India would love to just discuss. Their discussions are done for the sake of intellectual luxury. Urban and top cultured people try to find solutions through discussions. They try to find a way out at lunch, dinner, coffee and tea gatherings. It is their hobby. This has got its strength from the hotel culture. The people at the top have no idea of what the people at the bottom are thinking about it, what is happening on the ground. They keep assessing the situation of whole nation based on their knowledge about their house and their surroundings. People living in urban slums have TVs and transistors in their homes; they have electric bulbs; they keep experiencing the feel of heaven while leading a life of hell. They send their children to school by putting school uniforms on them. Do farmers of the village have this privilege? Even I am a person living in a village, a prosperous village, even then only two or three houses have TV. Crowds gather around to watch *Ramayana* and *Mahabharata*. This I have seen with my own eyes at my house. The village women, who put in lot of hard work, don't have the comfort having a toilet and bathroom in their house. I haven't seen it even in a wealthy state like Haryana when I was working for the party in that state. They go to the fields to attend to Nature's call and bathe at the tubewell of the field. Even then the posh people of cities assume that most of the people have TV and transistors and bathrooms in their houses.

How did crime enter politics? During freedom struggle Mahatma Gandhi made people suffer and they had to face hardships. After burning themselves in fire of struggle, they became *kundan*; meaning thereby there was an alchemy of their person. They kept themselves quite aloof from indulgence. Service to nation and human welfare had become their religion. Leader was Gandhi, who worked those talk, deeds and thoughts. He used to inspire people to go on the path of sacrifice not only through their words and actions but also through their mind. He used to inspire through food and also work. He used to be surrounded by top-class scholars, talented, noble people of the country. He was a bright star which shone like a big sun amidst many stars. Nation got Independence and they came into power; as they started enjoying the comforts of power, slowly all those followers of Gandhi started falling off their principles and ideals. It took a lot of time, their sacrifices of the past, sincerity and the name of Gandhi were stopping them from straying off the path. Still slowly, their downfall kept happening. Capitalists, administrators, corrupt people and businessmen started surrounding them and such people got encouragement from the top positions of power. People who fought against British were pushed to the back and those who supported the British started influencing the people in power. How come it happened? We should think about it. Gandhi was the leader of the freedom movement and struggle. Nehru became leader of struggle and power. As Englishness was dominating the power, we sent away the British, but adopted English and Englishness. This has slowly turned into an attachment and we kept sinking into that quagmire. Whoever had imagined Nehru as their ideal, did they ever try to ask the soul of the nation? Today there are many who are shedding tears over the downfall of the nation. But there are many among them who considered Nehru as their ideal. Opposition to Nehru was considered as opposition to the nation. Who were those people? The same urban and posh intellectuals, who sowed the seeds of racism, communalism and regionslism and those seeds have grown up as plants and are giving fruits. This is a chronic ailment which has become cancerous.

Communalism, corruption, racism and indulgence are at the root of criminalisation of politics. For the sake of power, a compromise has been done with these elements and an alliance has taken place. Starting from Nehru regime till date, whoever has been the Prime Ministers from Congress Party with the exception of Lal Bahadur Shastri, there were scandals in everybody's regime. Mundhada, Nagarpal, Bofors and Harshad Mehta scandals are most famous. Scandals like sugar, steel, cement and oil are hidden in the pages of history. The bricks of Parliament are all witness to these. At that time, socialists under the leadership of Dr. Lohia and communists separately and sometimes jointly used to fight against corruption, and this fight had given rise to many sharp leaders. There was continuity in this episodes of struggles. As a result, every year thousands of youth used to join the agitation.

In jails, they were given training and initiation into the ideals, policies, philosophy and activities; classes used to be conducted. The objective of building a society used to be there in front and workers were trained to achieve that objective. Young generation used to take the place of the old generation which was going away. New leadership and personality used to give new directions. There used to be sharpness in the voice, purity of character, expansiveness in personality, sharpness in intelligence. The fire of struggle could scorch and burn away all kinds of sleaze.

Then came the year 1967, the philosophy of non-Congress. A temporary strategy of greater devil and lesser evil, difference between the greater villain and a smaller villain. To kill the bigger villain to join hands with the smaller villain. Making people come out of Congress partners in power is like following the tradition of making Vibhishan the king to come out of Ravan's house. However, Vibhishan had surrendered to Rama.

He suffered as he was opposed to Ravan's injustice and immorality. However, due to non-Congress strategy, only those people came out of Congress, who didn't get the partnership in power or share in corruption. When they were removed from the partnership of power, they became rebels. They didn't become revolutionaries; rather they chose to become anti-party. They were not against the policies of Congress but angry at the behaviour of its leaders. Along with division of Congress Party, divisions appeared in opposition too. Socialists and communists got separated. As many leaders as those many parties. The time of struggle was over. The time of alliances, breakups and struggle for the sake of power had started. Just to get the majority, defections were promoted. People of principles were pushed to the back and opportunists started coming to the front. This opportunism has given way to criminalisation of politics. The colleagues of struggle used to fight within the party for policies, principles and ideals, which was not tolerated by the leaders in power. As a result, these people were pushed aside. Politics was imprisoned between groups and factions. Even the boundaries of groups and factions started shrinking. Slowly, it narrowed down to individual level. The politics of today is roaming in that *chakravyuh*. In the *Mahabharata* only one Abhimanyu was killed by deceit, but in the politics of today's Hastinapur, every day many Bhishmas, Dronas, Yudhishthirs and Abhimanyus getting killed. To take revenge on colleagues of one's own party, shaking hands with the people in opposition party, breaking up and joining alliances and mismatching union, have given rise to criminal tendencies in politics. A section of people are such that they forms gangs and wield weapons, kidnap people and commit crimes. The other type of people who don't carry weapons, they condemn the people taking up arms, but every day mentally and ideologically keep committing murders. Some kill with swords, some others kill with pen and with the art of behaviour. Every caste is included in this type of people. When the whole society is going down the hill, barring a few exceptions, everybody is included in it. Not only politics and politicians are at a loss of words, surprisingly, the whole society is left with no word.

People are using words like indigenous, self-rule, self-respect and self-dependence without knowing their meaning. When there is no dignity in the power of self, then whatever may be the word that is associated with the word self, exerts no influence. It is like insulting Brahma.

When there is no awareness of *swadharma* (self-righteousness and duty of the self) then how can anybody understand what is *dharma* (duty/righteousness). There is a big difference between self and ego. Ego is considered as self. Arrogance is considered as self-respect. Foreigners are hidden in people who talk about indigenous and strangers are hidden in indigenous people. Melody and intonation appear to be the same, but affection and inner voice are different. I got an opportunity to receive guidance from a political party by staying for a week at a pilgrimage centre in India. The topic of discourse was how foreign spies or Indian secret agents keep working in any institution or organisation. If I see with that perspective and on those parameters, I feel there are foreign spies all around me in some form or the other. What a big drama is going on! The party which opposed Pepsi, when it came into power, that same government gave licence to Pepsi and the same minister later on wrote a letter to the minister of the concerned ministry in the government that followed after it to cancel the licence of Pepsi. The author has a vast experience of socialism, nationalism, communism and non-Congress strategy.

There is no dearth of *Kalanemis* in today's society. Taking the name of Rama, ambassador of *Kalanemi* was posing obstacles in the duty of Rama. It was very difficult to identify and understand him. Only selfless and sincere sage could catch him. Do such people exist today? Somebody is doing the business of teaching and somebody is doing the trade of posts, some are doing the business of organisations, some are doing the business of devotional songs, some are doing the business of meals. If some are indigenous, some are foreigners. Some are on the top, while some are at the bottom. The way their leader and hero is, the volunteer and the organisation will be like that only. Gandhi, Lohia, Deendayal and Patel used to demonstrate their philosophy through their behaviour and actions. Their personality used to make their teachings effective. People by using beautiful words may not be successful in influencing people. To weave a web of words is the work of intellectual indulgence. To generate vibes through words is the work of saints and seekers. The voice from the top is not reaching the bottom. Similarly, the voice from the bottom is not reaching the top. Political drama is prepared at the top and people at the bottom are forced to watch it. When one has to select good from the inferior, then that good also will be highly inferior. Businessmen, writers, journalists, politicians, administrators, intellectuals and labourers are all travellers on the same path.

Institution has been made corrupt legally. MLAs and MPs are given funds every year for development activities. That fund gets utilised as per their recommendations. This has become a major cause for criminalisation of politics. In this, the person who takes the commission belongs to only one organisation. 80 to 90 percent of that fund is eaten away by politicians, bureaucrats and volunteers. Volunteers are also like leaders at their places. A trend of making the beneficiaries work has set in. This is what is happening in West Bengal, and now other states also are following suit. Beneficiary means the party cadre and order-following officer. In that journalists, writers and other professionals also join. The people who sing Kabir's *bhajans* sing, "*Raja se rank chor, sadhu se sant chor, baniya se vyapar chor, satguru shabd ke chor, in choron ke chor na kahiye, unki jo kalam se chorabat hai.*" Everyone irrespective of rank and status is downright corrupt. What is left? It's seen everywhere in every particle. They are facing Krishna; Krishna will give only questions to the questions of Karna. Answers have to be given by Karna only.

Speechless Karna had to bear the pain of piercing arrows at places where it hunt him the most. Principles are made to gain power. Nobody struggles to get power for the sake of principles. The slogan of complete revolution has come and gone. Those people who got power by taking the name of Jai Prakash during their rule only, at Gandhi Maidan, during the celebration of Amrit Mahotsav in Patna, shoes and sandals were hurled at Jai Prakash. The vehicle of the Defence Minister had to go in the reverse direction. They all were divided into hundreds of pieces and sunk into the quagmire of racism, drowned in the ocean of indulgence. They were building the islands of wealth in an ocean of poverty. If they were friends in the morning, by evening they were turning into foes. They were made instant saints and instant demons. Truth and respect ceased to be in existence for all practical purposes. The conscience doesn't accept when listening to the preachings and explanations of those people. Because of deceit, stratagem, cunningness and flattery, it has become the duty in this age to listen to the preachings and explanation of people sitting at the top. This is the reason why politics is Kalpataru and Kaamadhenu. Nation is suffering from fear and lure. This ego only gets hold of them. Writers and journalists are in union and they do the work of creating an image. Those who work hard day and night and try to bring awareness among villagers, farmers and the poor are buried under the soil; their voice is suppressed. In today's politics, adjustments are made. Nobody is projected; nature projects and then adjusts. Politics does adjustment and then pose obstacles in the process of projection. The root of Indian culture, philosophy and ideology is projection; continuously creating new forms from the old and keep worshipping the old. In today's politics, there is ample scope for a new leadership. Our organisations never try to improve the image; instead always try to tamper the image. Attempts keep going on to bring the shining people from other parties. This criminal tendency is more horrifying.

This episode can be prolonged as much as one wishes, but at the end of the day, it can be said that corruption, fear, lure, personal interests, lack of principles, race to grab power, negative ideology, falsehood, heavy top and weak base, no internal democracy, getting scared of holding elections to political organisations, carrying the process of nominations, making all democratic institutions corrupt, increasing the distance between public and the public representatives, promoting foreign capital, trade and promotion, cutting away nationality and culture from the society, creating disrespect towards ancient culture, running after modern indulgent and consumerist culture, conspiring to maintain one's influence over the top, making opportunistic alliances with equal ideologies, adopting corrupt election practices, make administration corrupt the elections, by giving privileges and comforts make journalists write in their favour, to make the top 5 to 10 percent of the population avail all comforts and privileges and exploit the people at the bottom economically, socially, politically, religiously, communally, administratively and ideologically are all crimes. Criminals are not only the people who intend to involve himself or herself in criminal activities but even those who commit and even give a fillip to such activities can well be termed as criminals.

*Aryavarta, Patna, 31 October, 1995*

□

# 56
# Society Building—Penance of Deendayal

This year too, 11th February has come the way it comes every year. Days keep coming by following their fixed rules of cycle of time. Some of the days become so important that they are remembered for a long time. A very great person was born on 25 September 1916 and after going through a long journey of life on 11 February 1968 he was sacrificed. He gained a lot during his journey of life and gave a lot to the organisation, society and nation. He set his direction according to his vision. He kept expanding his vision through practice and penance and went on setting the direction also. He started moving while holding a lamp in his hand and even in the midst of storms, he kept kindling the lamp. He never let the lamp get extinguished. Slowly the light of that lamp spread all over India. Many lamps were lit from that one lamp and covered the whole of India in that light.

The person who takes birth in a very ordinary family, he only gets to experience the bitter experiences of life. A person living without resources and poverty will show a new path to the whole universe. A person living in indulgence can never reach the peak of greatness. Energy through practice, devotion through worship and liberation through penance can be achieved. Those who didn't put themselves through hardships, couldn't remove their dirt. Penance will remove the dirt of a person and bring purity. Through cleanliness of the body and purity of mind, an individual gets a new light from within. A person travelling with the help of external light can't get permanent light. A dependent person can never be independent. He who doesn't have self-respect can't even have self-pride. A person who doesn't have self-pride can never give a new direction with a new vision to organisation, society and nation. Self-reliance and self-dependence are at the root of self-rule. Those who rely on others will also be under the control of others. Those who are under the control of others will be dependent on others; whoever is under the control of others is a slave. If we want to be free from slavery, then the human being has to be self-reliant. If lack of money pushes people down, then the influence of money can make people degenerate, unrighteous and commit treason.

There should neither be lack of money nor influence of money in the life of any individual. Today the world is getting grinded between these two. There are some nations which want to make other nations their slaves by virtue of wealth. Those which are lacking money are losing everything by enduring the unbearable pain of slavery. They are begging for money with folded hands. If money is put in constructive programmes then it will be for human welfare, but if it is used for indulgence, then it will destroy the society. Whole world has become indulgence-oriented. Man doesn't become dependent only from the economic point of view. Money is only one of the bases, there are many other bases, I such as political, social, physical, cultural, religious and ideological bases through which one can be dependent on others. Cultural and ideological slavery is more painful than economic slavery. One can get liberated from economic slavery but liberation from cultural and ideological slavery may take generations.

Social harmony is a must for democracy. Social harmony means there will be no inequality in the whole society. Inequality is also of different types. Dr. Ram Manohar Lohia had divided all these disparities into seven types and started initiatives for all these disparities, which he had named as *saptkranti* (seven revolutions). Similarly, for complete elimination of all disparities in 1974, Jai Prakash Narayan had given the slogan of *samagra kranti* (total revolution). Pandit Deendayal had given the philosophy of social harmony, which means whole society becomes even. If the ground becomes equal, then if we put water at one end, it will spread all over the ground. If the ground is uneven, then water doesn't spread equally. On a high ground as the water flows down there, the crops dry up and at low-lying areas, due to the accumulation of water, crops may get drowned. In the same way, society has been divided into highs and lows of different types based on gender, birth, colour, money, intelligence and technical knowledge. In India, society has been classified based on birth.

There is no value for capability, potential and experience. Human beings are considered as eligible and talented just because they are born in a particular caste. But however talented, potential and intelligent they may be, a person born in a particular caste is not assessed properly as the people assessing him are biased. A person born in a particular caste becomes imprisoned in that caste itself. He remains trapped in the bonding of the caste from birth till death and keeps sinking in that quagmire. However, liberal he may be through his words, but his actions are always bound by the caste and he can never get liberated from his caste bindings. Religious disparities can be removed easily but removing caste disparities is very difficult. It will be proved, if the pages of history are turned back, as the foreign invaders had got Indians to convert their religion. But even after converting to another religion, they couldn't end the values of their caste; as per Hindu society whoever was in whatever position due to caste system, they got the same order and position even after changing their religion. They went ahead to change the religion but they were given the respect only according to the caste system. If we see societies other than Hindu society, even among them there are higher and lower steps, which have to be seen very closely. This is a topic of study. As long as India, especially the Hindu society, is divided into categories of upper and lower till then, indigeneity, nationality and the feeling of unity will not come. When the feeling of equality comes, then a common goal will be set. When there is a common goal, then only collective direction can be fixed. Unless there is a collective direction, momentum doesn't come in the nation. Due to inertia of society, there will be inertia across the nation too. With the momentum of society, momentum comes to nation also. When society and individual become secondary to the nation, then nation is revived. But when for caste and the individual the nation becomes secondary, then nation becomes inactive, static and dead. All great people tried to make the nation full of life. Many religious and spiritual saints, sages and great people have taken birth, who gave messages to eliminate this disease, but with no result. People have been chanting against caste system, singing songs, and encouraging the society for its removal, but their own organisations and communities couldn't be freed from this caste system. This is a topic for introspection.

Politically, both Pandit Deendayal Upadhyaya and Dr. Ram Manohar Lohia worked hard to bring about social harmony and thus pave the way for an egalitarian society. Mahatma Gandhi tried to unite the whole nation and remove these inequalities. As long as Hindu society doesn't cure its leprosy called caste system, till then all its limbs will keep degenerating. What is the reason that people of Hindu society keep changing their religion and going out even today, but nobody comes into this religion? Hindu society is akin to a lake from which people may take as much water they need but there are no sources through which water from out can come into the lake. This is also a topic for serious thinking.

In India, Hindus are in majority. When the majority stays divided and separated, then how can there be unity in India? Social unity is essential for the unity of nation. Social equality is essential for social unity. Hindu society is like an erect ladder. From top to bottom, whichever caste is placed on that ladder, they will be treated in the same order as higher and lower castes in the social laboratory. Now if the society has to be made equal, the erect ladder has to be brought down. When the ladder is lying down, then even all would be sitting on their respective rungs, but they all will become equal. The day it happens so, society as a whole will become equal. Classes are formed with castes in momentum, whereas classes without momentum become castes. As long as there is momentum, water keeps flowing. Flowing water remains clean and stagnant water gets dirty and rotten.

The meaning of equal society as Dr. Lohia's *saptkranti* and harmonious society is the same. Mahatma used to run various programmes to create a harmonious society and abolishing untouchability was one of his major initiatives. He straight believed self-reliance is essential for marking the presence of the native self. As long as solidarity is not understood, till then there will be differences. How can oneness come when there is duality? Ego stops a human being from becoming harmonious. Due to the ego of position, intelligence, power, wealth and education, human beings want to keep themselves apart. Considering oneself to be superior because of birth is also in a way an apparent manifestation of ego. Ego comes with power also. Without purity and simplicity, how can equality be achieved? When people who talk about equality are given the authority to select or nominate, then they also get influenced by racial feelings. As long as there is no communion among preaching, thought and action, till then the vision of equality can't be attained. Awareness of equality comes only after vision of equàlity. With awareness of equality, the goal of equality will be formed. This philosophy is right from the spiritual point of view, but politically there is no value for all this. Power is only for selfish interest and selfish interest is for indulgence. People who fight for years for equality and who eat in one plate also when they achieve power, then they start cheating each other; very rare are there people who don't break the line of ethics. Whether it is an organisation, or government, or any other institution, the same is seen everywhere. There is luxury in simplicity, dirt in cleanliness. There is racism in nationalism, narrowness in liberality. Selfishness within the ultimate. Aggression within balanced behaviour. There is vice within virtue. Demon is there within human. Foreign within indigenous. Dependence in self-dependence. Slavery in self-rule, crookedness in softness, foul smell in fragrance, harshness within simplicity, roguery in scholarship, cunningness in fluency. This is the situation of politics today. Disciples of all great people worship their idols. They light lamps and incandescent and hail their principles. Raise loud slogans, but they forget all about their path, ideology, vision, direction and their work. Supporters and disciples also assassinate them. Holding on to body means the superficial and sacrifice the subtle means of ideology. This is what they feel internally. By founding institutions and organisations on their name, they fulfil their selfish interests. This is the fate of India. That's what is going on. Religion, culture, society and nationality are only meant for propagation. Socialism and communism became only a means to create hatred and tension. Decentralisation of economic policies and administrative system was only to shout slogans. Democracy became a drama of dynasty politics, individualism and racism. The safe and secure people are today preaching the unprotected and unsecure. People having privileges are opposing special opportunities and rebuilding the caste system once again. Whoever gets the opportunity, they give reservation to their caste. While some build a powerful circle of their caste people in the name of eligibility, talent, intelligence and potential, and some others in the name of population, exploitation, special opportunities and reservation reward the fanatics and extremists of racism. There are internal conflicts, tension and struggle in power, organisation and institutions. Without understanding the integral humanism philosophy of Deendayal, how can the stream of love and compassion flow out? You have struggled throughout your life. You undertook penance to strengthen the nation, practised to make it powerful and worshipped to get internal strength. Hey seeker, hey devotee, and hey ascetic and a dear son of India, I want to bow to you and touch your feet. I am not eligible to touch your feet as a minister to the Government of India, but being an Indian, I am touching your feet. Please bring Gandhi for once and Lohia along with you by acquiring the form of Trinity. Hey Rama, Krishna and Shiva, India is deviating from its axis; guide it into light from darkness. However useless I may be, but prayer to you is my right.

*Aryavarta, Patna, 11 February, 2001*

□

# 57
# In the Memory of Lohia

Like every year this year too on October 12, programmes will be organised to pay homage to Dr. Lohia. He will be remembered; his photos and statues will be garlanded. His supporters and opponents also will remember him and pay homage. So-called disciples of Lohia will organise meetings and formalities will be fulfilled. Lohia was a socialist thinker, who used to think in totality. He was a man who used to think deeply about all issues, such as politics, spirituality, culture, physical, ethical, personal and public. His ideology about nationality was very remarkable. He was influenced not only by Indian culture but also by Gandhi and Marx. He had done a balanced study of both Gandhian and Marxist philosophy. He always used to say, "An extensive study can't be done with a divided mind; all issues have to be seen in totality." About socialism, he said, "Principles are formless, programmes have form; programmes have to be designed by binding principles in time." Form and formless, spirituality and religion have been topics of thinking. Lohia presented a political explanation of them.

To abolish caste system, he used to organise break the caste rallys. As long as the caste system is there till then the pests of corruption would grow over the garbage of racism. Everybody keeps talking against racism and caste system but they never get freed from them in their actions and behaviour. According to Lohia, an individual's intention will be made clear when he gets to elect or nominate a person for the post of chief of any political organisation or institution. If there is no transparency, just by voluptuous talking no concrete results will be achieved.

They will nominate only their own caste people. Every chief would say the same thing—that he had selected on the basis of eligibility. While answering to such people, Lohia used to say that if they find eligible, talented and capable people only in their own caste that means he has a very narrow vision. A person thinking with whole mind and with expanded vision can see the whole society. After getting into power with the help of caste, if anyone overlooks caste while deciding on selection and nomination, then they can do welfare activities with that racism. Creating racial fanatics just to protect and retain his position and post is also a serious crime. Politicisation of caste, criminalisation of racism and socialisation of crime has happened. This is very problematic for India. Caste system is responsible for various malign tendencies, such as extremism, terrorism, corruption, directly or indirectly. If caste system ceases to exist, as many as 80 percent of India's ailments will be cured automatically. Whatever tensions and controversies have cropped up in the society due to some discrepancies in reservation system, they will also be removed. One of the solutions is to make inter-caste marriages compulsory for availing government service and other privileges. Choudhury Charan Singh also used to say the same thing, but the disciples of Lohia didn't try to do that after coming into power. Individualism and dynasty politics will take birth from the womb of the caste system.

Religion is long-term politics and politics is short-term religion, this is what Lohia used to feel and so was his philosophy. Religion says do good and it praises goodness. Politics condemns evil. Lohia used to say religion and politics will be complete only when they do good things and fight against bad things. Divided politics gives birth to quarrels and religion becomes the domain of the fundamentalist. When both religion and politics struggle for the same objective, momentum is maintained in society. That's the principal reason why Lohia used to say that there is a need for the battle of righteousness in India for fundamental and extensive transformation. Duty to the nation is by far superior to one's devotion and allegiance to a specific clan or even caste for that matter. Equal society was the philosophy of Dr. Lohia and harmonious society was the ideal of Pt. Deendayal. Children of both Brahmin and lower caste should get equal education. This will bring equality and shall invariably strengthen the feelings of nationalism. Everybody should be offered employment. In agriculture, services and in business, the principle of one person one job should be implemented. Monopoly of certain families has been established over wealth and employment opportunities. This must be done away with. The sources of employment and wealth have to be decentralised. Whoever doesn't have any one of these three means, they should be given one of the sources on priority basis. An Act should be given effect to. To decentralise the powers of administration and politics the four-pillared system should be implemented. Village, district, state and the Centre will be its four pillars. The rights of all the four poles should be divided and listed in the Constitution. The way there are lists for unions, states and borders, similarly there should be lists for village, district, state and Centre and the three entities should be given full independence and autonomy within their boundaries. The Constitution has to be amended to this effect. All the government servants working under the Panchayats have to be brought under the control of the Panchayat. All educational institutions, health centres, and other government servants falling within the purview of village Panchayat should be brought under their control. This will result in democratisation and localisation of governance and administration. Minimum and maximum income limits have to be fixed; 1 to 10 difference should be maintained; a cap on expenditure should be put. Concession on income and tax on expenditure should be given. Investments in nation building and employment-generating projects should be encouraged. The multidimensional benefits gained through the investment will be more than the amount collected through taxes. By respecting the national language, the foreign language should be removed from government affairs. Gender disparity and racial differences should be removed. Due to technological advancement, weaker nations are continuously moving towards poverty. Time has become the basis for international businesses. Due to technical expertise, a country may make a thing in one minute, but the same thing might be made in 10 minutes by a country lagging behind. Time has to be made the basis for pricing. There are many issues but how will they happen? People of Lohia have forgotten him. They forgot about removing the class disparities; in other words, economic disparities, and promoting caste disparities results in racial fanatics. According to Lohia, battle of righteousness is needed to establish equal society by removing all sorts of disparities. Independent India has witnessed many things; now it has to rise and transform India through the battle of righteousness.

*Vanchit Vani, Delhi, 12 October, 2003*

□

# 58
# About Farmers

Marathon discussions are being held relating to the problems of farmers. It is a good thing that the attention of illustrious people has turned towards farmers. The farmer is in focus. Since ancient times, India has been an agriculture and village-based country. There is a close link between villages, agriculture and animal husbandry. Indian agriculture is dependent on manual labour, agriculture machinery and other equipment drawn by animals. That's the reason why development of livestock was given priority. Primary attention has been given to ensure that there is stability and continuity in the productivity and fertility of land. In the hermitages of sages along with agriculture and animal husbandry, knowledge was imparted about science and other things. Agriculture, gardening and animal husbandry were combined with learning. To improve the quality of land and to convert the fallow lands into fertile ones, the dung of livestock and urine was used. Livestock was the basis for Indian agricultural economy. This is the reason why three very great people were animal keepers—cowherd Krishna, goatherd Prophet Mohammad and shepherd Jesus Christ who gave the message to the world; their influence is still on planet Earth.

A fight is going on between animal-drawn equipment vis-á-vis mechanical equipment. Manual labour is high in animal-drawn equipment; more hard work and a lot of sweat is involved. As a result, village life is very tough and goal-oriented. Because of animal husbandry, affection for Nature comes automatically. The beauty of Nature gets enhanced through gardening; it goes a long way in maintaining the cleanliness of the environment. Purity of body, mind and soul is also maintained. There won't be any pollution. Being Nature lovers, they have compassion and affection. But then the direction and situation of India has undergone a change. The mystery of who has changed it and why it has been changed is still to be uncovered. It is slowly getting uncovered and agricultural awareness is growing.

Because of fuel-run machines, the direction of agriculture has changed. Due to deep ploughing, deep irrigation and extensive use of chemicals, productivity has increased many times and prosperity has been in place, but due to prosperity, internal pain has aggravated like anything. Fertility of land, quality of water, and environment were badly affected by it. Now people are looking forward to getting out of this situation. The family of the farmer has increased and the size of the land has substantially decreased and the acreage of sowing has reduced. The land is very small and too scattered. In such a situation, farming with machines will never be profitable. Farmers are not buying tractors now because tractors have become unprofitable for them. If he doesn't use the tractor for other transport purposes, he can't repay the loan instalments in time and the burden keeps on growing on him. Due to the compound interest on loans leased by banks, the spine of the farmer has broken down. Those people are responsible for this situation who without understanding the long-term affects, have emphasised on modern techniques. Business of big industrial houses and modern technology-based Western agricultural policy is going in the wrong direction and it continues to go in that direction only. Thinkers like Dr. Lohia, Pt. Deendayal and Choudhury Charan Singh were neglected. Because of technical exploitation, the condition of farmers has become worse. New slogans were shouted and that took the people on a garden path, divided them into caste and community, showed the lure of grants and subsidies, and made them adopt Western techniques and misled them. The ill-effects of that are in front of us now.

According to the priorities advocated by Gandhiji, agriculture should rank first in the list of our priorities, cottage industries should come next and big industries on third position. India's economic policy should be formulated on that basis. Gandhi and Patel passed away, planners of later years put agriculture on the third position and decided to shut down cottage industries. As the cottage industries were neglected, employment opportunities of villagers kept on declining beyond measure. They also became dependent on agriculture; as a result the burden on agriculture increased. In the craze of urbanisation, industrialisation, and modernisation, people lost their senses. Attempts have been made to do agriculture in India using European techniques. There was no Indian orientation in the research. The agricultural research institutes and universities which were running on European grants and funds were imparting the same education as that of European countries. The agricultural infrastructure set up on European grants started cracking. More loans were needed to maintain it. Whoever was expert in getting the loan from foreign countries was considered that much efficient, talented and eligible. Agriculture techniques were not modified commensurate with Indian conditions; instead Indian agriculture was made European. Discrepancies and defects have started appearing since then and the dependence of population on agriculture has grown disproportionately. It became difficult to live on agriculture; the business of livestock also started dwindling; big dairy farms started coming up. But the traditional animal keepers were leaving animal husbandry. In 1951, for 1,000 people there were around 452 animals, by 1981; they were reduced to around 232. Who will answer this? Availability of milk has increased, but the population of cattle in proportion to human population has reduced to almost half. As cottage industries were closed down, traditional village professions also ceased. They all have migrated to cities. Small land, less investment, small farming, more manual labour techniques only proved more profitable to Indian agriculture. By modifying traditional techniques, they should be made superior and modern. Central Government alone can't do all these things. Political expenditure is increasing; state governments are spending money on political management and cheaper popular programmes. The funds received from Central Government are not being utilised for the betterment and development of agriculture; either that fund doesn't get utilised at all or gets utilised for other activities.

Some politicians, political parties, intellectuals and writers and media are engaged in passing the buck and even blame the existing government. **They are trying to push and politicise agriculture. They are influenced by prejudices and biases of varying kinds. They are dependent on grants and favours. They haven't seen villages, villagers and farmers. They don't have the experience of village life, village professions and village culture. They can't identify the breeds of species and seeds of crop. But unfortunately they have become the planners and advisors of India. They shout slogans about farmers but tend to favour the industrialists. They shout slogans of poverty alleviation but work to promote accumulation of wealth. In the garb of modernisation, liberalisation and globalisation they are mortgaging the country.** Whatever happened in Cancun, if India would have talked with such self-respect and pride in the first meeting itself, then this situation wouldn't have arisen. British rule and fifty years of independent India's rule have pushed agriculture towards inflation. Cottage and village industries have died down. This is the reason for unemployment, idleness and hunger deaths. Attempts are underway to improve the situation, but it will take some time. In near future, Indian farmer will establish his dominance in the world. With political will, strong willpower and public consciousness and awareness, the Indian agricultural policy is moving in the right direction now.

*Vanchit Vani, September, 2003*

□

## 59

# Human Beings Bear the Brunt of Corruption

The economy and political systems of the whole world are subjected to suffering because of worldwide influence of corruption. Corruption is like a hydra-headed monster staring in the eyes of every institution and organisation with its mouth wide open. Corruption is showing its presence in various forms and structure. If the actions go corrupt, then that person is called corrupt; but people won't become corrupt just by actions. Even before becoming corrupt by actions, they lose their path and become totally corrupt as they lose their principles. When ethics get corrupt, they become ethically corrupt. What is the reason behind it? We can't have solutions without knowing the reasons. When the roots get infected, all branches also get infected. There is a need for deep thinking about the fundamental reasons for getting corrupt. It doesn't cause that much damage when an individual becomes corrupt, but when an institution becomes corrupt, then it causes a lot of damage. It is an irony and an unfortunate thing that the democratic institutions have become corrupt. Corruption is omnipresent; as a result, situations of complete destruction have been created. Human being is a slave of situation, conditions and human weaknesses, but by fighting against them and by controlling and overcoming them, the human being can excel. But by taking the excuse of weaknesses and with their help, human beings go down the path of destruction. It becomes very difficult to halt once a person starts going down the path of destruction. It is very difficult to climb up, but it's very easy to climb down. Direction has to be set and goal has to be decided for climbing up, but it's very difficult to predict where the person, who is going down, will stop. The situation gets disturbed when one loses direction. Comforts, privileges and wealth are essential for life. But they make sense till the time they are in certain limits but once they cross the limits, then they will bring disaster. Money will make sense only when it is within a limit. But blindly running after money will result in disaster. There is an eternal fight between the paths of credit and pleasure. While simplicity, nobility and sacrifice are basis for the path of credit, indulgence, corruption and luxury are the basis for the path of pleasure.

Compassion, love and sacrifice are callousness in the heart. When the connection between mind and heart breaks down, the influence of cruelty, rudeness and hatred increases. When materialism freely exerts its influence, the influence of spirituality ceases to exist. Today materialism is influencing heavily the political, economic and administrative systems of the world. Materialism is one of the fundamental reasons for corruption, due to which individualism, opportunism, greed for power and selfishness have increased and the basis of compassion, harmony and equality has broken down. Prostitution is a part of corruption as both are related to actions. Because of this only, sexual assault is considered obnoxious and loathsome, but still prostitution continues. Prostitution and corruption are equally dangerous to society. People of materialistic mentality think woman to be a disposable commodity. In the name of freedom, they consume and consider women as a commodity only. They like to keep women on high pedestals instead of a puppet. Women and gold have a permanent relationship. In materialistic society, both of them are being used. When women will be able to guide the universe with self-respect and pride, that will be a fortunate day. That will be considered a golden time in the world. Draupadi is a glaring example of that. Draupadi used to keep all five husbands tied together and inspire them to achieve human goals. She was their companion on their journey from indulgence to liberation. She scripted the battle of Mahabharata against oppression and corruption. She challenged the power all alone. Today there is a need for Mahabharata in India and there is a need for women like Draupadi to erase corruption from India. Are we ready for them? If not, some Krishna must be preparing for the battle of imminent Mahabharata.

Caste system is another key factor supplementing the incidence of corruption. In the name of caste, the corrupt get hailed, respected and felicitated. From birth till death, they get tied down to their caste. Even if somebody wants to come out of it, he/she just can't afford to. They will be criticised and condemned by the political dispensation and agitations are done against them. But on social forums, they will sit next to each other. In one state, food has to be taken from the same plate. Politics and administration are two powerful pillars of government. Both of them get the protection of caste. Corrupt officers always help corrupt leaders. They will be fully taken care of. By taking good care of them, they will be retained in politics. They will get the protection according to the situation. Government changes, rulers are changed but administrators stay there only. They have to be there in that post for a fixed time. Being in positions of profit, they have to use it and consume it. The person at the top keeps changing but the vicious cycle of bureaucrats will not break. Because of caste system in every party, you get leaders of every caste. They get the protection of those leaders when required. By behaving according to the situation, they benefit. Who can spoil their game?

The author got to know this secret after forty years of experience in politics. This is true and everybody knows it and accepts it, but is unable to break this vicious cycle. Condemn racism, but stay linked to racism. As long as caste system is there, racism will be there. As long as individualism is there, the ego of the individual will be there. As long as ego is there, the masses will be like lifeless slaves to them, and the power to people shall continue to be a far cry. As long as people's power doesn't come, public welfare will not happen. Caste system is at the root of corruption, indulgence and fear. On the heap of garbage called caste system, the pests like corruption, indulgence and fear are born and nurtured and they eat up the society. On the path of nationalism, racism is a bigger hurdle than communalism. Identifying an enemy and destroying it will be easier than removing the obstacle. Due to the caste system, obstacles are created at every step. Nobody allows anybody else to progress. Whenever the link of caste system grew stronger, there was a downfall of India. History is a witness that whenever the caste system became weak, development occurred and golden period came in India. In India, Hindus are in majority but for a long time India was enslaved; a few invaders came and made India a slave. After suffering from slavery for thousands of years, for the first time India came together under the leadership of Mahatma Gandhi and because of their unity, the non-violent agitation became successful. Democracy has given equal rights to all of us, but feudal system is prevalent in the society. The leaders of caste are of feudalistic mentality. In comparison to the outsiders, they torture their own people. Whoever tries to protest for being within the caste, he has to to face insults and ridicule at every step. Even people of other castes also can't be of any help to him. Talent, knowledge, potential, eligibility and all other virtues are oppressed. Lack of character, aggression, violence, fanaticism, corruption are respected and worshipped. In comparison to the people in one's own party and organisation, they have stronger links with people of other parties and organisations. If one generation, on the basis of caste, worshipping a particular person gets to have power, the next generation worshipping some other political leader in the name of caste gets into power. Two castes have been made in every caste—one of the rulers and the other is of the ruled. The language and style of the rulers is same all over. India is suffering from the disease of racism. What Kabir said '*Ghar ghar dekha ek hi lekha vaid ke ghar me karan dekha* (the situation is same in every house; the reason was found in the doctor's house) is proven to be right. When people of a caste, leave the trademark of the party to take up other trademarks, they can't be trusted. Individuals are burning in the fire of superstitions. A person's character can be known by looking at the people he is surrounded by. Without eradicating this caste system, India can't be transformed. For this to happen, there is a need for big battles of righteousness. When racism gets eliminated from India, the Indianness will spread all over the world. There is a need for a Shiva who can drink this poison. Inter-caste marriages should be made compulsory for getting a job in government service and all privileges in the name of purity of blood should be discontinued. Hurdles are put in the path of national unity, integrity and the magnanimity of Hindutva. The youth of India has to tighten their belt and has to come forward to fight this battle of righteousness.

The economy of India aids corruption. A person who saves becomes a criminal and an indulgent person gets rewarded. Savings means getting into trouble with the income-tax demons. Income-tax promotes corruption, unethical practices and crime the most. People living in joint families, small families, leading unmarried life and saving money have to be rewarded. They talk about cooperation, but the Indian joint family system is based on the natural cooperation principle. That is crumbling. When a family gets scattered, the village gets scattered and when the village gets scattered, the country starts scattering. There is a direct connection between individualism and corruption. **There is a need to tax the expenditure rather than income.** The most corrupt people are sitting in income-tax department. The funds of MPs and MLAs are spoiling the cleanliness of the society. Worshipping the individual, brokering and commission-taking are growing in politics. Everybody knows it, but nobody is able to stop it. It can only be stopped by public revolt and through the battle for righteousness. The proportion of privileges, comforts and other things have to be decided on the basis of how much difference should be there between public and public representatives. Once retired from either government or judiciary services, nobody should take up either salaried or non-salaried government or non-government position. There is a need for banning this through legislation. This also helps in promoting corruption.

*Aryavarta, Patna, 04 May, 2000*

□

# 60
# The Objectives of Rule of Equality

Discrepancies have come up in the political, administrative, social, communal and educational systems of present day. All types of ruling systems have become unsuccessful and purposeless. They should get modified. Individuals and the universe should accept this modification naturally; otherwise the destruction of the world is certain.

Food and freedom, both are equally important for human being. Without food, the human being becomes weak and physically poor. If there is no freedom, he has to lead the life of a slave. If only one of them is available, life is incomplete. If agriculture is the root of food, then voice is the root of freedom. Both of them should get an opportunity to develop fully.

By setting immediate, short-term and long-term goals, Constitution and rules have to be prepared to achieve them. Agriculture is the basis of rural India. With long-term goals, equal society and world union have to be developed. As long as equality doesn't come in economic, social, political, administrative, educational and materialistic fields, till then the objective of equal society will not get fulfilled. The following Constitution has to be devised to achieve this objective.

To strengthen the agricultural and rural economy the following measures have to be taken on a priority basis:

- Distribution of land should be allowed up to such an extent only where farming is not uneconomical; which means land below 2.5 acres should not be allowed for distribution and the claimants should be encouraged to set up other cottage and small-scale industries.

- ☐ As farming on land less than five acres is uneconomical, no tax should be levied on farming up to five acres. Irrigation facilities should be provided free of cost.
- ☐ Electricity should be supplied for agricultural activities on a priority basis at very nominal rates.
- ☐ Priority should be given to the educated unemployed youth residing in villages to set up cottage and village industries. Subsidies should be given on farm equipment. Machinery that involves manual labour should be used for agriculture. Farming has been delimited but use of tractors is uneconomical and suicidal. Using hand-driven power tillers, farming should be done using Japanese technologies. Power tiller should be freed from all types of taxes. One-third of the cost should be given as grant and rest should be given as loan at a very nominal rate of interest.
- ☐ In every Panchayat, all shops providing high quality seeds, pesticides and fertilisers should be run by the Panchayat. Only farmers should be given the licence to sell equipment and machinery related to agriculture.
- ☐ Every Panchayat should have a *galla godam* (godown for storage of crops), where farmers would keep their harvest and take up to 80 percent loans from banks according to the existing prices. At the time of selling their crop, they can pay back the loans along with interest. As long as production, distribution and marketing is not secured and comes under the control of farmers, farmers can't be saved from exploitation.
- ☐ To achieve total self-reliance in food, imports of food material should be banned. Farmers should be encouraged by giving the money spent on import of food material.
- ☐ Export of products of agriculture should be given only to farmers. Villages will be transformed with agriculture science, intensity and prosperity will bring new light in the lives of agricultural labourers. While working on their own farm, they will be called farmers and while working on others' farms, they will be called agricultural labourers. But the line of difference between the two has become so

thin that it is very difficult to say when a person becomes farmer or an agricultural labourer.

- ☐ Clean and safe water is very essential to ensure the health and strength of the livestock. There should be a public pond in every village and arrangements should be made to supply safe potable water in that pond all through the year.
- ☐ In every village, a public shed should be constructed on Panchayat land to keep the livestock of the village and landless families be given a place in that shed to keep two animals.
- ☐ Every household is to be given grants and loans to set up a cottage industry. Textile production activities need to be given priority.
- ☐ It is to be made compulsory that industrial production of all equipment and instruments that will come in use of day-to-day life of rural people will be set up as cottage industries in villages only. Systems will be set up to end the competition between handmade and machine-made goods, so that machines will not snatch away the industry of handmade.
- ☐ Women will be provided with public toilets and playgrounds and learning centres will be made available for children.

### Education

A system of uniform education will be evolved for all the children, irrespective of status. Private schools will be closed down. The children of peasants and the poor will be imparted the same education from the same school. Education will be imparted, based on Indian culture, civilisation and ideals. By removing the differences between antique and modern, the foundation of education will be laid down on spiritual and scientific grounds. From there the inspiration for love, simplicity and sacrifice will be given. Education will be made compulsory for everybody's children. General level of education will be given to everybody. Higher education will be given based on the special qualities and talents of the children. Merit and eligibility will be the basis for higher education.

## Governance – Administration

Rulers keep changing at fixed intervals as per legislation. In an indirect way, administrators are the actual rulers. Elected representatives come and go, whereas, appointed representatives are permanent. The character of rulers keeps changing but the character of administrators remains permanent. Where there is a sense of stability, there ushers in stagnation. To add momentum to this, both governance and administration will be completely decentralised and made independent of each other. Governance will be set up on four pillars—village, district, state and the Centre. The rights and duties of these four will be fixed by the Constitution. There will be no interference from each other. Decentralisation of executive, judiciary and Legislature will be done on this basis only. Centre will get 40 percent, state will get 30 percent, district and village gets 15 percent each. The prototypes of the plans will be made by them only. Using a single procedure, the four pillars of governance and administration will be set up all over the country. Appointed officers will be under the authority of elected representatives. Village, district, state and the Centre will appoint officers according to their own legislation, policies and rules. The influence of All India Services will be very minimum. There will be appropriate representation of all castes, communities and groups in a decentralised system; whereas due to centralisation, Indian Administration Services are dominated by a particular class, caste, which is obstructing the heart of the nation.

Democratic processes and procedures are most complicated in the world. To get the practical experience and knowledge of them and this assumes the capability to handle them properly, Panchayats will act as mini units of Parliament. Rules will be made to give equal opportunities in government services to everybody, so that nobody will be able to exploit anybody. Intelligence and education is assessed by the mind, whereas humanity will be assessed by the heart. The feelings of caste ad community are in the heart. It is very difficult to investigate them, therefore inter-caste marriages would be made compulsory for government jobs. This would inevitably help to build a new society by breaking the stereotype caste system.

**Economic Policy**

Centralisation of economy has created an environment of disaster in every field. To reduce the economic disparities, minimum and maximum income limits will have to be fixed with a ratio of 1 is to 10. The national income will be utilised on a priority basis to take the lowest level to the highest level.

- Of the three sources, namely agriculture, job and business, only one will be allowed to one person. This will offer opportunities of employment to the unemployed.
- Urban assets will be delimited in order to maintain a balance between rural and urban economy and thus curb the element of dissatisfaction among people of a particular class.
- By putting a ceiling on expenditure, national income will be used for nation building rather than consumption. Maximum limit of expenditure will be not more than Rupees 1500/- per person. Whoever spends above that, tax will be levied according to the expenditure. Income will be totally free, but expenditure will be under effective control.
- There would be emphasis on modernisation of production but modernisation of consumption will be controlled.

**Industry**

Cottage industries will be accorded priority. After agriculture, big industries will be set in those fields where they are absolutely essential.

- Indigenous technology will be promoted and foreign technology will be reduced. With foreign technology, foreign investment will increase, which will weaken the backbone of the nation slowly. Because of growing influence of foreign investments and multi-national companies, various games are being played.
- By putting a control over production of luxury goods, priority will be given to producing goods of utility.

- The management of companies will be constituted proportionate to the loans given by governmental financing institutions. Though the share of private investments is less, yet big industrial houses are exerting influence over the management, thus making industries very sick. This system will be changed.
- Measures will be taken to ensure that consumers avail goods at a price which is one-and-a-half times higher than the cost. To estimate the cost, a commission will be set up by constituting representatives of consumers and experts as members. The commission will be called the National Commission for Price Control.

## Administrative Services

Although more than 80 percent of the population lives in villages and more than 70 percent are dependent on agriculture, still their representation in administrative services is negligible and very minimum. To increase their representation in these services, in all those institutions which appoint these officers, members from these sections will be increased according to their population. As long as there is no dominance of villagers and farmers in these appointing institutions, justice will not be done to them. People living and growing up in rural areas are not given due respect. Measures should be taken to change this attitude.

Reservations in administrative services are given on the basis of class along with caste consideration. To build a classless and casteless society, rules will be made to simultaneously eradicate both disparities.

## Wealth of Universe

Science has tied down the entire world into one. The influence of global incidents is expanding. Future of the whole universe is connected to one person. Some are wealthy, while some others are very poor in the whole world. While in one corner human beings are drowned in indulgences and at the other corner, human beings are dying due to hunger. The wealth of the universe is of the universe. All citizens of the world have equal rights over the wealth of the universe. The wealth of the universe will be managed and distributed through the Parliament of the world. It will be distributed as per one's requirements. Efforts will be made to set up a Parliament of the world. The existence of human beings and the universe is at stake and humanity is in danger. With the use of new experiments of mass destruction and killing, the entire environment and climate has been polluted. Because of this pollution, disparities and distortions are taking place in the mind. The protecting layer of the Earth is breaking up. There is a need for global cleaning up to take the world out of these dangers. The time has come to start systematic efforts to get the world out of the fear generated because of the culture of indulgence. When small units at the level of individual and large units at the top of the world are established, then only these problems will be solved. Disparities and distortions have come up in all systems of governance of the world because of internal conflicts. As a result they are getting destroyed on their own. All the systems have failed and have become redundant and useless. A new governing system and a new world order has to be created. An atmosphere has to be created to achieve these objectives. India will have a significant role in this. That's the reason why Indian parliamentary governance and administration has to be transformed. The process of change will not be complete without transformation. So, therefore, Indian voters have to vote actively and consciously in order to have a majority of such representatives in Parliament.

In order to ensure that the public representatives follow the orders from the bottom rather than the orders of the top, the election process will be modified accordingly. Candidates are selected according to the will of leaders of political parties, so the candidates follow the orders of those leaders. They don't care for the feelings, desires and behaviour of the people. When people's, representatives follow the orders of village gatherings instead of the orders of the bigwigs of political parties then only a true democracy will be established. As long as the system is under the control of public only then democracy will be there; right now people are behaving according to the system. Therefore, voters should be given the right to recall the candidates along with the right to elect them.

## The Objective of Awareness Tour

Faithless actions could never create trust. When an individual completely believes in the goal, objectives and ideals, only then he/she gets totally committed and performs the action. The biggest problem of the world is that today, in each and every field, human beings are doing actions without having any faith in them. As a result, the chain of trust is getting broken. When there is no faith in the self, then how can anybody have trust in others? Faith is not a thing to be attained; it has to be reposed. Faith can only be achieved when there is purity of action in the heart. To inculcate that faith, consciousness has to be awakened in every human being. Without consciousness, a human being is lacking faith and trust. Human being is awake but still in slumber. There is a need to wake him up. It is easy to wake up an illiterate, dumb and unintelligent person but it is very difficult to wake up a literate, intelligent and knowledgeable person who has forsaken his consciousness. Humanity is caught in this critical situation and is going in circles in the same situation. But one is not gathering enough courage to come of that situation. Whenever a moment of consciousness dawns upon him, one realises that without breaking the boundary and limits of circle, it is difficult to get out of the circle. But one still doesn't want to break the boundary because one is scared as one is not aware of the situation outside. One is going round in circles with this expectation that somebody from outside would break this circle and get him out of it. But this is a false hope, reason being that life itself tries to come out of the egg by breaking the shell. Attempts from outside may prove more dangerous to his life. It becomes a pious duty of every individual, institution and group which is trying to wake up the humanity, either directly or indirectly, covertly or overtly, anonymously to do so as a collective endeavour. There can be, if not fundamental differences, but procedural differences in whatever efforts are going on separately. Procedural differences can be eliminated. When proceeding in the field of action, while removing all prejudices, biases, self-assertions with calm thinking, the path will become easy and clear. When we forget about our personal profit and loss and think only about universal consciousness and have complete faith in that, all the differences will be removed. Our objective will be to awaken consciousness. When a human being becomes conscious, then he will find the path for himself. Paths are infinite; we can see only a few of them and are telling people about them. Unorganised efforts of liberation will not yield that much result. Thus, we should try with unity and in an organised way to bring consciousness in the collective. We can't be liberated alone while being tied down with the shackles of the world. We have to try to liberate the entire universe. So we have to forget our past forms, behaviour, actions and qualities. If we liberate ourselves from the memories of the past, worries of future and greed in order to grab the present, then we will be able to liberate the whole universe. With the combined efforts of liberated people, the path of collective liberation will open. Now the time has come to start an auspicious beginning of building a new age by forgetting the past and freeing ourselves from the doubts about the future and be in a state of emptiness in the present. In this context, a humble request is made to all those self-knowledgeable, materialistic and enlightened persons involved in accomplishing completeness along with righteous duties, wealth, desires and salvation in order to achieve that while protecting such activities and maintaining cordial relations with each other. Keep guiding with their flow of ideas. Indirect cooperation is considered better than direct cooperation. Keep giving full support even while being anonymous. When the opportunity comes, by revealing the identity and by giving internal and external support in order to keep trust in the objectives, impart direction and vision. The journey of conscious awakening is a global initiative rather than belonging to any one individual or institution.